PSYKHE

PSYKHE

KATE FORSYTH

VINTAGE BOOKS

Australia

VINTAGE

UK | USA | Canada | Ireland | Australia
India | New Zealand | South Africa | China

Vintage is part of the Penguin Random House group of companies
whose addresses can be found at global.penguinrandomhouse.com

Penguin
Random House
Australia

First published by Vintage in 2024

Cover images by BinGoTinGo/Shutterstock, mcmc/Shutterstock
and Roberto Castillo/Shutterstock
Cover design by Debra Billson © Penguin Random House Australia Pty Ltd
Typeset in 11.5/16.5 pt Goudy Old Style by Midland Typesetters, Australia

Printed and bound in Australia by Griffin Press, an accredited
ISO AS/NZS 14001 Environmental Management Systems printer

 A catalogue record for this
book is available from the
National Library of Australia

ISBN 978 0 14377 691 8

penguin.com.au

We at Penguin Random House Australia acknowledge that Aboriginal and Torres
Strait Islander peoples are the Traditional Custodians and the first storytellers of the
lands on which we live and work. We honour Aboriginal and Torres Strait Islander
peoples' continuous connection to Country, waters, skies and communities.
We celebrate Aboriginal and Torres Strait Islander stories, traditions and
living cultures; and we pay our respects to Elders past and present.

For Ella
my valiant joy

Part I

ōvum
Latin: 'egg'

. . . the youngest daughter was so strangely and wonderfully fair
that human speech was all too poor to describe her beauty . . .
Eros and Psykhe
Metamorphoses, Lucius Apuleius

I

The First Death

I was born blue, strangled by my own cord.

Everyone thought I was dead. My mother's midwife blew air into my lungs until I gasped and breathed on my own, alive once more. So I was named Psykhe, which means breath and soul and butterfly, words having many meanings.

Only gods die and return to this world alive. So as I grew into girlhood, many people began to think I too must be divine. They bowed low as I passed by and kissed their fingertips to the sky. Some even thrust gifts into my hands - flowers, fruit, or carved charms against harm. I did not like it. I clung to Brid's hand and hid my face against her robe which smelt of meadowsweet, mugwort and rue. Brid had been my mother's nurse, then her midwife, and now my handmaid. Sometimes I walked through the whole town with my face buried against her, too afraid to look up and see the curious eyes staring at me.

My mother had died when I was born. Her absence was the greatest presence in my life. I knew I looked like her because I was so very different from anyone else. The people of Rasenna were brown and sturdy, with dark eyes and thick curls, while my skin was pale as moth wings, my hair as fine and white as an old woman's. My sisters could run and play in the sunshine, and their arms and legs only became more golden. I burned and blistered and grew feverish, so Brid kept me inside, singing me songs and telling me stories as she crushed herbs between grindstones.

My sisters did not love me. Their mother had died of the plague when Khrysanthe was still a baby, and our father had married my mother soon after. I think they thought that was wrong. Certainly, Alektrona rarely spoke to me except to say something unkind. She once told me that a white-haired boy like me had been sacrificed and buried under the stones of the square. I did not like to walk there after that. I imagined the boy's empty eye sockets gazing up at me, his finger bones stretched in desperate appeal.

Alektrona scarcely spoke to Khrysanthe either. She loved only her milk-sister, a slave girl named Fatima. Alektrona and Fatima had suckled together and grown up together. The two girls spent all their time with each other, whispering, laughing, gilding their eyelids and twirling about with gauzy scarves as the slaves played their cymbals and flutes. I used to crouch on a cushion and watch them dance. My eyesight was blurry, and so often the two girls were just whirling shapes in the dim room, a susurration of silk.

Fatima's mother, Nasrin, wore her black hair cropped in a straight line across her forehead to hide her slave tattoo. Lord Cassius, my father, summoned her to his bed whenever he was at home, which was not often. He spent a great deal of time away, sailing on one of his ships in search of new treasures, or examining sacks of spices and strings of amber at one of his many warehouses. He was one of the richest lords in Tarchna, the walled town in which we lived, and had recently been chosen to represent it in the League of Twelve, the annual meeting of leaders from each of the dozen hill towns of Rasenna.

My life was constrained by the walls of the garden, where Brid and I gathered herbs in the cool of the dawn and the twilight, when the bright sword of the sun would not hurt my eyes. She made healing potions for the women of the town and taught me to do the same. Many times I heard her wish we had a bigger garden so she could grow more plants.

'We had a grand garden, your mother and I,' she told me.

'On the shore of the lake of the magic mirror in the pale mountains,' I chanted. Even the name of my mother's homeland seemed full of wonder and mystery to me.

'Yes, indeed,' Brid said. 'You should see the herbs and flowers that grow wild there in the spring! The air so sweet and clean, no-one could help being well. Not like here, with the evil air of the marshes.'

Brid had come to Tarchna with my mother, to serve her and guard her, when she came down from the pale mountains to marry my father. After my mother died, Brid stayed to care for me, even though she was a free woman who could have returned to her homeland if she had pleased.

'Why, Brid? Why did you stay?' I asked her once, when I was still just a little girl and as full of questions as a pomegranate is full of seeds.

She crouched by the fire, stripping thyme leaves to make a tincture for a racking cough. The answer was a long time coming, which was Brid's way. 'I should have saved her,' she said at last.

'Like you saved me?'

She nodded her head slowly. 'I could save only one,' she said after another long pause. 'And so I chose you.'

'Why, Brid? Why did you choose me? Did you not love my mother?'

'I loved her with all my being, with the very marrow of my bones. But I knew I loved you more.'

5

'But why?'

She smiled, her face as creased as old leather. 'Because I chose you.'

Brid often spoke in circles like that. Perhaps it was just a way to silence me. For I wanted to know everything. Why does the moon follow us home? What is smoke? Why do leaves fall in autumn? How does a caterpillar become a butterfly?

'How did you save me?' I asked her.

'I unwound the cord from about your neck. It still pulsed with life, but you were pale and unbreathing. I could not rouse you. I remembered the story of Isis, the goddess who resurrected her brother Osiris by fanning breath into his body with her wings. So I bent over you, and blew breath into your mouth. Your little chest rose under my fingers. When I stopped blowing, your chest fell. So I kept breathing into you until you gasped and cried out. I lifted you then to your mother's breast, but while I had been trying to save you, she had slipped away.'

'Where did she go?' I asked.

'Your mother's body was returned to the earth, as is fitting, but her spirit would have travelled to the underworld.'

'The underworld? Where is that? Can I go there? Would I see her there?'

'One day you will go there,' she answered.

'When? When might I go?'

'That is beyond my ken.'

I was silent. I knew it was no use questioning Brid anymore once she said that.

I was still only a little girl then, but I remember it well. It was the first time I ever heard of the underworld.

*

Because I had been saved, I tried to save others. I rescued drowning bees from the fountain, broke spiderwebs to free struggling butterflies, and crumbled the last of my bread for the ants to eat. When I was twelve, I saved the life of a dove. I did not know it was wrong, or how cruel my punishment would be.

It was summer, a time when I spent most of the day in the cool of my dark room. I could not bear the season when Sol drove his chariot too close to the earth. My skin burned, my temples throbbed, and the fierce light hurt my eyes. Alektrona was of an age to be married, though, and so I had to brave the heat to go to the shrine of Venus, the goddess whom the people of Rasenna used to called Vei, both names meaning 'desire'.

Tarchna was built on a high hill above the marshes and the saltpans, and the shrine to honour the goddess born of seafoam was down on the shore, so that sailors could pray to her for safe passage over the ocean. Venus was the goddess of love and marriage as well as smooth sailing, and every summer there was a festival in her honour in which all the young women of the town participated.

Richly dressed, adorned with jewels, they walked into the sanctuary, carrying little cakes made of honey and saffron that they had baked with their own hands. Alektrona's gown was lavishly trimmed with purple. Few could afford the dye, made from the crushed shells of twelve thousand sea snails. The festival was as much a chance to flaunt our wealth as Alektrona's marriageability. I followed along behind, my hand clasped in Brid's, shrinking in shyness from the stares of the crowd. My father frowned when he saw me, and turned aside.

'She looks too much like her mother,' someone said. 'As if she has frost on her eyelashes.'

The shrine had to be purified with the blood of a sacrificed dove, and so a flock of white-winged birds was released into the air.

7

I watched them soar into the sky, so transfixed by their beauty that I did not see the hawk being released. I saw only the shadow of wings, the sudden frantic attempt to escape. The hawk dropped like a stone, wings flaring, talons outstretched, and seized one of the birds. The rest of the flock soared away, and the hawk circled down to the shrine.

Overcome with pity for the poor bird, I let go of Brid's hand and ran forward, startling the hawk who released its cruel grip. The dove tumbled down to the ground. I dropped to my knees beside it and picked the bird up. Drops of blood glowed like rubies on its snowy breast. Its eyelids were shut, but I could feel the frantic beating of its heart against my palms. I bent my head and whispered a little healing charm Brid had taught me:

> Mend what is broken,
> heal what is ill,
> by this word spoken,
> and the strength of my will.

The dove opened its bright eyes, spread its white wings, and soared away.

I only realised I had saved a bird marked out for sacrifice when I heard the frightened murmuring of the crowd. They thought I had resurrected it from death. Nobody knew what to do. Miserably, I crouched in the shade as everyone shouted and argued. The shrine could not be sanctified now, the priests said. The festival was ruined, Venus would be greatly insulted, and it was all my fault.

Only a boy my own age seemed not to care. He sat on a wall nearby, singing to a small bird perched on his finger. The bird cocked its head, and trilled in response, its golden-red breast glowing like a sunset sky. I watched, entranced. The boy put the bird on his shoulder, then rose and came towards me, crouching beside me.

His curls were black, and his eyes merry and golden, almost the same colour as the breast of the little bird on his shoulder.

'It is not wise,' he said, 'to anger the gods.'

His voice was musical and sweet, but his words were terrifying. I was struck dumb, unable to respond or even move. He smiled at me, then rose and slipped away. I could have sworn a nimbus of light shimmered about him, like folded golden wings. But it must have been the all-too-familiar blur of my eyes.

A few days later, Brid died of a burning fever.

Sorrow is a sickness with no easy cure.

I felt her loss in every particle of my body, to the very pith of my bones. I should have been able to save her, as she had saved me. I should have known how to keep her from dying.

But I was only a child. I knew nothing. The only person who could have taught me what I needed to know was Brid herself. But she was dead, and her wisdom with her. It seemed as if a hole had been torn in the very fabric of the universe, as if I would never be able to recover from her loss.

All I had left of her was a spiral brooch. I pinned it to my dress and traced its spiralling path with my fingers many times every day.

Brid's death changed everything for us all, though it was my rashness in frightening away Venus's hawk that was the true cleaver for my family. Alektrona thought I was a fool and was angry with me for ruining her chances of marrying well. Khrysanthe wept because she hated people being angry. And my father feared the goddess's wrath and blamed me when things began to go wrong for him. Ships sank in storms, and his debtors clamoured for payments he could not make. He lost his position as Tarchna's representative to the League of Twelve, a demotion that he took as a personal insult.

'That girl has brought me nothing but misfortune,' he said one day when I was crouched under the table, hidden from view by the tablecloth. 'Indeed, I made a misstep the day I married her mother.'

'She was one of the Galli, my lord?' Lucius Julius asked carefully.

He was a tall young man with unruly dark curls and striking grey eyes, born into a noble Roman family. My father had hired Lucius to teach him everything he knew about Roma, which was growing wealthier and more powerful with every passing year. It was ruled by my father's cousin Tarquin the Proud, who had murdered the king and seized the throne four years before I was born. My father had never been much interested in Roma, since most of his wealth had come from trading with the Greeks, whom he professed to admire greatly. Hence our Hellenic names, and the great number of black-figure vases in our villa. Now he had lost his shipping fleet, though, he was looking to establish new markets with our richest neighbour and so was intent on becoming more Roman than the Romans themselves.

'Yes,' my father answered. 'I have never seen a woman so fair. By the Thunderer, I rescued her! But she never forgave me for taking her away from her home. As white as snow and as cold as ice, she was. And her accursed daughter looks just like her. I should send the girl back to her mother's people. Let her carry the gods' anger with her.'

'But she is only a child!'

'It would cost too much to send her back to the Galli, anyway. I need every coin for making a good show in Roma. I shall sell everything of worth and invest in men and weapons and put them to my cousin's service. It is a boon, in one sense, that my daughters have lost the chance of marrying well. I can use their dowries for other purposes.'

'But what of their futures? What will you do with them?'

'They're too old to be sent to Vesta. I will find somewhere cheap for them to live, at least until the scandal blows over and I have recovered my fortune. Stupid girl, interfering in the priests' business! I could strangle her.'

I crouched lower, trying to be invisible.

Over the next few weeks, my father sold his fine villa, his fat bales of silk and linen, his sacks of rare spices, his barrels of wine, his necklaces of amber and gold, his bronze mirrors, his engraved ostrich eggs, his monkeys and his slaves. Fatima and her mother, Nasrin, were to be sold too, but Alektrona fell to her knees at his feet and begged him to spare them. He looked Fatima over. She was fifteen, with sleek black hair and budding breasts. After a moment he said, 'The girl can stay.'

Nasrin was wretched, but there was nothing she could do. The guards took her away and she was sold at the market with the other slaves. Fatima wept, but my father had her beaten till she could scarcely stand, and after that she crept about the house with downturned face and swollen eyes. There was no more giggling, no more dancing.

When the villa was empty, any valuables he wished to keep packed up in heavy, bronze-bound trunks, my father announced that he was going to Roma to beg his cousin for his favour. 'Roma is no longer our enemy,' he said grandly, 'despite what the lords of Rasenna think. They would be wise to follow my example and throw their lot in with Tarquin the Proud, rather than holing up in their hill towns and hoping he doesn't look their way.'

'But what about us, my lord, where are we to live?' Alektrona demanded.

'You can go to Velzna,' Father said indifferently. 'I have bought an old watchtower there. It has a garden and an orchard. You will need to make do until I can repair our fortunes.' He cast me a look of dislike.

Khrysanthe began to weep. 'But that is so far away from all my friends! I will know nobody there.'

'That is a good thing. It will be a fresh start for you. Let us hope the rumours of the gods' displeasure do not travel with you.'

I stood, silent. I had known no other home. This is where my mother had given birth to me, where Brid had breathed life into me and saved me, and where both had died. I was the only one who remembered them, the only one who honoured them. On the day of the dead, when my father walked the house barefoot, throwing black beans over his shoulder and chanting, 'These I cast; with these beans, I redeem me and mine,' when he beat the gong of bronze and called to the restless spirits to go forth and leave our house, he spoke only of the ghosts of his fathers.

Once I was gone from here, who would venerate the ghosts of my mother and my midwife, the only ones who had ever loved me?

II

City of the Dead

In the dark of the night, I crept out of the house to go to my mother's grave. I went slowly, cold and afraid, wrapped in a heavy cloak and hood.

It was not far to the city of the dead, but I went by devious backways for the road that led to the tombs was where only the poorest lived, the pimps and pickpockets and prostitutes. I had a small lantern with me, but kept it sheltered within my cloak. I wanted no-one to see me.

Somewhere, an owl hooted.

A row of cypress pines cast dark shadows. I flitted from one to the next, my ears alert for any sound other than the wind. At last I reached a small gateway. I slipped through and hurried down an alleyway lined with great stone tombs shaped like beehives. Doorways like dark slits gaped on either side. I uncovered my lantern, casting a low glow so that I could peer at the emblems carved on the lintels. The stone coping above the door of our family tomb bore the face of Hercules, his head enclosed in the ferocious jaws of a dead lion. My father never failed to take any opportunity to remind the world that he was descended from the hero.

Small as I was, I had to crouch to enter the doorway. My heart was beating uncomfortably fast. I crept down the steep steps into the crypt. The air was cold and smelt damp. Shadows sought to blow out the frail flame I carried. The light flickered over bright frescoes of people dancing, feasting, making love. The people of Rasenna took great care to honour their ancestors so that their dissatisfied spirits would not return to haunt them, and so the homes of the dead were as elaborately decorated as the homes of the living. As always, my father took pleasure in proving our wealth and consequence; our family tomb was one of the biggest and grandest in the city of the dead.

I came to the chamber where my mother's bones lay beneath her sarcophagus. The stone was carved with spirals and ravens, emblems of her people. There she lay, as if turned to stone by sorcery. In one hand, she held an egg. I touched her cold face, then kissed my fingers and pressed them to her cold mouth. It was as close as I could ever get to my mother.

I wanted to ask her for a boon but did not know how to say what was in my heart.

'Let me be loved,' I whispered at last. 'Oh, please, let someone love me one day. Let there be someone to mourn me when I am gone.'

My fingers shook as I unfastened Brid's spiral brooch and left it there for her. I had learned there must always be a price to be paid.

The next morning a cart was loaded with our few remaining possessions, and my sisters and I rode away from the hill town of Tarchna where we had lived all our lives. Lucius Julius and a small contingent of guards trotted alongside, their bronze breastplates moulded to their muscular forms, while Fatima trudged behind, shivering in her thin slave's tunic.

'I am so glad you are with us, Lucius,' Khrysanthe said in her sweetest voice. 'They say the road is infested with bandits, but none will dare attack while you are with us.'

'Minerva's spear, we have nothing worth stealing!' Alektrona said. 'Father has left us with nothing. We'll be lucky not to starve this winter.'

'I am so afraid of what lies ahead. You will help us, won't you, Lucius? You do not need to return to our father straightaway, do you?'

Lucius frowned. 'I'm afraid I must, my lady. Lord Cassius was very clear in his instructions.'

Khrysanthe sighed. 'Whatever is to become of us? Leaving our beloved home forever! I have such fears for the future.'

'I will do my best for you while I can, my lady,' Lucius promised her, and led her horse through the crowded streets towards the town gates.

Fatima struggled to follow, her sandals slipping in the mud. Alektrona looked back, then said impatiently, 'Come, ride with me, we will take forever at this rate.' She held down her hand to the slave girl, who set one foot upon her boot so she could be pulled up in one swift, graceful movement.

Khrysanthe frowned. 'It is not seemly to ride with a slave. Father would be most displeased if he saw.'

'Father is not here,' Alektrona said indifferently, and undid her cloak so she could fling it about them both, keeping Fatima warm.

Our small party turned away from the sea and followed the road as it wound through the marshes. It was cold and grey. Somewhere a melancholy bird called. I looked up anxiously, dreading another

15

evil omen, but the skies were empty. We seemed free for now from the gods' malevolent gaze.

It took us four days to reach Velzna.

Enclosed within high walls of golden stone on the summit of a towering rock, the town floated high in the heavens. As we came close, I had to crane my neck to see it. It glowed in the last light of the day, spilling out from a rift in the purple-massed clouds. The wind was bitter, and Khrysanthe had her fur-lined cloak wrapped close about her. Lucius rode beside her, turning often to gaze into her face as they spoke together in low voices. Fatima still rode behind Alektrona, the slave girl's arms wound tight about my sister's slim waist. I had heard tales of magical beasts made of different creatures, like the horse with the wings of an eagle, or the chimera that had the face and forequarters of a lion but the tail of a lashing serpent. My sister and her slave were like one of those mythical beasts, two girls sewn together as if they were one.

I rode alone at the end of the procession. Even in a crowd, I was always alone.

The road rose steadily through terraces of small bare-leaved vines and olive trees, the gnarled trunks wrapped warmly in sheepskins against the frost. The cliffs soared upwards like an immense wall. Small caves had been hand-hewn into its base and fitted with rough wooden doors, for storing tools and supplies, I guessed. Above, small square holes had been dug for doves to nest. They flew in and out, cooing, and I shivered. I had not liked Venus's birds since Brid's death.

It was dusk by the time we reached the heavy wooden gate, barred and studded with bronze, and guarded by two burly men in leather. They demanded to know our business, and Lucius strode forward to show them my father's seal, the head of Hercules enclosed within the gaping jaws of a dead lion. The guards looked at us with sudden fearful interest.

I had drawn my cloak around me, head lowered. As the guards came to search our cart, one looked up at me and jerked back in surprise.

'An ice witch?' He clutched his spear closer. 'What does she do here, so far from the pale mountains?'

'She is the youngest daughter of Lord Cassius of Tarchna, who owns a residence in this town,' Lucius said coldly.

'He married one of the Galli,' one guard muttered to the other. 'All witches and warriors, that lot.'

'Watch your tongue!' Lucius said. 'I would not wish your ill manners to cause any discord between my lord and yours. Now let us pass.'

'You will need to pay the gate tax,' the guard replied in a sullen tone. Lucius tossed him a small piece of stamped bronze, but the guard shook his head and demanded more. Angrily, Lucius gave him another heavier coin. The guard weighed the coins carefully, recorded their value, and locked them away in a strong box.

'The lord of Velzna is rich as Croesus,' Lucius said as the guard lifted a huge hammer to knock the bolt from the gate. 'Yet still he charges a hefty price for entry to his town!'

'What do you expect?' Alektrona said scornfully. 'He is of the Rasenna, and you are Roman. Everyone knows the king of Roma wants to bring the League of Twelve to heel. He probably thinks you're a spy.'

Lucius gestured around him. 'I think Velzna need not fear the king just yet. Look at this place, it's impregnable.'

The gateway had been hewn from living rock, so that we rode through a deep shadowy tunnel to enter the town. The road tilted steeply upwards, our horses' hooves clattering on the cobbles. Small houses made of stone and wood and thatch crowded close on either side. Swallows darted through the sunset sky. I kept my hood drawn close to my face, conscious of many curious glances. Children dropped their ball to come and stare and point. An old woman stopped sweeping her doorstep, and another paused in her spinning. Two men looked up from their game, the thrown dice still spinning, gazing at me open-mouthed in surprise.

I hated it. Hated being stared at, hated the pointing fingers. I dropped my gaze, drawing my hood so close I could scarcely see a thing.

The market square was at the height of the rock, a temple at one end and a grand palace along the southern side, guarded by tall, muscular slaves with bronze breastplates. A deep cistern had been carved from stone in the centre of the square, with women chattering and laughing as they filled their buckets with water. Beyond were the terracotta roofs of the villas of the great families, as always built to face the east and the rising sun. Automatically we rode that way but, sombre and frowning, Lucius halted us, indicating we needed to turn down an alley on the left. Khrysanthe and Alektrona looked at each other in horror. North was the least propitious of all directions. The entrance to the underworld lay that way, and so too the cities of the dead.

The alley was dirty and potholed, lined with mud huts, smoke trickling from the thatch. Someone tossed the contents of a chamber-pot out the door, narrowly missing Khrysanthe. She shrieked, making her horse shy, then held her nose.

At a crossroads, where the road split into three, Lucius drew his horse to a standstill. In the high stone wall was a massive wooden gate, banded and studded with bronze. A gorgon's head was carved on the stone lintel. Lucius rapped on the door with the hilt of his sword.

A deep bark sounded, making me flinch and the horses rear and sidestep. Then a wooden panel of the gate slid open, and a brown wizened face peered out. It was an old woman, holding a flaming torch in one hand. Unsteady light flickered over the crevices of her face and made an aureole of her frizzy white hair.

'Who is there?' she croaked.

'Lucius Julius, guardsman in the service of Lord Cassius Tarquinia of Tarchna, accompanying his daughters to their new home.'

'Show me his seal.'

Lucius drew out the wax medallion, imprinted with my father's insignia, but the old woman insisted he dismount and move closer, so she could examine it by the light of her torch. Impatiently he complied, though the barking increased in volume and ferocity with every step he took.

'Hush, Nera,' the old woman said. At once the dog fell silent.

She examined the seal closely, then looked with curiosity at us all. 'Three daughters,' she muttered. 'One will wed for hate, one will wed for gold, and the last will wed for love.'

My heart thumped hard in my chest.

'What was that?' Khrysanthe said, leaning forward eagerly. 'One to wed for gold? Who? Which one of us?'

The old woman looked up at her with dark hooded eyes. 'Seek not to know your fate, child. Remember Croesus, who was told if he went to war, he would destroy a great kingdom. So he went to fight, not realising it was his own kingdom that he would be destroying.'

I gazed at her wonderingly. It was an odd coincidence, having this old woman refer to the long-dead ill-fated king that Lucius had mentioned earlier.

'Stop your mumblings and let us in,' he ordered. 'It's as cold as Hekate's tit out here.'

19

She cackled with laughter and shut the wooden panel. We stood shivering in the street, waiting, wondering if she meant to admit us. Just as Lucius's patience broke and he reached to pound with his fist on the door, we heard the turn of a key in the lock and the rusty screech of bolts drawn back. The gate creaked open.

A huge black dog bounded out. The horses shied away, hooves slipping in the mud. Khrysanthe screamed, and Alektrona wrenched her horse's head around. Lucius cursed and drew his sword.

'Stop!' The old woman hobbled into the street, raising one urgent hand.

'Keep that dog under control or I shall kill it,' Lucius commanded.

'No need for killing.' The old woman clicked her fingers and the dog returned obediently to her side. Its massive head was higher than her elbow. 'Nera is here to guard your master's house, both from the living and the dead.'

Our guards made the sign of the horns, their middle fingers folded down and tucked under their thumb, index and little fingers extended downwards. It was an instinctive gesture against bad luck that I had often seen directed at me.

'What do you mean?' Lucius kept his sword raised.

'This house is built above the graveyard. Not all who lie there sleep peacefully.'

Khrysanthe gave a little cry. 'Oh, I want to go home! I don't want to live in some miserable hovel haunted by ghosts. Lucius, take us home.'

'My lady, I cannot. I'm sorry. Your father's orders were very clear. Do not mind the old hag, she seeks to frighten you.'

'Not at all. I simply speak the truth.'

'How dare you speak to us so!' Alektrona spurred her horse forward. 'Out of my way!'

The old woman held up one gnarled hand, and the horse shied. 'Beware how you speak to me, child, for you are a stranger in this town but all here know and trust me. I am the gatekeeper here, and it is I who chooses who may enter and who may leave.'

There was a long moment of silence, the old woman barring the way, the great dog standing by her side, hackles raised, growling menacingly.

Lucius said irritably, 'Then let us enter, gatekeeper, before our balls are frozen off!'

She laughed and dragged open the heavy door. I had expected it to open into a room, but instead I saw a tangle of brambles and briars, sharply silhouetted against the twilight sky. Beyond soared the dark shape of a tower with a pointed roof. It was the last moments before the sun sank away, and the light was eerie and greenish, giving everything a strange patina.

My pony was still skittish and afraid, so I slipped down to the ground to calm and comfort her. I was so stiff and sore after the days of riding that my legs almost buckled beneath me. Lucius led Khrysanthe's horse through the gate, and Alektrona spurred on her own mount, Fatima clinging to her waist. The gate was just wide enough for the cart, though the guards had to manoeuvre it through the stone pillars. I hung back, waiting, stroking my pony's velvety nose. No-one paid me any heed.

'What is your name, little one?' the old woman asked out of the shadows.

'Psykhe,' I answered shyly.

'Welcome to your new home, little butterfly.'

Her voice was so gentle, I lost a little of my fear and peeked at her from behind my pony. Her face was brown and wrinkled as a walnut, and her black eyes were deeply hooded. She wore a long black robe. 'Would you like to pat my dog? I know she's big, but she's very gentle.'

Timidly, I came a little closer, and reached out one hand to stroke the dog's velvety soft fur. She turned her big ugly head and licked my hand.

'You have ridden a long way these past few days,' the old woman said. 'Make sure you have a hot bath tonight, with as much salt as you can hold with both your hands. Toss in some rosemary and stinging nettles too. You will find them both growing in the garden by the kitchen door.'

Nodding in silent thanks, I wondered what her name was but did not dare ask.

She smiled at me. 'You may call me Mistress Nocturna.'

Nera and Nocturna. Names that meant night.

'Go in now,' she said. 'It is cold and soon will be colder still. Snow is on its way. Light a strong fire tonight.'

I nodded and led my pony through the gate.

Very gently, she said, 'I hope you will be happy here.'

I turned, frowning. I did not know what happiness would seem like.

She smiled. 'Remember, Psykhe, all things are possible in all possible worlds. Even happiness.'

I thought about that as the guards forced a way through the brambles with their swords, cursing as the sharp hooks tore their skin. *What would happiness be like for me?*

Love. Safety. Kindness.

Beyond the brambles was the tower, with a thatched house on one side. A wall ran along the edge of the cliff. I ran to climb and look over its edge. I saw a misty landscape of fields and forests, so far below it was like we were on an island floating in the sky. To the west was a smear of red. To the north, bruise-coloured peaks rising so high they looked like storm clouds.

My heart jumped. Could they be the pale mountains where my mother had been born?

'It's an old watchtower,' Lucius said. 'Looks like it was abandoned long ago. These briars would protect it from attack from within the

22

town, and the height of the cliff would protect it from attack from without. Let us find somewhere we can eat and sleep.' He crossed to the house and forced open the door, pushing aside dead sticks and breaking spun cobwebs. 'It's bloody cold,' he said, lifting his lantern to show a dark cavernous space.

'It's going to snow,' I said, breathing so deeply the air hurt my lungs.

He glanced at me in surprise. 'I think the child speaks true. Men, gather up as much firewood as you can.'

I relinquished my pony's reins into the hands of a guard, and took a few steps away from the door. I could smell rosemary. An evergreen hedge ran alongside the path, enclosing a tangle of frost-bitten weeds and a round well.

'A garden,' I said in delight. As I broke off a few rosemary twigs, I felt the burn of nettles on my bare skin.

'Not much of a garden,' Alektrona scoffed. 'More like a bramble patch.'

But I did not listen. Already I was imagining the garden I would make here, like the one my mother had when she was just a girl like me.

I would grow all the healing herbs and flowers I could find. I would make sure no-one I loved ever died again.

III

The Month with No Name

When I woke in the morning, it was to find our bucket of water lidded with ice. We had all slept about the central hearth in the hall, a dark vaulted space with rafters stained black with smoke.

It was my fault that our father had lost his fortune and that we had been banished to this hovel, so I did my best to make amends for my folly. I dusted the shelves, scrubbed the table, fed the fire with wood, and scrubbed out a pot and put some water on to boil so I could wash the dishes. I was hungry but did not know how to make anything to eat. The slave who had been our cook had been sold along with all the others.

Khrysanthe sat as close to the low flames as she could, hunched within her cloak, while Alektrona angrily ordered the men to dig the snow away from the door and to gather us more firewood. Then she told Fatima to make us something to eat.

'I don't know how to cook!' Fatima protested. 'My mother was a dancing girl, not a kitchen slave.'

'How hard can it be?' Alektrona said. 'Surely you just throw it all into a pot and stick it on the fire? I'm hungry.'

Fatima made a little helpless gesture with her hands. 'I will try, my lady, but . . . do we have any food to cook?'

We had eaten at roadside inns on our journey and had been too tired the previous night to do more than find somewhere to sleep. We were all very hungry now, but the pantry was bare.

'Minerva's spear! Does our father want us to starve to death? There's not a crumb in the house!' Alektrona called to Lucius. 'You! Send your men to the market to buy us some food.'

Lucius looked uncomfortable. 'I am sorry, my lady. Your father did not give me any instructions other than to bring you safely here. We are meant to march directly to meet him in Roma.'

'Father will not know if you leave at dawn or at noon. Would you abandon us here in this filthy place, freezing and starving? What kind of man are you?' Alektrona challenged him.

Khrysanthe raised a pitiful face. 'Will you not help us, Lucius? It is not fair that I am punished too.'

Lucius bowed. 'Very well, my lady.' He instructed the men to gather as much firewood as they could, then took Fatima to the market to buy supplies. I kept on scrubbing.

It turned out that throwing handfuls of meat and barley and vegetables into a pot and boiling it fast does not make a very palatable meal. We forced it down. Then, despite all Khrysanthe's pleas, Lucius and his men left, taking our horses with them. We were left alone in this strange old house, with its garden of thorns.

I wrapped my cloak about me and went out to explore. The house was built from a lattice of woven twigs and reeds, daubed heavily with a mixture of clay and straw, with a steeply pitched thatched roof. Laid out before it was a small kitchen garden, set around the well. The water was so dark that I could see my reflection, as pale and ethereal as the moon.

Through an archway to one side of the house was an orchard, full of bare trees and weeds. The old tower stood on the other side of the kitchen garden. I had to force my way towards it through the briars. The key was in the lock. It took all my strength to turn it. Within was a small round room, piled high with broken furniture. A ramshackle ladder led to the next floor. I climbed up, testing each rung carefully before I put my weight on it. One broke, making my heart lurch, but the rest were sturdy enough and soon I was at the top of the tower.

In one corner was a bed shelf, piled with rotting straw. Two stools were set near a vast stone hearth, filled with cold ashes. An old winding horn hung on the wall above. I went to the window, hauled back the broken shutter, and looked to the north where distant mountains soared into the sky.

Could they be the pale mountains where my mother had been born?

Once, Brid had told me, those far distant peaks had been as brown as any other rocky outcrop. Then the prince of the land had fallen in love with the daughter of the king of the moon, and married her. At first they were blissfully happy, but slowly she began to pine with homesickness. Every day she grew thinner and whiter, till he was afraid she would dwindle away altogether. One day he met the lord of the *silvani*, wild forest-dwelling spirits with the power to cast enchantments. The *silvani* lord promised to help the young prince in return for refuge in his land. Seven of his brethren worked together all night to spin the silvery radiance of the moon into a vast shining veil which they hung from every peak. When the princess saw the mountains glimmering as white as the moon, she smiled for the first time in months.

The guard at the gate had called me an ice witch, and wondered what I was doing so far from home.

Are there others in the pale mountains? I wondered. *Other girls who look like me?*

*

It was the month that had no name, the coldest time of the year when it seemed the earth was dead. I was only thirteen and growing fast. I was hungry all the time, but we had little food and did not know how to cook what we had.

Often as I went about my daily chores, I looked down to the rounded barrows of the graveyard that lay at the foot of the cliff. The city of the dead, where bones lay in crumbling heaps, their names forgotten, their souls sucked away. I wondered why my father, usually so proud, owned such a tumbledown old tower, a place where only the poorest would live?

The ravens circling in the wintry sky had no answer to give me.

One day our last sack of beans was empty, and nothing was left of our smoked ham except scraped bone. The sun had come out for the first time in days, so I wrapped myself in a warm cloak and went out into the garden. All was cold and still, glittering with frost. The sharp air made me cough till my chest hurt and I was breathless. I pressed my hand to my sore ribs. When I used to get sick as a little girl, Brid would tuck me up in bed and make me soup with chicken and leeks and sundried plums and parsley, which always made me feel better. But Brid was dead, and we had no chicken and no plums. Perhaps there were some leeks lying buried under the snow, or some old parsley that I could boil up. I was so hungry I felt faint. I scrabbled about in the snow, but found only dead nettles and some rotten turnips.

The wind shifted, bringing the smell of something delicious. My stomach grumbled loudly.

Alektrona came to the door, calling to me to gather more firewood.

'Can you smell that?' I said eagerly. 'Someone is cooking! Do you think they would give us some if we asked them to?'

'We are not beggars,' Alektrona replied haughtily. 'We are Lord Cassius's daughters, and do not deign to plead for alms.'

I sniffed the air. 'It's coming from Mistress Nocturna's rooms. Perhaps she would not mind sharing a little with us?'

'She is our slave. She should have brought us some!' Alektrona began to stride forward through the winter-bare garden, but then cursed as her mantle entangled in the brambles. Being smaller and thinner, I slipped through more easily and hurried towards the blue haze of smoke rising from the boundary wall.

Through an archway I found a small herb garden centred around a pomegranate tree. A long narrow house was built into the thick wall, with regular slits of windows to let in the light. The door stood open, and the black mastiff slept on the sill. Nera must have heard my step, light as it was, because she sat up and regarded me. She was almost as tall as me, and loops of drool hung from her jaws. I backed away.

'Nera just wishes to greet you.' Nocturna's voice surprised me so I jumped. She came towards me, carrying a basket full of rosehips red as rubies. 'Let her sniff your hand, so that she knows you are a friend.'

I held myself steady, holding out my hand. The dog sniffed it thoroughly, then solemnly licked me. I smiled, then turned aside to cough.

'What do you think of your new home?' Nocturna asked.

I thought for a moment. 'It is very old.'

'Indeed it is. Like me.' She laughed, her face crumpling with a thousand wrinkles.

'Is this where you live?' I dared ask.

'Yes, me and Nera. This is our garden.'

I recognised a few plants that Brid had grown, even though little remained of them but a few frostbitten stalks. 'Comfrey,' I said, pointing. 'And lemon balm.'

'Very good. You know your herbs. Most unusual for a lord's daughter.'

'My nurse Brid taught me.' My throat was thick. I had not spoken her name in months.

'She is gone?'

I nodded.

'I am very sorry. May you meet her again one day.'

I thought she had misunderstood me. 'I'll never see her again. She's dead.'

'Nothing ever truly dies,' the old woman said. 'Look at those stalks of lemon balm. So brown and shrivelled. It seems impossible they will ever grow green and vital again. But come spring, they'll return to life once more.'

People were not like plants. A wave of sadness overcame me, and I turned my face away.

'You are shivering. Come in out of the cold.'

I followed Nocturna inside, pausing for a moment on the step to let my sight adjust after the thin brightness of the sun on the snow.

Within was a long room, only a few steps wide. It had warm rugs on the floor and embroidered hangings on the stone walls, and wooden shutters that could be slid over the window slits. Down the far end was a bed shelf, spread with a warm patchwork quilt.

Nera trotted in and lay down on a rug before the charcoal brazier. Nocturna gestured to me to come closer and warm myself. I noticed that, while most of her nails were cut short, the middle one on her left hand was long and sharp. I wondered why but did not dare ask.

'Are you hungry?' she enquired. 'Here, taste of my rosehips while I stir the stew.'

I must have looked puzzled, for she raised her eyebrows. 'What, you've never eaten a rosehip before? No wonder your cough is so nasty. Let me show you.' Smiling, she plucked one of the rosehips and - holding it so I could see - she gently squeezed the hip till a soft red pulp oozed out. Hesitantly I caught it on my fingertip and popped it into my mouth. It was tart but delicious.

Just then Alektrona strode into the room. 'What is that you are cooking? You have meat? And beans? Minerva's spear, you are nothing but a slave, it is wrong that you should eat and we should go hungry!'

'I am not a slave,' Nocturna replied sternly. 'I am as freeborn as you, and this is my home. You have no right to command me.'

Alektrona was at a loss. She had never had anyone refuse to do her bidding before.

'I am willing to share my supper with you,' the old woman said, 'but you must pay for it.'

'We have no money!' Alektrona cried. 'Our father has left us with nothing.'

'Then you must pay for it in kind.'

'What do you mean?'

'You must work for it.'

'Work?'

Nocturna smiled at her astonishment. 'Yes, work. I am old and my joints pain me. I shall help you if one of you helps me.'

'What help do you need?' Alektrona's lip curled in scorn. 'No-one ever comes here. It's not as if you need to open the gate a dozen times a day!'

'Being your father's gatekeeper is the least of what I do,' Nocturna replied. 'My true work is that of helping the women of the town. I ease the passing of their babes into this world and the passing of their grandmothers to the underworld.'

She was a midwife like Brid!

I must have made a little sound of surprise, for both Nocturna and Alektrona looked at me. My sister said, 'Very well then, let Psykhe help you, just so long as we get some supper. My stomach is as hollow as a sucked egg!'

Nocturna smiled at me and lifted the pot of stew off the stove with a thickly folded cloth. 'Carry it carefully, else you'll burn your hand,' she told me. 'When you have all eaten, bring me back my pot and we will begin.'

An hour or so later, I returned with a full belly and an empty pot. Nocturna scoured it clean and put it back on the stove. 'First, I will teach you to make soup, so you can nourish yourself and others. Then I will teach you to make a healing syrup with rosehips and honey to banish that cough. And then we shall go together, you and I, into the town to visit the sick, and those who are with child, and those who have just given birth, and do whatever we can to help.'

I bit my lip, torn between my desire to help and my fear of what the women of the town would say when they saw me.

Once again, Nocturna understood without me having to speak. 'Do not be afraid, little butterfly. They will not care if your hair is white like mine. They will only care that your heart is kind and your hands are gentle.'

I gathered together my courage and took the basket she gave to me. Within me was a bright new eagerness. Nocturna was a midwife, just like Brid. She could teach me everything I needed to know to defy death.

Nocturna's wisdom encompassed every stage of life, from the first cry to the last gasp. Every day she initiated me into the mysteries of healing herbs and expected me to learn their secrets off by heart. I never knew when she would expect me to recite what I had been taught.

One day we sat together in her room, my head bent low over some embroidery. Midwives needed to know how to sew with neat, tiny stitches, Nocturna said, so they could repair any damage done to a woman's body by the convulsions of birth. And giving birth often took a long time. A midwife needed work for her hands and her mind while she waited to be needed. Sewing was hard for me, though, with my blurry eyesight, and so I had to bring my nose almost to the cloth to make my stitches small enough to please her.

'So, Psykhe, do you remember how to make rosehip syrup?'

I screwed up my face. 'Harvest the hips, wash them, remove all the leaves and stalks and the brown spiky bit from the bottom. Chop up fine. Pour boiling water over the chopped hips, then leave to steep overnight . . .'

'How much water?' she asked, then sighed at my apologetic shrug. 'One part rosehips, two parts water. Then what?'

'Simmer it?'

'How long do you simmer it for?'

'Till half the water is gone!'

'Very good. Then what?'

'Strain it through linen a few times.'

'Why?'

'To get all the hairs out.'

'Why?'

'Else you'll get an itchy bottom!' I laughed, then hid my mouth with both hands.

'Exactly. Those tiny hairs can irritate every part of your digestive tract, from your throat all the way through your body. Very well, what do you do once you've strained all the hairs out?'

'Mix with honey, equal parts,' I chanted.

'Very good. And what is our rosehip syrup good for?'

'Colds and coughs and fevers and sore throats.'

'Well done, Psykhe! I'm proud of you. I'll teach you some more remedies we can make with rose petals in the summer. But for now, let's concentrate on what we can forage in winter. I want to teach you about a rare and magical plant that we harvest in the depths of winter. It has golden-green leaves, growing in pairs, small golden flowers and, later, white berries. Do you know what it is?'

'I've seen it before, I think. Sprays of white berries hanging over people's doors and windows.'

'People hang it for protection against malevolent spirits,' she told me. 'It's called mistletoe. There's no other plant like it in the world, for it flourishes green and strong in winter, and fruits in the frost when all the other trees are sleeping. And it has no roots. It does not touch the earth or draw sustenance from it.'

'How does it grow then?'

'It hangs high in the branches of trees and draws its strength from them. Some say it draws out the soul of the tree in which it swings, and that is why it is so magical. It is known as all-heal because it is a natural remedy for so many illnesses, even though every part of it is poisonous.'

Nocturna had my attention now. I stopped practising my stem stitch and stared at her. 'How can a poisonous plant be healing?'

'Many poisons are panaceas. Belladonna, foxgloves, hemlock, poppies, stinking nightshade, mandrake, to name just a few. It's all in how much we give. One drop can heal and ten drops can kill.'

I thought about that. 'But how do you know?'

'You listen to me.' She pointed at the cloth in my hands. 'Why are you not sewing? Your hands can do one thing and your ears another, you know. Keep your stitches as even in length as you can. I will teach you about poisons another day. Today I want to teach you about mistletoe. It's a sacred plant, linked to fertility and death. Proserpina, the queen of the underworld, wears a crown of white berries and her mistletoe wand revives the dead. Because of this, a sprig of mistletoe is the best protection against ghosts and witches.'

I nodded, repeating silently to myself, *Mistletoe, underworld, ghosts*.

'We harvest all-heal in midwinter, at moonrise, six days after the new moon, with a blade that is not made of iron. You must take great care that no part of it touches the earth, else all its power will be lost. When was the new moon?'

I did not remember.

Nocturna frowned. 'A midwife must always know the phases of the moon, Psykhe. It's how we keep track of time. The moon was dark six days ago.'

'So it's time to harvest mistletoe?' I asked eagerly. I much preferred going foraging with Nocturna to sitting still and sewing.

'It is. Get your cloak and boots. We have a long way to go, for mistletoe is hard to find indeed. We shall need to go deep into the woods.'

I ran to get my cloak from its hook by the door. Nera stood up too, tail wagging. She knew the word *go*. 'What shall we do with the mistletoe once we have it?'

'Women who wish to have a baby carry a sprig in their pockets or drink a tisane of mistletoe and mugwort. We also use it with verbena and vervain for those suffering nervous exhaustion and make a salve for those who have sores or ulcers on their skin. And we'll sell bunches of it at the midwinter fair.'

'For people to hang above their doors and windows to banish ghosts.'

'Yes, though a great many girls will want a sprig to put under their pillows on midwinter's eve.'

'Why do they do that?'

'To dream of who they're going to marry in the spring.'

I made a face. 'We'd better not tell Khrysanthe that, or she'll take it all!'

34

IV

Roses of the Muses

A few days later I went with Nocturna to the midwinter fair. As she had predicted, our bunches of mistletoe sold swiftly and our basket was soon so heavy with bartered produce that I needed both hands to carry it. A few people paid with misshapen bronze coins, stamped on one side, and Nocturna treasured those as it meant she could buy some of the more exotic ingredients brought by the pedlars from faraway lands.

At one stall she purchased a gnarled old root, saying with satisfaction, 'Ginger, Psykhe! Very good for colds. Grind the root, mix with dried elderflowers, and steep in boiling water, then add a good dollop of honey. Or you can stir some in with your rosehip syrup.'

Every purchase was a lesson, and I was afraid my head would burst from trying to remember it all.

An entrancing phrase of music lilted through the bustling crowd, unlike anything I'd ever heard before. I turned, peering to see. An old man sat on the stone edge of the cistern, playing a flute made of reeds bound together with leather. He wore a long brown robe, patched and torn, and his wild grizzled hair was matted into elflocks that hung past his waist. His beard looked as if it had never seen comb or scissors.

A boy with black curls and hazel eyes ran out, juggling four small golden balls. I caught my breath, an odd twist in the pit of my stomach. I knew that boy! He was the one who had spoken to me after I'd saved the life of the dove at Venus's temple. *It is not wise to anger the gods*, he had said.

He saw me at the edge of the crowd, caught his balls, and cartwheeled over to me, landing gracefully right in front of me, laughing.

'It's you,' I said stupidly.

'Yes, it's me.'

'What are you doing here?'

'Performing for my supper,' he replied. He waved a hand towards the wild-haired musician. 'That is my great-uncle Silviano. Give me a moment. I must collect what I can before the crowd wanders off again.'

He grinned at me over his shoulder as he ran round the crowd, begging for alms. I watched shyly. One or two tossed him a coin, but most gave him something from their shopping baskets – a bread roll, a handful of currants, an onion.

'I'm Ambrose,' he said in a friendly way. 'You?'

'Psykhe,' I managed to say.

'Pretty name. I've never heard it before. Psykhe.'

It sounded pretty in his mouth. As if he was singing it.

'I've come to visit my grandmother. At least, she's not really my grandmother, but I call her that. Don't I, *nonnina*?' He grinned over my shoulder.

'I'm the closest thing to a grandmother you'll ever have,' Nocturna replied.

I jumped in surprise, not having seen her coming towards us.

36

'Ambrose is my niece's adopted son,' she explained. 'He often comes to visit me. Not usually without warning though.' She looked past him to the musician. 'Silviano, what do you do here? Is something wrong?'

'The boy was curious,' Silviano answered in a low voice, glancing at me. 'He wanted to know who dared defy *her*.'

He spoke the last word with emphasis, and a quick darting look around as if he feared being overheard. I do not think he meant for me to hear what he said. But my hearing had always been sharp, perhaps because my eyesight was dim.

'I was tired of always having to be my mother's messenger boy,' Ambrose said defiantly. 'I wanted an adventure.'

'Well, it is always good to see you, Ambrose,' Nocturna said. 'Does your mother know where you are?'

'No,' he replied. 'But she will not care. She has a new lover.'

'I see.'

'Please don't tell her! She will make me go home. I don't want to.' In his alarm, Ambrose grasped her arm, looking pleadingly into her face.

'You will need to let her know you're safe. She'll be worried about you.'

Ambrose looked sceptical, and Nocturna smiled at him. 'I'll send her a messenger tonight. Now you and Psykhe go and play while I catch up with Silviano.'

Ambrose rolled his eyes derisively. 'We're not babies, *nonnina*! We don't *play*.'

'Then take Nera for a walk. She needs a good run. Off you go and try not to cause any trouble for once.' Nocturna waved her hand dismissively.

As I followed Ambrose and Nera away through the crowd, the musician said to Nocturna, 'It is good to see you. What news?'

'Evil portents in the sky,' she replied. 'I fear war is coming.'

'When?'

'Not yet. We have a little space of time.'

I heard no more, for Ambrose turned to me, his eyes dancing with mischief. 'Come on! Let's explore.'

I nodded shyly, afraid and enchanted in equal measures. I had feared he was some messenger of the gods, with his warning that had brought such tragedy into my life. But Nocturna was his adopted grandmother, I reminded myself. He was just a boy.

'Do you like it here?' he asked, leading me through the crowd.

I nodded, too timid to speak.

'Why?'

'I like the garden,' I ventured. 'And the tower. And the view to the mountains. I like helping your *nonnina*. And I love Nera!'

Nera heard her name and lolloped towards me, wagging her tail, long loops of drool swaying from her jaws. She jumped up to lick my face, and slobber flew all over both me and Ambrose. We laughed and rubbed our faces clean.

'Your fault – you wear it!' Ambrose said, threatening to wipe his hands on my clothes. I shook my head, backed away, and tripped over Nera, landing on my backside in a puddle. That just made us laugh even more. Ambrose pulled me up and began to run, pulling me along by the hand. I ran with him, breathless, my hair falling out of its plait, clutching my muddy skirts with my free hand. Nera pranced alongside, barking with joy.

I had never had a friend. My sisters did not like me much, and the children of Tarchna had always been afraid. Perhaps they knew the story of the white-haired boy who had been sacrificed and buried beneath the town square, or perhaps it was simply because I had died and been brought back to life. Ambrose knew neither of these tales, so he treated me just as if I was an ordinary girl. He made me laugh by walking on his hands, and by pretending he was a fine lord wanting to buy me an amber necklace, rather than a ragged boy without a piece of silver to his name.

We passed the fullers at their work, treading on the town's dirty laundry in their deep troughs and scraping at the stains with hedgehog skins. Ambrose saw one of the fullers coming back from the winehouse with a ceramic jar full of urine, gathered for its power to cut through grease and dirt on fabric. Ambrose ran towards him, dodging sideways at the last moment so the poor man slopped the jar's stinking contents all over himself. I could not help laughing.

'At least it's easy for him to wash himself clean,' Ambrose said, holding his nose in comic exaggeration at the smell.

The man chased after us, shaking his fist. Ambrose grabbed my hand and we fled. Ahead was the lord's palace with its grand colonnade of arches. Guards stood by the great front door, so we veered away and ran down a side alley, the man still chasing us. A half-open doorway revealed a flight of steps. We scrambled down, Ambrose kicking the door shut.

The steps were narrow and steep, and light ripped strangely on the stone walls. I could smell dampness and hear water lapping. We came out on a stone platform beside an underground cistern. Light shone down in narrow rays from cracks and holes in the stonework above, touching the water with ripples of gold. To one side was a deep basin, connected to the cistern by a delicate stone lattice so the water flowed in and out.

Nera trotted forward and lowered her head to drink from the basin. Suddenly she yelped and leapt away, her tail between her legs.

'There's something in the water. Look, eels!' Ambrose cried.

I crouched down, peering, and to my amazement saw a multitude of pale sinuous creatures writhing through the water.

'Careful, don't fall in.' Ambrose put a steadying hand on my shoulder. 'Eels have a nasty bite. I wonder why they keep them here. Maybe the lord likes eel pie?'

'Maybe it's to keep the water in motion so it doesn't become stagnant? And it'd stop mosquitos breeding.' I knew all about that, having grown up near the swamps of Tarchna.

He looked at me in sudden swift admiration. 'That would be it. Clever. Look, there's a tunnel. Come on, let's see where it leads.'

The tunnel led to other chambers and cellars, filled with boxes and sacks. One had a small millwheel driven by water that gushed down a deep channel gouged in the rock. Another contained wine barrels, sacks of grain, jars of pickled fruit and vegetables, and yet another had doves nesting in little niches, with a small opening to the sunset sky. Ambrose frowned at the sight and turned abruptly away. 'Come on, it's getting dark, we should be getting back.'

He put out his hand to guide me, and I took it gratefully, for twilight was falling fast and I could see little. He must have had eyesight like an owl's, though, for he led me rapidly through the maze of cellars.

'There's enough water and food here for the town to last a long siege. Who is the lord here?' Ambrose asked.

'Lord Quintus. He's the leader of the League of Twelve and very rich.'

'I'm not surprised. He makes it a law that we must come inside the city walls to sell our wares, then charges us all a hefty entrance fee!'

'I have never seen him, but your *nonnina* attends his wife sometimes.'

'Nocturna's not really my grandmother,' Ambrose said. 'And my mother's not my true mother either – she adopted me and a whole lot of other boys too. I don't know who my real parents are, or where I came from.'

'Doesn't your mother . . . your adopted mother . . . know?'

'If she does, she won't tell me. She likes having me at her beck and call all the time.'

'It was kind of her to adopt you,' I said tentatively.

'Was it? I suppose so. Kind is not the word I usually associate with her.'

'Is she cruel to you?'

'Not cruel. Not really. She just . . . she likes to get her way, I suppose, and is angry whenever anyone stands up to her. That's why . . .'

'What?'

'Why I ran away. I wanted to stand up to her somehow. No-one ever does. Except . . .' Once again he stopped abruptly.

'Except who?'

'Except me now, I suppose. Oh, she's going to be furious.' Ambrose laughed, shaking off his sombre mood. 'Come on, let's hurry, they'll be wondering where we are.'

We ran together through the narrow streets, Nera bounding alongside. I had lost my ribbon, and my long hair rippled free. Ambrose cast me an admiring glance. 'I've never seen hair like yours before. It's like moonlight on the sea.'

I laughed and tossed my head, for once not trying to hide it away.

Silviano sat on the edge of the stone cistern, playing a wild and merry tune on his reed flute. Ambrose caught my hand and we ran to join the crowd of dancers, spinning under the hundreds of swift-winged swallows that darted through the twilight sky. Stars began to glimmer overhead.

At last it was too dark to see. The stallholders began to pack up their wares by the light of smoky tallow candles, and a slave lit the oil lamps outside the lord's villa, sending golden light rippling across the deep water of the cistern. Silviano lowered his flute, and bowed to the departing crowd who flung coins and favours into his soft hat. He beckoned to us. 'Ambrose, my boy, Nocturna has gone to the lord's villa, his wife is unwell. Will you run and get her? It is time for us to go and I do not want to leave Psykhe here alone.'

Ambrose nodded and ran off. Silviano smiled and patted the stone. 'Come, sit with me. Do you like music? Let me sing for you.'

He drew a lute out of a leather case and began to strum its strings. The song was delicate and strange and sad.

> When you die, you will lie forgotten,
> No memory of you left behind, nor longing,
> for you have not eaten the roses of the muses.
> You will drift invisible in the underworld,
> A shade among the shadowy dead.

The words worried me. What did it mean? I did not want to lie forgotten, I did not want to drift invisible among the shadowy dead. I wanted to be remembered forever.

I summoned all my courage and wriggled a little closer. 'Please,' I whispered. 'Your song? What does it mean?'

He looked down at me kindly. 'To eat the roses of the muses means to sing and tell stories and remember the past, seeking to radiate the light of knowledge into this dark world.'

I smiled, liking that idea. Silviano reached into his pedlar's pack and drew out a narrow scroll of paper. 'Here is the song. It was written by the poetess Sappho long ago.'

He unrolled it for me, and I gazed down at the dark marks upon the paper. They meant no more to me than the squiggles left behind on leaves by certain moths.

'Can you not read?' he asked gently.

I shook my head. My father had seen no point in paying a tutor to teach mere girls.

He spread the scroll on his knee, pointing to each collection of marks and telling me what they meant. Roses. Muses. Underworld.

'Are there marks for everything?' I asked.

He nodded.

I looked at the swallows darting through the crimson sky.

'How do you write "bird"?'

The musician drew the marks on the muddy ground with the end of his crooked stick, and I crouched so I could trace them with my finger. 'They don't look much like swallows.'

He laughed. 'There are an infinite number of phenomena in the universe, my child. It would take an infinite number of lifetimes to learn them all. No, the marks do not represent the thing itself, they represent the sounds we use to speak their name.'

One by one he traced the marks again, pronouncing each sound slowly and distinctly so that I could hear how they linked into a word. I clasped my hands together. 'What about *me*? What are my marks?'

'You want to know how to write your name?'

I nodded eagerly.

He bent and drew four deep marks on the ground.

Ψυχη.

'Psykhe,' he said.

I carefully traced the marks with my finger. I wanted to learn my name by heart and never forget it.

Spring came, and the garden stirred back into life. Sweet-scented violets grew beneath the plum trees, and the pomegranate put out tiny crimson buds like drops of blood. I felt a quickening of life within me as if the green sap that sang in their stems sang also in mine.

Most of my days were spent in the garden. As well as providing us with food, it was a medicine chest for the people of Velzna. Nocturna and I did our best to help anyone who needed it, and it was a rare morning when someone was not on our doorstep at dawn, begging for the remedy for one ailment or another. Sometimes they paid with a basket of fresh figs or a loaf of new baked bread, other times with help in the house and garden. With my eager help, Nocturna was able to produce a great many more salves and tinctures than before. We worked side-by-side, planting countless healing plants in the garden and harvesting and distilling their essences. Gradually we repaired the broken walls, the rotting thatch, the table with its uneven leg. The weeds and brambles were tamed, and the garden restored to order.

Last to bloom were the rose briars. Furled buds opened into delicate pale blooms, flushed faintly with pink, with golden hearts the bees loved to dive within. I rushed to gather a handful but pierced my finger on a hidden thorn and had to suck the blood away.

'Roses are like love,' Nocturna said. 'You must dare the thorn to pluck the blossom. That is why they are Venus's flower. Created from seafoam like the goddess herself.'

I looked at Nocturna enquiringly. 'How could a goddess be made of seafoam?'

She leant on her pitchfork, her black dog lying peacefully at her feet. 'Do you not know the story?'

'I know she was born of seafoam, I just don't know how.'

'Ah, you are curious, a seeker of knowledge, a questioner. That is good, particularly for one who wants to cure people.'

I tilted my head to one side. 'Cure and curious. They sound the same.'

'That's because they grow from the same root, which is the word that means to care.' She smiled at me. 'Would you like me to tell the story to you?'

'Yes, please.' I sat down cross-legged on the grass, picking daisies and dandelions and weaving them together into a crown.

'Long, long ago,' Nocturna began, 'Gaea was born out of the void, the first and oldest elemental being. Her body is the earth on which we live, and all living things were born from her, and so we call her Terra Mater, our earth mother.'

I laid my hands on the warm earth wonderingly.

'Gaea was lonely, so she created the sky god to be her consort. She lay beneath him and they conceived many children. It had been foretold, though, that he would be dethroned by one of his offspring, and so the sky god forced his children back inside her womb, causing her great anguish and pain. At last Gaea begged her children for help. Saturnus, her youngest and most dangerous son, was the only one who dared confront his father. He castrated him with a stone sickle, then flung his balls far across the sea.'

I made a face. 'Why? That seems a mean thing to do.'

'He was angry and wanted revenge. Remember, his father had kept him and his siblings imprisoned for a long time. Now where was I?'

'Stone sickle,' I prompted, not wanting to say the other words.

'Oh yes. Saturnus cut off his . . .' Nocturna saw my expression, and made a vague circling motion with her hand. 'His father's private parts. They flew across the sea and landed with a great splash. Out of the foam, Venus was born in a cascade of white roses. Many years later, she became besotted with the young mortal prince Adonis, a heedless young man who loved to go hunting. One day, he was gored by the tusks of a wild boar. Venus ran to help him, but she trod on a fallen rose and its thorn pierced her heel. Wounded, she could not reach him in time and so Adonis died. The goddess's blood stained the rose petals red, a reminder that love must hurt.'

'That's a sad story. Why are so many stories sad?'

'Because sorrow is a part of life. And so is work. Pick me a basket-ful of those roses and I shall teach you how to make a healing salve to put on your finger.'

V

Hidden Thorn

On the next full moon, Nocturna taught me how to weave willow stems and roses together to make a wreath to hang above our hearth. It was so beautiful my sisters exclaimed with pleasure, and their compliments – so rare – made my heart sing.

'Can you make more?' Alektrona said. 'For I see girls selling posies in the market that are not half as pretty as yours.'

So I made half-a-dozen rose wreaths which we carried to market in a little handcart. They sold out fast, and Alektrona sent me home to make more. Fatima was kept busy running back and forth, snatching each wreath as soon as I finished weaving it. By the end of the day, our handcart was piled high with sacks of beans and flour, a hock of ham, a wicker cage of chicks, a skep of bees, and ceramic jars of vinegar and oil. Alektrona and Fatima laughed as they dragged the handcart through the gate, and Khrysanthe smiled for the first time in months.

'Make some more,' she ordered. 'I badly need a new cloak, my old one is so shabby. And a new dress! And some of those new sandals with the gilded leather thongs.'

'You will need to help then,' Alektrona said. 'You can wear a wreath and smile at all the boys and convince them to buy their sweetheart a posy.'

Khrysanthe dimpled. 'Happy to help,' she answered demurely. 'As long as I can have an ivory comb for my hair too.'

I soon discovered the season of roses was marked by many rites and rituals which would keep me busy in the garden and still-room I had set up in the lower level of the old tower. There was the spring equinox festival, then the Lemuria when all worked to appease the restless ghosts of the dead. After they had been helped on their way to the underworld, it was time to honour those who lay quietly in their graves. The people of Velzna washed themselves in rosewater, then carried great garlands of red roses down into the city of the dead to adorn their family tombs. They would return to a feast of brains cooked with sweet wine and rosewater, cakes heavy with rose-petal syrup, and an intoxicating mead made from rosehips and rose-steeped honey called *rhodomeli*. At that time, the scent of roses hung heavy in the air, so that festival was named the Rosalia.

After that came the Vestalia, when every donkey and every millstone in town was garlanded in honour of the goddess of the hearth. Then it was the season for weddings. Young men wore wreaths of roses and violets and lilies, while young women wore crowns of marjoram under their long yellow veils. All summer I worked hard, for the season of roses was brief and the winter long. Once the rose petals began to fall, I knew our fortunes would too.

My work with Nocturna continued, for there were always babies to be born and the sick to be tended. I still had much to learn too. As well as recipes for medicines, Nocturna taught me to honour the plants that I harvested and to thank the goddesses that helped us in our work. Gaea, mother of all living things. Luna, deity of the moon and women's cycles. Hekate, goddess of witches and midwives, who stood at the boundary of life and death and guided our souls to the beyond with flaming torches. Proserpina, queen of the underworld.

Though I looked for Ambrose and Silviano every time I went to market, they did not come to Velzna again, much to my bitter disappointment. I wanted a friend of my own, someone I could talk to as easily as I had with Ambrose, and I wanted to laugh and sing and dance again. I wanted to learn more words too. I had read the scroll of poetry Silviano had given me till the papyrus was cracking from being unrolled so often.

I soon discovered that other pedlars carried treasures in their packs. I wished for two things. Seeds and stories. I planted the seeds, and in time discovered their true nature. The stories were much more difficult. So many marks I did not know, so many words to learn. Whenever I had a spare moment, I unrolled one of the scrolls I had bought and tried to decipher what was written upon it, even though the letters wavered before my eyes, and soon my temples were pulsing with pain. I was determined to master this strange magical art, meaning hidden within marks of ink. So I read late into the night, my nose bent almost to the scroll, till at last the words were nothing but a blur and I had to stop, sick with weariness.

One day, I put a posy of flowers in an old glass bottle on the table and noticed that the stalks within seemed much larger. So I experimented and discovered that, if I filled a glass jug with water and slowly moved it over the letters, I could see their shape more clearly. After that it was much easier. As I learned a new word, I practised writing it with ink I made from walnut juice, often drawing a little picture beside it to help me remember.

As the moons waxed and waned and the seasons turned and turned again, my collection grew. Poems and prayers, recipes and remedies, songs and spells, I read them all. Every day was a new and joyous discovery.

I should have remembered that every rose hides a thorn.

My father came to the tower without any warning a few months after my eighteenth birthday.

I had worked by Nocturna's side for five years, my strong young hands able to do much that she no longer could. I laboured at her instruction in the garden and the stillroom, I listened to all she had to teach me about the art of saving lives, and many times I went with her to the bedside of a woman in labour. Sometimes we returned in silence and sorrow, the scent of blood heavy in our nostrils. More often, though, we returned weary but content, smiling at the thought of the mother with her new child cradled in her arms.

I had even begun to dream of having my own baby one day, perhaps one with black curls and merry golden eyes. For I often thought of Ambrose, wondering what he would be like now that he was a man. The very thought was enough to make me blush hotly. Sternly, I told myself not to be a fool, that he had long ago forgotten me. I could not help hoping, though, that one day in the market-place I would hear a strain of wild music and see a young man juggling golden balls. He would cartwheel towards me, laughing.

'It's you,' I would say stupidly.

'Yes, it's me,' he would answer and draw me close to kiss me.

I was thinking about Ambrose that day as I came into the garden. It had been the midwinter fair when he had come last time, and now another winter had passed with no sign of him and it was spring again. I was too proud to ask Nocturna if she had word of him, though I had asked after Silviano casually, wondering if we would see him at the fair that year.

'Who knows what he's doing?' she had replied, shaking her woolly white head. 'He could be anywhere. He was always a wild one, my brother! No tying him down.'

What of your adopted grandson? I wanted to ask. *Is there no tying him down either?*

But I dared not reveal my secret heart, not even to Nocturna.

It was still cold, my breath pluming white before my mouth. The bare briars of winter were swelling with buds like tiny, cupped hands. One had opened its fragile petals. I cut it gently and laid it in a basket, then went down the steep road to the gateway, hewn out of the living rock. I would have to pay the gatekeeper for the right to return, but the sacrifice of the first bloom had become an important ritual for me. I walked around the base of the towering crag until I came to a graveyard, laid out just like a true town but in the smallest of scales. The homes of the dead were tiny, though each had a peaked roof and a front door just like a real house. The name of each occupant was engraved above the door.

I walked along one of the narrow streets towards a shrine built under the overhang of the cliff. A small statue of a naked woman stood there, surrounded by wild roses and myrtle. She was carved from rare white marble, and wore golden earrings hung from holes pierced through her earlobes. The earrings depicted a little winged boy with a bow and quiver of arrows. One of the statue's marble hands grasped a dagger as if about to strike a blow, and the other was lowered to hide her womanly cleft. In that hand she held a marble egg.

I had discovered the shrine by chance one day, searching for rosehips to propagate for my garden. The egg in her cupped hand made me think of my mother, so every spring I honoured the statue with the first rose.

An enchanting trill of music interrupted my thoughts. I paused, looking about, but there was no-one to be seen. Quietly I climbed the overgrown steps, careful not to stumble on the broken stones, and peered through the mossy branches of an old myrtle tree.

An old man sat cross-legged on the ground, playing a flute made of reeds. His matted locks of hair fell down his back almost to the ground, tied here and there with beads and feathers.

'Silviano!' I cried in delight and amazement. 'I was just thinking of you!'

Nimbly he leapt to his feet and held out his hands to me. 'Psykhe! Look at you, little butterfly, grown into a woman.'

'Silviano, it is so good to see you. It has been so long. Where have you been?'

'Where have I been? Travelling the world, my dear, singing and playing my flute and filling my pack with new treasures to sell.'

'Is . . . is Ambrose with you?' I looked about, trying not to seem too eager.

'Alas, no. His mother wishes him to be always by her side, and he finds it hard to escape. She is not easy to defy, you know.'

'But . . .' I changed my words at the last moment, saying, 'what are you doing here?' I gestured at the lichen-grey tombs, the marble statue.

'I have brought a gift for Venus.' His expression turned sombre. 'Many people forget that she is the goddess of hate, as well as of love, and when she is angry she can be merciless. It is not good for her shrine here to be so neglected. Nothing enrages her more.'

A sinking sensation in my midriff. 'This is a shrine to Venus?'

He cleared away the nettles to reveal an engraved bronze plaque that read: *Vei*. The Rasennan name for Venus.

'The implacable goddess of desire,' Silviano said. 'She rules all longings of the human heart, the wish to hurt as well as to heal, to sunder as well as to save. Once she was revered here. But now the god of thunderbolts rules everywhere, and she is thought of as no more than a beautiful face and a beguiling body. Her shrine has been allowed to fall into ruins; she is forgotten and neglected. I do not want her to punish Velzna, when I have loved ones here.' He smiled at me. 'So I have brought a rare and fabled rose for her. I found it in the far city of Damascus and have endured much danger and hardship to bring it back here. I planted it bare-rooted, in the month that has no name, and have come back now to see how it grows. Look, is it not beautiful?'

A rosebush had been planted so it could greet the sun rising in the east. Never had I seen such a rose. Elaborate frilled buds abounded, a few already bursting open into a multitude of sweet-scented white petals, tightly whorled about a stigma the colour of the sea.

'A thousand-petalled rose,' Silviano said with satisfaction. 'The green eye is said to protect against evil, and bring luck and love, and the flower blooms from the last snows of winter to the first.'

'How much does such a rose cost?' I asked shyly. I wanted one badly. Not just because such a beautiful and unusual rose would help me restore my family's fortunes. I longed for it because it was rare and strange, like me, and because I wanted to be loved so much.

'A fortune!' Silviano answered. 'Not to mention the difficulties of bringing it back the thousand leagues between here and Damascus!'

'I'd give anything for a rose like that.'

'For you,' he said, plucking one of the long stems with its blowsy white rose and two fat rosebuds.

I took it with reverent hands. 'Thank you,' I said. 'Will you come back with me and see Nocturna? We could give you lunch.'

'I would have to pay the gate tax,' he said, 'and I have no silver to spare. The rose cost me everything I had. Will you give my regards to my sister and tell her I will see her soon?'

I promised to do so, said my farewells, and carried my stem of roses home with great care, so as not to lose a single petal. I put it in a jug of water on the table in my stillroom, marvelling at the delicacy of its multitude of white petals, its unusual green heart.

The skirt of my dress was already muddy, so I decided I would work in the garden a while before I washed and tidied myself. I began in the kitchen garden, weeding and clearing away dead leaves and foliage. Nocturna came to help me, the black mastiff at her heels as always. Nera lay down nearby, her chin on her paws, her tail beating the ground every time we came near.

I was telling Nocturna about my unexpected meeting with Silviano when Nera lifted her head and growled, looking towards the gate. Then she sprang to her feet and began to bark. The bell clanged, and someone hammered their fists on the door. Nocturna and I looked at each other in surprise. Most people who came to ask for our help did not knock with such authoritative force.

Nocturna unlocked the gate and dragged it open, and my father trotted in on his grey warhorse. At first I hardly recognised him. He had shaved his beard and cropped his dark hair in the severe Roman fashion, and wore a simple white tunic and a red cloak. But then his frowning dark eyes swept the garden and saw me. He twisted his mouth in displeasure, and I knew it was him.

Three other men rode with him. One was a big man with a foolish grin. His reins hung loose on the horse's neck and he carried a toy wooden sword and shield, waving them aloft as if pretending to be in the cavalry. I was filled with pity. I had heard of men who remained like a child all their lives, but had never seen one before.

The other two men were younger. One wore a long purple cloak and a proud look, while the other was a slim young man with a soft face and long curls. Behind came two dozen men, led by Lucius Julius, the young Roman soldier who had brought us to Velzna. The soldiers' horses trampled the garden underfoot, and the men drew their swords and hacked at the roses, cursing as their cloaks were torn.

54

'Stop it!' I ran forward. 'Please, stop! You're wrecking the garden. We need those herbs and flowers, we cannot help anyone without them, people will get sick, they'll die. Stop!'

They paid me no heed. Nocturna drew me aside, one arm about my shoulders, the other on Nera's collar. I could tell by the stiffness of Nocturna's stance that she was angry, but she did not speak.

Dismounting, Father looked at me with distaste. 'You look like a beggar's brat, Psykhe. Is this how you greet your father? Come and make your obeisance.'

A hard, angry lump rose in my throat. My sisters and I had not seen my father in five years, nor had any communication from him. We had been left to fend for ourselves in wretched poverty, we could have starved or frozen to death or come to all sorts of harm, and his first words to me were as cold and uncaring as ever. For a moment, I stood still, my fists clenched and my jaw set. Then I lifted my grimy skirts as if they were silk, dropped to one knee, and bent my lips to the hand he held out to me.

'Now go and dress yourself more fittingly for the daughter of one of the Tarquins!' He looked at the other men with a deprecating smile. 'Please excuse my daughter, we have obviously caught her unawares. Psykhe! Order the slave girl to bring us some wine.'

'If you had given us warning of your coming, we would have been properly prepared,' I answered coolly. 'Unfortunately, Fatima has gone to the market. I will bring you something to drink.'

He frowned, displeased. I hurried away to my tower room where I hastily washed my face and hands, changed into my best dress and combed the tangles out of my hair, braiding it into a long thin plait that hung past the small of my back.

When I came back into the garden, most of the men had gone through to the orchard where they were setting up camp. My father and the other three lords had dismounted, and their horses had been led away to the stables. They sat at a table under one of the old olive trees, bare legs stretched out in the sun. There was no sign of Nocturna. She must have retreated to her little house within the wall.

I offered my father a cup of well-watered wine, pale and sweet. I expected him to drink at once, but instead he indicated that I offer the wine to the proud young man in the purple cloak.

'Make your obeisance,' he said sternly, 'to Sextus Tarquinius, son of the king.'

Startled, I did as ordered. The young man drank deeply, then looked me over in open curiosity. 'She is indeed as striking as you promised, Cassius.' He looked at the youngest of the men with a sneer on his face. 'Are you not afraid, Collatinus, that lying with her will freeze your cock so it blackens and falls off?'

I was so mortified that I could not look at any of them.

'Psykhe! Take the wine and offer it to our other guests.'

I did not know who to offer it to first. My father indicated the large man with the toy sword. 'The king's nephew, Lucius Junius.'

'Better known as Brutus,' Sextus said with a snigger. 'On account of his stupidity.'

The large man giggled. 'No, it's not. Silly Sextus. It's because I'm strong!' He waved the wooden sword.

'Would you like some wine, my lord?' I offered him a cup.

Brutus grabbed it and lifted it to his mouth. As he drank, he spilled wine all over himself. He then looked inside the cup, puzzled. 'All gone. Where did it go? I want more!'

Wearily my father indicated I pour him more. Once again Brutus drained it to the dregs. 'Want more!'

'That's enough, Brutus. Your cousin has not yet had any refreshment. Psykhe, this is Lucius Tarquinius Collatinus, son of the king's cousin.' My father indicated the youngest of the men. I passed the cup to him, and he looked me up and down with such open interest

I felt as if he stripped me in his imagination. I kept my eyes lowered, but could not stop a hot flush climbing my neck and face.

As I lifted the tray to carry it back to the kitchen, my father rose and drew me aside with a tight grip on my arm. 'We have come for the spring festival,' he said in a low voice. 'All the great lords of Rasenna shall be here, and we wish to woo them into signing a peace treaty with Roma.'

I stared at him in surprise. Tarquin the Proud did not offer peace treaties, he attacked and burned and conquered. I wondered if the so-called peace treaty was really a thinly veiled threat, an act of intimidation.

'My cousin does not wish to expend too much time and money on a long war, and knows how difficult it would be to defeat the League of Twelve. These hill towns are virtually impregnable.' He made a gesture at the watchtower's massive walls and the precipitous fall beyond.

'The king wants the league to submit to him, and he has paid me well to ensure it. If I succeed, he has promised to tie our families more tightly together through marriage. This is a great thing for us, Psykhe. It will make you all princesses, and me father-in-law to the richest and most powerful men in Roma. I warn you now, any defiance or misconduct from you or your sisters, and I will whip the skin from your backs. Do you understand?'

I nodded, and he released my arm. Trying to calm the uneven thumping of my heart, I went back to the kitchen. I feared my father, I feared what lay ahead. I wished he had not come home.

VI

A Hare Hunted by a Hawk

Khrysanthe was waiting for me in the kitchen. 'Is that Father?' she asked incredulously. 'What is he doing here? Who are those men?'

'Sons and nephews of the king,' I answered shortly. The thought of being forced to marry one of them sickened me.

'Did you see if Lucius was with them?' she asked. 'You know, the guard who escorted us here?'

I nodded. She smoothed her curls and pinched her cheeks; then, smiling, carried the tray with a fresh flagon of wine through to the men in the garden. I followed with a platter of smoked meats, cheese and olives.

Lucius stood nearby, a sword at his belt. He looked very handsome in his moulded bronze breastplate. Khrysanthe sent him one brief glance, before pretending to ignore him. He kept looking her way as she poured wine for the men. His grey eyes were bleak.

'Where is your sister?' Father demanded.

Khrysanthe shrugged. 'Who knows, my lord? Probably gone to the market with the slave girl.'

His lips thinned. 'She should have more decorum. Once she is married, she will have to learn to act as befits her rank.'

Khrysanthe looked up at once. 'Married? Who is she marrying?'

'It is past time you were all married! You can make your bow to Sextus Tarquinius, the king's son, his cousin Brutus, and second cousin Collatinus. They have come to petition the league to sign a peace treaty with Roma.'

Colour flared in Khrysanthe's face. She made a graceful bow. 'Welcome, my lords.'

'She's pretty,' Brutus said. 'Is she mine? I want her, she's pretty.'

Khrysanthe cast him a look of undisguised horror.

At that moment, the bell rang. Nocturna hobbled out and unlocked the gate, Nera pressed close to her side. Alektrona and Fatima came in, laughing and talking gaily, carrying a heavy basket between them. Their smiles faded at the sight of Father. Alektrona came forward to greet him, dropping to one knee to kiss his hand, while Nocturna withdrew once more. I would have loved to have gone with her, to sit by the fire in her narrow room and be comforted, but I dared not leave without my father's permission.

Fatima made a clumsy obeisance and hurried away, heaving the basket with both hands. Father looked after her, rubbing his chin. 'Well, she's grown into a little beauty. Tell her to come to us tonight. We shall have some fun with her.'

'No!' Alektrona cried.

He clouted her, and she fell. 'How dare you deny me?' His voice was cold as steel.

'I'm sorry!' Alektrona sat up, holding her face. 'It's just . . . Father, she's not . . . she's not ever had to . . .'

'She's a slave. My slave, to do with as I please. I see I have been away too long, and you have all run wild. You will need to be properly schooled.'

Alektrona bowed her head. 'I beg pardon, Father.' Her voice was constricted. When she got up, there was an angry red mark on her face.

I stood stock still, my throat thick. For the first time I truly realised what it meant to be a slave. Fatima had been with us so long, I had forgotten that she was owned, like the fine horse my father rode or the chickens that had scattered under its hooves. She had been born into slavery, born to serve us and do our bidding. Her mother had been a dancing girl, bought by my father for the sole purpose of entertaining and pleasing him, then sold at market when he had no further use for her. Slaves were everywhere in Rasenna, running errands, guarding the palaces of the rich, digging trenches and graves, tending vineyards and olive groves, so much part of the fabric of the everyday they seemed inevitable. But the wrongness of it struck me now, palpable as a blow. Yet I could not speak out, could not protest, without being punished too. My fear of my father kept me silent, much to my shame. I looked down at the ground, blinded by tears.

'The lord of Velzna is holding a feast tonight to celebrate the festival of Fortuna,' Father said. 'He holds to the old ways, where women and men dine together, and so you have been invited too.'

'Women at a banquet!' Collatinus grumbled. 'Who wants to look at some fat matron while you eat?'

'There are some compensations,' Sextus responded, his eyes on Alektrona, who gave him a cold and haughty look. He smiled in a way that made my skin crawl.

'Will there be pig to eat?' Brutus asked. 'I like pig.'

Father ignored him. 'I have arranged for seamstresses and hair-dressers to come and tend you this afternoon,' he said to me and my sisters. 'You must look your finest. We have hired a villa in town for ourselves, though I must say this place is not such a hovel as I expected. I will send Lucius Julius to escort you at sundown.'

He bowed and gestured for us to withdraw. As soon as we were out of sight, I rushed to help Alektrona. I took her to my stillroom, bathed her face, gave her a cold compress to press to the bruise, then rubbed in some salve made from comfrey and calendula. She was trembling.

'What can I do?' she muttered.

'There is nothing you can do. And you were a fool to provoke him so,' Khrysanthe reproved her. 'You know he cannot bear to have his will thwarted.'

Alektrona was as close to weeping as I had ever seen her. 'I hate him!'

'I for one am pleased he's come back. I thought I'd die here, unwed and untouched, considered a peculiarity by all. I was ready to fling myself off the cliff.' Khrysanthe sighed melodramatically. 'Though being unwed can't be any worse than being married to that fat fool. Surely Father cannot mean to marry me to him?'

'I don't want to be married!'

'Well, you are peculiar. What else is there for a woman to do? Wash your eyes and put on some chalk powder, and, for Juno's sake, try not to scowl so much.'

For the rest of the afternoon, we were scrubbed and brushed and plucked and oiled, then my sisters were made to stand as folds of soft linen were pinned about them. Khrysanthe wore a dress of her favourite yellow, and Alektrona chose royal purple. I, however, was brought a dress unlike anything I had seen before. It was severely made from finely spun white wool, without any folds or flounces. Its neck was square and edged with silver stem stitch, and long sleeves flared out from my elbow. A silver girdle was fastened about my waist, hung with a soft drawstring pouch embroidered with silver flowers. With it was a hooded cloak of white fur.

'Lush,' Khrysanthe said, stroking the hood. 'Why do you get an ermine cloak and I don't?'

'Your father's orders, my lady,' the seamstress said.

The dress looked like the long white robe Brid had once worn. I touched the embroidery with one finger and wondered if the dress had belonged to my mother. It smelt faintly of thyme and meadowsweet.

I was not allowed to darken my eyebrows and eyelashes, though my sisters did so. 'Your father wants you white as snow,' I was told. The hairdresser curled my sisters' hair and piled it high, but mine was left loose, the hairdresser saying to me ingratiatingly, 'I have never seen hair so fine and fair. It is as lovely as Venus's.'

'Do not say so,' I whispered fearfully.

Nothing but evil could come of such words.

Finally we were laden with jewels. Gold and amber earrings, necklaces, bracelets and anklets for my sisters. For me, a heavy silver torc that fitted close about my throat, decorated with two owls that rested on the knobs of my collarbones, tiny moonstones for eyes. It must have been worth a fortune.

'He wants you to look like a barbarian,' Alektrona told me, an edge in her voice.

A flare of something deep inside, some emotion I did not recognise. I went to my room in the tower and plaited my hair into its usual long braid, then coiled it about my head. I took the spray of roses Silviano had given me out of the jug of water. I stripped away the thorns with my paring knife, then quickly wove a delicate wreath of willow tendrils entwined with the roses. I laid it on my head, hiding my hair as best I could.

'Psykhe! Psykhe!' My sisters called me.

I went to join them, heart thumping uncomfortably hard at this small act of rebellion.

*

Fatima stood by the gate, dressed in dirty old rags, her face pinched and miserable. She had always been neat and clean in our old clothes, and I wondered why she would suddenly go about like a beggar. As I came closer, I saw that a heavy iron collar was clasped tightly about her neck. It had been hung with a medallion that said, 'I am a slave. I belong to Lord Cassius of Tarchna. If you find me, whip me well and return me.'

I stared at her in horror. The iron ring had been fitted to her throat and soldered shut. Father must have ordered it done while we were being bathed and dressed.

I felt the weight of the torc on my throat. At least I could easily take mine off. It was made of twisted silver wires that simply flexed open and shut. The only way for Fatima to remove hers was for it to be sawn open.

Her neck was red and bruised. I stepped close and whispered, 'Fatima, I'm so sorry. I will find some salve for you when we get home.'

She tried to smile in thanks, but her face was bruised and swollen. She had been beaten.

'It's my fault,' Alektrona said. 'If only I had not spoken!'

'At least you tried.' Fatima's voice was hoarse, as if her throat hurt her.

'When he is gone, we shall cut it off,' Alektrona promised.

Fatima cast her a look of blatant disbelief.

Lucius stepped forward. 'Your father sent me to escort you to the feast. Will you come now? It would not do to keep him waiting.'

'No, Minerva forbid that my father should ever be kept waiting, or be made uncomfortable in any way,' Alektrona responded sarcastically. She took Fatima's hands between her own. 'I will fix this, I swear it.'

'How?' Fatima replied dully. 'I am a slave. There is nothing you can do.'

Alektrona let go of her hands and strode to the gate, calling angrily for Nokturna to come and unlock it for us. She limped out, leaning on her stick, looking bent and worn out, her wrinkled face drawn with worry. As I passed her, I tried to smile. 'Be careful, little butterfly,' she whispered. 'These are not good men.'

I nodded and pressed her arm briefly. It felt very thin under the heavy black cloth of her robe. Nera whined, and I bent and fondled the soft flaps of her ears. How I wished I could stay with them! But I dared not disobey my father.

As we walked along the narrow cobbled laneway towards the square, Lucius fell into step beside Khrysanthe. 'You are looking very beautiful tonight, my lady,' he said in a low voice, not looking at her.

'Thank you,' she said demurely. 'It is so long since I have seen you, I daresay I am greatly changed.'

'Not at all,' he said. 'You are as lovely as ever.'

She cast him a look of admiration from under her lashes. 'You haven't changed either, Lucius. I thought you might have come to visit us, make sure all was well with us.'

'Your father has kept me very busy,' he answered in some confusion.

'I'm glad you are here now.' She smiled, and his olive skin reddened.

Father was waiting for us by the cistern. He jerked back at the sight of me, blood ebbing from his face. It was as if he had seen a ghost. That was when I knew that I wore my mother's clothes. He did not speak to me, but made a gesture to the princes who stood, idle and bored, by his side.

'My daughters,' he said. 'Rich prizes indeed.'

A throng of gaily dressed men and women climbed the steps to the front door of the palace. In the dining room, low tables groaned with platters of food and pitchers of wine, men and women reclining on couches while slaves filled their goblets. As unmarried daughters, my sisters and I had to sit bolt upright on hard stools at the foot of our father's couch. Two boys sat as uncomfortably near Lord Brutus, looking as if they would rather be anywhere in the world but there.

Lady Arathea beckoned me to come and join her. I had attended her many times, and she knew me well. A thin stooped woman who had suffered many miscarriages, her only pleasure in life was gossip, and she was avid to hear all I could tell her of my father's highborn guests.

'I believe those boys are the children of Lord Brutus, the king's nephew,' she said. 'Their mother died recently, poor things. I have heard that he is looking for a new wife?'

I gave a little shrug, knowing anything I said would soon be all over town.

'Well, he is rich as Croesus, though how he managed to gather such a fortune is a mystery. He's simple-minded, you know. It's odd, when the rest of the family are such cunning schemers. Did you hear what the king's son Sextus did to Gabii?'

I shook my head.

She bent closer. 'Sextus pretended to rebel against his father and fled to Gabii, which was resisting this so-called treaty of theirs. He begged the lords for shelter, and they welcomed him. He wormed his way into their confidence, then – when he had learned all their secrets – sent a messenger to his father in Roma, seeking his guidance on how to seize control of the city. Tarquin the Proud was walking through his garden when the messenger arrived. Instead of answering, the king hacked off the heads of the tallest poppies with his stick. Sextus understood his father's meaning and ordered the assassination of all the most powerful men in the city. Soon Gabii had no choice but to sign the treaty.'

I looked sideways at the king's son. I was afraid of him. We had heard such terrible stories of his parents' ambition and ruthlessness. Tarquin the Proud had assassinated his own wife and brother so that he could marry his sister-in-law, and then he and his new wife had conspired to kill her father, the king. His henchmen had stabbed the old man to death in the street, and then she had whipped up her horses and galloped her chariot back and forth over his body till she was splattered with his blood. How could Sextus Tarquinius not be monstrous, born of such cruel and pitiless parents?

Lady Arathea leant closer. 'The whole family is a nest of vipers. Even young Collatinus is greedy and cruel, for all his soft looks. He's the son of the king's cousin, I believe. Born into a poorer branch of the Tarquins, and determined to make his fortune. I've heard he's on the hunt for an heiress.' She looked speculatively at the heavy torc about my throat, and I raised one hand to touch it. Who had my mother been, to own such a rich and rare piece of jewellery? And if Collatinus was poor, why did he wish to marry me?

The lord of Velzna rose, calling for a toast. 'We extend greetings to Prince Sextus, younger son of the king of Roma, and remind all that the laws of hospitality forbid any hostility tonight.' He laid a faint stress on the final word.

Sextus got to his feet, smiling, hands spread. 'We come in peace. Do not forget that it was our ancestor Tarchon, the grandson of Hercules himself, who founded the League of Twelve. We wish only to assure you of our willingness to offer you our protection, and to come to your aid if war should arise.'

'War begun by you!' a young man cried.

The prince's narrow face stiffened. 'Sign the treaty, and there shall be no need of war.'

My father stood up then, speaking smoothly and suavely of the potential for prosperity if the league threw in its lot with Roma.

A loud hum of conversation rose. It seemed not all wished to reject the possibility of a peace treaty with Tarquin the Proud. My father watched the crowd with intent eyes, noting who was in favour and who argued against the treaty. Sextus looked angry, and my father soothed him with soft words.

More wine was brought, and the room was cleared for dancing. I retreated to the shadows, where no-one would stare at me, but my sisters joined the revelries. Alektrona danced with light-footed grace, every step and gesture perfect, but Khrysanthe romped like a child, laughing and clapping her hands with delight and almost falling over at one point when she tried to spin too fast.

'She's pretty,' Brutus said. 'I get her, don't I?'

'Yes, that's right,' my father agreed. 'Look at those curves! She will have no trouble bearing you many more children.'

Brutus gave a foolish grin. 'She's the same age as my boys. They can play together!'

'As long as you play with her too,' Father said with a thin smile. 'You'll need to bed her, as well as wed her. Though I suppose you know about bed sport, having sons already.'

Brutus stared at him blankly, his mouth hanging open, then got up and shambled off, calling for a slave to bring him more pig.

My father turned to Sextus and said in a low voice, 'It's a shame Brutus is such a drooling idiot. But his sons seem sensible enough, so hopefully it's not bad seed, but the injury done to him as a child.'

'For such a fool, he has infernal luck! He won another stack of gold from me this afternoon, playing knucklebones, for Jove's sake! I should have known better.'

'You'll gamble on anything that moves,' Father replied, smiling. 'So what do you think of my eldest daughter, Alektrona? She's not as pretty as her younger sister, but not as foolish either. You will find her intelligence an asset to you in the machinations of the court.'

Sextus regarded his polished fingernails. 'I hope she will not be so foolish as to seek to influence me in any way.'

'No, no, of course not,' my father said hastily. 'Alektrona's a sensible girl, and has been properly trained, I assure you.' He turned to Collatinus. 'What about you? I promised you a rare beauty in Psykhe, did I not? Have you ever seen such dazzling fairness?'

'She is indeed fair,' the young man said slowly. 'But . . .'

'Fair and rich! I shall dower her well, and you know her mother was a princess among her own people. In that barbaric world, women are permitted to inherit if there are no brothers, and Psykhe's mother was an only child. Her father was king of a great land, of exceeding fruitfulness. Any man who marries her naturally gains her inheritance too.'

I sat as if struck by lightning. My father had never spoken of any inheritance to me. I wanted to touch the silver torc about my neck again but felt the men's eyes upon me and so sat quietly, pretending to be unaware of their conversation.

'But who wishes to go and screw their wife's dowry out of the Galli?' Collatinus said discontentedly. 'Are the men not all warriors and the women all witches?'

'What of it?' my father said haughtily. 'Are you trying to tell me you haven't the balls for it? No matter. There will be many a young man eager both for the girl and her inheritance.' He made a dismissive flicking gesture with his fingers and drank deeply. Collatinus frowned and looked unhappy.

'I must admit I'm tempted to take the youngest, instead of the eldest,' Sextus said. 'I have never seen such icy perfection in all my life. I'd like to see if her blood runs hot, or if she's as frigid as the snow.'

'Well, you can't have her,' Collatinus snapped. 'She's already been promised to me.'

68

'At least the eldest one is more likely to burn me than give me frostbite,' Sextus said. 'She has a proud look. I shall enjoy breaking her in.'

'Excellent! Then we are all agreed. Alektrona for you, Khrysanthe for Brutus, and Psykhe for Collatinus. I shall have the marriage contracts drawn up in the morning.' My father clapped his hands for more wine.

'Had we best not be sure the league will sign the treaty first?' Sextus said smoothly.

'Oh, they will. I'll make sure of it, one way or another,' my father replied. 'Let us drink to our future fortunes!'

All drank deeply. I sat, unmoving, afraid. My mind was like a hare hunted by a hawk, darting one way, then another, trying to find a way to escape.

But there was none.

VII

The Green-Eyed Rose

The music ended. Khrysanthe returned to her stool, laughing and fanning her hand in front of her flushed face. Alektrona followed, cool and scornful.

'My beloved daughters! Come!' Father cried. 'Look at you, women grown. It is past time you were married! Fortuna is smiling on us, the gods are pleased. Your dowries will be rich indeed. I wish to give you all a gift, as a sign of my regard for you all. What would you like? You may ask me for anything.' He made a broad, expansive gesture.

For a moment, we were silent with surprise. He made another gesture, his brows drawing together in displeasure.

Khrysanthe said, with spurious sweetness, 'Dear Father, your regard is worth everything to me, and I need nothing else. But if you truly wish to reward me, may I ask for a new distaff and loom so that I may busy myself spinning and weaving all I will need for my new life as a wife and mother?'

Alektrona choked back a snort.

Father was pleased. 'Your wish will be granted in the morn.'

He looked at Alektrona.

'I want Fatima.'

Father's smile disappeared.

'You said I could ask for anything.' Alektrona was defiant, her hands gripped in fists.

'Indeed I did. And of course you may take your slave girl with you when you are married. She can be part of your dowry. I'm sure your husband shall appreciate such a pretty piece about the place.'

'I will,' Sextus said.

Alektrona's look of fierce triumph faded away. For a moment she was silent, then she said, 'If Fatima is mine, then I shall free her. I shall have the right.'

'Enough! You forget yourself.' Father turned to me. 'What about you, Psykhe? Jewels? Fine silks? That is what you girls should be asking for!'

'I would like a green-eyed rose.' I kept my eyes lowered and hands folded.

'A rose?' He was surprised.

I nodded. 'Yes. A rose with blooms like the ones in my hair. It has a thousand petals, and the sweetest of scents, and its green eye is said to ward off evil and bring luck and love.'

Despite myself, colour rose in my cheeks. I do not know why I asked so boldly for what I truly wanted. Perhaps I hoped my father would have to travel far, far away to find me such a rose, perhaps even all the way to Damascus. Perhaps I hoped that my audacity would distract him from his anger towards Alektrona.

My father's eyebrows had shot up. 'I must admit all three of my daughters have surprised me. I was expecting to be asked for jewels, but instead one wants a distaff, another a slave girl, and the third a rare rose. Most unexpected. But I have given my word, and so my promise must be honoured.'

I should have been pleased. All I felt was cold, creeping dread.

*

71

We returned to the tower in silence. As we came to the gate, my father said, 'Send the slave girl to my villa.'

Alektrona started. 'But, Father, you said you would give Fatima to me!'

He gave that false smile of his. 'So I did. But you forget that you too are mine, Alektrona. All that you have, from your toilet sponge to those golden anklets you wear, is mine. I can do with you as I wish, and I can most certainly do as I wish to your pretty little slave girl. Including beating her to death, if I so desire. So I suggest you do not anger me any further. Send her to me now.'

Fatima was pressed close to Alektrona's side, trembling. There was a long moment of fraught silence, then Alektrona said, 'Go with my father.'

Fatima hesitated.

'Go.'

Fatima went to stand by his side, her eyes wide and terrified.

'Go to your own beds, my daughters, and keep your doors locked. I can hear my men have grown a little rowdy. I would not want you to be disturbed.' He waited till we had obediently walked away, then called Lucius to him, giving him a string of instructions in a low voice that I could not hear.

In the orchard, Father's men were sitting about their campfires, singing, shouting and eating their way through our winter reserves. My sisters went in, quiet and subdued, and I climbed the ladder to my small room in the upper level of the tower. I had long ago made it comfortable, with a warm rug on the floor and embroidered hangings on the walls. I had a little stove there, and shelves to hold my scrolls, and a comfortable bed with feather-stuffed pillows and soft blankets that smelt of herbs and sunshine. I read for a while by the light of my small lantern, slowly unrolling the scroll from one rod to the other, but the words swam and flickered. At last I put the scroll away and blew out the flame. I could not sleep, though. I was sure something terrible was going to happen.

Many hours later, I was jolted out of a half-doze by the sound of the tower door scraping open. Everything was dark, though a few coals in the stove blinked sleepily. I lay motionless for a moment, my heart thumping hard, then crept towards the hatch and peered down.

A few dark figures came in. I could tell by their height and bulk that they were men. Paralysed with fear, I crouched low. What was their intention? How had they got in? I had the only key, and I had carefully locked the door that night. I looked around for something to defend myself, but all my tools were laid out neatly on the table below. I put my hands on the ladder, ready to fling it down if anyone tried to climb up.

Light flickered. A lantern had been unshuttered. I crouched down, scarcely breathing. I saw the gleam of bronze breastplates, the long narrow shadow of a spear. The men began to shift furniture about. Bottles clattered. One fell and broke.

'Quiet, fool!' Lucius's voice.

They gathered by the fireplace. Lucius made pressing movements with his hands along the wall, and suddenly, to my astonishment, a narrow aperture appeared. A secret door. One by one the men slipped through and disappeared.

My curiosity overcame my fear. I wrapped myself in a dark cloak, slithered down the ladder, and through the doorway. Rough, uneven steps led down. I felt my way in the darkness, listening for any sound of the men returning. It was pitch-black, and I could not see a thing. Many times I stumbled, or stubbed my toe, or cracked an elbow, but I pressed on. A sense of space around me, the touch of fresh air on my face. I crept onwards. My fumbling hands felt piles of boxes and sacks. When I bumped into one, it gave a dull metallic clank. Ahead, a faint easing of the darkness. It was the cave's mouth, little more than a crack, half-hidden behind the twisted roots of an old cypress tree. I wriggled through.

Below me, the city of the dead. The low mounds of the tombs were unmistakable, even in the darkness. I took a hasty step back, in sudden superstitious dread, then stood shaking with cold and fear. I did not know what to do. I did not want to be caught. Should I keep following the men, find out what their plans were? Or should I creep back to my room, and pretend I never saw a thing?

I heard tramping feet approaching, and turned and scrambled back into the cave and up the stairs, hands groping before me. The faint flicker of their lantern followed me far too close. I flew up the ladder as if I wore Mercury's winged sandals and scrambled into the safety of my bedroom.

'What was that?' Lucius demanded as he pushed his way through the secret doorway, followed by a great many men, far more than had left. 'I heard something.'

'It'll just be a rat,' someone else said. 'Place like this would be overrun with them.'

'Right, men. Come through. Now, remember, not a sound. If things go the way my lord wants, there'll be no need for any bloodshed, and we can all go home. But if the lord of Velzna refuses the alliance, then we'll have a job on our hands. I've seen Lord Quintus's men – they're tough, and will defend the town to the death. So be ready.'

I lay flat, trying to calm my racing heart. So this was why my father owned the watchtower! It hid a secret route into the old walled town. He and his men could come and go, without having to pay any taxes. He could store goods and weapons here, he could sneak men in, he could fortify the watchtower, he could aim a spear-head of soldiers straight into the heart of Velzna.

One by one, the men slipped out the tower door and into the garden. Our land was entirely enclosed behind high stone walls. No-one would see them; no-one would know.

Lucius stopped a few of the men with a gesture. 'Wait, there's another small task for us tonight. The ice witch wants a green-eyed rose. It is our mission to get it for her, no matter the cost. Be alert. We must go again to the city of the dead.'

He gathered up some of my tools – a spade, a pruning knife, a wooden bucket, some sacking – then led his chosen party back through the secret door. I followed them unhappily.

It is not wise to anger the gods, Ambrose had said to me once, a long time ago. The green-eyed rose had been planted to honour Venus. She was well known for her petulant rages. Once again I had thoughtlessly offended her. Surely she would seek revenge? What price must I pay for wishing for a rose given in her honour?

I kept as close to the men as I dared. By now my bare feet were bruised and cut, my body aching, but I did not falter. I followed the men through the cave to the city of the dead, then round the base of the great crag to the other cemetery, overgrown with nettles and wild roses.

I had been so afraid that was their destination. How had my father known? He must have sent Lucius to interrogate the guards on the gate. They must have told him what direction I had come from that morning, carrying the branch of roses.

The sky was beginning to lighten to the east. I hurried as much as I could, but my body was so weary I could scarcely stumble along.

A sudden cry of alarm, then a panting scuffle. A sword clanged against something hard. I heard a few sharp curses, then a scream of pain.

'Stop!' Lucius ordered. 'Don't kill him, for Jove's sake! We want no trouble here. Hurry up, dig up the blasted rose and let us be on our way.'

I crept closer, hiding behind a tomb, peering to see. The men dug up the rose and swaddled it in sacking, then carried it back towards the town. I waited till they had passed, then picked up my skirts and ran towards the shrine. I was worried about Silviano. Was it he who had screamed in pain?

I found him, lying motionless by the shrine. The statue lay toppled, broken. One bloodstained marble arm lay near Silviano's head. Blood leaked down the side of his face, clotted his wild beard. I flung myself to my knees, cradled his head in my lap. I wiped away the blood with my skirt, felt all over his skull for the wound.

My questing fingers found two small, hard horns, hidden by his matted hair. I recoiled. I saw then his sprawled legs, revealed by the rumpled robe. Hairy, goatish, ending in hooves. For a moment, the world seemed to tilt.

He opened his eyes and looked up at me. 'Psykhe,' he whispered. 'Who . . . who . . . what?' I could scarcely speak.

An expression of infinite sadness crossed his face. 'She will be angry. So angry.'

Then, with a sudden lithe twist, he was up on his hooves, galloping away.

I sat, frozen, trying to understand. Was Silviano a faun? But how had I not noticed before? How had he kept his horns and hooves hidden? Was it magic? And were fauns not wild creatures of the forest? What was he doing here in Velzna?

I got to my feet, feeling strange and shaky. It was as if some kind of mask had slipped sideways and showed me the world was not as I believed it to be. I wanted Nocturna badly, but I was afraid too. If Silviano was some wild spirit of the forest – a faun or a satyr – what was Nocturna? And what of Ambrose? I had thought he was just a boy. I had dared to dream he might come back for me one day, that my only friend could become my only love. But now? That seemed more impossible than ever.

He's adopted, I reminded myself. Nocturna is not really his grand-mother, Silviano not really his great-uncle. But I was not comforted. The world seemed askew, and everything a sham.

VIII

The Barrier Between the Worlds

Slowly I limped home, keeping my cloak drawn over my hair. I wanted no-one to see me or know that I had left the tower. At last I was safe back in my stillroom. The men thought they had put it all back in order, but they did not know how I liked things, arranged in utter beauty and order. Bottles were misaligned, scrolls shoved back in the wrong shelves, my tools not set out neatly from smallest to largest.

Wearily I began to tidy up.

Urgent hammering on the door made me look up, then I heard the panicked sound of my name. I hurried to open the door. Alektrona crouched on the step, Fatima in her arms. The slave's tunic was torn and bloodied. We half-carried her inside. I sat her down on a stool and did my best to tend her. My father and his friends had not been gentle with her.

'I am so sorry,' I whispered as I stitched the worst of her wounds. My words were so inadequate. I wished I could promise her she would never be so hurt again. I wished that I could wrench the iron ring from her neck and fling it far away. But I could not.

'Please,' she whimpered, clutching my hand. 'You must help me. I must not have a babe. I can't! I can't! They are monsters. I do not want their seed in me. Clean me out, I beg of you.'

I touched her shoulder lightly in reassurance, then carefully weighed and mixed a potion made of ground rosehips, rue, wormwood and yew berries, diluted with wine and sweetened with honey. Alektrona held the cup to Fatima's lips while she drank, then I made us all a calming tisane of chamomile and elderflowers.

'Will it work?' Fatima asked desperately.

'You will not have a babe, I promise you that. You will be very sick, though, I'm afraid.'

She shrugged. 'What does it matter now? Nothing matters anymore.'

'He'll never touch you again,' Alektrona cried. 'I won't let him!'

Fatima cast her a look of scornful incredulity. 'How?'

Alektrona seized her hand, but Fatima snatched it away. 'Don't touch me!'

The potion did not take long to work. Alektrona and I did our best to help Fatima, but there was little we could do, except wipe her face with a damp cloth and wrap her in a blanket I warmed by the stove. At last she lay quietly, curled into a ball.

'Let her sleep,' I whispered to Alektrona. 'She needs time to recover.'

We tiptoed out of the tower. 'Do not let them see how much you care,' I said. 'They will hurt her more for the pleasure of your distress.'

Alektrona looked at me with frowning eyes. 'Thank you,' she said abruptly. Her thin hands moved restlessly, then she jerked out a few more words. 'I'm sorry.'

I nodded.

It was then I saw the green-eyed rose. It had been dropped against the wall of the tower, its roots still wrapped in sacking. I went and gently touched one of its frilled buds. What had I done, asking for the goddess's rose? What price must be paid?

I needed to talk to Nocturna. So much I did not understand.

But she was nowhere to be found. Her door was closed, her stick gone from the wall. Had she been called out to a woman in labour? I did not know of any babe due to be born that day. Had she needed me and not been able to find me? I stood, hesitating, on her step, wondering if I should go in search of her. Someone would have seen her go by.

I went out into the garden and saw that the little door in the gate stood ajar. Frowning, I went to shut it. I had never known Nocturna to leave it open before. I felt on edge, anxious. My thoughts returned to Silviano. He had been badly hurt. Had she known somehow, and gone to care for him? Perhaps he had sent a messenger? It had taken me a long time to walk back from the grave-yard, and then I had been busy tending Fatima. But I had not heard the bell ring, or Nocturna call for me. It was strange.

Walking through the garden, I tied up broken branches and gathered fallen rose petals. At least I could make some healing salve with them. I took a basketful to the stillroom to steep in olive oil, opening the door as quietly as I could, so as not to disturb Fatima.

She was not there. I looked around in surprise. She had been badly hurt, barely able to walk. Where could she have gone? I began to search for her. Nowhere in the garden or the house. I knocked on Alektrona's door, trying to calm the needling of fear.

'I can't find Fatima anywhere,' I told her. 'Is she with you?'

'No. I thought she was sleeping. What do you mean, you can't find her?'

'She's not in the tower, or the house, or the garden. I even went to the orchard just to check. She's left.'

'You think she has run away?' Alektrona said. 'Father will have her whipped to death.'

'We must find her!'

We slipped out the little door and searched the surrounding streets, then went to the town gate and asked the guards if they had seen her. They had not.

'Where could she be?' Alektrona asked, acute worry in her voice.

I was anxious too. I kept seeing the utter despair in Fatima's face.

Ahead, a hubbub. People running, calling out for help. We ran too. A man carried a girl's limp body, long black hair dripping water. 'She was in the cistern! I think she's dead.'

He laid her down on the ground in front of the temple steps. I knew at once it was Fatima. The long black hair, the slender brown limbs, the heavy slave collar about her throat. Dropping to my knees beside her, I wiped away the wet tendrils so I could see her face. Her lips were blue, her face deathly pale. She was not breathing. I laid my fingers on her clammy neck, just below the sharp angle of her jaw, where the force of life should thud most strongly. It was still.

'She's dead, she's dead.' Alektrona flung herself on Fatima's body.

Time seemed to slow.

You were still and pale and unbreathing. I could not rouse you. I remembered the story of Isis, the goddess who resurrected her brother Osiris by fanning breath into his body with her wings . . .

Brid's voice was as clear in my mind as if she knelt beside me. I pushed Alektrona away, then bent and put my mouth to Fatima's. I blew until my lungs were starved, took another breath, blew again. People argued and gesticulated above my head. I barely noticed. Breathe, blow. Breathe, blow. Breathe, blow.

Fatima's lashes fluttered. She coughed. Moved her head weakly. Coughed again.

'She's alive,' Alektrona sobbed as she chafed Fatima's cold hand, then lifted it to her mouth and kissed it.

Fatima tried to sit up. I raised her so she was leaning against me and wrapped my cloak about her. She coughed, then vomited a gush of water. Alektrona and I rubbed her icy limbs dry, my sister murmuring endearments in a broken voice.

'You saved her!' she said to me. 'Thank you, thank you! I can't believe it. She was dead but now she lives. How? How is it possible?'

Her words caused a ripple of amazement through the crowd.

'That slave girl was dead,' the man who had found Fatima said, staring at me incredulously. 'The ice witch brought her back to life.'

'It's a marvel!' said someone else. 'The gods must have acted through her.'

'She kissed the girl and awakened her from the dead! Never have I seen such a wonder.'

I had not known I could do such a thing. No mortal had ever before brought the dead back to life. Orpheus had tried and failed. Odysseus had raised the ghost of his dead mother but could not embrace her. *It is the nature of the dead,* she had told him. *When life has left the body, the sinews no longer knit flesh and bones together, the spirit has flown . . .*

But here was Fatima, alive again.

A clamour of voices rose around me. I heard only snatches.

. . . ice witch . . . born dead . . . brought back to life . . . impossible . . . is it a sign?

'Is she a goddess?' a child's high voice cut through the noise.

The word was taken up, spreading like flame on spilled oil.

No, I wanted to cry. I am just a girl! An ordinary mortal, just like you. Do not name me goddess! The gods will be angry. They will think me arrogant – they will punish me. Please, do not call me such a thing!

But I could not speak. I was so tired and cold, and shivering so violently, I had to clench my jaw to stop my teeth from chattering. Alektrona knelt at my feet, sobbing, 'Thank you, thank you.' She kissed Fatima's cold cheek, stroked back her wet hair. Fatima looked up at me, eyes dark and enormous.

Somehow I managed to get up. The man who had found her in the cistern bowed to me, hands pressed together in a gesture of supplication. He offered me his cloak, and I clutched it around me with numb fingers. 'Need . . . to get her warm,' I managed to say to Alektrona.

My father must have heard the commotion, for he and his friends strode towards us. The crowd parted before them, many bowing low. He saw me, Fatima and Alektrona crouched at my feet, and heard the clamour of the crowd.

Someone asked what the slave girl was doing in the cistern, anyway. I said as clearly as I could, 'It was an accident. She stumbled and fell. See the bruise on her face?'

'Likely story!'

'She had no need to cause herself any harm. She was given her freedom only last night. Wasn't she, Father?' I fixed him with a warning glance.

'Then why does she still wear a slave collar?' a man asked.

'It will be cut off just as soon as we can find a blacksmith,' Alektrona cried.

I saw the moment my father decided what to do. He had been frowning, his muscles tense, his hand on his sword. But he rearranged his face into a smile, flung wide his arms, and said, 'People of Velzna! The gods have acted through my daughter and saved the life of this poor drowned girl. It's a sign! The gods wish you to sign the treaty with Roma. We are not your enemy, we are your friends. Has my daughter not worked here among you these past few years, tending your sick and saving your lives?'

How did he know? I wondered. *How could he possibly know?*

But then I remembered Lucius and his men, tramping through my stillroom, knocking over my bottles, disarranging my tools, asking the town guards about my movements.

My father was continuing smoothly, persuasively: 'That is all the king wishes to do, to help and assist you as my daughter has helped you and helped this poor drowned slave girl. The gods have worked their will through her – they have spoken. Sign the treaty!'

His words were taken up, passing quickly through the crowd. A mood of jubilation replaced that of fearful awe.

'What about Fatima?' Alektrona challenged. 'Her slave collar will be cut off and her liberation papers signed, won't they, Father? Today?'

'Yes, yes,' he said, smiling thinly. 'Once the treaty is signed.'

I suddenly realised what I had done. Saving Fatima's life meant the peace treaty would be signed and my father's plan to marry us to the Roman princes succeed. A wave of despair rocked me.

A litter was brought, and Fatima laid tenderly within it and carried home. Alektrona walked beside her, clinging to her hand. The crowd followed us, buzzing with excitement. My father made the most of it, proclaiming that he would sacrifice a white heifer to Apollo, the god of healing and patron of Roma, that very day. 'And then tonight we shall sign the treaty and drink to peace and prosperity!'

The crowd cheered.

Why is it, I thought, *that beasts to be sacrificed must always be white?*

I felt a hot flare of anger and defiance. I leant forward and said to him, 'I gave Fatima poison today, to wither any fruit of your body that may have taken root within her. If you fail to free her as you promised, I will give the poison to you, I swear it.'

I did not look back to see the effect of my words. I went to the tower, closed and locked the door behind me, jammed the secret door shut with my chair, stripped off my drenched clothes, and climbed into bed. I lay curled up tight, knees to chin, trying to calm the shivers that racked me. I saw Fatima's face, the closed eyelids, the blue lips, her limp hand, her unmoving chest. I had blown my breath into her mouth, and her chest had risen and fallen, risen and fallen. Then had come the moment in which her faltering life force caught and blazed up again, like a spark into tinder. How thin, how very thin, the barrier between the worlds. A moment of falling. No more.

'Psykhe.'

I jerked awake.

He stood in the window embrasure, the last light of day creating a golden nimbus around him. He was a man now, but I would have recognised him anywhere.

'Ambrose.'

'Psykhe, you must beware. Do not forget life and death are the affairs of gods, not mortals.'

Part II

larva
Latin: 'ghost, mask'

*An early stage of growth for butterflies, which emerge wingless
from the egg, before undergoing a process of transformation
into their final form.*

*. . . the commands of heaven must be obeyed,
and the unhappy Psykhe must go to meet her doom . . .*
Eros and Psykhe
Metamorphoses, Lucius Apuleius

I

Truth Hidden Deep in the Shadows

I clung to the window frame, straining to see in the darkness.
Nothing but a shooting star, far, far away.

My whole body fizzed with nerves. What was real and what
was not? Had I truly seen Ambrose standing in the tower window?
How? How could I have seen him? The window of my tower bedroom
was many dizzying feet high, set on the edge of the cliff above the
necropolis. He must have flown. He must have wings. Had I truly
seen them, golden and airy, folded back along his back? Or had my
eyes just been dazzled? Had he truly spoken to me, in the charged
voice of a god, or had I longed for him for so long that I had somehow
conjured him into existence, a figment of a maddened imagination?

I had to get out. I needed the peace and calm of my garden.
I wrapped myself in a thick cloak against the chill and slipped quietly
down the ladder and out into the night. I walked back and forth
under the trees, my bare feet icy from the dew, and looked up at the
moon, Luna's silver chariot.

I had always loved the night and its luminous edges. When I was
a little girl, I had thought the moon followed me, guarding my steps.

'Help me understand,' I whispered to her now. 'What is he? Is he a god? How can that be possible?'

All things are possible in all the possible worlds . . .

It was as if I heard Nocturna's voice, repeating what she had once told me long ago. I walked slowly back towards the tower, deep in thought, my cloak drawn close about me.

A man's voice. 'I have a gift for you.'

I stopped abruptly, heart uncomfortably fast. I peered about me and saw two dark figures standing close together in the shadows.

'I know . . . I know I should not . . . but I wanted you to know how I felt . . .' the man said. I recognised the voice but could not quite place it. Not Ambrose, as I had thought just for a moment.

'What is it?' a woman asked eagerly. It was Khrysanthe.

'Earrings, as golden as your skin, forged in the shape of Amor, god of desire. I . . . I wanted you to have something to remember me by.' I recognised the voice now. It was Lucius. He held something out to Khrysanthe, something that gleamed in the moonlight.

'But how?' Khrysanthe asked. How could he afford to buy such a gift for her, she meant. Common soldiers were not paid much.

'Think of it as war booty,' he whispered. 'A reward for my loyalty. I cannot bear to think of you being forced to marry that oaf. I want you to wear my gift, and know that if you ever need me, all you need to do is call me. I would die for you, my lady.'

'Oh, Lucius, thank you,' she whispered, raising herself on tiptoe so she could kiss him.

'My lady, what are you doing?' Lucius's voice was uneven.

'I'm kissing you,' she answered, laughing, and following her words with the action. A long fevered moment, soft gasps and sighs.

'My lady, please . . . I can't . . .'

'Don't you want to?'

'Of course I want to! But . . .'

She kissed him again. I tiptoed past, holding my breath, feeling my way forward with my feet. They were so deeply absorbed in each other they did not see me in my dark cloak.

'If I am to be married to some fat fool old enough to be my father, let me have just one night of love,' Khrysanthe whispered. 'Please, Lucius.'

'We cannot.' He groaned as she pressed herself against him. 'My lady, think what you do . . .'

'I know what I do.' She loosened the ties of her bodice, took his hand and pressed it to the pale curve of her breast. 'Lucius, please.'

'Your father . . . if he knew . . . he would cut off my balls . . .'

'He will never know. Lucius, please. I know you want me. Let me have just one night. One night of pleasure. What harm can it do?'

He groaned, deep in his throat, and pushed her back against the wall. I hurried away as silently as I could, wondering if I should have stopped them. Lucius was right. My father would punish him severely if he knew. How could they take such a risk? How could they dare so much for love?

I must have slept, somehow, for I woke in the morning to find my blankets in a tangle and my hair a mess. My head was full of dreams I could scarcely remember, yet which still had the power to bring the blood surging to my face. I looked at the window, where I had seen Ambrose standing, blazing with golden light. Where had he come from, where had he gone? How could I call him back?

Stop being such a fool, I told myself. It was just a dream, a feverish imagining, a kind of moon madness.

I dressed and went out. Everything seemed too bright, too alive. I drew my hood over my head to shade my eyes. The stable yard was teeming with activity. Men were bridling horses, harnessing surly-looking oxen to a dray, and scurrying back and forth, loading the contents of our storerooms. My father watched the men, a whip held in one hand. He was dressed for travelling.

My steps quickened. 'What in Hekate's name are you doing?'

'We prepare to ride for Roma.' My father's voice was as cold as I had ever heard it. My heart sank. I had threatened him, I remembered. Told him I would poison him. I must have been mad. My father would never forgive such insolence. He would find a way to punish me – I'd suffer for it for the rest of my life.

'But . . . our food, our grain. We shall starve.'

'You are coming too. All of you. I have no use of this house anymore; the treaty has been signed. I shall sell it. To help pay for your dowries.'

My chest was too tight to breathe, blood pounding in my ears.

'Sell . . . you want to sell our home?'

'Your home will be with Collatinus once you are wed. Till then, I shall have to suffer your presence in my villa in Roma. Get your things together. I plan to be on the road before noon.'

He gestured for me to go.

With leaden steps, I returned to the tower, preparing to pack a trunk with my tools and scrolls, my jars of salves, my potions and brews. I did not want to go, but I did not know how to stay. I was only a woman. I had to do as my father commanded, regardless of my own wishes. He had the right to kill me or sell me into slavery if I displeased him. Deep inside me, a flame of defiance burned. Why? Why must I submit my will to another? Why did I not have the right to choose what I did with my own life?

As I came close to the tower, I saw the green-eyed rose, still propped against the wall. Proof that I had not dreamed the terrors of the night. It was real, and the cost I must pay for it was all

90

too real. Once again I had lost my home and my teacher, once again I was dispossessed.

I packed quickly, not bothering with many clothes – there was no room for them except to safely swaddle my bottles and jars. Lucius helped me stow my belongings on the oxen cart. I swaddled the green-eyed rose carefully and put it where its branches would not be crushed. I would find somewhere to grow it, far to the south in Roma.

My father ordered me to hurry my sisters along. I went to Khrysanthe first. She was in a dither, trying to squeeze all her favourite clothes and sandals and combs into one chest. 'Though I hardly need these old things! My husband will buy me whatever I want. He is very rich, did you know? Rich as Croesus, rich as King Midas. I shall have whatever I want.' Her voice was over-shrill.

Golden earrings dangled from her ears. I had last seen the jewellery adorning the marble statue of Venus in the sanctuary by the graveyard. The statue now lay broken, her shrine plundered.

How could they be so foolish?

Yet there was no way they could have known. It had been dark, and Lucius was not from Velzna. He did not know it was a shrine – just as I had not known. To him, it was just an old statue in a forgotten graveyard. Perhaps it had toppled in the brawl, perhaps he had seen the jewellery glinting in the torchlight, and grabbed it, unthinkingly. And how could Khrysanthe, preening in her hand-mirror, know that she wore jewels stolen from a goddess? They could not know, and it did not matter. They would pay the price. That I was sure of.

I could not bear it. I left her without a word and went next door to Alektrona's bedchamber. She was walking back and forth, talking passionately, while Fatima quietly packed her chest. The slave collar had been cut from around her throat, and she had wound a scarf about it to hide the marks it had left on her skin.

91

'Come with me,' Alektrona begged. 'Why should we be separated now? You are free, free to do as you please!'

'Go with you? Live in the same house as that man? Do you know what he did to me? I would rather die than be near him again.'

'But . . . Fatima . . . please . . . I can keep you safe . . .'

Fatima shook her head. 'You have no power to keep me safe. I love you. I pity you, to be married to such a man. But I am powerless to help you, and to go with you would be to put myself in danger.'

'But we swore we'd never be parted! We swore to be together forever.'

'I'm sorry. I can't. I shall go in search of my mother, and do my best to buy her freedom too. I will leave as soon as you and that man are gone. I only wish I could buy you free too.'

Alektrona sank to the ground, hands over her face. 'I hate him! I hate him so much.'

Suddenly I remembered what Nocturna had predicted the first time she met us, so long ago. *One will wed for hate, one will wed for gold, and the last will wed for love.*

It seemed the first two would come true. My sisters were to be married, one with hatred in her heart, and one filled with greed for gold. But what of me? I was not to be wed. I remembered the way the men in the yard had shrunk away from me, the fear in their faces.

It seemed impossible that I could ever be wed, let alone for love.

I had to see Nocturna.

So much had happened, so much had changed. I needed to say farewell to her. The thought was enough to make me weep. I ran through the garden to her rooms, built within the wall. She was waiting for me on the step, Nera sitting dolefully by her side.

92

I cast myself into her arms. She stroked my hair silently as I tried to tell her all that had happened. All I could manage was a few shuddering words, broken phrases, incoherent sentences. 'I don't want to go, I don't want to! What can I do? Can I stay here with you? Please?'

'I too need to find myself a new home,' she said. 'I do not own this place. I live here in return for my duties as gatekeeper.'

I saw that she had a small sack by her feet, and her gnarled walking stick. 'What will you do, where will you go? I do not want to leave you. Nocturna, please, can't I stay with you . . . I'm afraid . . .'

'Do not fear, little butterfly. It is time. I have taught you all I can.'

'But . . . Ambrose, I saw him, how could I have seen him, in the tower room so high? And Silviano? Is he a faun? I don't understand. Is he . . .? But you? You're not? Are you?'

I could not say the words. The implications were too huge for me. I had thought her the wisest woman I had ever known. I had thought her, possibly, a witch. I had not thought she could be a magical being, a fauna or a dryad, or even perhaps a goddess. The gods were terrible.

'Psykhe, there are many stories told about me and my kind. Many are untrue, but some carry truth hidden deep in the shadows and those are the ones that shine the brightest. I need you to trust me. I came here, to this place and this time, for you. I have waited long for your coming.'

'You and your kind? So you . . . you are a goddess?' I stared at her. She looked just like a very old woman, bent and frail, with dark crumpled skin and cloudy white hair, one fingernail grown long and filed to a sharp point for the breaking of a baby's birth sac.

'That's one word I've been called. Believe me, I've been called many others. Keeper of the Keys, Warden of the Crossroads, Night-Walker, Fate-Spinner, Torch-Bearer, Guardian of Souls, She

Who Transforms, She Who Throws Down the Gates, She Who Walks Between Worlds.'

I stared at her in disbelief. I knew those titles. They were some of the many names for Hekate, goddess of the night and the dark moon. I had to cling to the side of the table for support, my legs trembling. The ground felt unsteady, as if it was rocking under my feet. My knees loosened, and I crumpled to the ground, pressing my face to the stone.

She bent and raised me up. 'They are just names, little butterfly. All you need to know is that I was your teacher and guardian.'

'Was?' I asked faintly.

'Yes. My work here is done – I can do no more. I have given you everything I can. You are not a child anymore, you are a woman grown. It is time now for you to walk towards your destiny.'

I laughed. 'My destiny! To be married to a man I do not even know? A man who makes my skin crawl?'

'I think you will find that is not your destiny, Psykhe.'

'Then what? What is my destiny?'

'Do not wish to know that which is in the hands of the Fates.'

For a moment I was frightened of her. The flickering firelight leapt over her wizened face, her eyes glittering out of deep shadowed sockets. Then Nera whined and licked my hand lovingly. I crouched, burying my face against her neck, driving my fingers deep into her silky black fur.

'What of Silviano? Is he a god too? What of Ambrose?' I spoke his name only with the greatest difficulty. For it was clear to me that he was of her kind, whatever that was, and that made him far above me, impossible to ever dream of reaching.

'Silviano is one of the oldest of the gods and one of the wildest. Ambrose . . . Ambrose is young, like you. He has his own journey to make, his own struggles, his own choices.'

'But he is a god. And I am just a girl.' My voice was flat with desolation.

Nocturna took my hand. 'You are a child of Gaea, as I am and as Ambrose is. All living things carry a fiery spark of the divine within.'

I shook my head. I did not believe her. My cheeks were hot with shame and embarrassment. What a fool I had been, dreaming of love, deluding myself that he was just a boy, that he longed for me as I longed for him, that one day we would meet again, touch, kiss, caress, lie together, make a babe together, build a life. Just because he was the only boy to ever look at me as if I was a girl like other girls, a warm, living, feeling person instead of a ghost.

'Psykhe, mortals call us gods because we do not die easily, because we move between worlds, because we have powers that seem impossible to you. But the blood of mortals and immortals have mingled for aeons. Some immortals hate and fear this, thinking it will dilute or sully their power. I am not one of them. Many a mortal has joined the ranks of the gods, and many gods walk among mortals in disguise.'

'Like you? Why? Why did you come here? You said you came for me, that you'd been waiting for me. Why?'

Nocturna was silent for a long moment, her dark eyes hooded. 'I wanted to teach you. I wanted you to know the mysteries, to remember, to teach others.'

'But why me?'

She smiled at me, her skin creasing into a thousand wrinkles. 'Because you once saved the life of a dove.'

I did not understand. Did she mean I had shown compassion, kindness, gentleness of heart, and so she thought I would make a good healer? Or did she mean I had been brave? Willing to risk the anger of the gods? If so, she was wrong. I was not brave. I was so afraid of the future I could scarcely breathe.

'Do not be afraid, Psykhe. You have a dark and difficult road before you, but I promise you we shall meet again. This is not farewell, just fair journey.' Nocturna tugged me down so she could kiss my cheek, then she reached into her basket and withdrew two small knives, sheathed in leather.

One was made of silver, its ivory handle decorated with a crescent moon, its blade honed to a sharp edge. It was used to harvest herbs, to sever the umbilical cord after birth and, sometimes, to cut the mother to make the baby's passage into life easier.

The other was made entirely of whetted obsidian and was decorated with the round blackness of the dark moon. It was used for cutting a dead baby into parts so it could be hooked out of the mother's womb. I had seen Nocturna do it once when both mother and baby were dead. I had never done it myself.

I took the two knives reverently. The gift comforted me a little. Perhaps I could continue to do my work in Roma. Perhaps I could build a garden. Perhaps I could be of use.

'You will find your way,' Nocturna promised me. 'Now go. You do not have much time and neither do I.'

II

Hellebore for Hekate

I had been apprenticed to the goddess of witches, and not even known.

What a fool I had been, what a child.

But I knew now.

I went out into the garden, cutting and harvesting herbs sacred to Hekate with the silver knife she had given me.

I wanted to cast a spell.

Nettle, rosemary, black hellebore, hemlock, wormwood, cypress and yew. Herbs for protection and guidance. I cut seven leaves from each herb and put them in a small glass bottle along with seven black dog hairs, plucked from Nera's head, and seven white hairs, plucked from my own. A handful of ashes scooped from my hearth, and three iron nails – one prised from the front gate, another from my tower door and the last from Nocturna's. Finally, I mixed it all together with seven drops of my blood, my finger pierced with the tip of the silver knife.

Brid had taught me many charms when I was a child, and Nocturna had taught me more as I had grown into a woman. I had heard others muttered in fear by sickbeds or shouted in rage in the marketplace. Some of the darkest and strangest I had deciphered from tattered scrolls and broken lead tablets. This spell, though, was the first I had ever invented myself and the first I had uttered since the little healing chant that had saved the life of a dove so long ago.

Everyone called me an ice witch. Let me be one then, and harness what power I could. I knelt in the garden, facing the west, and spoke the words of the spell.

I call on Hekate, the goddess crone
She who sits upon the dark throne
Protect me always, and my blood and bone.

I call on the Torchbearer, Hekate
Be brightness in the dark for me,
Light my way and guard me on my journey.

I call on the goddess of the threshold,
Give me courage, help me be bold,
So I may serve you as you have foretold.

I sealed the bottle with black wax, bound it three times with black ribbon, and buried it beside the step.

I had been aware of the men watching me as I worked, but I did not care. Such spells were best done in the midnight hour, when there was less chance of watching eyes, but I did not have time to wait for darkness. I had to cast the spell now, before I left forever. At last it was done. My hands were grubby with dirt, my hair and dress dishevelled. I went to the well to wash. The men all fell back to let me through, diverting their gaze. A few made the sign of the horns with their fingers.

Among them was Collatinus, son of the king's cousin. His face was so drawn and sweaty with superstitious terror I knew Nocturna had been right, and that marrying him was not my destiny.

I smelt the city of Roma before I saw it. The sickly-sweet reek of rot.

For days we had been tormented by a sly wind with needle-sharp claws that raked our faces and found every gap in our clothes. Now the sky darkened, thunder rumbled menacingly, ravens flew over, croaking. My uneasiness grew.

To our left the river surged, brown and foamy. We came over the crest of a low hill. The nauseating stench hit me like a blow to the stomach. I covered my nose and mouth with my cloak, looking around to see its cause.

The first thing I saw was a great earthen rampart built along the opposite shore of the river. The town beyond was hazed with smoke, a few terracotta roofs rising above thatched huts. A great temple was being built on the highest hill.

The road ran towards a wooden bridge, supported by narrow sticks driven deep into the mud. Alongside was a long row of strangely cropped trees, each hung with a limp bundle of cloth. I peered at them, wondering why anyone would shear trees so they had just two horizontal branches, spreading out on either side of the trunk. They would not bear much fruit that way. And what were those limp bundles? Some method of frightening away the ravens? If so, it did not work. The great black birds were everywhere, swooping over the river, screeching at the verge of the road, perched on the trees, pecking at the ragged bundles.

'What is that smell?' Alektrona exclaimed, covering her nose and mouth with her hand. 'Is there something dead on the road?'

I recoiled in shock. We drove through an avenue of corpses, hung on crossed staves of wood for the carrion crows.

99

My stomach lurched. 'But . . . who? Why?'

Lucius glanced at me. His face was stern.

'The king exhibits the bodies of any slave who dares kill himself, so that his ghost may never find rest.'

'But . . . so many? So many kill themselves? Even knowing they'll be denied burial?'

He nodded. 'They would rather be dead and wander the world forever than work any longer in the king's employ.'

I pressed my hands over my face, unable to bear either the sight or the smell, until the clatter of the dray's iron wheels on wooden palings told me we were at last upon the Bridge of Stilts, the only way to cross the river into the city. I drew my hands away. Ahead was a bronze-studded gate. Lucius paid the tax, and we drove under the stone parapet and into the city. The gate slammed shut behind us, and heavy oaken bars were driven into their sockets by the huge hammer wielded by the guard.

The streets of Roma were crowded with laden donkeys, pedlars with packs on their backs, swaying litters carried by sweating slaves, and soldiers marching in precise formation, their tunics as red as blood. Pigs rooted in the rubbish, thin dogs gathered to lap up blood from under the butchers' hooks, and flies buzzed drunkenly above the piles of dung left to lie in the road.

Khrysanthe covered her nose with her hand. 'It stinks!'

'The king is building a great sewer,' Lucius told us. 'It will be large enough for boats to be rowed along it. When it is done, the city will not reek so badly. Or so he says. Many slaves have died in the building of it. And the temple to Jove.' He nodded at the great building being erected on the high hill to our left. 'There were many shrines there before to other gods and goddesses. Older gods. But the king has ordered them all knocked down to make room for his temple to the Thunderer.'

Silviano had said the goddess Venus was enraged that her shrines and temples were being allowed to fall into ruin. Uneasily I wondered what other gods and goddesses were angry.

Many of the houses were simple thatched huts, like the ones I was used to in Tarchna and Velzna. As we entered the Forum, the architecture changed. Taller buildings, with shops below and apartments above, many with washing lines strung between them. A raised platform, with cages underneath where gaunt ragged men crouched, hands held through the bars begging for alms. Hordes of people walked past them, not even noticing them. I had never seen so many people. I kept my cloak drawn over my head, but nonetheless many turned to stare at me. Even here, in such a multitude, my white hair and skin were strange.

The Forum was built in the valley between two hills. Many palatial villas had been built on the slopes, surrounding one tiny mud hut with a thatched roof.

'What is that?' Khrysanthe asked with a little trill of laughter. 'Some plebian hovel? You'd think they'd knock it down.'

Lucius cast her a warning look. 'That is where Romulus and his twin brother Remus were raised by a kind shepherd, my lady. Whenever the hut is damaged in a storm, the priests have it rebuilt exactly as it was.'

This quietened her. It was the tone of his voice, the cautioning glance. It did not do to mock Roma's sacred sites.

It was a strange story, how Roma came to be founded. Twin brothers, born to a vestal virgin raped by the god of war. Her wicked uncle put her babies into a basket and threw them into the river. Swept downstream, their basket washed ashore at a place where seven hills guarded the only ford. A she-wolf found the twin boys and suckled them, saving their lives.

In time, Romulus and Remus grew into men and decided to establish their own kingdom. They could not agree on which hill to build their city, or what it should be named. They decided to settle their dispute by seeking a sign from the gods. Each established a lookout on their chosen spot, Romulus on the hill near the cave of the she-wolf that suckled them and Remus further south. He saw six vultures fly overhead, birds sacred to Mars, their father. He ran to tell his brother he was the one chosen by the gods.

But Romulus had seen twelve vultures soaring in the sky. Both claimed the kingship, Remus because he saw the birds first and Romulus because he had seen more. The tension between them turned into bitter rivalry. Romulus began to plough the boundary of his new settlement, but mockingly Remus leapt over the furrows, making some remark about how easy it was to breach his walls. In a sudden rage, Romulus drew his dagger and stabbed his twin to death, shouting, 'So perish any who dares to leap my walls.'

Roma was a city consecrated with blood. No wonder the Romans prided themselves on their fierceness.

The crowds were so thick, our progress was slow. Lucius kept up a running commentary of all that we passed. The shrine of Vulcan, built well away from any houses for fear of fire. The temple of Saturnus, the god of sowing and reaping. It was he who had castrated his father with a stone sickle and set free the gods. The small temple of Janus, the two-faced god of boundaries and beginnings, with its big double doors open wide. 'The doors are unfastened in times of war and closed in times of peace,' Lucius told us, 'but since the king is always at war with someone, I have never seen them shut.'

We passed a deep circular pit. 'That is the navel of the city. It is said to be a gateway to the underworld. You'll be taken there tomorrow, to throw in a handful of dirt from your homeland. All new citizens must do so.'

'But we did not bring any dirt,' Khrysanthe said.

'I brought some for you,' Lucius assured her.

'You think of everything,' she responded, wide-eyed with admiration. His lean cheek reddened.

The round temple to Vesta, where virgins dressed in white tended the everlasting flame of the goddess of the hearth. Taken when only children, they would never know the touch of a man's hand, the deep kiss of desire, the swelling of a child in their womb, the suck of a babe on their breast. This seemed terrible to me. Not the lack of such things. I had never known them either, though I longed for them. It was not being allowed to choose for themselves that most troubled me.

Khrysanthe asked some coquettish question about what happened to a vestal virgin who was caught breaking the rules.

'She is buried alive,' Lucius answered tersely.

Beside the temple was the long narrow house where the virgins lived, and near it, another oddly shaped building, which Lucius told us was the Regia where all the records were kept, and also shrines to Mars and Rhea, the goddess of fertility, daughter of Gaea. Next door was a magnificent villa of soft cream stone, with vast pillars like a temple, set behind a high, thick wall.

'The royal palace,' Lucius said, 'and our destination.'

'We're going to the palace?' Khrysanthe bounced on her seat in excitement. 'But I'm not dressed for it!'

He smiled at her. 'You will not be presented to the king and queen tonight, my lady. Your father has his own quarters within the palace complex. He instructed me to take you there for now.'

Khrysanthe thrust out her bottom lip in an exaggerated pout. 'I suppose it's for the best. I must look a sight after all these days on the road.'

'A most pleasant sight,' he assured her, and she dimpled prettily.

We did not go in through the main entrance, but through another small gate around the side, guarded by men with the lion-hooded

103

face of Heracles on their shield. Within was a dark garden of stiff cypresses, set about a fountain lined with lemon trees in terracotta pots. The colonnade was set with cushioned couches and low stools, and in a side garden was a smaller pool where eels swam, ready to be caught for supper. I had a sharp shard of memory. Ambrose and I, exploring the lord of Velzna's cellars. Ambrose's look of admiration, the warm strength of his hand. Then nothing, for years, till he appeared in my window, blazing with unnatural light. Do not forget that life and death are the affairs of gods, not of mortals, he had told me.

I could never forget.

The rest of my father's quarters were just a blur. I was so tired, so shaken, so overwhelmed. I could not forget those poor slaves, hung like bags of meat for the birds and the beasts to fight over. We did not see my father, thankfully. We were taken to our rooms by obsequious slaves, brought warm water scented with lemon, washed as if we were babes, shown to beds heavy with richly embroidered counterpanes, given sweet warm wine, left alone to sink into soft pillows stuffed with goose feathers.

I lay staring into the darkness. What fate lay here for me, in this city founded on bloody murder and revenge?

III

Stargazer

I was unhappy in Roma. I missed Nocturna and Nera with an incessant gnawing ache, and it was difficult to undertake my work when no-one knew me as a healer. I found the heat and stench of the city overpowering, and the constant round of royal banquets and processions exhausting. I longed for the peace of my herb garden and stillroom, for the satisfying weariness at the end of a day spent in purposeful labour.

My sisters were married, wearing crowns of marjoram I wove, to the men my father had chosen for them. Thankfully no-one wanted to marry me. My father brought many to look me over. I think they came out of curiosity, rather than any desire to wed. Collatinus had married a sweet-faced, pious young woman named Lucretia, who made a surreptitious gesture against the evil eye every time she saw me. I wondered what Collatinus had told her. Whatever it was, I suspected he had told everyone, for there was a hush, a huddle, a drawing away of hems everywhere I went.

I did not much care, as long as I was left alone. I spent a lot of time in my bedroom reading with the help of a jar full of water, studying my library of scrolls for stories of mortals who fell in love with gods. None ended well.

My bedroom had doors that opened out into the garden, with its splashing fountain and lemon trees in pots, its spear-like trees and statues of muscular gods and heroes fighting. A small space, no more than a few steps, had been left bare. When I first arrived, I had cultivated it and planted it with seeds and cuttings I had brought with me from Velzna. I put the green-eyed rose facing east, to the rising sun, amidst other silvery-white plants that would glimmer in the moonlight. When Luna came, driving her chariot, my shadowy garden glowed with unearthly beauty.

I looked up at the great wheel of blazing stars above. Nocturna knew the name of every cluster of stars, every constellation. I had been born under the sign of the weighing scales, she had told me, carried by the goddess of justice. The month of my birth was the balancing point between summer and winter, day and night, warmth and cold, light and darkness, joy and sorrow. That was why I needed order and symmetry, why I could not bear any injustice. That was why my father's crooked ways upset me so much. Everything he did was wrong, disordered.

Summer passed, the year turned towards winter, and still I spent much of my time alone. My father was always in attendance upon the king, which meant he was often away at one of the ceaseless war campaigns waged by the Tarquins. They seemed determined to conquer the world. My sisters lived with their husbands elsewhere in the palace, and even though there was always a feast or a festival I was expected to attend, I went only when physically forced. We met when we could, which was not as often as I would have liked. Khrysanthe's belly was growing rounder by the week, and Alektrona was growing thinner and harder and ever more bitter. Sometimes I saw bruises on her throat and arms. Silently I would bring healing salve. Silently she would take it.

Near the end of the month that had no name, on a cold and frosty night, Lucius came to fetch me. 'Khrysanthe is in labour! She's having a difficult time. Will you come?' He was white with suppressed anxiety, unable to stand still. I nodded and went to fetch my cloak and basket.

Brutus's apartment in the palace was one vast floor crammed with riches. My sister's slave Ancilla was waiting for me anxiously, a lantern held high. As she hurried us down the corridor, I could hear high-pitched cries. We came into the bedchamber, and saw Khrysanthe writhing on the bed in pain, her face contorted. She saw me, and gasped, 'Make it stop, make it stop, make it stop.' Then another paroxysm gripped her, and she screamed.

I went to her at once, felt her forehead, touched my fingers to the urgent beat of blood in her wrist. Her hair was falling out of its plait, her face was white and strained, sheened with sweat, and her lower lip was swollen and bloodied where she had bitten through it.

I raised my eyebrows at Ancilla in an unspoken question.

'It has been many hours already,' she confessed. 'It seems to start, then stop, then start again. I thought it was a false labour, but it's been going on so long, and nothing seems to help.'

I nodded and put my hand on her shoulder in comfort, then knelt beside my sister, gently turning her face to mine. 'I'm here now. Look at me, Khrysanthe. Breathe with me.' I took a deep calming breath and nodded to her, squeezing her hand. At last she seemed to understand. We breathed together, deep and slow, in through the nose and out through the mouth. She began to calm. I saw the moment in which the contraction began again. I accelerated my rate of breathing, exhaling in short swift pants through my mouth. She gripped my hands, her eyes fixed on mine, copying me.

When the contraction at last died away, I unpacked my basket, laying each object in its place on the clean cloth. Bunches of herbs, jars of salves and scented oils, a cheesecloth bag of salt, a bottle of sweet wine macerated with wormwood, glass vials of opium milk and deadly nightshade, my knives. I stoked up the fire, set a pot of water on the fire to boil, dampened a cloth with verbena water to bathe her face and neck, and gave her a bunch of dried lavender to clench so that its scent might calm and comfort her.

Then I went swiftly around the room, unshuttering the windows and throwing them open to the sweet night air, unfastening all ribbons and ties, unplaiting her hair, unknotting the string of her nightgown. I unhooked the golden earrings from her ears, and put them away in her jewellery box, out of sight. Deep inside me was an awful fear that Venus was punishing me, punishing my sister.

Khrysanthe was exhausted, her pulse weak and uneven. I felt all over her belly with gentle fingertips, then sat back, troubled. The baby was a stargazer, facing upwards towards the sky instead of downwards towards the earth. Most babies were born heads down, facing their mother's spine. That way they passed more easily down the birth canal. When a baby lay sideways, or came down feet first, or – like this little one, faced upwards – the labour was much more gruelling.

Her contractions came in ever-quickening waves, but still the baby did not come. I did everything I could. I massaged the immense tight belly with clary sage oil, then held my hands before Khrysanthe's nose for her to breathe in the fumes. I supported her as she walked up and down, sobbing all the while. I sat her in the birthing-stool with a bowl of hot, steaming water beneath her to warm and relax the straining muscles. I asked her to crouch on all fours, rocking from side to side, a heated stone on her lower back. I squatted behind her, pressing hard on the small of her back to lift and open the pelvis, allowing more room for the baby's head to descend. It was no use. The baby's head was jammed at an awkward angle, its chin tilted up instead of tucked to its chest.

I put the wide end of a hollowed-out ram's horn against Khrysanthe's swollen belly, and bent and pressed my ear against the other end. I could hear the baby's heartbeat. It was frantic, uneven, like a bird with a broken wing. My own heart speeded up. If the child was not born soon, I could lose them both.

Nocturna would have broken the baby's caul with the long sharpened nail of her middle finger if she had been here. Mine had not been filed to a point like hers. I had to use a long hook instead. Liquid gushed out. It was yellowish-green. I bit my lip. Not a good sign.

Nothing I did could free the baby. He was trapped in the birth canal. After one particularly harrowing round of contractions, Khrysanthe fell back limply and we could not rouse her.

'Is she dead?' Ancilla cried.

I held a small bronze mirror above her colourless lips. The faintest of mists.

A strange eerie calmness. Everything seemed very clear and focused. I rolled back her shift so that her belly was exposed, then picked up my knives.

'No, no, you will kill them both.' Ancilla started forward.

I hardly heard her, looking down at the knives. Silver or obsidian? Which one did I need?

She dared not try to stop me. She was a slave, and I was a lord's daughter. 'The master! I must go and tell the master.'

I nodded absent-mindedly. Ancilla ran out the door. 'She plans to cut the baby out! You must stop her!'

Lucius rushed in. I shook my head, holding out one hand emphatically. He came to a halt, looking from me to Khrysanthe, lying unconscious on the bed.

'Is she dead?' His voice broke.

'No. But death is not far away. I'm trying to save her life! Please, can you keep them away?'

Lucius nodded. As he went out, I heard Ancilla asking a house slave to go and find his master.

'He's watching the gladiators,' a boy's voice piped.

'Run! Run and fetch him. Tell him the witch-girl means to cut open his wife!'

All my attention was on the task that lay ahead. I remembered the story of Apollo, the god of healing, music and prophecy. He had cut his son Aesculapius from the womb of his dead mother, and the boy had survived to grow up into a great healer himself.

Could it be done? If so, how?

I imagined Nocturna was here. What would she do? I could almost hear her voice. *Care for the mother first*, she would say. *Preserve her life if you can.*

I measured a tincture of opium and deadly nightshade into some warmed wine, then dripped some into Khrysanthe's slack mouth. It ran out the corners. I held some powdered hartshorn to her nose. It revived her just enough for me to lift her, and help her drink the drugged wine, then she slipped back to sleep.

Consecrate your tools, Nocturna would say. *Offer a libation to the gods.*

I picked up my knives again. Silver or black? Life or death?

I laid down the black blade, amazed at the steadiness of my hand.

After washing my hands and arms thoroughly, I scrubbed the silver knife all over with salt. 'By earth, I cleanse and bless you.'

Passed it nine times through the steam of the boiling water. 'By air, I cleanse and bless you.'

Held it in the flame till its tip glowed red. 'By fire I cleanse and bless you.'

Dipped it deep into the bubbling pot. 'By water I cleanse and bless you.'

I then poured a cupful of the warm wine over my sister's belly, praying to Hekate, goddess of midwives and witches. *Please, great goddess, help me! Help me save my sister.*

I was calm, cold, remote. With the tip of the knife, I made an incision down the centre of my sister's belly, slicing open the layer of skin. Below was fat and connective tissue. Carefully I cut through them, trying to keep the edges of the wound clean and neat. Below was a thick band of tightly knitted muscle. I did not want to cut this. Damaged muscle never fully recovered. I took a moment to breathe and think what to do. I was vaguely aware of running footsteps, of men shouting and women sobbing. I slid my fingers into the band of muscle, finding a way through, panting at the effort it took. Below was a thin membrane, almost translucent, stretched tight. I cut it open. Beneath were various meaty-looking organs. I delved below and found the wall of the uterus. My arms and shoulders were burning now, my legs trembling. My hands were deep in my sister's body, blood welling everywhere, I could not see. I had to staunch the bleeding with swabs of clean linen, then sprinkled yarrow powder into the wound.

I felt the round shape of the baby's head, the staccato thud of his heart. I cut through the casing, using just the tip of my knife. I looked down and saw a tiny hand reaching up. I laid one finger in the baby's palm. His fingers closed reflexively upon mine.

'Well met, little one,' I whispered.

I drew my finger free, cradled his warm head in one hand, and eased him out. It was difficult. I had to push down on my sister's uterus, then negotiate his small, curled form through the narrow slit. The blue, pulsating cord was looped around his neck. I loosened it, clamped it, cut it. The baby wailed, high and thin. I wrapped him and laid him down while I found and removed the placenta. My arms were bloodied to the elbow. I washed myself thoroughly, then bent over my sister. Her eyes were moving rapidly under her eyelids, and her breath was short and rapid. I consecrated my needles with salt and water and smoke and fire, then began to sew her together again, one delicate layer at a time.

At last it was done. I was so exhausted I could barely stand upright. I swayed, but could not rest till my sister's wound was bound with clean linens, and she was as safe as I could make her. I did not have the strength to change her bloodstained sheets. Besides, the baby was crying. I gathered him up. My nephew. He gazed at my face with unfocused eyes, puckered his brow, made a sucking motion with his mouth. He was covered with muck and blood. Gently I washed him. He was perfect. I wrapped him in clean linen, warmed by the fire, and we sat together in a cushioned chair, gazing at each other. I had never seen such a thatch of dark curls on a baby, or such unusual grey eyes. My heart sank a little. He looked like Lucius. What would happen if Brutus thought so too? The Romans were as pitiless in their punishment of adultery as they were in everything else.

The sound of shouting, a scuffle, the door banging open. Brutus rushed in, surrounded by his men, swords drawn. Lucius got up from the floor, massaging his jaw. I cast him a quick look of gratitude, stood up and went to Brutus, unswaddling the little boy and laying him naked at his feet.

He was astonished. 'The baby's alive?'

I nodded. Brutus gazed down at him. 'A boy,' he said. 'Thank Jove.'

He bent and looked at the boy more closely. A quick frowning glance at Lucius, who stood imperturbably by the door, his grey eyes lowered. My heart was thudding thickly in my throat. If Brutus repudiated the baby, it would be left out in the street to die.

Brutus looked towards the bed. My sister lay unmoving, in the bloody shambles of her bed. 'Khrysanthe? Is she dead?'

I shook my head. Brutus strode to the bed. He bent over his wife, checking her pulse and her temperature. He folded back her shift. Linen bandages wrapped her from ribs to hips. He stared, transfixed, then gave me a look of such deep frowning calculation I was afraid. What would he do?

For a moment, he stood, silent, inscrutable, then picked up the newborn baby, now squalling loudly, his little arms and legs jerking. He held him expertly, but without any tenderness or wonder, and passed him to me to be wrapped up warmly again. Relief flooded me. He had accepted the baby as his.

Suddenly his face changed. His jaw loosened, his mouth hung open. 'Baby got cut out,' he said in his old childish manner. 'Got cut out of his mammy's tummy. Like a god! He's a lucky baby. Lucky for him and lucky for me.'

'Very lucky,' I said shakily. I could not understand the change in him. A moment ago he had been all focused action, his manner and words just like any other man. Suddenly he sounded like a fool again. Was that moment of frowning calculation a momentary parting of the mists that clouded his mind, or had I seen a glimpse of the true Brutus, hidden behind some kind of mask?

All his men were staring at me. I knew it would not be long before the whole city heard what I had done.

'I am very tired,' I managed to say. 'Lucius, will you escort me home?'

'Of course, my lady.' He sprang forward to take my basket. He cast one look at the tiny, grey-eyed baby, now sucking his fist in his cradle, then led me away. As soon as we were out of sight, he surprised me greatly by dropping to his knees before me and kissing my hem. 'Thank you, my lady, thank you for saving them.'

'Please get up, Lucius,' I said wearily.

'It's a miracle. My son must have some great destiny, to be born in such a way.'

'I couldn't let them die.'

My limbs were leaden with weariness, but I could not bear to stay within my father's walls. I walked out into the garden. The sky was pale green, the luminous gate between dark and light.

113

The thin moon shone silver as a freshly whetted scythe. Bees danced in the white lemon blossoms. Above the glowing horizon one bright star blazed.

The beauty of the dawn made me feel precariously close to tears. I had saved my sister, I had saved her son, now I must brace myself for the cost. I drew my cloak more closely around me and lay down on the stone seat. A bird sang somewhere. I closed my eyes and slipped towards sleep.

A rush of feathers, a light and buoyant step. A shadow fell over me. Someone bent and brushed my mouth with theirs. It was the most delicate of touches, soft as a butterfly's wing yet burning like a brand. I startled awake.

Ambrose sprang back. A pair of great golden wings snapped open, lifting him from his feet. In one hand he held a golden arrow.

I reached out one hand to him, but in a flurry of wingbeats he was gone.

IV

The Sibyl

The memory of Ambrose's kiss haunted me.

The touch of his lips on mine, the flash of light along the golden arrow. What did it mean? Had he come to kiss me or wound me?

The golden arrow was the weapon of Amor, whom the Greeks called Eros, god of desire. He shot it into the hearts of men and women so they would fall madly, desperately, in love. Those hard gleaming arrows had caused much havoc and war throughout history. Why had Ambrose come to me with one in his hand? Was he Venus's wild son, Amor? Did he come to me to punish me at his mother's command? If so, why had he not stabbed me? Why had he kissed me, and then fled? If only I had been quicker. I could have wound my arms about his neck and held him to me, I could have kissed him back.

He's a god, I told myself sternly. Loving him will bring nothing but hurt. Stop dreaming of him.

But I could not.

*

Nine days after his birth, my sister's son was named Lucius, Brutus's first name. I hoped no-one remembered it was also the first name of my father's bodyguard.

Most people nicknamed him Cesar, meaning 'to be cut'.

Every day I went to tend my sister and care for the baby. He was my greatest joy. Every squint, every yawn, every pucker of his little face was a source of wonder to me. *I saved him*, I'd think. *If not for me, he'd be dead.*

Khrysanthe was relieved her husband had not repudiated him. 'It's a good thing Brutus is so stupid!' she said to me, lying in bed while I rocked Cesar to sleep. I was troubled. I did not think Brutus was really a fool. So why did he pretend?

I began to ask about him, trying to understand. Slowly I pieced together his story.

Brutus was the only son of the king's sister. He had been adopted by Tarquin the Proud after his father had been murdered. Some people whispered that it was the king himself who had ordered the deed done, after Brutus's father had protested Tarquin's violent seizing of the throne. Only a boy, Brutus had witnessed his father's murder. Some said he had always been a fool, and had greeted the assassins with giggles, trying to fight them with his little wooden sword. Others said that he had been born a bright boy but had been struck such a heavy blow to the head by the assassins they had left him for dead. He had been found unconscious, lying in his father's blood, his toy sword in his hand.

Whatever the cause of his simple-mindedness, the boy had been brought to court to act as a kind of fool for the king and his sons. He had grown up in the palace, galloping about on a hobby horse made from a stick, seeming never to grow any older in his mind even as his body grew into that of a man. He was fond of games of chance, bet heavily on the races and gladiators, and somehow had won himself a fortune. Tarquin had married him off to his first wife to keep him out of trouble, and to everyone's surprise he had fathered two sons before she had died. Somehow he had flourished in the court of the Tarquins, when so many others had perished.

I watched him covertly, and slowly my suspicion that he was not as foolish as he seemed grew. I did not have much to go on. A kind of theatricality in the inane way he behaved before the court, a half-smile or a flash of contempt when he thought no-one was looking.

If it was true, if he was not a simpleton, why did he pretend to be one? He would have to have maintained his pretence for a very long time. Did he seek at first just to survive, and then found he dared not risk discarding his mask? Or did he enjoy hoodwinking them all? Did he use his reputation for foolishness to trick his way into richness, or did he have some deeper game to play?

I did not know. I just knew I now feared him too.

Lucius had made himself my personal protector. Everywhere I went he accompanied me. I needed him. Word had spread, and I was the object of much curiosity and wonder. The sick and the lame crowded in the streets outside the palace, waiting for me. Every morning I went out with a basket of remedies, doing my best to help, but there were always more, calling my name. Others turned away, surreptitiously making the sign of the horns. They were the ones who called me a witch.

Snow turned to sleet, then to icy rain. The river flooded, and the walls of the sewer collapsed. The common folk had to wade thigh-deep through filthy water to go about their daily business. People fell ill with a bloody flux, raging fevers, blinding headaches. I did my best to help, but it was difficult. How I missed my garden and stillroom, my big mortar and pestle, my distillation pot.

'The gods are angry,' people whispered.

I was afraid. Was it my fault? And even if it wasn't, would I be blamed?

I was full of foreboding. Had I done wrong in saving Cesar's life? Perhaps the gods were angry with me for daring to reach my hands into my sister's womb and pluck forth her living baby?

Life and death are the business of gods, not mortals, Ambrose had said.

My will hardened. The gods gave us our hands and our eyes and our brains for a purpose. It would have been much more wrong to know that I could have saved their lives and done nothing.

The king's great temple to Jove went ahead, despite the rain and the floods. I wondered if he sought to atone in some way too. If he too feared the anger of the gods. Day after day the slaves toiled in the mud, day after day they stumbled and died, and more slaves were brought in to take their place. Slowly the heavy pillars were hauled up, and the massive steps laid.

One day a severed head was discovered buried under the temple works.

'Apparently it was still quite fresh,' Khrysanthe told me, rocking Cesar in his cradle. 'Can you believe it? What does it mean?'

'It means some poor man was murdered and his body dismembered,' Alektrona said harshly. She was looking thin and nervy, and her face was heavily painted. 'They'll probably find the rest of him dumped all over the city.'

'Urrgh, Alektrona! Must you?'

'Would you choose to hide parts of a dead body under a temple to the king of the gods?' I asked. 'Wouldn't you be afraid of angering him? Unless, of course, it was some kind of ritual killing . . .'

'Like a blood sacrifice?' Alektrona looked at me with sudden alarm. 'You think the king . . .'

'Sssh!' Khrysanthe hissed, glancing about. 'Best not speak of it. Slaves have ears too, you know, and tongues for spreading rumours.'

'It's not a good omen,' Alektrona said heavily.

Soon it was announced by the king's priests that the severed head belonged to a warrior, miraculously appearing by divine intervention, to show that Roma was meant to be the ruler of the world.

Yet still the arrows of plague bombarded the city. I worked as I had never worked before. Day and night, I ground herbs between grinding stones, made up healing tinctures, went out into the poorest districts of the city, eased pain and fever and grief wherever I could.

Word spread. Every morning, more people clustered outside my father's gate. They stretched hands through the bars, left posies of flowers and clumsily-made clay figurines in my honour, dropped to their knees and kissed the ground as I went past. 'Fairer than Venus,' they called me.

One day in the square I was attacked by a flock of pigeons. Their wings beat around my head, their talons raked at my arms and head as I did my best to protect my face. Lucius laid about him with his shield and the flat of his sword, but still the birds swooped at me, pecking and screeching. Suddenly, a gust of wind blew from the west, scattering the flock. Borne on the wind was a bright-breasted little bird who came to rest on a wall beside me, warbling sweetly. I spun, looked eagerly about me. People were chasing after their hats, holding down their swirling skirts, picking up overturned stools. Only one figure seemed unperturbed by the chaos the wind had caused. A slender young man, dressed in filthy rags, a tattered hood drawn over his face. He looked straight at me.

I would have known those golden eyes anywhere. 'Ambrose!'

He lifted one finger to his mouth, and slipped away. The robin darted after him.

I was as stunned as if I had been punched in the stomach. Questions clamoured in my mind. But no answers.

After that, I thought I saw Ambrose everywhere. Just a glimpse through the crowds. A shadowy figure slipping away into the shadows as I came home from the markets, a certain languid grace in the movements of a beggar, a charge of electricity in the air like a storm front coming.

Perhaps I had just imagined him. Perhaps I had conjured him out of my loneliness and longing. He certainly troubled my dreams every night, and disturbed my every waking hour.

I woke one morning to the riotous sound of clattering wood, like a thousand drumsticks being knocked together. It continued without ceasing. I rose and dressed, and went out to see the cause of the noise. No-one knew. I called for Lucius, but he was already waiting for me, his grey eyes full of trouble.

'What is it, what's that noise?' I asked him.

'The spears of Mars are rattling,' he told me. I did not understand. 'The spears kept in his shrine. If they vibrate, it is a sign that something terrible will happen. They've been vibrating all night. The king's priests say it is a sign that the god of war smiles on us, but word is spreading, and the people of Roma are uneasy. Crowds are gathering, and the mood is ugly. The king has called for you.'

'Me?' I shrank back. 'Why me?'

'My lady, you must do as he bids.'

The king's assembly hall was thronged with richly dressed people, arguing and gesticulating. I was led through the crowd, people clearing the way for me, everyone staring at me with curiosity. I saw Collatinus and his pretty young wife, Lucretia. Both made the sign of horns at me. Khrysanthe stood beside Brutus, her golden cupid earrings catching the light as she scanned the crowd. A nursemaid stood behind her, holding baby Cesar. He cooed at the sight of me and held out his chubby arms. I smiled at him, but could not stop to cuddle him. His face screwed up, and he began to cry. I could hardly hear his wails over the clanging of the spears of Mars. The reverberation shuddered through the palace, causing doors to rattle and vases to totter and fall. My whole body felt jangled, my jaw aching with the effort of keeping my teeth from chattering.

At the far end of the room, the king's sons lolled in their ornate chairs, dressed in elaborate robes of royal purple. Alektrona sat on a low stool at Sextus's feet, her downturned face a mask of make-up that did not quite cover a bruised and swollen eye.

I held my head high and my step steady, determined to show no weakness.

The royal podium was guarded by twelve strong, hard-faced men armed with axes. The king reclined on a couch, a cup of wine in his hand. A heavy man, fleshy with too much good living, he wore a long purple cloak and red shoes. My father lounged next to the king, close enough to whisper in his ear and laugh at any remark he made. He too wore red shoes, an affectation I had never seen him don before, and gold rings on all his fingers. The queen sat on a low cushioned stool, her hair arranged in elaborate oiled curls, her back straight as a ruler. I had never been so close to her before. She looked me over coolly, measuringly, as I dropped to my knees and bowed my head.

The king regarded me with heavy-lidded eyes. 'Indeed, she is most fair. I see why you succumbed to the wiles of her mother, Cassius,' he said to my father. 'Is it true she cut a babe from the womb, and both mother and babe lived?'

My father smiled ingratiatingly. 'Yes, sire, it is true. The gods were guiding her hands.'

'And is it true she brought a drowned slave girl back to life? And goes among the people of Roma, healing them with her hands?'

'Yes, sire, it is all true.'

I looked at my father with startled eyes. I wanted to protest, to tell them all it was not me but the medicines I made, but I dared not speak.

'So, girl, tell me, what do you think it means, the rattling of the spears of Mars?' the king asked me.

'I am no Sibyl,' I answered, 'to understand the signs of the gods.'

The king reared back, surprise and suspicion on his face. 'You speak of the Sibyl! You too believe I should give her an audience? What do you know of her coming last night? I asked it to be kept secret!'

I had wanted merely to deflect the question, to stop any more intimations that I was somehow an instrument of the gods. But I saw now I had erred. The king thought I had inner knowledge of some kind.

'Please forgive me, your highness, I know nothing of the Sibyl,' I hastened to say. 'I simply meant that I cannot read omens. I know nothing of the gods' will.'

'I am the king of Roma,' he proclaimed. 'I do not deign to hold audience with some witch, just because she crooks her little finger at me.'

'You mistake me! I do not know the Sibyl. I have no connection to her.'

The queen suddenly spoke. Her voice was silky and caressing. 'The girl knows nothing, my liege. It is I who summoned the Sibyl. She speaks with the voice of the gods, does she not? We should listen. Be as wise as the serpent, my love, let the oracle approach you.'

The king scowled but made a flicking motion with his hand. I was permitted to retreat, and the order was given for the Sibyl to be brought to the king.

A distant clamour of music, wild and insistent. Everyone's heads turned. The king raised himself up on his elbow.

A long procession of dancers came into the hall, spinning and leaping, shaking cymbals and banging hand drums. Musicians played flutes and double pipes. They all wore short loose tunics with their hair long and wild under wreaths of leaves and flowers. Some spun flaming torches around their bodies, others did handsprings and backflips. Some young women ran, leading great spotted lynxes with tufted ears and slanted eyes. Another had a monkey on her shoulder, leaping up and down and gibbering.

A young woman danced at the centre of the procession, dressed in a long saffron dress embroidered with vines, flowers and sheaves of wheat. Her skin was the darkest I had ever seen, her eyes the blackest, her masses of curls so thick and heavy I wondered how she could force a comb through them. On her head she wore a crown of poppies. Heavy necklaces of amber hung about her neck, and golden bracelets in the shape of snakes wound up her upper arms. Every step she took rang with the tiny bells she wore about her ankles. In one hand she carried a large tambourine set with tiny metallic cymbals, and she shook it with a kind of ecstatic fury. Everything about her spoke of strength and pride.

The crowd stared and whispered, and the bodyguards moved as one, stepping forward with weapons crossed before the king.

The young woman in the saffron gown ignored them.

'O king,' she cried in a clear carrying voice. 'The lances of Mars are rattling in their sockets, and still you do not come to me. I speak with the voice of gods – they reveal their intentions through me, and still you do not listen. Your priests speak untruths at your direction. Do you think the gods do not know?'

Red with anger, the king began to bluster and threaten.

She raised one hand. 'Be silent! I am the Sibyl of the Tiburtine. Three times I have sent for you, and three times you have refused me.

So I have come to you. This does not mean that I obey you. I obey only the great goddess, she whose giant snake was slaughtered at her shrine at Delphi, she whose shrines lie empty and abandoned, she whose celebrants are hunted and stoned, she who is angry. I bring to you the nine books in which are inscribed your future – yours, O king, and that of your city of Roma. You wish to know how to appease my goddess? For the cost of three hundred pieces of gold, the books will be yours, and so too the answers.'

The king laughed.

The Sibyl tossed her giant tambourine to one of the dancers and took his fiery torch. With a dramatic gesture she flung it on the ground, then threw a handful of some kind of powder upon it. Green flames leapt up. I recoiled at the smell. Stinking nightshade. I knew it well. It was said that the dead wore the purple-veined flowers as crowns in the underworld.

Simultaneously every single one of those wild, frenzied dancers dropped to the floor, faces pressed to the stone. Even the wild cats lowered themselves to their haunches, while the monkey hid within its mistress's robe. I crouched down too, covering my nose and mouth with a fold of my cloak. I knew what that foul-smelling smoke meant.

Only one person remained standing beside the Sybil. There was no way of knowing if they were man or woman, young or old, human or giant. I had never seen anyone so tall. Dressed in a long black gown, they had jet bracelets stacked up their wrists and jet earrings hanging from their pendulous earlobes. Every single hair on their body had been shaved or plucked. Under their crown of stinking nightshade, their skull shone as if polished, and their eyelids were gilded. They carried nine wooden staves, with ancient-looking papyrus scrolls rolled thickly about them and tied securely with black ribbon. They passed the Sibyl three of the scrolls, and she flung them onto the fire. In seconds, they were devoured by flames.

Cries of alarm resounded from the watching crowd. The king was on his feet, wine spilling from his fallen cup. 'How dare you! I am the king of Roma . . .'

'And I am the Sibyl of the Tiburtine, and hold no allegiance to any man, but only to the great goddess and her chosen consort.' She bent and breathed in the poisonous fumes. Her arms rose above her head, sinuous as serpents, her eyes turning up in their sockets.

The smoke swirled about the room. People were coughing, gasping, their eyes watering. Some were staring at nothing, their eyes dilated. Some clutched their throats, choking. Others screamed and pointed, 'Snakes! Snakes!'

Vipers slithered from the Sibyl's dress, writhing away into the crowd. Two more wound up her arms, the bracelets come to life. People stampeded, shoving and shouting. The bodyguards sprang forward, striking left and right, trying to keep the snakes away from the king. The queen leapt up onto her chair, screaming.

I could scarcely believe what I was seeing. A snake in the house was the worst of omens. Dozens of them was a calamity. The Sibyl must have carried the vipers hidden somewhere within her clothes. Was she not afraid? Of the king's anger, of being bitten?

At that moment, the vipers on her raised arms struck viciously, sinking their fangs into her throat. Her eyes rolled back. The Sybil began to sway from side to side. Strange wild words poured from her, punctuated by long pauses in which she wailed and ululated.

> Great Goddess, mother of us all, speak with my tongue.
> Arrogant king, your time is coming to an end.
> Empty your throne shall stand, nothing left but ashes.
> All of your seed shall perish with fire and sword.

Dying snakes thrashed on the floor, blood smearing the mosaic. The Sibyl stopped wailing and said to the king, 'Only six books remain.

You wish to know the future? For the cost of three hundred pieces of gold, the books will be yours.'

'But that's how much you wanted for nine books!' the king protested.

The Sibyl held out her hands. The black-clad giant passed her three more scrolls, and she flung them on the fire. In seconds they too were devoured by flames.

'Are you insane?' the king screamed.

The foul-smelling smoke billowed through the hall. I kept my mouth covered, trying not to breathe it in. My eyes stung.

'Only three books remain,' the Sibyl intoned. 'Three books in which your future is told. For the cost of three hundred pieces of gold, the books will be yours.'

'I will pay, I will pay,' the king gabbled. 'Give me the books! Do not burn any more.'

Silently the Sibyl stood, snakes writhing about her throat, till the chests of gold had been brought and laid at her feet. Her followers lifted them up and carried them away, as the musicians began to beat their drums and blow their pipes once more. The dancers paced slowly, with lowered faces and gazes averted from the dying snakes, the pile of glowering ashes on the floor. The Sibyl stumbled forward, the black-clad giant steadying her with reverent hands. Then she swayed and fell, only a handspan away from me. Instinctively I reached to help her.

One thin hand seized mine. I looked into her eyes. Unfathomable black. She began to speak, in a low hissing voice, punctuated by the same strange wild ululations.

Alas, you shall never wed one born of mortal seed.
Mount the highest crag where your dread bridegroom
    awaits you.

One feared by all who live, even the mighty gods.

Ruin of all, none can escape his arrows of flame.

My father missed little. As soon as we left the throne room, he twisted my arm and demanded to know what the Sybil had said to me.

'She said I would not marry,' I replied, struggling to free myself from his grip.

'Tell me exactly what she said.'

'I do not remember.'

'Don't lie to me, Psykhe.'

So I told him the words branded on my memory.

'Mount the highest crag? Arrows of flame? You sure that is what she said?'

When I nodded, he whispered, 'So the hour of reckoning has come at last.'

V

First to Embrace His Mother

That night the king was struck down with the plague. I was
bid to attend him.

It was strange to see he was just a man, as afraid of death
as anyone. He sweated and shivered, his bowels running like water.
Livid blotches spread over his back and stomach. I had not seen
the like before. I did what I could to ease his pain but feared the
worst.

'Will he die?' my father demanded.

'He might. I do not know.'

'How can you be so cool? Do you not know our fortunes will die
with him? Save him, you stupid worthless girl.'

'I would if I could, Father.' I was so weary from lack of sleep that
I could scarcely frame the words.

The king's eldest son, Arruns, took charge, ordering slaves to
gather up the dead and bury them in a communal pit outside the
city. Sextus protested vehemently. 'Our father is not dead yet. You
have no right!'

'I am the eldest.'

'The order in which our mother shot us out of her womb means nothing! The king is chosen by the gods.'

'So let us ask the gods,' Arruns responded. 'I'm willing to bet you a sack of gold they'd rather have me than you.'

'Enough!' my father cried. 'The king is dying. Should we not be asking the gods to spare his life, rather than squabbling over who shall succeed him?'

'Better ask the Sybil,' Brutus said.

Sextus stared at him. 'That witch, with her snakes and her lies? Do you know how much damage she's done? Half the city believes the time of kings is over, and the throne shall fall. I wish I'd run her through with my sword.'

Brutus grinned. 'More than half.'

'What?'

'More than half of the city believes the time of kings is over.'

Sextus glared at him. 'Watch out, else I'll run *you* through with my sword.'

'Should go ask the other Sybil,' Brutus said.

'What?'

'The other Sybil. The one with the dead snake.'

'He means the oracle at Delphi,' my father said. 'It's not such a foolish idea as it seems. The Tiburtine Sibyl is clearly half-mad and follows the old religion. The Delphic Sibyl is far more civilised.'

'But just as expensive, no doubt,' Sextus said. 'Very well. Let us go to the Sibyl at Delphi and ask her who shall inherit the kingdom of Roma.'

'Is that a good idea?' Arruns said, frowning. 'If we go to the Sibyl, all will know our father is dying. Our enemies will gather like vultures at a battlefield.'

'You don't need to come,' Sextus said.

'If you go, I go,' Arruns replied, glaring at his brother.

'I will travel with you also,' my father said in his smooth way. 'Best to have an independent witness, don't you think?'

I could only be glad that he would be going, though I felt sure his decision had something to do with the Sibyl's mysterious prophecy. What had my father meant when he said the hour of reckoning had come? What mistake or misdeed had he made that needed punishment? And how was it linked to the Sibyl's strange, fevered words?

She had been drugged with smoke, I told myself. Delirious with snake venom. Perhaps the message had been garbled. Perhaps the goddess did not truly speak through her.

I could only hope.

The king did not die, though I felt the cold presence of Orcus, god of the dead, all around him. Slowly Tarquin the Proud recovered, angry with his sons for their absence. I was given gold in thanks for saving his life, and used it to buy the ingredients I needed to make medicines for the sick. With Lucius keeping me safe, I set out to all the poorest parts of the city, carrying my laden basket with both hands. I returned exhausted, my basket empty, only to spend half the night working to make more.

One day I was in the palace courtyard, overseeing the unpacking of a crate of medicinal supplies, when I heard a clatter of hooves in the square and an imperious voice shouting, 'Out of my way! Open the gate!'

The palace slaves ran to unfasten the heavy bars and drag the gate open. Sextus galloped in, with his brother and cousin close behind. Their horses were lathered with sweat, eyes rolling white-rimmed. Sextus leapt down from the saddle, bellowing to a slave, 'Where's my mother? Answer me, fool! Where's the queen?'

Arruns jumped down seconds behind him. 'Mother! I need you.'

Both rushed towards the queen, who had come out to greet them. They shoved at each other, trying to reach her first. I gazed in utter astonishment. Neither had ever shown much affection for her before.

I turned at a sound behind me. Brutus had tumbled from his horse and lay on the ground, his arms flung wide, his face pressed into the earth. I ran at once to help him, but he sat up, rubbing away the dirt. His dark eyes blazed with fierce exultation. I faltered in surprise. At once his face slackened. 'I'm such a stupid fellow! Always falling over my own feet.' He was hauled to his feet by two slaves and shambled forward, grinning as the two princes reached the startled queen and fiercely embraced her.

My father galloped into the courtyard, his stallion blowing hard. He jumped down before the slave could grab the bridle, striding towards us. 'Who reached the queen first?' he demanded.

'Sextus, I think. Why? What does it matter?'

'The oracle told them that whichever young man was first to kiss his mother would rule in Roma. Hence the mad rush.'

But why had Brutus thrashed his horse close to death in the race with the two princes? He had no mother. She was dead. Unless, of course, you counted the Great Mother, the earth from which all living things came. I stilled, as the thought grew in my mind. An oracle always spoke in riddles. Perhaps the Sibyl's message was never meant to be taken literally. Perhaps the first person to embrace Gaea was the one destined to rule. Perhaps Brutus had not stumbled but had fallen deliberately, so that he could kiss the soil. In which case, it was Brutus who would be king.

I shook the thought away. I was reading too much into a simple clumsy misstep. Besides, I had other more urgent things to worry about. I raised my eyes to my father's face. 'What did the oracle say?'

'The same,' he answered. 'The gods have made their wishes very clear.'

I clutched my arms about myself. 'What does it mean?'

'Did I ever tell you how I met your mother?'

Startled, I shook my head.

'I had travelled north to the pale mountains to try to open trade routes with the Galli. I knew they loved wine and olive oil, and I wanted their weapons and amber. It was the middle of summer, the only time it is truly safe to travel in those high snowy wastes. I arrived to the sound of weeping and wailing. You see, every Midsummer Eve they sacrifice a maiden to the dragon that inhabits the highest peak, the one they call the crystal mountain.'

Cold dread crept through me.

'The king's daughter had drawn the short straw. Her father could not bear the prospect. He paid me handsomely to take her away in the dark of night. She did not wish to go. She thought it wrong that other young women had sacrificed their lives for the safety of their kingdom and that she, the king's daughter, should be spared. But by the time she woke from the sleeping draught she had been given, we were many miles away.'

I could not believe my father would be so moved by pity that he would rescue a barbarian princess. He smiled wryly at my expression. 'The truth is I saw her, I wanted her, and so I took her when she was offered to me. I see now that it was wrong. The gods have frowned on me ever since. I have pondered the oracle's prophecy the whole way home, and I believe it means I must send you back to your mother's people and make sure that you take her place and redress the wrong.' He paused a moment, then said, not looking at me, 'I'm sorry.'

It was only then that I realised what he intended to do. I drew in a sharp breath.

'Say your goodbyes. I will book you passage on the next ship sailing north.'

*

132

I sent a messenger to my sisters, telling them I was to leave Roma in the morning and asking if we might have supper together.

My father had told me I need not bother packing, that I had no need of anything but clothes to travel in. He gave me a small chest. Within was my mother's white dress and cloak and the silver torc.

After he had gone, I sat gazing at the neat pile of clothes on my bed. I lifted the dress to my nose. It smelt faintly of thyme and meadowsweet. I carefully unpicked the side seams, and sewed in long, narrow pockets in which to hide my knives. The silver knife on the right side and the black knife on the left. I practised sliding my hand in and whipping the knives out. I imagined stabbing them into living flesh.

Could I do it?

I did not know.

My father hired guards to accompany me, and bought me a mare to ride. She was as white as a marble statue. He had always had a flair for the dramatic.

I went to say farewell to my sisters. I sat in Alektrona's sitting room, holding Cesar in my arms, breathing in his sweet milky smell. He yawned and blinked up at me and gripped my finger tightly. I could not bear to leave him.

'Thank heavens our husbands are away,' Khrysanthe said. 'We can be comfortable!'

'But they have only just got back from Delphi! Where have they gone?'

'The king has sent Sextus on an errand to Ardea, I think to keep him from his brother's throat,' Alektrona answered. 'You know the siege there has dragged on for ages – he wants Sextus to find some way to break through and take the town. I only wish it was further away. Ardea is close enough for him to ride back any time he wants.'

133

'Brutus has gone too, thank Juno!' said Khrysanthe. 'He was so strange all day, huddled together with his men, whispering, and sending out messengers.'

Once I would have been curious, but now I just sat, listening, thinking this was the last time I would see my sisters, the last time I would see Cesar. A heavy fatalism weighed on me. I could see no way of escape. The oracle had spoken. We must obey.

My sisters did not understand my father's intention. They thought I was returning to my mother's people to find a husband. I did not know how to tell them the truth. But one thing I had learned from Nocturna was that it was best to deliver bad news swiftly. So I said simply, 'I do not return to my mother's people to be wed. I go to my death.'

My sisters stared at me in shocked silence.

'The Sibyl says I must be left on the highest crag for the dragon that lurks there. My mother was meant to be sacrificed there, years ago, but Father rescued her and took her away. He thinks substituting me will appease the gods, somehow.'

'Juno save us,' Khrysanthe whispered.

Alektrona did not speak. I glanced at her. She was struggling to hold back tears.

'Don't cry,' I said. 'It cannot be helped. The gods have spoken.'

'Why does he not sacrifice himself then, the bastard? Why is it always some girl that has to die? Minerva's spear, I hate men!' Alektrona scrubbed her eyes and blew her nose.

'I quite like them,' Khrysanthe said. 'Men, I mean. Not my husband, of course. He's such a lumpen fool. And has no idea how to please a woman in bed! But other men can be quite bearable, sometimes.' Her face took on a dreamy look.

'Khrysanthe, stop thinking about your lover and concentrate. Our sister's in dire trouble here. Psykhe, can't you run away?'

134

I made a helpless gesture at my face. 'How can I hide? Anywhere I go, people notice. Father would have no trouble finding me.'

'We could stain your hair and skin with walnut juice.'

'I cannot hide my eyes, Khrysanthe.'

'No. I suppose not.'

'You could bind a bandage around them, pretend to be blind,' Alektrona suggested.

'But then I would need someone to lead me everywhere by the hand. Who could I ask?'

'I'd go with you – I'd do it!' Alektrona declared.

I stared at her, utterly taken aback.

'You . . . you'd do that for me?'

'We could go in search of Fatima,' Alektrona said eagerly. 'I need to find her – I need to beg her pardon. Surely she'll forgive me?'

'We'd be beggars, at risk of being taken as slaves ourselves.'

'You worked as a midwife before, why not again?'

'I'd need a garden, a place to make my remedies, tools . . . where would we get the money for that?'

Alektrona gave a wild laugh and waved her hand at the silver goblets and platters. 'I will steal it from my husband.'

'Alektrona, you couldn't!' Khrysanthe was shocked. 'He'd kill you.'

Her shoulders slumped. 'No, I couldn't. He would hunt me down wherever I fled. Psykhe would have a better chance of escaping without me.'

I swallowed hard. For one shining moment, I had begun to imagine escape.

'Let us have no tears,' I said. 'It's hard enough. Give me some happy memories of you. Let's have wine and song and tell funny stories about our childhood. Let's dance!'

So we did. It was a very strange thing, that I had such a happy time the night I told my sisters I was doomed to die.

The flame had sunk low in the lamp when the door suddenly banged open. Sextus and Brutus staggered in, arms about each other's shoulders, closely followed by Collatinus, a wine jar dangling from one hand. They were sweaty, dirty and very drunk. 'See, this is what our wives do when we are away,' Sextus slurred. 'What kind of good faithful wives are they, ordering such a splendid banquet while we are off fighting?'

Indeed, the table was strewn with dirty dishes and empty flagons of wine. Khrysanthe waved one hand at her husband and said, 'Oh it's you. What are you doing here?'

Brutus gave his familiar foolish grin. 'We were laying bets on who had the goodest wife. I swore it would be you, but for some reason my cousins thought that was hilarious.'

Khrysanthe's smile faded away.

Alektrona rose, her hands clasped so tightly together her knuckles showed white. 'Sextus, what do you do here? I thought you were at Ardea . . .'

'So I see. Is this what you get up to while your husband is at war? Feasting, drinking? Who else has been here? Any lovers hiding under the table?' He kicked it over with a great crash. My sisters screamed and jumped. The baby woke and began to cry. I lifted him into my arms, soothing him.

'By Jove, Sextus, I think we've lost the bet,' Brutus said. 'Neither of us have the goodest wife. We'd better pay up! Collatinus wins the day!'

Sextus narrowed his eyes. 'He's not a winner yet. We haven't yet seen what Collatinus's wife is up to.'

'We'd better find her with a lover in her bed! That's the only way Collatinus will lose now.' Brutus guffawed, slapping his cousin on the back.

Both Sextus and Collatinus were furious.

'Lucretia is the most virtuous woman in Roma,' Collatinus declared. 'She would never cuckold me.' He cast a scathing look at my sisters, as if to say he had his doubts about them.

Alektrona was ashen. 'I swear, my lord . . .'

'Shut up. Did I bid you speak?' Sextus turned on her angrily.

'We'd better go and see what Lucretia is doing. We'll sneak in on tiptoe and catch her in the act!' Brutus chortled.

'There'll be no act to catch her in!' Collatinus protested. 'She'll be in bed asleep at this hour.'

'But is she alone?' Sextus asked.

'Of course she's alone!' Collatinus shouted.

'Then let's go see,' Brutus said. 'Maybe she'll still be awake and will give us a warm welcome.' He sniggered.

'A warmer welcome than I ever get from my wife!' Sextus flicked Alektrona a contemptuous look. 'I'm sure Lucretia will be far more amenable.'

Collatinus bristled. 'My wife would never even look at you, Sextus! She's far too pure and good to ever want to sully herself with a weasel like you.'

'Is that so?' Sextus was smiling thinly. 'Well, we shall see, won't we? Who wants to raise the stakes?'

'Me!' Brutus crowed. 'I'll bet a thousand gold pieces that Lucretia doesn't sleep alone tonight.'

The men clanked off again in their armour, but our celebratory mood had been broken. I bid my sisters goodnight and went home to bed.

The next morning, I went to the throne room to give the king's attendants the tinctures I had prepared for him. To my surprise, the long hall was crowded with men. Usually, few were awake at this early hour. Tarquin the Proud was taking audience, my father in attendance as always. The king looked displeased to be roused from his bed and slouched in his chair, drinking wine from a golden goblet while an old magistrate droned on about some injustice enacted in the king's name. I recognised him. It was Spurius Lucretius, Collatinus's father-in-law. His was the only face I knew, apart from the king, my father and Brutus, who was standing with a large group of men, all in long cloaks and hobnailed boots. The mood was tense, expectant.

A sudden stir at the doors. I looked around. Collatinus's wife Lucretia stumbled into the room, her hair dishevelled and her sleeping robe torn and bloodied. 'Help me,' she whimpered. 'Oh, please, help me.'

Her father hurried towards her, hands held out. 'Lucretia, what is it, what has happened?'

'He said he would kill me if I did not submit. He said he would kill my slave too and put our naked bodies together in my bed and tell everyone he had found us so and that he killed us to defend my husband's honour. That, I could not bear. He . . . he had a knife . . . he pressed it into my throat . . . oh oh oh, it hurt, it hurt! He hurt me!'

Without thought I had started forward to help her, but Lucretia saw me and recoiled with a scream. 'No! Not the witch! She is his sister-in-law – she will poison me to shut me up. Oh please will someone not help me?' Her voice rose into a hysterical shriek.

Her father grasped her arms. 'Who? Who did this to you?'

'The king's son! Sextus Tarquinius! He forced me.'

Suddenly Lucretia drew out a dagger and slashed at her own throat. Blood spurted out, and she crumpled to the floor. Her father tried desperately to staunch the arc of blood. He raised an anguished face. 'Help me, please! Won't somebody help me?'

I fell to my knees beside him, my hands across the terrible gaping wound. It was no use. A crimson tide of blood flowed inexorably out across the floor. Lucretia's head lolled sideways, her eyes vacant. Gently I shut her lids, shaking my head.

Her father staggered up, clutching the bloodied knife in his hand. 'Who will help me avenge my daughter?'

The hall was in an uproar. Men shouted and shook their fists, and the king had started up in horror, his goblet spilling wine across the floor.

'Where is the prince?' Brutus shouted, drawing his sword. 'Where is Sextus Tarquinius? He must pay!'

'They all must pay!' cried one of his companions. 'Down with all tyrants!'

'Down with the Tarquins!' cried another, grabbing a knife from his belt.

'Sextus must be found! He must pay for this crime with his life! Who will help me ensure justice is done?' Brutus had raised his sword high in challenge.

I gazed up at him in horrified amazement. He had a fire in his eyes I couldn't have imagined possible. He could not have been more different from the shambling, slack-jawed drunkard who had interrupted my farewell feast with my sisters the previous night. He had seemed Sextus's friend then, flinging his arm across his cousin's back, laying bets with him about whose wife was the most virtuous. It had been Brutus, I remembered, who had suggested paying Lucretia a visit, who had insinuated that she would be open to their sexual advances. Yet here he was, only a few hours later, completely sober and steely-eyed, calling for the death of his cousin.

Had it all been an act, his drunken needling of Sextus and Collatinus? Had Brutus hoped to provoke Sextus to rape Lucretia? But why? Why would he do such a thing?

'Who will stand with me against these arrogant Tarquins, who think they can take anything they want?' Brutus cried. 'Let us throw them down and end their tyranny forever!'

139

All through the room, men drew swords and daggers out from under their cloaks. 'Down with all tyrants! Down with the Tarquins!' they chanted and charged at the podium, where the king and queen cowered behind a wall of bodyguards. I scrambled out of the way, as Lucretia's body was dragged aside, cloaks flung down on her blood so the men's feet would not slip.

Realisation hit me like a blow. This whole scene had been carefully planned. These men had come to the throne room that morning, weapons hidden in their clothes, waiting for their chance to rise up against the king. Lucretia's rape was just an excuse. Brutus had ruthlessly manipulated the whole sequence of events. What a terrible, devious, cold-blooded scheme. All those years, pretending to be an amiable fool, Brutus had been secretly plotting to have his revenge for the murder of his father by overthrowing his uncle's throne. And poor innocent Lucretia had been his sacrificial lamb.

Brutus and his men struggled with the king's bodyguards, swords clanging against their axes. Tarquin the Proud shouted for someone to kill his lying, treacherous cur of a nephew, while the queen and her ladies ran screaming out the back door. My father held the king back, urging him to flee. One by one, the bodyguards were cut down. My father hustled the king out the door, not sparing me even a glance.

Brutus leapt up onto the podium. 'I call you all to witness that I swear to pursue Tarquin the Proud and all his seed, with fire and sword and any means I can! Down with kings, I say! Down with tyrants and despots! For too long we have suffered under the yoke of this cursed family. Who stands with me? Who will fight to overthrow the king?'

A great surge of men, shouting and fighting. I had to get away. I crept along the wall and squeezed out the door past the soldiers seeking to get in. I was knocked to my knees, but crawled away.

My hands left streaks of blood on the floor. I managed to get up, though my legs were trembling violently.

Ahead was the courtyard door. I hurried forward, lifting one hand to the latch.

A hand clamped over my wrist.

'Not so fast!' my father snarled. 'You think to escape? You think wrong. This is all your fault – you've been bad luck from the hour of your birth. The gods are angry and must be appeased. To the dragon you'll go if I have to drag you there by your hair!'

VI

Seafoam

Lightning flickered in clouds as black as the sea. The sail was full bellied, creaking under the strain. Above us, great white gulls wheeled, shrieking raucously. On each long oar, four men strained to keep the boat steady. The horses whinnied and fought, but they were lashed tight within their pen. I clung to my mare's halter and tried to soothe her with my voice, but I could not conceal my own terror.

Venus had been born from the seafoam, the spume of her father's castrated manhood.

She had used her power over the waves to devour my father's ships and leave us close to starving. The Sibyl's prophecy had surely been given at her directive. She was my enemy, and now she sought to drown me.

Barefoot sailors swarmed over the boat, shouting warnings to each other, pulling on ropes, dragging up another small sail over the pointed bow. The ship should have reached the port at Lerici the day before, but so strong was the wind that we had been swept off course. Cliffs towered as far as I could see. The ship's captain peered through the spray, his hand shielding his eyes. Night would soon be here.

The boat crested the wave and smashed down. I braced myself. Water raced over the deck in a welter of white. A great crack. The mast broke, splintered, fell into the deck. The boat tilted and the sea rushed in. I slid one hand into my pocket and withdrew my knife. A flash of silver as I sliced through the ropes. I thrust the silver dagger back, but had no time to secure the loop about the handle. The ship was sinking fast. I seized my mare's mane and leapt onto her back. She reared and plunged, as the deck fell away below her hooves. She struck out, swimming. I bent low over her neck. Behind me, timbers groaned and shuddered. A backward drag threatened to pull us under. My valiant mare forged on, churning the water into white. I crouched lower, concentrated all my strength into holding on.

Ahead soared the cliffs, sheer faces of rock with their feet in the ocean and their heads in thunderclouds. There was nowhere to scramble ashore, nowhere even to grasp a handhold. My mare was tiring, barely able to keep her head above the waves. Her hooves flailed at the unforgiving stone, slipped back. I was plunged under water, all breath driven from my body. I clung to the mare's mane, kicked with all my strength. A wave lifted us and hurled us against the rock. My mare neighed shrilly, only to be swamped by water again.

I fought upwards and gasped in a breath as my head broke free of the water. To the east a sliver of moon was rising above a towering headland. *Hekate, goddess of the dark moon, I beg you, help me.*

A rattle of stones. Peering through the dusk, dashing my hand across my stinging eyes, I saw what looked like a broken shelf of rock. I kicked my heel into the mare's side and wrenched at her mane. 'Come on,' I urged, struggling to keep my head above the churning water. 'Swim, my darling, swim.'

I struck out towards the rock, one hand still entwined in her mane. She turned and swam with me. I banged my knee on a rock, felt something sharp slicing into my arm. I struggled up and forward. The mare found a foothold. Slipped back. Found another. She surged up, and I went with her. Water cascaded over my legs, then I pitched forward, landing heavily on rocks, breathless, bruised and shaken.

Alive.

I woke in the dawn. The sky was aflame with light. Only a few feet away, waves surged upon angular rocks. Cliffs stretched as far as I could see. Somehow we had found the only place it was possible to clamber ashore.

I hurt all over. Everywhere I looked, bloody scrapes.

The mare sprawled nearby, her legs splayed. I crawled to her. She lifted her weary head, whinnied in response to my anxious voice. I ran my hands over her, but apart from a few nasty scratches, she seemed uninjured. I took her halter and encouraged her to her feet. With a heave, she staggered up then stood, head drooping, one hoof cocked.

No sign of the ship, or of my guards. Had they all drowned? Had they died because of me? I stared out to sea, searching desperately for any sign of life. Nothing.

I could not move for a long time. But the mare whickered encouragingly and nudged me. I laid my forehead against hers. 'You saved me,' I whispered.

She looked at me with great dark eyes, pawed the ground.

'I will call you Salvatora,' I told her.

Step by slow limping step, we made our way up the rocks, away from the sea. My sodden dress and cloak seemed unbearably heavy, dragging at my aching limbs. Someone had built rough, uneven steps, and carved the occasional handhold. These signs of human habitation spurred me on.

Above was a wall made from uneven boulders and stones, with a sturdy wooden gate which stood ajar. I managed to heave it open, and led Salvatora onto a high, narrow promontory. Huddled into the headland was a village of stone huts thatched with reeds, terraced gardens rising in steps to a fort at the top of the cliff. A tamarisk tree shaded a stone water trough where a donkey dozed. To the left was a harbour, protected from the fast running strait by two rocky break-waters. Boats bobbed up and down in the water, and a few had been drawn up onto the rocks. At the far end of the promontory, built on a natural rocky rise above the sea, was a small shrine.

A woman was gathering seaweed from the shore. She saw us and straightened, shielding her eyes against the rising sun.

'Please . . . help us . . . our ship . . .'

I choked, unable to say more.

She took me into her house, helped me strip off my icy sodden clothes, rubbed me dry with a rough cloth, wrapped me in a warm quilt, and made me a hot brew.

'My horse . . .'

She assured me with nods and smiles, poured me more chamomile tea. It was immensely comforting.

The cottage was soon crowded with villagers. The men were driven out with orders to scour the coast for survivors. My tangled hair was combed free of knots by one toothless old woman, who exclaimed over its colour. Like moonlight, she said. A dress was found for me, my own clothes hung steaming before a fire of driftwood.

I felt untethered.

Where did I come from? Where was I going? Who was I?

I hardly knew.

I did my best to answer, indicating I came from the south and was heading north, and that my name was Psykhe. 'Where am I?' I asked.

'Portovenere,' the old woman answered. 'It means haven from the sea goddess.'

My heart lurched. 'Venus?'

They all nodded and made little sounds of recognition and encouragement. 'Yes, yes, Venus. Goddess of the sea and the fair voyage, goddess of want.'

'Our holy place is there by the sea,' the old woman explained. 'A shrine where we make our offerings.'

'To spare us,' another explained.

'And our loved ones.'

One woman whispered to another and was swiftly shushed, with a quick glance at the door. She must have heard a familiar step for the door swung open and a man's bearded face looked in. He shook his head and shrugged. No sign of the ship or any survivors.

A low murmur of sadness and commiseration.

The old woman rose. 'Let her sleep. Next market day, we will hear any news to be had.'

I lay back, overwhelmed with exhaustion and horror.

All dead because I, in my foolishness, had incurred the wrath of the goddess of love and hate.

It seemed to me I had three choices. I could return to Roma, to the life I knew. I was sick with worry for my sisters and my nephew, and desperate to know what had happened. Were they safe? Had Brutus overthrown the king and seized the throne? Or had he been defeated and imprisoned? Were my sisters married to men now at war with each other? So many questions, and no way to answer them except by returning south.

Roma, however, meant my father and my father meant death.

I could continue my journey north, seek out my mother's people, ask them for shelter and support. That had been in my mind from the beginning. Surely my snow-white hair and my silver torc would reveal me as one of them? Perhaps they would welcome me; perhaps among them I would not be an oddity.

Or perhaps they would be glad I came, so they did not need to sacrifice a girl they loved to the dragon, offering me instead. So going north could mean death too.

My third choice was to run. To go anywhere but south or north. To wander the world until I found a place where I could do my work in peace. I did not need much. A roof over my head, a patch of earth to plant a garden, babies to help into the world and the old to ease out of it.

The third choice was the hardest way, the loneliest. It meant casting off everyone I knew and loved, rejecting all ties and all responsibilities. I had been told by the gods that my fate was to be given to one who hurt all that lived, one who was stronger even than death. All our lives we were taught that we must submit ourselves to the gods' will, that we must placate them or be punished. To run was to deny the gods themselves.

History was full of those who tried to avoid their ordained fate. What was the point of even trying?

To live, my anguished heart cried. I must try to live.

In the end, my decision was easy. I let go of my breath in a long sigh, lay my cheek on my hand and closed my eyes.

Tomorrow I would take my horse and go. I would disobey the gods and defy death.

*

147

I woke and lay for a moment, not sure where I was. All was quiet and still. The fire had sunk low, and the room was full of shadows. I raised myself on my elbow and peered around me. No kettle hung on its hook above the driftwood fire, no cat slept on the bed shelf. I got up and put on my dress, left neatly folded on a stool. Automatically I slipped my hands into my pockets, to check my knives were securely fastened within. One pocket was empty. The silver dagger Nocturna had given me, the knife I had used to cut Cesar free, was gone. It must have been lost in the sea. Tears stung my eyes. It was a bitter loss.

It was cold, so I drew on my stockings and boots and wrapped my cloak about me before going out into the street. It was twilight, I realised, not dawn. To the north-west, the sky was red. The whole village was eerily quiet. No children played in the street, no women sat on their steps spinning wool, no old men played board games under the trees, no chickens scratched in the dust. The curve of pebbly beach was empty of all boats. I walked down and stood on the rocks, looking out to sea. No sails.

Cold fear stole over me. Where was everyone?

I went down the street, calling hesitantly, knocking on doors, looking into every house. All empty.

I thought of Salvatora. I ran back to the shed where she had been stabled. To my relief she was still there, with a bucket of fresh water and some grass. I stroked her satiny neck. 'What's happened to everyone?' I asked. 'Where are they all?'

She shook her mane and pushed her nose into my shoulder.

'I think we should go now. We should just go.'

But I hesitated. It felt rude to leave without thanks. They had been kind.

The silence was so heavy, so strange.

'Let's go,' I said, and tried to unknot the rope that tied my mare. My fingers shook so much I could not get it unravelled.

Boom. Boom. Boom. A slow drumbeat. I could not unknot the rope. I slid my left hand into my dress, and found the hilt of the obsidian knife. The knife for cutting and releasing the dead. I drew it.

Still the drum pounded, steady and inexorable. I cut the rope in such haste, the dagger sliced deep into my palm. I did not notice the pain. Sliding the knife back into its hidden sheath, I led my mare out into the street. Without a saddle, I could not easily mount her. I looked for a step, a stone, something to stand on.

Boom. Boom. Boom. I did not know if it was my heartbeat that thundered so loud in my ears, or the imperative beat of the drum coming closer and closer. I gripped the mare's mane with both hands, and somehow scrambled up. My palm was hurting now. I had left bloody handprints on her shoulder.

The drumbeat quickened. A skirl of pipes, the sound of keening. I turned my mare about and kicked her forward, heading up the narrow path away from the sea.

I was too late.

A procession wound its way down from the headland. Women dressed in simple white shifts carried a bier heaped high with blood-red flowers. Other women danced before and behind, tearing at their clothes, beating their bare breasts, sobbing in grief. On their heads, wreaths of crimson roses and anemones with deep purple hearts.

I could not go forward without riding through them and so I slid down from my horse and stood, head bowed, waiting for them to pass. The women carrying the bier walked with unnaturally slow, measured steps, their eyes downcast, their feet stamping in time with the drum. I began to hear words in their wailing.

> Sweet Adonis is wounded, O Venus,
> Cruel are his wounds and cruel the wound to your heart,
> All the world laments with you, O Venus,
> O weep, weep, weep for Adonis, let us weep.

The women saw me and their step faltered. One or two lowered their flutes from their mouths, glancing at each other in consternation. The old woman had been pacing at the head of the procession, carrying a flaming torch. She frowned at the sight of me, then set her mouth grimly, drawing a dagger from her belt. She came towards me, the flame dancing in the bright surface of the blade. She stopped before me, saying in slow measured tones, 'Blood on the way is the price to pay.'

I did not understand her. Shrinking away, I raised one hand in defence.

The old woman spoke again, but now her voice was different, light with surprise and relief. 'You've paid the toll. Safe is your soul.'

I frowned in puzzlement. She pointed with one crooked finger to the deep, red-lipped cut on the palm of my hand. She sheathed the dagger, took my uninjured hand, and led me to the bier. Then she squeezed my other hand till my blood flowed freely once more, dripping down onto the face of the body that lay beneath the mound of red flowers.

I had expected the corpse of some great lord or king. Instead, I saw an effigy woven of straw. It was like a crude doll, or a puppet. It had no eyes or mouth, but a fennel stalk indicated where its manhood would rear.

I looked at the women, trying to understand, and saw that they all had bloodstained cloths bound about their left hands. They bobbed their heads at me in acknowledgement and began once more to play their drums and flutes. The old woman bound my hand for me and gestured for me to join them. I could have shaken my head, I could have ridden away. But, leading my horse, I walked with the other women down towards the little shrine by the sea.

When the women began to sing once more, I joined the refrain.

Sweet Adonis is dying, O Venus,
His blood drenches the soil, your tears run like rain,
Beat your breasts, O Venus, tear your garments,
O weep, weep, weep for Adonis, let us weep.

The women carried the bier to the shrine. Within crouched a heavy white boulder, roughly carved into the shape of a woman. Her pendulous breasts and womanly cleft were clearly delineated, but her eyes and mouth were mere cracks in the stone. The ground before the shrine was stained with what looked like blood. Small offerings were pushed into every crack and hole: dead flowers, ragged feathers, nuts and shells of all shapes and sizes, carved stones, triangular flints, tiny dolls made of twigs and grass, long ribbons made of braided wool, a few tarnished coins, a tattered snakeskin.

Each of the women laid some of their flowers about the goddess's clawed feet, then collected driftwood to pile high around the effigy. I tethered Salvatora in the shade of the tamarisk tree, making sure she could reach the water trough, and went to join them. As the sun sank into night, the old woman lit the pyre with her fiery torch. The blaze crept along the driftwood and devoured the effigy, a crown of flames where once there had been a crown of flowers. The women danced and sang and mourned. Some women danced slowly, bent with age. Others spun and leapt as lightly as dandelion seeds in the wind. I danced with them, swaying and twisting and spinning, while the sparks flew like fiery bees towards the stars.

Your sweet lord is lost to you, O Venus,
You have lost your love and lost all happiness,
Never again will you kiss his honeyed mouth,
O weep, weep, weep for Adonis, let us weep.

151

Tears slipped down my face. I wiped them away, but still they came, unstoppable. I thought of the story of Venus and Adonis. The goddess who loved the young mortal, even knowing he must die. The young man, gored to death by a boar's tusk, his lifeblood soaking into the earth. The first anemone springing up where he had lain, its heart the colour of pain.

Dawn broke. The old woman rose stiffly to her feet, and we all rose with her, sombre and hollowed out with our grieving. She hobbled to the edge of the cliff and threw her wreath of blood-red flowers into the ocean. The flowers bobbed up and down in the waves, rushing into shore, then being swept out again in a trail of broken petals. One by one the other women followed suit, from eldest to youngest, all singing, 'O weep, weep, weep for Adonis, let us weep.'

'Let us weep for Adonis,' the old woman intoned, 'let us weep for all whom we love, for all those who must die.'

The goddess loved and lost her love. Surely she should wish to spare others such hurt?

I watched as the red petals floated and swirled and sank, swallowed by the seafoam. Behind me, the women raked the embers into terracotta pots, then walked among the little gardens and fields, scattering ashes onto the roots of the olive tree and the vine, the rosemary and rue. I could not understand why the goddess was so cruel, to me and to so many others. I thought of Myrrha, Adonis's mother, who had been cursed to lust after her own father. How could the goddess cause such pain and heartbreak when she had suffered such grief herself?

She feels a need to hurt how she was once hurt. She wants me to suffer.

I rose to my feet, afraid once more. *I need to go,* I thought incoherently. *I have escaped her net, she will seek once more to kill me.* I went to my horse and untethered her.

152

The slap of a sail alerted me. I turned. Out of the morning mist sailed the fishing boats, returning from wherever the men had retreated for the night of the women's mysteries. Standing in the prow of the biggest boat was Marius, my father's captain of the guards, his keen eyes searching the shore for me.

VII

The Pale Mountains

Stone pinnacles soared high on either side, wreathed in mist. The narrow path led alongside a swift torrent that raced over icy boulders. We were forced to ride in single file, me in my white cloak upon my white mare, the soldiers in their bronze armour and scarlet cloaks strung out before and behind me.

Quite a few of my father's men had been drowned in the shipwreck, and many horses and weapons lost, but enough had remained for me to know it was no use to struggle or try to flee. The villagers of Portovenere had been glad for me, thinking I had been found by friends. I said nothing to disillusion them. *Maybe I can still escape,* I told myself. *Maybe my chance will come.*

At first the road had been good, and there had been inns where we could stay. We had rested a few days at Parma, named for a soldier's round buckler, for it was the final shield of the Rasenna against the Galli. While there, news came that the royal family had escaped the palace. No more kings, Brutus had sworn. Roma was now a republic.

'I need to go back,' I begged Marius. 'I need to find out what has happened to my family.'

He shook his head. 'It makes no difference, my lady. Your father's orders were clear. To the dragon you must go.'

So on we rode, into the wild uncharted lands of the Galli. I ate when food was placed before me. I lay down where I was directed. I slept little, utterly bone-weary and sore. Day after day it was the same. Nobody spoke to me except to tell me what to do. The men were not unkind, just aloof and disciplined. They made and broke camp with ruthless efficiency, and rode for as many hours as there was light to see. I fixed my eyes on the horizon, where the dark shadows of the mountains grew greater with every mile we travelled.

Now the stony peaks loomed above us, implacable as the gods. The men rode with their hands on their weapons, watchful and alert. At night, they took turns to stand guard. I tried to remember the stories I had heard about the Galli. They were fierce, they were proud, they worshipped trees, it was a dishonour for them to die peacefully in bed. My fear was like leaden weights tied to my limbs. I dragged myself through each day and tried not to think about the dragon.

One morning the wind brought swirling snowflakes.

'It's supposed to be bloody midsummer,' one of the guards muttered.

That night Marius and our guide spent a long time poring over the crude map he had drawn up for us. Named Cerdo, he was a bent old man with faint blue markings on his face and hands, and snowy-white hair and beard he wore in long braids. My father had bought him at the slave markets in Roma so that he could show us the way and translate for us.

'Into the mountains we must go,' Cerdo said, 'following the river. We will come to a valley surrounded by great mountains on all sides. One of those is the crystal mountain you seek. On its far side lies the lake of the magic mirror, where the dragon flies.'

'How will I make contact with the leader of the barbarians?' the captain of the guards asked.

'The Raven will contact you, my lord. He knows already that you come.'

The captain glanced about uneasily. 'But I've not seen or heard anyone near.'

'The Raven has seen and heard you. He knows all that happens in his realm.'

That night, the captain doubled the watch.

A few days later, we rode into a valley encircled by towering snow-capped peaks, just like the old man had described. That night the cold was piercing. I woke with a fine crust of frost on my blanket. I remembered how someone had once said of me, 'It is as if she has frost on her lashes.'

Will there be others like me here? I wondered, then thought drearily, *What does it matter?*

'Which peak is the crystal mountain?' I asked the guide, who was busy gathering handfuls of wild thyme.

He pointed towards one of the massive ridges of stone, set to the north-east of the valley. It looked like a clenched fist.

'Why is it called that?'

'The rock glitters like crystal when it catches the light,' he answered, stripping the leaves from the thyme stems and tossing them into a little pot of boiling water.

'And why is the lake on the far side called the magic mirror?'

'It's an old tale of my people. The mirror once belonged to the wicked sorcerer who lives beneath the crystal mountain. If you looked within, you could see into your own soul, and the soul of anyone else you wished.'

He stirred the pot and added a tiny piece of honeycomb from a jar. 'The daughter of the king wanted the magic mirror for her own and so she gave her father no peace until he promised to get it for her. The king went to the sorcerer and begged him for the mirror. The sorcerer agreed to give it to the king on the condition that he turned himself into a great mountain that would cast a shadow over the whole valley. The king loved his daughter dearly and could not deny her heart's wish and so he agreed.'

I looked up at the grey, towering peak. What would it be like to have a father who loved you so much he'd sacrifice his own life for you? Tears stung my eyes, and I brushed them away angrily.

'The sorcerer gave the princess his magic mirror and she gazed into it for so long, she did not notice that her father was changing and growing, and that she was being lifted higher and higher and higher.' Cerdo lifted his arms into the air, touching his fingertips above his head.

'When at last she looked away from the mirror, it was to find herself standing on top of a stone pinnacle that was thousands of feet tall. She screamed and fell to her death. The magic mirror flew from her hand. It tumbled down to the floor of the valley and smashed. Her father was so grieved, he wept and wept. His tears flowed down over the broken mirror and transformed it into the lake that still reflects his sorrowful stone face.'

'That's a sad story.'

'Many of our tales are,' Cerdo answered, and carefully poured me a cup of wild thyme tisane. 'Drink up, my lady, you are looking very pale.'

'I am always pale.' I tried to smile, but my lips were so stiff it must have looked more like a grimace.

After a scant breakfast of flatbread and cheese, we rode on, the pathway rising through a dark forest of fir and spruce, brightened with the airy green of larches. Clouds hung heavy over the mountains, and the wind's icy fingers probed through my clothes. That night we all huddled about the fire, our hands held to the blaze, the darkness breathing down our necks. 'Not far now,' Cerdo said, his rheumy blue eyes gleaming with excitement. I did not sleep that night, lying on my back and watching countless stars wheel above the snowy peaks. Never had I seen so many stars.

The next morning we rode through the narrow pass between soaring cliffs. Far below, a long stretch of jade-green water was set like a shining jewel in dark stands of pine trees. The tall pinnacles were reflected in a perfect mirror image. I thought of the tale the guide had told me, and wondered if I would see my own soul if I looked into the water.

Far above, a high-pitched shriek. A golden sinuous creature wheeled on currents of air, its ribbed wings widespread. It shrieked again, then folded its wings and dived, the light flashing off its scales.

'The dragon grows hungry,' Cerdo said.

My stomach lurched. I could not catch my breath. I swayed, clutching at my horse's mane.

'Catch the maid,' he cried. 'She faints.'

The men hurried to help me. I was lifted down from the mare, half-carried to the shade, set down on the ground. I pressed my face into my arms. Cold sweat prickled my scalp.

Cerdo brought me water to drink. My fingers shook so much I could not grasp the leather bottle. He held it to my mouth. I drank and swallowed. It eased the constrictive pain in my throat, but still I shivered, black spots swimming before my eyes.

'Are you ill, moon maiden?' he asked. 'What ails you?'

I looked at him in astonishment. Did he not know that I was to be sacrificed to the dragon? Then I realised that, of course, my father had told him nothing. Why would he?

'Nothing,' I replied harshly. 'I . . . I am just weary.'

I closed my eyes, and he moistened a cloth with water and put it in my hand. I thanked him, pressing it to my face and neck. In the bright light of day, the markings on his face and hands showed clearly – intricate circles and spirals and crosses. I wondered what they meant.

'Why do you call me moon maiden?' I asked.

'Because you look like one of the descendants of the princess of the moon.'

'I know that tale. She got so homesick for her home that the wild men of the forest spun the moonlight into a silvery gauze that they flung over the peaks. That is why the rocks here are white, instead of brown.'

'Who told you that story?' He spoke sharply, his eyes intent on my face.

'My mother's midwife, Brid.'

'I once knew another young woman who was as pale as you. She disappeared long ago, along with her handmaiden, Brid.'

I gazed at him in wonder. 'Was that young woman named Alba?'

He nodded.

'She was my mother. I never knew her – she died when I was born. What was she like?' I clenched my hands against my chest.

'Well, she was tall and slender like you, with hair like snow and eyes as pale as ice. Many were in love with her, but she cared for none of them. She walked like a queen, her head held high, and her footsteps were so light she hardly left a footprint behind her. I never saw her lose her composure, not even when she chose the dragon stone. I am glad she escaped that night, and that she gave birth to another moon maiden, no matter the cost.'

'You know I am to be sacrificed in her place?' My voice cracked.

Cerdo jerked back, astonishment on his face. 'Is that why you are here? To atone for her flight?' He fell silent, his gnarled hands twisting together. Then he spoke in a low voice, not meeting my eyes. 'It caused much distress and heartache, the flight of your mother. If the dragon is not fed, it brings storm and fire against the town. Many die. So all the other young women who had thought themselves safe had to go through the ordeal of choosing again, and this time it was the Raven's beloved who chose the dragon stone. She died in the place of your mother, and he grieved very deeply for her. Much anger was felt, that your mother fled when she had been chosen . . .'

'She did not flee!' I protested. 'She was taken by my father against her will. They drugged her . . . her father and a servant . . .'

Brid? I suddenly wondered. *Was that why she could not return to her own people after my mother died?*

'I see,' the old man answered. 'Well, we shall tell the Raven so and perhaps he will not feel so bitter towards your mother anymore.'

'What does that mean, the Raven? Is he a man or a bird?'

'Do you not know? The Raven is the king, the warlord. He's your mother's cousin and was named Raven when your grandfather died.'

'Will he help me?'

'It is the Morrigan who chooses who goes to the dragon, not the Raven.'

'Who is the Morrigan?'

He looked at me in fearful astonishment. 'Why, the goddess of fate and prophecy and death, she who speaks doom.'

I did not sleep much that night. It was too cold, and I was too afraid.

Such a restlessness in me. I wanted to feel everything there was in the world to feel. I wanted to run, to dance, to spin and spin like I had as a child. I wanted to laugh till my ribs ached, I wanted to shout with joy, I wanted to weep because the world was so beautiful. Most of all, I wanted to love and be loved. What would it be like to lose oneself entirely in another? Lucius and Khrysanthe had risked everything to have one night together. Alektrona still grieved the loss of Fatima a year after they had parted. I wanted that kind of love. I had never been touched by a man, I had never even been properly kissed. Only that brief touch of Ambrose's lips on mine, the morning after Cesar's birth. Yet afterwards he had fled. Why? Had I so repelled him? Had his touch kindled me to fire and my touch turned him to ice?

I could leave my cold lonely bed and creep into someone else's. My guards all kept their eyes averted, careful never to let their hands brush mine when they passed me a bowl or helped me down from my horse. If they were truly indifferent, they would surely not take such care to avoid me. I could choose one, and go to his bed, and lie with him, and discover what it was to be touched by a man. I'd be a maiden no longer, dragon bait no longer.

But what would happen to the man I chose? What would be the cost?

And perhaps the man I chose would not want me anyway. Perhaps my touch would freeze him too.

In the morning, I rose early and told Marius I wished to bathe and make myself tidy before I faced my mother's people. He was reluctant to let me out of his sight, but I gave him my word I would not try to run away. 'Where would I go?' I asked, waving my hand at the immense pinnacles and towers of stone that loomed over us.

I mounted Salvatora and turned her head away from the camp. The path led down to a green meadow. I urged my mare into a canter, and then into a gallop. My hair whipped behind me, the wind coaxed tears from my eyes. A small torrent of water leapt down the hill, falling in thin cascades over the white stones. It was the palest green I had ever seen. I stripped naked and stepped into the water. The cold was shocking, a thousand silver pins. I splashed myself all over, unbraided my hair and combed it out. Tingling all over, I dressed myself in my mother's white dress, then walked barefoot through the meadow, picking wildflowers. The airy umbels of cow parsley, dandelions like little suns, glossy golden buttercups, forget-me-nots like tiny petals of sky, pink clover, the dark violet bells of columbine, crimson alpine roses. I hung a garland about my mare's neck and made myself a delicate crown.

I heard the soldiers calling me. It was time to go. As I rode down towards the lake, my mare paced solemnly through the forest, her head held high. I sat straight, my white hair rippling down my back. I wanted to be as proud and fearless as I imagined my mother would have been.

My guards trotted close about me, eyes wary, hands on their sword hilts. We passed through a grove of birch trees, the dark marks on their trunks like uncanny watching eyes. The lake was as bright as cloth-of-silver, rippling under a catspaw of wind. My mare fidgeted sideways, her ears turning back.

I bent to caress her neck and saw a swift movement in the shadows under the spruce trees. Suddenly men rose from the undergrowth, seizing our bridles, spears held threateningly towards our throats. Salvatora reared and I almost fell. Someone caught her rein and soothed her with soft words in a language I did not know.

Dressed in thick furs and leather, their long hair and beards twisted and braided with carved wooden beads and feathers, the men seemed part of the forest. Their faces were marked with dots and lines like painted masks of beasts and birds. Many had bare legs and arms, despite the cold, and the same intricate markings encircled their biceps and calves. Their spear hafts were made of wood, with leaf-shaped blades of bronze whetted to a glinting edge.

162

Cerdo cried out in his own language and was answered with rapid-fire questions while the Galli warriors looked us over suspiciously. He pointed at me, pointed at the mountain, then the sky, made a prayerful gesture. I sat silently, enduring their stares.

At last one of the Galli grunted and made a beckoning gesture.

'He says the Raven will see us and decide our fate,' Cerdo said.

VIII

The Dragon

My mother's people lived at the far end of the lake, in a hillfort enclosed by a high palisade of great pine trunks, their tops carved into sharp points. Smoke hung in a blue haze over the town, wreathing it in mystery. A wooden watchtower guarded a heavy gate which opened at our approach. A stag's skull crowned with antlers hung above it, and great bunches of raven feathers tied with bones and stones pitted with holes.

Within were small round houses with steep thatched roofs that reached almost to the ground. Women sat in the doorways, spinning thread, or grinding grain into flour. Their pale hair hung in long braids that swung as they worked. A giant of a man with red hair, naked to the waist, shaped hot iron at a forge, and a girl guided a herd of bristly black pigs with a switch. A group of tow-haired children played with an inflated pig's bladder, batting it back and forth with sticks. Young men practised fighting with long staves, and a woman worked at a potter's wheel, her skilful fingers creating a pot out of a lump of wet clay.

As I rode past, they rose and bowed their heads gravely, making a signal with their right hands. Thumb and index finger met in a circle, the other three fingers held straight.

'What does that gesture mean?' I asked Cerdo.

He hesitated, glancing about him to make sure no-one was listening. Then he replied in a low voice, 'It is the rune of the birch tree, the first letter of our alphabet. Birch means "to shine bright", because its bark is as silvery as the moon. It is the first tree to grow leaves after the dead of winter, and so birch means spring, rebirth, new beginnings.'

'But why do they make this sign at the sight of me?'

'Why do you think, moon maiden? They know who you are and that you come to make reparation. They honour you for your courage.'

I was silent, filled with a kind of fearful awe.

The path led us straight up to the crest of the hill, where the thatched roof of a huge round building towered above the rest.

'The mead hall,' Cerdo said, 'where all meetings are held.'

The double doors stood open, but inside all was dark. I dismounted, one of my guards taking Salvatora's reins and leading her away. Only then did I realise that the people of the town had followed us in a great, silent throng.

'The Raven waits within.' The old man gestured for me to precede him.

I took a deep breath, smoothed down my dress, and went through the doors. My guards followed close behind. For once, I was glad of their presence. The people of the town filed in after us, Cerdo in their midst.

My eyes were dazzled by the light outside, and so it took a moment for my sight to adjust. I saw a vast shadowy space, held up by rafters of polished tree trunks. In the centre of the room was a round fire pit where crocus-coloured flames danced in the dimness.

165

Smoke stung my eyes. I moved forward uncertainly, the hem of my dress whispering against the rushes and sweet-scented herbs strewn over the earthen floor.

It was then I saw him. A man sitting quietly, his hands resting on the carved arms of his high-backed chair. The firelight played over the heavy golden torc he wore about his throat. I faltered.

'Welcome, moon maiden, daughter of Alba, granddaughter of Bran,' he said in a deep, calm, resonant voice. I was startled. I had not expected him to speak the same language as me, or to know who I was.

He raised one hand and gestured for me to come closer. I obeyed. My guards followed, hands on their swords.

'Tell your Roman dogs to surrender their weapons,' the Raven said, 'else we shall need to wrest them away by force.'

I looked at the captain of the guards. Reluctantly he unbuckled his dagger and sword and gave it to a tall, fair-haired warrior with blue markings on his face like a wolf. When all the weapons had been collected and taken away, the warrior said, 'You may now approach the Raven.'

I walked into the warm glow of the fire, my eyes fixed on the man on the throne. He was tall and lean and much the same age as my father. His hair was grey and braided into a neat bun at the back of his head, and his beard was red and wild. His face was marked with the curving beak and wings of a raven. By his side stood an old man and an old woman, both robed in white and leaning on tall staffs of wood hung with bones and skulls and feathers. The old man had the shape of a sun marked between his eyes, the old woman a crescent moon. I thought they must be what Brid had called druids, the priests and priestesses of the Galli.

'So, you have travelled far to see us, moon maiden. Why?' the Raven asked.

The captain of the guards began to speak, but I put up my hand and stepped forward, raising my voice to drown his out. 'I have come to ask for sanctuary, my lord.'

The Raven's frowning gaze was fixed on my silver torc. 'Your mother betrayed us. She chose the dragon stone and should have been chained on the mountain peak as sacrifice. But her courage failed her, she fled, and another was forced to take her place. Your mother is no longer one of us, and neither are you.'

'She did not leave willingly. She was drugged by her father, and given into the care of my father, a merchant who was staying here.'

The Raven frowned. A low murmur rose from the crowd.

'How do I know if you speak the truth?'

'My father has no reason to lie.'

'Lord Cassius returns her to you as atonement for his act,' the captain of the guards cried. 'There is plague in Roma, and the spears of Mars rattle day and night. The oracle in Delphi was consulted, and it bade us bring her here to be sacrificed. The oracle speaks with the tongues of gods. They must be obeyed!'

The Raven's frown deepened. He turned and spoke in an undertone to the two druids. I waited, fixing my gaze on his face, willing myself to show no weakness.

The Raven spoke again. 'Your father says he seeks to atone for his act, and so offers you up as sacrifice. Yet you say you seek sanctuary. Your words are at odds with your father's will and with the will of the gods. Why?'

I moistened my dry lips and croaked, 'I do not want to die.'

The druid spoke grimly. 'None wish to die, but death comes to all in time.'

'One day. When I have lived my life. When I am old and ready. Not now. Please not now.'

'None of us may know the time or manner of our death,' the druidess said.

Struggling for composure, I gazed pleadingly at the Raven.

'I hear and understand you,' he said slowly. 'You do not feel you should carry the blame for your mother's escape from her ordained fate, and so you hope I will embrace you as kin and protect you from your father's intention.'

'Yes, my lord.'

He rose and came towards me. I tensed in every muscle. For a moment he stood before me, frowning, examining me from head to foot, then he smiled and embraced me. 'Welcome home, my cousin's daughter.'

A rush of relief so weakened me I almost fell. The Raven had to steady me, hands on my shoulders. I looked up into his face and saw it was set hard as iron. My lips trembled, and all strength seemed to leave my limbs. I steeled myself, waiting.

'You are one of us now, you have our protection.' He turned and bowed to the captain of the guards. 'You are released from your duty. Leave now, return to your own people or face my wrath.'

The captain tried to speak, but the Raven made a gesture and he fell silent. He and the other guards were shown out, and soon came the sound of retreating hoof beats.

'Let us give our warmest welcome to the moon maiden, returned at last to her own people.' The Raven turned me to the crowd, who murmured in amazement. Some smiled, some called greetings to me, some stood, frowning, arms crossed. I stood stiffly, trying to smile, trying to believe it was true.

Then the Raven's voice rang out across the hubbub. 'Of course, as one of us she too must submit herself to the Morrigan. Tomorrow is Midsummer's Eve. At dawn, we shall see who of our maidens shall draw the dragon stone.'

*

The next morning, as the east began to lighten, a line of young women walked through the forest. We were all dressed in loose white gowns, our hair unbound, wreaths of wildflowers on our heads. We were led by the druidess, small and spry, her mass of silvery hair hanging down her back to her knees. Behind came the Raven and the druid and all the people of the town.

One of the young women turned to me. She was fair-haired and blue-eyed, and wore a silver torc like mine. 'My name is Misurina,' she said shyly. 'My father is the Raven, so that means you are some kind of cousin to me.'

'I am pleased to know you,' I answered, just as shyly.

'I am sorry we must meet like this.' She gestured to the sombre procession of young women.

'It is a dreadful thing,' I burst out. 'Why do your people do it?'

Misurina looked at me in surprise. 'We all must serve in whatever way we can. The warriors risk death every time they ride to war – should we be less courageous than them? If the sorcerer is not pleased, he unleashes a storm of lightning upon the mountain. The earth shakes, trees fall, many houses are destroyed, and many people hurt. Old people, babies.'

'Sorcerer? Like in the old tale about the magic mirror? He still lives?'

'Oh, yes. The dragon is just one of his many forms.'

'Has no-one ever tried to defeat him?'

She nodded. 'Once, long ago. The queen of the land had twin daughters. One was hidden for safekeeping, the other raised as a warrior. The spirits of the forest made her silver chainmail that no weapon could pierce, and a silver trumpet, and a quiver of silver arrows that never missed their mark. With these gifts, she was invincible, and it seemed the shapeshifting sorcerer would at last be defeated.'

She paused, looking sad. I said softly, 'So what happened?'

'She fell in love with one of the sorcerer's knights. For love of him, she swore never to fight again. She gave away all her silver arrows to hungry beggar children, not knowing they had been sent by the sorcerer to trick her. Her father was ambitious and greedy, though. He forbade her to marry and banished her lover. He wanted to defeat the sorcerer and win his riches, hidden away under the mountain. There was a great battle, and the warrior princess knew that her people would be defeated. She rode into battle one more time, even though her chainmail had turned black and she knew that meant she would die. The sorcerer shot her with her own enchanted arrows, and she fell.'

'That is so sad.'

Misurina nodded, her face grave. 'The blind queen and her daughter fled through a secret gateway into the underworld, where they have lain in an enchanted sleep for hundreds of years. Once a year, on the night of the midwinter solstice, the gate to the under-world opens and they row out onto the wild lake in a black boat. It has been prophesied, you see, that one day the silver arrows will be found again, and then the sorcerer can be killed. On that day, the silver trumpet will sound and the queen and her daughter will wake and fight to win back their land. Till then, though, we must pay our tithe to the shapeshifting sorcerer.'

She made a helpless gesture towards the sombre procession of girls, then said in a quick low voice, 'I am sorry my father has made you join us. This is not your home – you do not understand our ways. I hope you do not choose the dragon stone.'

'I wish none of us had to,' I answered, and she nodded.

The procession wound up a hill to a circle of grey stones, each twice as tall as a man. They were eerie in the pale light, natural cracks and crevices looking like eyes and mouths. My skin prickled with unease.

As the sun rose, the stones cast long shadows over the hill. One ray of light blazed through a hole in the tallest of the stones like a star. The druidess bowed before it, then turned and gestured to us to stand in a ring within the circle of stones. She carried a small leather bag. She shook the bag so it rattled, then walked around the circle of young women. The first to draw was the eldest, a thin young woman with a long brown braid and a tense anxious face. She drew a stone from the bag, turned it over and showed its smooth white surface. She gasped with relief, then ran into the arms of a young man waiting in the crowd.

'They have wanted to marry for a long time,' Misurina told me, 'but no girl is permitted to wed until she has stood the midsummer test. Now she is free of the fear of the dragon, free to live her life.'

The druidess rattled the bag again and offered it to another girl, who chose an unblemished stone. She ran to her mother's waiting arms and was hugged close. Unexpectedly a lump rose in my throat.

Another girl, another unmarked stone, another family released from fear. Another, then another, then another.

The bag moved ever closer.

Misurina stared straight ahead, her face tense and white. Without looking at me, she said unhappily, 'Last year my best friend Rosa chose the dragon stone. She was chained to the highest crag. The next day, nothing was left of her. Not a bone, not a drop of blood. Nothing left to bury. Where does her soul roam since she was denied the descent to the underworld? Is she condemned to haunt the crystal mountain forever?'

The druidess rattled the bag and offered it to Misurina. She chose a stone, withdrew it. Pure unblemished white. She sagged with relief, then ran to her father who held her close, weeping.

I swallowed. My turn now. The druidess shook the bag and offered it to me. Taking a deep breath, I slid my hand within and groped for a stone. The old woman looked at me steadily, her sunken blue eyes filled with sorrow and pity. I had to choose. I ran my fingers over every stone. All were smooth to the touch, all seemed the same size. At last I chose one.

It was painted in ochre with the shape of a winged dragon, its tail an intricate spiralling knot. The old woman took the stone and held it high. 'She has chosen the dragon stone! Today she dies.'

All around me, people hugged and kissed, laughing and weeping together in joy and relief. I stood alone. I was cold, giddy, light-headed, as if all strength in me had drained away. It was as if I stood within a glass bottle, the outside world looking wavery, sound and light reaching me distantly, distorted.

The druidess put her arm about me, supporting me. 'I am sorry, my child. The goddess has spoken. Her will must be done.'

I shook off her arm and stiffened my body, keeping myself from swaying. I would go proud and fearless to my death, if that was indeed my fate. But already I was thinking about how I could escape. I did not believe that Hekate herself had taken me as an apprentice if my destiny was to die on a bare mountain top. She told me she had wanted me to know the mysteries, to remember and teach others. Well, to fulfil her wish, I had to live.

The druidess brought me a hot tisane to drink. Under the chamomile and honey, I smelt poppy juice. I shook my head and poured the drink on the ground. She gave me a frowning, thoughtful look, but took the empty cup away without protest.

Then began the long climb to the highest peak. The world seemed very clear and bright, as if newly rinsed. I tried to cram my senses with life – the scent of pine and thyme, the sound of birdsong, the chill caress of the wind, the shadowy reflection of the mountains in the mirror of the lake. A long procession of people accompanied me, chanting and drumming. I endured it all in silence. Every now and again came the shriek of the dragon, the flash of light along metallic wings, and everyone would freeze and duck, then hurry me along faster.

The path grew narrower, in places little more than a ledge with a dizzying drop below. In other places we had to climb, clinging to rough-hewn steps just wide enough for a hand or a foot. The druid and druidess were nimble and light-footed despite their age, their bare feet seeming not to mind the sharp stones at all. We came to ice and snow, and laboured across, clinging to branches of fir. It was cold now, the shadows lengthening. My whole body trembled, my teeth chattered.

Eventually we came to a steep ridge that we had to scramble up on all fours like goats. It was twilight, and the setting sun dazzled my eyes. Ahead rose a high slanted rock. The world fell away in all directions, shadows gathering below the fire-touched peaks. At the very apex of the highest crag, an iron chain hung from an iron loop.

There I was shackled and there I was left to die.

Part III

pupa
Latin: 'girl, doll, puppet'

A stage in the life cycle of a metamorphic insect such as a butterfly or moth in which it is enclosed in a cocoon or protective covering, while undergoing internal changes that lead to a final profound transformation.

You say well that he is some strange beast . . .
Eros and Psykhe
Metamorphoses, Lucius Apuleius

I

The Dread Bridegroom

My hands were manacled together. I could not reach the hilt of my obsidian dagger.

I spat on my wrists, trying to lubricate the skin so I could slip one hand through the fetters. I tried jerking the chain out of the rock. I tried breaking the chain. Nothing was any use. In the end I sat, my head bowed, so exhausted in body and soul I could scarcely stir a finger. I watched the red light creep across the stone and fade away. Darkness fell. I was alone.

Hours passed. I fell into a half-doze, my mind wandering. The sound of wings roused me. I looked up, scanning the night sky. Far above, a vast panoply of stars. Something dark, moving fast. A rush of wind, a clanking of my chains. My wrists were jerked painfully. I screamed and scrambled away.

'Sssh! Lie still!'

I froze, every muscle tensed, trying desperately to see. A figure bent over me. Huge and misshapen. I shuddered and scrambled away. A hand caught my shoulder, held me motionless. 'Be still . . .'

Another jerk and clank, and suddenly my wrists were free. The chains fell with a clatter.

Strong hands drew me up, clasped me close. I cried out, struggling to be free.

'Be careful! It's a long way down!'

I stopped struggling. 'Ambrose?'

He did not reply, holding me immobile in an embrace as strong and unbreakable as the chains. He leapt and fell into darkness. Wind whistled in my ears, my hair streamed upwards. I screamed again and clutched at him. The next moment, a rush of air, the clench and spring of muscles under bare skin, and a swoop upwards that made my stomach drop.

The sound of feathery wings, as if we were held aloft by a flock of great birds. I twisted my head, trying to see. 'Hold on, dear heart,' the voice whispered. 'Not far now.'

Above, stars. Below, black earth. The rim of the world tilted. Tears ran from my eyes and were swept away by the wind. I clung with all my strength to the warm body that held me. My cheek pressed into the curve of a strong shoulder, a muscular arm embraced my waist. I felt the rise and fall of a human chest, the pumping of a human heart, the clench of human muscles under smooth human skin. Above my head, strong wings beat rhythmically.

'Don't be afraid,' he whispered. 'We will soon be safe.'

I clung more tightly. He turned and dived. The dark world hurtled towards us. I gasped and pressed my face into his chest. His wings spread wide. Our descent slowed, and then he landed lightly on his feet. My knees crumpled, but he caught me and laid me down on the earth, kneeling beside me.

'Ambrose?' I asked again, my voice unsteady.

'Sssh. Do not speak. No-one must know where you are.'

'But . . .'

Again he admonished me to be silent. I could see nothing of him in the darkness. I reached to touch his face, to be sure it was him. Swiftly he kissed the palm of my hand. I felt the shock of it all through my body.

'Lie still. Rest. I will come again when I can.'

His wings unfurled and he leapt into the air. The wind of his passing made my hair swirl about me. I sat up, staring after him. My heart was racing as if I had drunk a potion of foxgloves. All around me the night was still and dark. Slowly I lay down again, curled myself up against the cold. Pine needles underneath me pricked me through my cloak. I slid my hand into the slit in my dress, drew out my obsidian knife, and held it close. Slowly, slowly, my tense muscles relaxed. My eyes shut. Somehow I slept.

When I awoke, it was late morning.

I sat up in a panic, looked around me. I was alone. I was safe. Sun slanted through the dark branches of the pine trees. Birds twittered. Sudden giddy relief flooded through me. I was alive. Ambrose had saved me.

I'm alive, I'm alive, my heart sang.

Through the tangle of branches I could see the steep grey peak of the mountain where I had been chained and left to die.

What would the dragon do? I wondered. *Would it punish my mother's people with arrows of flame? Would it demand another girl, another sacrifice? Would they hate me for not dying, as they had hated my mother?*

I could not be sorry. It was wrong. Barbaric. My mother's people needed to band together and defeat the sorcerer. In the meantime, I had escaped, and I needed to make sure I was not found. I tried to get to my feet, and only then realised I hurt all over. My legs ached, and I was covered in cuts and bruises. My throat was sore. I had to haul myself up, grabbing onto a low branch for help. I hobbled a few steps, my heart jerking at the rustle of my own footsteps in the pine needles.

What should I do? Ambrose had said he would come again when he could. Should I just stay here, waiting for him? But I was parched with thirst, weak with hunger. I needed to find water, food, shelter of some kind. I had lost everything except my obsidian knife. I picked it up from the ground and hid it once again in my pocket.

A bird twittered above me. I glanced up. A robin looked at me with a bright and merry eye, flew a few feet, perched on a twig, looked at me again. He sang robustly, then flew a few more feet. I followed.

The robin led me to a gate in a high stone wall. It stood ajar. I stood for a while, listening. The robin chirped, flew over the wall, then returned, waggling his tail encouragingly. I pushed the door with one hand. It swung open soundlessly.

Within was a garden in full summer bloom. A path led to a small white castle with two round towers, their roofs made of silvery-grey slate. Beyond, dark forest and soaring ramparts of stone. No sound but the distant tinkle of water and the robin's sweet song. Water, I thought, and tiptoed up the path. The little bird hopped and darted ahead. It led through an archway into a courtyard. In the centre was a well with a quaint pointed roof of thatch above. It had a shaft and chain, but no bucket. Drooping in disappointment, I looked around me.

On one side was a long white building, its wooden door and shutters firmly closed. Smoke drifted from its thatched roof, and a kitchen garden was planted before it. There were rows of cabbages, sorrel and beans within low hedges of rosemary starred with tiny blue flowers, beds of mint and thyme and marjoram, a neatly clipped bay tree in the centre. The robin perched on its dark globe, tilted its head, then flew over the wall.

I followed it through another archway into another, larger courtyard. Opposite was a barn, its white walls and thatched roof mirroring that of the kitchen which it faced. An avenue of linden trees led to an immense iron-bound gate with hinges forged into the shapes of leaves and lilies. I turned the other way, though, towards the castle. A few wide steps led up to an arched door, decorated with the same ornate hinges as the gate. It stood open invitingly. The robin perched on the top, cocked his head and regarded me, then flew inside.

I knocked tentatively on the door. No answer. I peeped within. A long hall, with soft rugs on the floor. A lantern stood on a carved sideboard, casting a warm radiance. Hesitantly I stepped within, calling a greeting. A sweet warble answered me. I followed the sound and found myself within an arched dining-room with a fresco on the wall of a man and woman feasting. A table was laid with a ceramic soup tureen, bowls of bread and cheese and fruit, a silver salt-cellar, a decanter of wine and another of water, a silver goblet, knife and spoon, and one empty bowl and plate.

Surely no-one would mind if I had a little to drink? I was so hungry and thirsty. The robin flew down and pecked at a piece of bread. I called out again and looked through the rooms nearby. An arched doorway led through to one of the towers, which housed a library with a circling spiral staircase at its centre, and shelves to the peaked roof filled with neatly tied scrolls. A desk was set under the window, looking out into the garden. I saw a wax tablet and stylus laid down on its smooth surface, as if the writer had only just risen from their seat.

Another doorway led into the kitchen wing with its wall ovens and big hearth, where a fire crackled merrily. A pot of soup hung

181

above it, the smell making my stomach growl hungrily, and a table was laden with baskets of fresh herbs and vegetables, a bowl of eggs, and glass bottles of wine, oil and vinegar. But no person, no living creature except the robin who had accompanied me from room to room. He perched on the back of a chair, head cocked, chirping comfortingly, then flew out the door once more.

I followed him to the dining table and poured some water. It was cool and clear. I drank greedily, poured some more, drank till my thirst was slaked. The robin pecked away happily at some grapes in a bowl. I took a slice of bread. Just one wouldn't matter, surely? And the soup would be getting cold. Again I looked out into the hall. No movement, no sound. I sat down at the table, served myself, ate hungrily, served myself some more, then wiped up the last of the soup with some more bread.

Feeling much better, I got up and began once more to search for the owner of the castle, wanting to explain and apologise and to offer to pay in kind, if I could. The robin flitted away through a window, its shutters sliding open to let in the pure fresh air.

In the other tower I found a round sitting-room with a cushioned chair by a fire and an open workbox neatly packed with thread, needles and a leather thimble. A small loom was set against the wall by a narrow window looking into the rose garden, and the walls were hung with beautiful tapestries of woodland beasts and birds and flowers. By the fire was a low table with a scroll resting upon it. I sat and unrolled the papyrus. It was a collection of love poems. I read for a while, savouring every word, stopping occasionally to listen for a footstep or voice. The only sound was birdsong and the wind in the pine trees.

At last I laid the scroll down again, and made myself rise. It was difficult, as I was bone weary, and the chair was so comfortable. One of the embroidered hangings had been drawn back and tied with a green tassel, revealing a narrow spiral staircase hidden behind. I was surprised I had not noticed it before. I peeped through, wondering where the steps led. After a moment I tiptoed up. I found myself in a bedroom, beautifully furnished with a wide bed spread with a patchwork quilt in shades of softest blue-green, silvery-white and rose, patterned with birds and butterflies and stitched with a design of flower petals.

A fire of pinecones burned on the hearth, and before it stood a deep metal bath filled with steaming water. A linen towel was draped over a stool with a bowl of salt and dried lavender flowers. On the bed was laid a white silk nightgown with a warm robe trimmed with ermine, two slippers set neatly on the floor below. I gazed at the bath longingly. I was so tired and dirty and sore.

But the bath had been drawn for someone else, not me. I went back downstairs, looking everywhere for some sign of the castle's owner. I explored every corner but saw nobody. At last I went back to the dining-room, thinking to have another drink of water. The remnants of my meal had been cleared away, and a steaming tisane of linden blossom sat waiting, a honey cake on a plate beside it.

The back of my neck prickled.

'Hello?' I called. 'Is anyone there?'

No answer.

With quick steps, I went back into the garden and hurried down the path. The gate I had entered was shut. I tried to open it, but it was locked. I wrenched at the handle, twisting it one way, then the other. I shook it. Kicked it. Nothing budged it. I tried to climb the wall, but the stones were fitted together so closely there was nowhere for my fingers and toes to cling. I ran down the avenue of linden trees and heaved at the front gate. It was locked tight. For more than an hour I roamed the garden, seeking a way out. I found a summerhouse overlooking a wide pool where huge golden fish swam beneath the waterlilies, and an orchard of mossy apple trees with wildflowers growing in drifts below. No gates in the wall, no trees close enough to climb. No way to get out.

I came back to the garden at the base of the round tower. A seat was set there to catch the last rays of the sun. Wearily I sat down. Only then did I notice the roses. White as snow, with dozens of petals curved protectively about a small green stigma.

My green-eyed rose.

Stupidly I sat, staring, for a long time.

Then I went back to the bedroom in the tower. An oil lamp had been lit, filling the room with soft moving shadows. The bath still steamed enticingly. I undressed within the cumbersome protection of my cloak, had a long hot bath, drew on the nightgown and climbed into bed. A hot brick wrapped in flannel warmed my cold toes. I had tucked my obsidian knife under the pillow. I lay down, touched its hilt, and waited.

'Dear heart?'

I opened my eyes. It was so dark I could not see a thing.

'Ambrose?'

'No names!' he said.

'Why?'

'Names have power.'

'I don't know what you mean.'

'When you say a name, it has the power to call that person to you. It helps people find you.'

'But you are here,' I objected sleepily, then sat up, grabbing for my knife. 'You are Ambrose, aren't you?'

'Please! No names.'

'But I need to know who you are. Where am I? Why have you brought me here?'

'You're safe now, isn't that enough?' He sounded a little disgruntled.

I said steadily, 'I don't feel safe. Why am I locked in?'

'Locked in?'

'The gates are all locked.'

'Oh. That is to protect you, to keep you safe.'

'I don't like being locked in.'

'I'm sorry. Please believe me, it is for your own safety.'

'Why should I believe you? Why should I trust you, when you will not tell me who you are?'

'I'm . . . I'm your friend. I mean you no harm, I promise. I . . . can you not just trust me?'

'What do you want with me?'

'I don't want anything with you! I just wanted to help you, to save you.'

'Thank you,' I said. 'I don't mean to be ungrateful. It's just . . . it's dark, I cannot see you. Can I just light a lantern? I would feel safer if I could see you.'

'I'm sorry, I can't let you do that.'

'But why? Why don't you want me to see you?'

'I can't, it's dangerous.'

'Dangerous for whom?'

'For me, for you, for both of us,' he answered rather wildly. 'Please, I cannot explain why. Can't you just trust me?'

'Trust needs to be earned. You won't let me see your face or know who you are. How does that win my trust?'

'You know who I am, don't you?' he replied after a long moment. 'In your heart, don't you know who I am?'

'I . . . I think so.'

I sat in silence for a minute, trying to see, trying to be sure. All I had for a clue was the sound of his voice, the way he said my name as if he was singing it. I had known Ambrose as a boy. As a man he had spoken only a few words to me: *Psykhe, you must beware. Do not forget life and death are the affairs of gods, not mortals.*

'Did I know you once? A long time ago?'

'Yes.'

'Did you kiss me?'

A long pause, then he answered, very low. 'Yes.'

'Why? Why did you kiss me and then flee? And why am I here now? Why did you save me?' I battered his silence with questions.

'I don't know!' The words seemed to burst from him. 'I don't know why I feel this way. I've never felt it before. This ... this longing, this ... this ceaseless desire. Nothing eases it. I think about you all the time, I wonder where you are, what you are doing, thinking, feeling. I want to tell you things, things I've never told anyone before. I want ... I want to ...' His voice broke.

My soul leapt within me. I gazed towards where I thought he must be. 'Ambrose,' I said unsteadily.

A few quick steps towards me. He knelt beside me, one hand rising to touch me. 'Please, no names! She will hear, she will know.'

'Then what am I to call you?' I took his hand.

'My darling, my heart, my treasure, my life, my twin soul ...'

I bent forward and kissed him. His breath caught, I felt him jolt. Then he caught me into his arms, pressed me back onto the bed, kissed me as if he wished to devour me. 'Psykhe,' he whispered, his mouth moving to my throat, my breast. 'Oh, Psykhe, I've wanted you so long. Are you sure?'

I ran my hands over his bare back, underneath his shirt, kissing wherever I could reach. 'Yes, yes, oh please.'

It was a kind of death. The utter loss of myself in him.

II

Ruin of All

One feared by all who live, the Sibyl had said. *Ruin of all*.
My father had thought she meant the dragon. But the
Sibyl had meant love.

I was delirious with desire. Each day I counted off the daylight
hours, waiting for night and his arrival. As soon as the darkness
was absolute, Ambrose would come to me. The sound of his step was
enough to make my stomach lurch. I'd hold out my empty arms to
the shadows and he would fill them, fill all the empty places within
me, all loneliness, all longing. I loved the smooth softness of his
skin, the way it dampened with sweat, the taste of salt on my tongue.
I loved the way he held me close afterwards, my body moulded to
his, feet hooked together.

Every morning I woke and found myself alone again.

Or not quite alone. Invisible hands poured hot water into
a bowl for me to wash and laid out clean clothes for me, beautiful gowns of silk so fine I could have drawn them through a
ring. As I walked through the castle, doors would open before
me, lanterns would light. If I was hungry, food was laid out for me

in the dining-room. If I wanted something to read, scrolls would magically unroll for me.

'Who are you?' I asked. 'What's your name? Will you not show yourself to me?'

Never any answer.

'Who are my invisible attendants?' I asked Ambrose one night, lying in his arms in the darkness.

'Household spirits,' he answered in surprise.

I was surprised too. All my life we had tossed a few crumbs of bread onto the hearth before a meal, but somehow I had always thought the ants ate them.

'Do your household spirits always wait on you hand and foot?' I asked, half-teasing.

'Of course,' he answered.

Is he truly a god? I asked myself. *How can that be?*

I dared not ask him. Everything felt like a dream, and I did not want to wake.

My days were long without him. I lay abed, reading, then wandered the garden. I fed the fish with crumbs from my table and picked bunches of herbs to make healing teas, though there was no-one who needed them. I was just passing the time. There was nothing to do, not a weed to be pulled, not a doorstep to be scrubbed. At last the sun would sink below the rim of the world, and I could go to bed and wait for darkness and his coming. Afterwards we would lie, hands lazily tracing the unseen contours of each other's bodies, and talk.

'Where are your wings?' I asked, stroking his smooth bare back. 'You do have wings, don't you?' For I was still unsure what was real. It was hard not being able to see him.

'I have wings if I need to fly,' he answered. 'But I don't need them for bed sport. They'd rather get in the way, don't you think?' He spun me over so he lay flat on his back and I sat astride him.

He coiled my hair about his hands and drew my face down to his, so there was no more talking that night.

'Why did you kiss me?' I asked another time. 'That time in Roma.'

'I could not help myself,' he answered. 'I had longed to do so for a very long time.'

'But you fled me,' I said. 'You kissed me and then you ran away.'

'I had to. I knew she would be angry. She spies on me.'

'Your mother?'

'Yes.'

'But why would she be angry?'

'She wants me to love her and only her. But hush. Let's not talk about her. She always knows, even when she is not named.'

'But how . . .'

'Enough talk. I have better uses for your mouth.'

He drew my head down, and my question was forgotten.

Another time I told him how long the days were without him.

'Mine too,' he answered. 'I count off the hours till I can come to you.'

'What do you do all day?'

He shrugged. 'Whatever my mother wants me to do. Most of it is a bore.'

I made a restless movement. 'I'm bored too. I'm used to working all day.'

'No need for you to work anymore.' He caught up one of my hands and kissed my palm. 'No need to ever work again, my darling. I will look after you.'

'I like working,' I told him. 'I like helping people.'

He was kissing his way down my body and paid no heed. I sighed and slid my hands down his back. *It doesn't matter*, I told myself. *To have him here in my arms is all I need.*

I began to walk the perimeter of the wall every day, looking for a place that I could climb and see what was on the other side. I could hear running water, the sound of the wind, but never another human voice. Where was I? Was I near the crystal mountain? I never heard the shriek of the dragon or saw it fly over.

I wondered greatly about what was happening in the world outside the garden walls. Where were my sisters? Were they safe? Was Cesar babbling his first words yet? Had he rolled over, sat up on his own? I was missing so many moments in his life. I yearned to hold him in my arms, to breathe in his sweet baby smell.

The garden had seemed so big when first I had come. Now it seemed stiflingly small.

'Where do you go all day?' I asked Ambrose.

'Home,' he answered, with a note of surprise.

His words hurt me. 'But where is your home?'

'It's . . . elsewhere.'

'What is that supposed to mean? Is it far away? Can I go there?'

'Gods forbid!'

I sat up, pulling the sheet around me. 'You don't want me there?'

He sat up too, putting his arm about me, drawing me close. 'I didn't mean it like that! It's just . . . well, my mother is there.' He lifted my hair away so he could kiss my bare shoulder. 'It's best not to remind her that you exist.'

'She's going to have to know one day,' I told him. 'Or do you plan to keep me locked in here forever?'

'Of course not! I'm just waiting for the right moment.' He kissed me.

I drew away, troubled and unhappy.

'But why do you need to wait? If she knew, then you would not always have to leave me here alone.'

He answered impatiently, 'You know why, darling. It's to keep you safe.'

'But why can we only meet in darkness? What harm would it do to kindle a lantern? We could eat supper together, talk properly.'

'We don't need light to talk. There are some things that are best done in darkness.' His voice was smiling. 'Let me show you.'

Once again I was willingly seduced into silence.

The next day, as I wandered about the garden, I noticed that all the petals of the white rose had fallen. I gathered them up, thinking to steep them in almond oil to make a sweet-scented salve. But then I let them fall from my hands. What was the point? There was no-one whose pain would be eased by my balm. I wondered again about my sisters, hoping they were well, hoping they were happy. I wondered about my father. Had he fled Roma with the royal family? Did they fight to win back the throne? The white castle in its walled garden seemed out of time, a world unto itself, and my other life utterly remote.

'Do you know what is happening in Roma?' I asked Ambrose that night.

'No,' he answered in surprise. 'I have not been there since you left.'

'Can you get news for me? I want to know how my family is.'

'If you like.' He traced his finger down my nose to my lips, down my chin and throat, down the cleft of my breasts, down my stomach and into my navel, following his finger with his tongue. I sighed and sank my hands into his curls.

The next evening, as I lay with my head cradled in his shoulder, I asked him eagerly what news he had heard.

'News?'

'Of my family.'

'I'm sorry, sweetling, I forgot to ask.'

'You forgot?' I asked.

'My mother is suspicious. She keeps me by her side all day, doing endless trivial tasks for her.'

'But it's important to me. Please, can't you find out?'

'What does it matter? You've left that life behind you now. Besides, they were always so unkind to you. Ordering you about, calling you names.'

'They're my family. All sisters squabble sometimes.'

'I'll see what I can find out,' he promised.

I turned my back, pretending to sleep. Inside, unhappiness smouldered. I spent all day alone, longing for him, while he was at his mother's side, at her beck and call, unable to even remember a small task for me. He pressed himself against me, his arm about my waist. Usually I would have wriggled closer to him, wanting every inch of my skin to touch his. That night I lay still, unresponsive even when he stroked his hand over my belly. He sighed and rolled away.

I was sorry the next morning, when I woke and he was gone. Questions needled me all day. I wandered about listlessly, tried the handle of the gate again. It was still locked. I went to bed at the usual time but left the little lantern burning by my bed. I wanted to see him, wanted to see his expression when I kissed him, wanted to see his face when I asked him about my family. I watched the dancing flame sink down, growing ever bluer. Then it sank away into darkness.

I stared and stared, but I could see nothing. An eternity of waiting. At last the sound of his light step, the weight of his body sinking down the side of the mattress, the touch of his fingers like a brand on my skin. 'My darling, my treasure,' he whispered. 'All day I have longed for you.'

I melted into his arms. I could not help myself. When our passion had been slaked and we lay idly in each other's arms, I asked him

192

again, 'Dear heart, have you discovered news of my family? Truly I fear for them.'

'Oh, I meant to tell you. I have heard no news of them. But Roma is at war, that I do know. Besieged by your king who wants his throne back.' His voice was light. He felt me stiffen and draw away. 'What's wrong?'

'War is not a joke,' I said coldly. 'People are dying.'

'I'm sorry,' he said after a moment. 'I forget sometimes that the lives of mortals are real, and not some pageant designed for our entertainment.'

I felt all at once how alien he was to me. 'Our lives are just idle amusements to you?'

'No, dear heart,' he said apologetically. 'Not to me. Not anymore.'

I hardly listened, thinking of all the stories I had heard about the lives of the gods, the bacchanalian feasts, the drunken orgies.

'It is different in our world,' he tried to explain. 'Your lives are so short – you live with such intensity. Our lives are long. We do not fear death in the same way.'

'Your world?'

'Yes.'

'Where is your world?' My voice was cool.

'Very close. As close as I am to you now.' He slid his hand down my belly. I pushed it away.

'How do you get to your world?'

'Sometimes it is easy to find the way. A crack in a cliff guarded by an elder tree is likely to be a doorway, or a cave that can only be reached through water. Certain times of the day are easier to pass through, like dawn or dusk, the gateway hours. And certain times of the year are easier too. Midsummer, midwinter, the equinoxes.'

Is that why he leaves before dawn? I wondered. *So he can get through the gateway?*

193

'Time works differently in the different worlds,' Ambrose went on. 'One night in our world can equal a hundred years in yours. And the gateways between the worlds can lead anywhere, anytime. You need great strength of will and steadiness of purpose to travel at will between the worlds.'

My mind reeled. How many worlds were there? How many gateways?

'Sometimes the doors will close against you,' he continued, 'and then you can spend a lifetime searching for a gate, eaten out with longing for the otherworld but never able to find the way through.'

I lay in silence, thinking. 'Will I ever go to your world?' I asked at last.

'I . . . I hope so. One day. My mother will surely relent in time. I just need to think how best to win her over.'

Then Ambrose whispered, as if to himself, 'I just need to feed the monster.'

That night I did not sleep, but lay awake, his arm heavy on my body. I wished there was somebody else I could talk to. I tried to imagine what Nocturna would say. She was the wisest woman I had ever known.

Open your eyes, my child . . .

A high sweet warble. A robin sang just outside our window. I startled awake and strained my eyes, but there was no lessening of the darkness. It was not yet time for the dawn chorus. Beside me, Ambrose stirred. I felt the moment in which he came fully alert. Very slowly he slid his arm from my body and turned back the coverlet. The air was chill on my skin. He eased his way out of my bed, then stood, tucking the coverlet around me with a gentle hand.

'Ambrose, don't go,' I whispered.

'No names!'

'Please, don't go.'

194

'I have to.'

I sat up, reaching for him. 'Stay with me.'

'I can't. Let me go.'

When I clung on, he jerked his hand away. I heard him dressing. I threw back the coverlets, jumped up, groped my way through the thick darkness. I had no tinder and flint to spark a light, no burning ember kept safe in a tin, no way of lighting my lamp. My groping hands found him. 'Please don't go.'

He drew me close, and kissed me. 'Go back to bed. You must trust me – I cannot stay. Please, dear heart, let me go.'

The robin sang more robustly. Ambrose bent and picked something up. Faint metallic clinks. His quiver of arrows? I fell back a few steps, suddenly afraid.

I heard his quick tread on the steps, the faint squeak of the door. I caught up my robe, flung it about me, and followed as quickly as I could. I hit my hip on the side table, banged my shoulder against the wall, almost fell down the stairs. Usually, wherever I walked through the castle, lamps kindled before me and were snuffed out behind me. There were no lamps now. The invisible spirits of the household obeyed him, not me. I reached the ground floor and hurried down the corridor to the great oaken door. I could see the faintest lessening of darkness where it stood open. I rushed outside.

A vast arc of stars above. The pine trees beyond the wall showed black against the flush of saffron and rose to the east. There was no sign of any living thing. The stillness and silence were eerie.

I went back to bed. The sheets were cold. I curled my knees to my chest, wrapped my arms about myself. I felt very alone.

He did not come to me that night. I wept myself to sleep. The next day dragged even more slowly than usual. Again he did not come. I began to fear he would never return. I swore that next time he came I would love him so thoroughly, he would never want to leave. The third night he did not appear, I told myself things had to change. I needed a life of my own, a purpose, a source of happiness besides Ambrose. I needed to be my own person again.

That night I did not lie in the darkness, straining my ears for any sound of him. I turned on my side and began to make plans. I would need to find the key to the gate, I would need to explore the countryside. Surely there would be a village where I could sell some of my healing tinctures? Perhaps I should disguise myself. Dye my hair and skin as Alektrona once suggested. I'd wear my plainest gown, ask my invisible servants for some sensible boots instead of the thin-soled silken slippers they put out for me each day.

'Darling?'

The unexpected sound of his voice startled me. I gave a little cry of fear. He dropped to his knees beside the bed, reached for my hand. 'I'm so sorry, I'm so sorry. I could not get away. She watches my every movement – I did not dare risk it. Please forgive me.'

He lifted the quilt and slid in beside me. My skin yearned for his, but when he moved over me, seeking to kiss and touch me, I held him away from me. 'Not now, dear heart.'

He drew away. 'What's wrong?'

I did not know how to say what was in my heart. At last I said, 'I missed you so much. You were gone for days. Don't you realise how lonely I am when you are not here?'

'I missed you too,' he cried. 'I could not bear being away from you for so long!'

'But are you lonely?'

'Yes,' he said fiercely. 'Though my mother's court is full of people, I always feel alone.'

'But nonetheless there are people with you, people you can talk to. I have no-one.'

'I'm sorry I could not come! You know I wanted to.'

196

'But I don't know. How can I? You come only at night, in darkness. You will not let me see your face, you will not let me leave or see my family, you will not let me do my work. You expect me simply to trust you and obey you, but you do not tell me why.'

'You know why.'

'No, I don't. Why must I never see your face?'

'She will know.' His voice was so low I could hardly hear it.

'Your mother?'

'Who else?' Ambrose had lifted away his hand and lay beside me, cold and remote.

'But I don't understand why it matters. Doesn't your mother want you to be happy? Is she truly so unkind?'

He moved restlessly. 'She's very kind to those who please her. When I was a little boy, I thought her the most wonderful woman in the world. I thought I was so lucky to have her as my mother . . .'

His voice trailed away.

'But? What happened?' I prompted.

'Well, I grew up, I suppose. Things changed.' He shuddered, like a horse shaking off a stinging fly.

'And that upsets her? That things have changed?' I felt my way forward cautiously.

'I suppose so. She knows I don't adore her like I used to, and she wants me to. She adores to be adored.' His voice was bitter. 'So she punishes me by making me dance attendance on her all the time, and pouts if I'm away from her side for more than a minute.'

I kissed his shoulder. 'At least your mother didn't try to sacrifice you to a dragon like my father did.'

I spoke lightly, but he responded with an angry rush of words. 'That was her too. She watched me, making sure I didn't go back to see you again. And then, when I did, after you saved the life of that drowned girl, she ordered me to shoot you with one of my

197

golden arrows, so you would fall in love with the first man you saw. I had to go to you at dawn, when your father was on his way home from one of his parties. She wanted him to be the man you saw, the man you lusted after.'

I recoiled from him. 'What?'

'It's a trick she's used before. On a girl called Myrrha who was so beautiful people called her a second Venus. I had to shoot her with an arrow so that she was cursed with lust for her own father. Myrrha seduced him in the darkness so he did not know who she was. When he discovered the truth, he tried to kill her. My mother thought it a pretty revenge.'

'You . . . you shot Myrrha? You cursed her?'

'I didn't know what I was doing! Please, you have to believe me. My mother just told me she wanted to teach the girl a lesson, and I was to go to her house at a certain time and shoot her with one of my arrows. I would never have done it if I had known.'

'But it's such a terrible thing to do to someone!'

'I didn't know.'

'And she wanted you to do it to me? To make me fall in love with my own father?' I felt sick.

'I wouldn't have done it, dear heart.'

'But you came. I remember. You had an arrow in your hand. You meant to strike me with it.'

Ambrose sat up, grasping my shoulders. 'You fool! Of course I meant to strike you with it. I wanted you to love me too. I've been in love with you for so long. But you never seemed to miss me or think about me. I thought I would prick you with the point of my arrow and then wake you, so that I would be the first man you saw. But then I couldn't bear to. I wanted you to love me for myself!'

He tried to kiss me, but I held him off with both hands. How I wished I could see his face, read his expression. 'Are you telling me the truth?'

'Yes! Why do you not believe me? I kissed you, because I love you, and that is why my mother hates you. I disobeyed her, and that she can never forgive. That is why she wanted you sacrificed to the dragon.'

'So the Sibyl was your mother's tool?'

'The Sibyl sees all possible futures. The moment my mother decided you must die, it became possible. So too did the future where I would try to save you, where I would want you for my own.'

I was silent, struggling to understand. 'But surely, if she loves you, she'd want you to be happy? Why would she want to kill me if she knows you love me?'

'Do you know what the gods fear more than anything else?' Ambrose said.

I thought of the Sibyl's words. *One feared by all who live, even the mighty gods.*

'Love?' I asked.

'Yes, they fear love because what is loved can be lost. A god's grief is a terrible thing. But love is not what they fear most.'

'What, then?' I asked.

'Being forgotten. A god only exists as long as they are worshipped. Each time someone prays to a god or makes sacrifice to them, the god gains in strength. That is why she fears you when they worship you instead.'

I sat silently. It was true.

What is remembered lives.

What is forgotten dies.

III

Three Gifts

In the morning, I woke to find three gifts on my bedside table. A key. A golden ring. A silver bowl with a long, slender handle embossed with a woman's face looking in three directions. A note was tied to the key.

Dear heart, the key unlocks the gate. I was afraid for you, and wanted you all to myself, but I should not have kept you locked away from the world. Forgive me. You can go out if you like, but I beg you to take care. Let no-one know who you are or where you live or that I am your beloved. You must trust me and obey me in this, else all will be lost. The ring is enchanted. Twist it three times in the direction of the sun and it will take you wherever you wish. It will work no more than three times, so use it only in your hour of greatest need. Finally, the scrying bowl allows you to see what is hidden. Fill it with water from the lake of the magic mirror, and then, on the night of the dark of the moon, kindle a light and gaze within. Say, 'Flame so bright, open my sight, let me see, what's unseen by me', while thinking of those you wish to perceive. Take care while using, guard yourself as best you can. It can be dangerous to see secrets.

The note was signed with a scrawled A. I read it through twice, and pressed it to my heart. I slid the ring onto my finger, threw on my plainest dress and cloak, and hurried to the gate in the wall. The key turned easily in the lock, and I was able to step outside the castle grounds for the first time since I had arrived.

The castle had been built at the end of a long, green valley surrounded on three sides by steep unclimbable peaks. A waterfall tumbled from the heights, cascaded over rocks in a wide curve around the castle, then fell in a series of foaming rapids to the lake. The tears of the stone king, I thought.

I explored the valley, then scrambled down a precipitous track beside the waterfall, clinging tightly to the steep rocks. I came out on a flat crag that jutted into space. Carefully I edged forward. I had a view across the whole panorama of soaring pinnacles and plunging ravines. Far below, the lake of the magic mirror reflected the forest and the snow-streaked peaks. Smoke drifted over the steep thatched roofs of the hillfort. It seemed as if all was well there. I heaved a sigh of relief, even as I wondered why the dragon had not taken its revenge. I had been so afraid another girl would be sacrificed in my place.

I saw more smoke rising from the forest to my right. I scrambled that way, and after an hour or more of rough walking, came to a small alpine meadow where four or five small wooden houses faced each other across a yard with a well and a big beehive-shaped oven. Each house had its own barn and pigsty behind the house, and a plot of carefully tilled land where crops grew. The whole hamlet was surrounded by a protective hedge of thorny shrubs. I lay on an outcrop of rocks, hungrily watching its inhabitants go about their business, shaking out rugs, milking a goat, thatching a roof with birch twigs, spinning wool, grinding grain. I saw a young woman rocking a squalling newborn baby in her arms. She looked exhausted. Fennel tea, I thought, and proper swaddling. An old man digging with a fork stopped and stretched, fists in the small of his back. Arnica and mint salve, I thought. I'll need beeswax and almond oil.

When the shadows began to stretch long, I turned for home. It was a hard scramble back to the castle, and if it had not been for the waterfall showing me the way, I would never have found it again. The green valley was completely hidden from view.

As I clambered, I collected handfuls of flowers and leaves. Some I would transplant into the garden, others I would lay out to dry before steeping in oil. I wondered if my invisible servants could bring me the equipment I would need. Glass jars and bottles, a funnel, some grindstones. Perhaps I could ask the potter at the hillfort to make me an earthenware distillation pot like Nocturna's. Then all I would need was beeswax. It'd be best to have bees of my own. I'd have to establish a hive.

Desperate cheeping broke into my thoughts. I looked around. Squatting on a narrow ledge nearby was a grey bundle of fuzz with round orange eyes and a tiny, hooked beak. It had the most comical expression of astonishment on its face, and enormous fluffy claws.

'Have you fallen from your nest, little one?'

Above, on a shelf in the cliff-face, was a rough nest of old twigs. Below, a dizzying fall of rocks and rubble. If the owlet took even a few clumsy hops, it would fall to its death.

I had been using the skirt of my dress as an improvised basket for the herbs I had been collecting, with the hem twisted up through my sash while I climbed. It took me only a moment to scoop up the baby bird and tuck him among the leaves and the flowers.

He squawked indignantly, then glowered at me as I began to climb again, this time holding the gathered hem in my hand so that the owlet was not squashed. I spoke to him gently, saying, 'Not far now, little one. You'll soon be safe. Where's your mama?'

A warning shriek, then a huge shadow passed over me. I shrank back against the cliff. An immense owl was flying overhead. It had marigold-coloured eyes, ferocious ear tufts, and wings as wide as a man's outstretched arms. It carried a struggling hare in its feathered talons. I knew I had only a few seconds before it turned and swooped on me. Quickly I scrambled the last few feet, tipped the owlet into its nest, then scrambled away, taking shelter behind an outcrop of rock. There was a whoosh of wings, the flash of pale feathers, then the owl landed in the nest where her baby was jumping and squeaking in excitement. As she began to tear at the hare with her great curved beak, I crept away.

That night, bubbling over with excitement, I told Ambrose about the owl. 'It was the biggest owl I have ever seen! Honestly, it was as big as an eagle.'

'I've seen one before,' he said, stroking his fingers over the curve of my hip. 'With eyes like the full moon when it's just risen. I've heard them called eagle owls because they are so big.'

'The baby was so big, I could barely carry it! And so clumsy and ungainly. The only problem is that it crushed all my herbs to bits. I can salvage some, but I'll have to go and gather some more. The thyme and nettles and dandelions are easy enough, they grow everywhere, but I only found that one mint plant and I want it to make that muscle balm for the poor old man in the village . . .'

'Wait! What? What man?'

'A man I saw in a village in the valley. He was in pain. I thought I'd make him some salve to rub into his aching joints. Arnica and mint are the best, but mint is rare up here . . .'

He was silent. After a while I quietened too. 'What's wrong?' I asked.

'Darling, I'm sorry, but you must not be seen by anyone. You can't go into any of the villages.'

'I thought I could disguise myself,' I said after a moment, my throat constricted. 'Hide my hair, darken my eyelashes.'

He snorted. 'Don't be a fool! No disguise will hide what you are. Even if you could, everyone would know you were a stranger. There'd be talk, gossip. Word would spread.'

Ambrose was right. I knew he was right. I lay down with my back to him.

'Don't be upset.' He stroked my thigh. 'It's not forever.'

'So when? When will I be free to come and go as I please, to work if I want to? I'm not a doll, Ambrose, to be left lying in the toybox when you've finished playing with me. I need more.'

'I'm not enough for you?' He sounded hurt.

'I only get half of you,' I snapped. 'I want the daylight half as well as the night-time. I want to have breakfast with you, and walk in the garden with you, and read out bits of books to you. I want all of you, and I want you to have all of me.' I pushed away his hand, and sat up, wrapping myself in the sheet even though it was pitch-dark, and he could not see me.

'I tell you what,' I said. 'You say you need to find the right time to tell your mother about me. Why don't you go and do that? Tomorrow is the night of the dark moon. I will go down and gather water from the lake, and I'll take a look and see how my family is doing. You go and do whatever it is you need to do, and when you're ready to share the whole of yourself, come back and see me.'

'Psykhe,' he said in an anguished voice, but I began to push him out of bed, crying, 'Go on, go!'

Ambrose stood silent for a moment, then said gruffly, 'Be careful, dear heart.' I thought he meant to take care no-one saw me when I went down to the lake, but then he added, 'The scrying bowl shows much that is hidden, even that which is deeply concealed within the human soul. Not all wish to be watched, not all wish to be known.'

The following evening I left the castle as the sun was going down. It took me more than two hours to walk down to the lake, and the last part of it was done in darkness. I went slowly, carrying a shuttered lantern, illuminating my way with the smallest beam of light I could manage. An owl hooted, flying over my head with muffled wings. Otherwise, the only sound was the wind in the pine trees. My thoughts kept returning to my argument with Ambrose. So many things I should have said, but did not. To distract myself, I wondered about my sisters and baby nephew. I would finally get to see them that night, even if they could not see me. I imagined them somewhere safe, firelight glowing on their smiling faces, Khrysanthe rocking Cesar's cradle and singing a lullaby, Alektrona stirring a pot and laughing.

The lake lay before me, glimmering faintly in the starlight. I knelt on the pebbly shore and filled my leather bottle to the brim. The water was icy. I was thirsty and drank a mouthful, and my throat ached with the cold. Then I turned and trudged all the way back to the castle. It was a dangerous and difficult climb in the darkness, with only my little lantern to show me the way. All the landmarks I had memorised looked different. My legs were trembling by the time I finally locked the gate behind me, and went into my sitting-room. A fire glowed on the hearth, and a steaming hot tisane stood waiting for me. I drank it gratefully, warming my chilled fingers, then poured the water into the silver bowl and set my lantern beside it. Looking down into my own eyes, pale as water over ice, I spoke the words of the spell:

205

Flame so bright,
open my sight,
let me see,
what's unseen by me.

Dizziness overcame me. I felt like I was falling. Spinning like a leaf in a flood. Then I saw myself, a newborn baby, my face small and crumpled, my white eyelashes lying still on my ashen skin. Brid bent over me, tilting back my head with its tufts of white hair like a dandelion clock, blowing into my mouth. My chest rose and fell, rose and fell, rose and fell. Suddenly my closed eyes flashed open, my startled hands flew out. I gasped my first breath.

I watched myself grow, a frail child who hid under tables, watching the world through my fingers. I tossed and whimpered in bed, my face flaming, my breath coming fast and uneven, as Brid wiped my face with a damp cloth and said, 'You must not go out in the heat of the day, Psykhe. The sun will burn you up!' I sat alone in the shade of a tree, making tiny gardens out of leaves and twigs and fallen flowers, playing with a ragdoll Brid had made for me with white wool for hair. I lay curled in my bed, clutching Brid's hand, begging for just one more story, please, just one more, watching in terror as she closed the door behind her, and the flickering shadows of my lantern transformed into ogres with claws and fangs.

'What is wrong with her?' other children asked, pointing at me as I went by. 'Why is she so white? Is she a ghost? Does she suck blood?'

'She's god-touched,' some parents would say, drawing the child away. Others whispered, 'She's like a creature from another land, a dryad or a fairy.' Once I heard someone say, 'She should have been abandoned on the mountainside as a baby!'

Everywhere I went, I carried the burden of the stares of strangers. A woman came one day with a sick baby, hoping Brid could help.

I was sorry for the little girl and held her tiny hand while Brid mixed up some salve for her. The next day, the hot red blisters were gone, and the mother told everyone it had been my touch that had healed her child. After that, many people came, wanting me to put my hands on them. They thrust little gifts into my hands, or under my door. Sometimes people would rush up to me, grabbing my hand and pressing it to some weeping sore on their bodies. I had always hated leaving home, but after that I began to dread it with every particle of my body. The very thought made me sick.

Even at home I was not safe. My sisters pinched me, or mocked me by snatching away my doll and holding it above my head so I could not reach it. They called me a mealybug and a termite, and stamped on my pretend gardens. One day, after I was given a golden coin, Alektrona said with a cruel twist to her mouth, 'You know they sacrificed a white boy just like you? They buried him alive under the marketplace.'

Again there was that whirling sensation, as if I was falling. A boy, spectral-white, stumbling as he was dragged along by a crowd of people chanting to the gods. He fell, twitching as if struck by lightning. They dropped him into a pit, and heaved a stone across. I descended into the hole with him. I heard the thudding of his flailing limbs against the rock, his scream.

Think of someone else, think of someone else.

Cesar, Cesar.

Spinning, swirling, spiralling.

My baby nephew lay in my sister's arms, his screwed-up face crimson, his little fists flailing. He wore nothing but a filthy nappy. Khrysanthe crouched on the floor, rocking back and forth, her hair a matted mess, a torn robe falling off her bare shoulder, muttering, 'Shut up, shut up, shut up, shut up.' A loud knock interrupted her. She looked up, fear stark on her face, then laid the screaming baby down so she could open the door. A heavy-set man stood outside, dressed in a bloodstained tunic and a thick belt. He pushed Khrysanthe into the room, kicking the door shut behind him. She cringed away, hands held out in appeal, but he only laughed and thrust her back against the wall.

I exclaimed in alarm and flung out my hands, striking the scrying bowl and rocking it. Water spilt, and the awful vision dissolved. With shaking fingers I steadied the bowl. *Where is she?* I thought. *Why is she alone? She needs help. Where's Alektrona?*

Again, I spoke the words of the spell, and again the water spun. I saw my elder sister plodding along a dark road, a lantern in one hand. Behind her were the lights of a town. Ahead, the humped shapes of beehive tombs. I recognised the place. Graveyard Street, in Tarchna, our childhood town. It was where the poorest and most wretched whores plied their trade. I could see them in the shadows, dressed in rags, sores clustered in the corner of their lips. Some came forward to accost Alektrona. Hopefully, she asked them all, 'Do you know a girl named Fatima?' When they shook their heads, she moved on, shoulders slumped.

Some of the whores followed her, exchanging laughing looks. One seized her about the throat, the others roughly stripped her of her coin purse, her gilded sandals, her necklaces and earrings. Alektrona struggled but they slapped and punched her. She fell to her knees. They kicked her and tore her fine woollen cloak from her shoulders. She curled into a ball, trying to protect her face. Blood trickled from her nose.

I could scarcely breathe, my emotions in turmoil. *What has happened while I've been gone?* I cried silently. *How can my family be in such danger?*

The vision shifted and swirled. I saw a struggling crowd of men in the Forum, the royal palace burning, smoke staining the sky brown.

Lucius with a bloody sword in his hand, fighting his way through, Khrysanthe following close behind, eyes wide with terror, clutching her baby son. A vicious sword thrust, and Lucius staggered and fell. Khrysanthe screamed, and tried to run to him, but his body was trampled under the feet of the fighters. The man who had killed Lucius hustled her away. She was taken to her husband, examining a long scroll in a room full of sober-faced men. Brutus glanced at her, said indifferently, 'I hereby divorce you,' and returned his attention to his scroll.

Khrysanthe sobbed. 'But, my lord, what am I meant to do, where am I meant to go?'

He shrugged. 'That is not my concern anymore. Go back to your father or find a new lover. I want no association with those of Tarquin blood.'

'But I don't know where my father is!' Khrysanthe cried.

'I imagine he is with the rest of our enemies, plotting against us. You may take him a message from me. The Roman kingdom is no more. The people of Roma are free now of tyranny and there will never again be a king in our land. Now leave. I do not wish to see your lying, faithless face again.'

'But, my lord . . . Brutus . . .'

He jerked his head, and his servant manhandled Khrysanthe from the room. The door was shut in her face, and she was left weeping outside, jostled by the angry mob, her baby son screaming in her arms.

'How could he?' I cried. 'The pig!'

Hot impotent rage seethed inside me. Where was our father? *Did he not care what happened to us?* The vision in the bowl quivered and dissolved. I saw my father, lying on a dishevelled bed, his head wrapped in bloody bandages, one arm in a makeshift sling, a sheen of sweat on his face. He looked deathly ill.

I jumped up, sending the table rocking and water slopping everywhere. I had to go, I had to do something. But what? How?

'Help me,' I said through stiff lips, hardly knowing to whom I was calling.

The lamplight glimmered on the puddle of water lying on the table. A face formed within. An old, old face with a thousand wrinkles and a frizzy aureole of white hair. Fathomless black eyes looked directly into mine.

'Nocturna,' I whispered.

She stood before the gate of the old watchtower, Nera by her side. In her hand was the heavy iron key. She bent painfully, lifted up one of the stones of the gateway, and slid the key beneath. The stone fell back neatly into place, hiding the key from sight.

Then she looked at me again and drew a spiralling shape with one finger. The vision in the water swirled away, and I was alone again.

IV

Return to Velzna

I knew what I had to do.

'Tell him I've gone to help my family – they need me,' I told the air, and then I threw a few things into a satchel. My obsidian knife, the scrying bowl, my leather water bottle, the bread rolls put out for my breakfast, some clean linen. I caught up the ermine cloak, drew its hood over my pale hair, and set out through the garden gate, locking it securely behind me.

I was tired after my long night, and so I went slowly. It was a cold blustery day, and brown linden leaves blew against me. I noticed the larches were tipped with gold. The season was turning towards autumn – I must have been at the castle for weeks. I had not kept count of the days.

I did my best to stay within the shadows of the trees, to move quietly and surreptitiously, for I could not forget how the Raven's men had risen out of the undergrowth, spears to our throats. At last I reached the lake. I crept forward and knelt, filling my water bottle to the brim. Then, hidden by the tall straight trunks of fir trees, I turned my ring three times, saying huskily, 'Take me to the old watchtower.'

An odd sensation, as if I was the still hub of a great spinning wheel. Then the world steadied around me, and I was standing outside the heavy oaken gate in the wall, the gorgon face glaring down at me. I bent, and lifted the stone. The key lay in a small cavity carved specially to fit it. I used it to unlock the gate, and stepped once more into my garden.

I had hoped, against all reason, that Nera would come bounding towards me, barking joyously, Nocturna hobbling after, calling my name in welcome. But the garden was wild and overgrown, great hoops of briars once again clawing at the sky. I had to make my way carefully, stopping often to unsnag my cloak. Anger was growing inside me. My father had lied to me – he had told me the watch-tower had been sold. He must have kept it, wanting the secret way into Velzna in case of need. He cared nothing for my misery and homesickness, cared nothing for the garden, once so productive and beneficial, cared nothing for the many people we had once helped. He cared only for himself.

Nettles overran the kitchen garden, but there were still a few brave herbs struggling underneath. I drew some water, lit a fire, made myself a hot tisane and tried to make plans. I would go to Roma first, for Cesar was only a baby. He would die if not cared for. When he and Khrysanthe were safe, I would go to Tarchna. I would find Alektrona and see what I could do to help her, and I would seek news of my father. The king and queen would most probably have taken refuge there since it was their ancestral home. Someone in their court must know where he was.

I would need money. A woman could not travel through the war-torn land by herself. I'd need a horse, guards, supplies. I looked through the house and garden in a kind of numb despair. All our provisions had been taken by my father, and there was not a crumb left in the pantry. My chickens and bees were long gone, and the garden was a tangle of weeds. The orchard, at least, had some fruit, but I could not live on plums alone. And there was so much work to do before I could begin earning again. It would take me some time to harvest what was left, and to start making salves and tinctures. And I felt so very tired, as if I had run all the way from the mountains rather than being transported by magic.

I dressed myself in old clothes, tied up my hair in a scarf, and got to work. That night I was so sore and worn out I could not climb the ladder to my old bedroom. I made up a rough bed by the fire in the hall and ate one of the bread rolls, crumbling a portion of it onto the hearth stone in silent thanks for the household spirits.

I woke at cockcrow, dragging up my aching body to begin again. There was nothing to eat but the last of the rolls I had brought from the castle. I tossed some more crumbs down for the ants, smiling a little at the memory of how I'd teased Ambrose about being waited on hand and foot. Every thought, every action, led back to him somehow. I missed the touch of his hand, the feel of his skin against mine, his clean male scent. I hungered for his kiss. Was he missing me as much as I missed him? It seemed impossible. I had to harden my heart, focus on what I had to do to help my sisters.

I was hungry too. I had no money to buy supplies, nothing of value but my golden ring, my scrying bowl and my obsidian knife, and they were worth too much to me to sell. I made nettle soup and dandelion salad, foraged for wild mushrooms and blackberries, and drank endless cups of lemon balm tea.

Nine days later, when the market was held in the town square, I had a little pile of produce to sell - wreaths of rosehips and ivy flowers, posies of harebells and wild clematis, bottles of elderberry syrup, baskets of sweet chestnuts gathered from the forest. I loaded up the handcart and trundled it through the cobbled streets of the town to the marketplace. The whole way I had a strange sense of dislocation. Everything was the same, and yet I was not. I was irreversibly changed, a child no longer. I had cradled an unborn babe in my hand, I had thought I was about to die, I had felt the rapture of utter surrender to desire. It was the time of the autumn equinox, the month when the world once again tipped towards winter and darkness. Soon I would be twenty.

In the main square, many people recognised me and stopped to ask me where I had been and what had happened since I had been gone. I answered as briefly as I could, and turned the subject by asking them for news. There had been plots and counterplots, I heard. The king had attempted to regain the throne by force, and then by stealth. Brutus had gradually taken more and more power into his own hands, until he was nearly as much of a tyrant as his uncle had been. He had even ordered his own sons to be executed when they defied him.

'What of the king?' I asked.

'He is in Tarchna,' they told me, 'trying to raise an army strong enough to defeat the might of Roma.'

'His sons?'

'Prince Sextus is dead. He fled to Gabii, hoping to raise support there, but the town remembered his reign of terror and he was stabbed in the street one night.'

I reeled with surprise and relief. Alektrona was free. And surely she was her husband's heir? I added researching Roma's inheritance and divorce laws to my ever-growing list of things to do.

Two weeks later, I rode for Roma. I was tempted to transport myself with the magic of the ring, but I knew I could only use it three times. I had already used it once. It would be best to save the spell for when I was in dire need.

It seemed ironical, returning to the city I dreaded and from which I had escaped. I found lodgings in a rough but clean inn near the Forum. I needed to wait until the next dark phase of the moon before I could look in the scrying bowl again, so I spent the next few days looking for my sister and trying to find out what had happened while I had been gone. Nothing was left of the royal palace but piles of rubble and a few charred timbers, though the Forum seethed night and day with activity as messengers came and went, and the great families of Roma vied with each other to gain power in the void left by the fall of the king.

I went back to my father's villa, but the place had been ransacked, Brutus having ordered the seizure of all of the Tarquin family's possessions. Only a few of my scrolls remained, the oldest and most tattered. I took them with me, and hunted through the markets for more. Once I had wanted books about gardens and healing. Now I wanted to find out everything there was to know about the gods.

Roma was very different under the rule of Brutus. He had dropped all pretense of amiable foolishness, and ruled with cold efficiency. Soldiers marched everywhere, the pound of their sandalled feet echoing off the stone walls. Men wore their hair cropped short, and shaved twice a day. Women kept to their homes, and vied with each other to prove their modesty and chastity. Lucretia was extolled as the perfect Roman wife, preferring to die than be shamed. I needed a guard to accompany me everywhere I went. He reminded me of Lucius, and I felt again a deep pang of grief.

I hated being back in the city. The noise and the crowds were hard to bear after my long months spent in virtual solitude, and the smell made me retch. I made myself a small bag filled with fragrant herbs and kept it pressed to my nose, but I felt faintly nauseous all the time.

On the night of the dark moon, I poured a measure of lake water into the silver bowl, lit an oil lamp and gazed within, forcing my mind to stay focused on Khrysanthe. I saw her sleeping in a nest of rags with her son, cooking a meagre meal over a smoky fire, tossing the contents of a chamber-pot out a window with broken shutters, gnawing on a heel of dark bread to soften it for Cesar, laughing as he pulled himself up to stand. She could have been in any poor hovel anywhere in the world. I needed more clues. So I listened carefully. During my time in Roma I had visited many different parts of the city, as I had done my best to help the sick and the poor. Each quarter had its own distinctive soundscape.

The crow of roosters, and the bellow of cattle being taken to the slaughter. The rumble of carts on the road, the clang of a temple bell, hawkers calling out their wares. Any district of Roma had such sounds. I had to listen harder. I noticed the babble of many different languages. Somewhere outside Roma, then, or perhaps the area around the river dock where many foreigners lived.

The slap of oars in water. So she was somewhere near the river, perhaps near the docks. Then I heard it. The distinctive rattle of iron wheels on a wooden bridge. She was near the Bridge of Stilts.

I wanted to go to her straightaway, but it was too dangerous to venture out into the streets of the city at night. I forced myself to lie down and try to get some sleep. As soon as dawn came, I summoned my guard and set out for the bridge. I asked everyone I met if they had seen her, but there were too many young women with brown curls and babes in their arms. All day I wandered the streets, till I was footsore and weary.

As dusk came on, I saw a heavyset man trudging along, a bloody haunch of meat on his shoulder. He wore a belt as thick as the width of my hand around his ample waist. I went as close as I dared, needing to see his face. I was almost sure he was the man I had seen in the first vision of my sister. I followed him through a maze of narrow, crooked alleyways to a sprawling tenement in which dozens of people lived, each occupying one small room reached by rickety wooden staircases from the street. He went into one of the rooms on the lower floor. I stood in a doorway opposite, my cloak drawn close about my face, and examined the building carefully. On the highest floor, there was one window with broken shutters.

I climbed the staircase and knocked on the door, calling, 'Khrysanthe, Khrysanthe!'

My sister opened it, mouth open in astonishment. 'Psykhe!'

Then she fell into my arms, weeping.

I sat with Cesar cradled on my lap, hardly able to believe how big he had grown. His dark hair was a riot of curls, his grey eyes full of wonder as he stared at me, one hand grabbing at my long plait.

'The first thing we are going to do when we get home is give you a bath,' I told him. 'You stink!'

'So do I,' Khrysanthe sighed, gathering together her few belongings. 'Oh, Psykhe, I can't believe you are here. How did you find me? What happened to the dragon? How did you escape? And where did you get that divine gown?'

'It's a long story,' I answered. 'Plenty of time for that once we get you home safe.'

'But where's home?' she asked like a piteous child. 'I've lost everything, Psykhe. Everything. Even the jewels Lucius gave me!' She began to weep again. 'I had to pawn them to pay the rent. And I got practically nothing for them! The landlord is a pig! Oh, Psykhe, what am I going to do? He says I owe him so much money.'

'Don't worry, I'll pay him.'

She brightened. 'You have money? How much? Can we go and get my jewels back?'

But after I had paid the surly landlord, I had barely enough money to get us all back to Velzna. The journey was slow and difficult, for it rained without cessation and the road was a quagmire. Cesar cried and struggled, arching his back and trying to throw himself out of my arms. He wanted to crawl.

'We'd probably get along faster if we all crawled,' Khrysanthe complained, standing by the roadside, shivering in her old cloak, while our carriage was dug out of the mud once again. 'Can't we find a nice dry inn to stay in, Psykhe? I'm soaked to the skin.'

But I did not want to wait. I had to see Khrysanthe and Cesar safe, I had to find Alektrona, I had to make sure their futures were secure. Because only then could I go home. Home to Ambrose.

At last we were back in Velzna. Khrysanthe had a kind of nervous collapse and took to her bed. I found her crying under her blankets. Lucius had been murdered in front of her, I remembered, and her husband had spurned her and cast her out in the street. She had endured a great deal. I let her rest and kept Cesar with me while I worked.

Somehow I had to raise enough funds to go in search of Alektrona and to make sure Khrysanthe and Cesar survived the winter. It was now mid-autumn and the grapevines were scarlet against the golden fields. It was the time of the Armilustrium when soldiers' weapons were ritually purified and stored for the winter. Garlanded with flowers, the town's battalion marched through the streets to the sound of drums and trumpets. Few flowers were left in the garden, so I went to the forest early and gathered wild clematis and ivy flowers, and wove as many wreaths as I could. I foraged for berries, sweet chestnuts and mushrooms, and made cough tinctures from elderberries.

My work was not made easier by Cesar, who was now able to crawl at an astonishing rate and was always reaching up to pull things down on his head. He was a bright, curious boy, and loved to bang metal cups together and play peek-a-boo. It gave me a curious pain around my heart to sit with him on my lap at the end of the day, telling him stories as he sleepily sucked his thumb. It was hard, sometimes, to give him back to Khrysanthe.

I could not leave her when she was in such low spirits. I made her soup and lemon balm tea and, after a week or so, she began to recover. She rose from her bed and sat by the fire, wrapped in a shawl, rolling a ball to Cesar or playing clapping games with him. As her interest in the outside world revived, so too did her questions. I found it harder and harder to avoid answering them. I wished I could just tell her the truth, but Ambrose had made me promise not to tell anyone about us.

I realised I had a great many secrets.

V

Dancing Girls

Damp mists hung over the marshes. The hill town of Tarchna slowly rose ahead of me, huddled inside its stone walls, the grey sea beyond almost indistinguishable from the wetlands. I had been riding for almost a week, and was stiff and cold and aching in every muscle. I thought longingly of a hot meal and a warm bed, but knew I could not afford such luxuries. Most of the money I had raised had been left with Khrysanthe, the rest paying the hard-faced guards who rode with me. I could have stayed, tried to raise more, but I could not face any more questioning from my sister. Besides, Alektrona needed me.

Sullen and orange, the sun sank into the water. A flock of gulls swooped overhead, shrieking. The wind smelt of salt and swamp. I shivered. I did not like being so close to the sea.

'We should pick up the pace,' the leader of the guards said. 'Night closing in, and a sea fog rising by the looks of things.'

I nodded and kicked my tired horse into a canter. The fog was faster, though. It rolled over us, cold and dank, till we rode in a strange kind of twilight. The sun was nothing but a red smear. Then it disappeared, its light unable to pierce the thickening mist.

'Stop!' I called to the men. 'We can't canter in this. We'll lose the road and get lost. We could stumble into the quagmire and be dragged down.'

I dismounted and ordered my guards to stay close. Then I led them forward, feeling my way with a long stick. Again and again my foot slipped into squelching mud. I could see nothing but vague shadows. The town seemed to have disappeared. Water was sliding over the road and my hem grew damp and heavy.

'We've lost our way – we're on the beach!' the guard said. 'I can hear the surf.'

I could hear it too. A wave crashed on the rocky edge of the road. I was splashed to the knee.

It's the goddess, I thought. *She knows I'm here. I have come too close to her territory. She's bringing in the sea to drown me.*

'Hurry!' I cried. 'But take care not to stray off the road.'

We stumbled forward, the horses shying and fighting the rein, water swirling about their hocks. Solid ground shifted under my feet. I almost fell but grabbed at my horse's bridle to steady myself.

An eerie greenish light rose to our right, floating like a lantern carried by invisible hands.

'That way!' one of the guards shouted. 'I can see a light!'

'It's an illusion,' I called back. 'Don't follow it. Stick to the road.'

The swampy smell grew, till I was close to retching. There was cold water up to my knees, up to my thighs, up to my hips, the current threatening to drag me away.

Hekate, shine your torch, show me the way, I prayed.

The mist swirled and parted. To our left, warm lights glowed fuzzily through the fog. I veered that way, clinging to my horse's bridle. The ground grew firmer under my feet, the road began to tilt, the marshes fell away. I struggled on till I could see the road rising before me. Then I dragged myself up onto my horse's back again. 'Come on! This way!'

Our small party began to gallop up the road. The sea sucked back, back, back, then surged forward again in a great cresting wave. Unnaturally high it rose, then crashed down on our backs. A welter of freezing dark water all about us, sea spray in my mouth, in my eyes.

I urged my horse on. We raced up the road. The town wardens were dragging the gate shut. 'Wait!' I cried. 'Please!'

My horse had her neck stretched out, foam flying from her muzzle, her eyes rolling white. Her hooves pounded the earthen track. The wardens paused, peering into the darkness. 'Wait!' I panted.

We pelted the last few feet, clods of mud flying behind us, while the sea sucked back, paused, flexed, then rushed in once more. I heard the thunder of it behind me. I crouched lower, and my valiant mare leapt through the gateway. My guards were only seconds behind. The wardens slammed the gate shut, and drove the bolt home with a single blow of the immense hammer. The wave crashed against it. The heavy oak took the shock, shuddered, held firm. Foam rushed through the gap beneath, clawed at our horses' hooves, then slid away in a rush of white bubbles.

Our horses stood, shivering, chests heaving, in puddles that gleamed with the gold of the wardens' torches.

'Never,' one said, 'have I ever seen the sea come so high.'

'Never,' his companion echoed.

'The lady of the sea is upset about something,' the first said with a sideways look at me.

The second warden nodded and grunted in agreement.

'Thank you,' I said shakily, and paid them both the last coins in my purse.

I was wet, exhausted, badly shaken, and penniless. With an effort I straightened my spine and lifted my chin. 'Would you be so kind,' I said, 'as to direct me to the residence of the king?'

The wardens gazed at me in amazement, bowed low and pointed out the way.

I inclined my head graciously, then rode towards the main square. My guards fell into place at my back.

The streets were full of the king's soldiers, many of them drunk and rowdy. They all turned to stare at me as I rode past, and muttered to each other. I ignored them. I had too much else to worry about. I did not even know how to begin looking for Alektrona. I needed money, a place to stay, advice on divorce and inheritance laws. My father was here somewhere, and I dreaded seeing him. And I was shaken and terrified by the rising of the waves. Venus, goddess born of seafoam, knew I was here.

I did not want to appear at the royal court wet and bedraggled and shivering with cold, but I had no choice. I had nowhere else to go.

A sweet warble of music. I jerked around.

A robin sat on a bare branch hanging over a wall. It cocked its head, warbled again, then flew a few paces down a side alley. I turned my horse's head and followed it.

The little bird led me to a small inn, scrupulously clean, with a kind-faced woman who took one look at my bedraggled state and came rushing out with a warm blanket. 'Soup!' she yelled over her shoulder. 'Hot water! Mulled wine! And be quick about it.'

'I have no money,' I said faintly. 'At least, not now. Tomorrow, I hope.'

'Then pay me tomorrow. Vesta's flame, what happened to you? Did you fall overboard?'

I smiled faintly and shook my head. Making clucking noises, she ushered me in to the inn while a boy led the exhausted horses to the stables and a dimpled serving-maid brought the guards a mug of spiced wine warmed with a hot poker.

All night I dreamt the sea was rising through the town, cascading along the laneways, seeping in under my door. I woke with a jerk. The light was grey, and outside a robin was singing. I sighed, rolled over, closed my eyes and slept again.

I woke mid-morning, feeling well rested and better able to tackle the problems that lay before me. I rose, washed, dressed in my freshly laundered clothes and went down to a lavish breakfast of new baked bread and cherry jam. The innkeeper was full of curiosity about the tidal wave that had almost swept us out to sea. She told me seaweed had been found draped on the town gate, and that half the road had been washed away. 'It'll take a while to fix,' she said cheerfully, 'so you're stuck here in the meantime.'

My heart sank. 'May I stay here? I will arrange payment for you today.'

'Of course,' she answered. 'I know you'll not cheat me. I remember you from when you were a little girl. You held my daughter's hand when she was sick and helped make her better. I'm glad to have a chance to help you now, and say thank you.'

I smiled and nodded, feeling a little teary. I had not expected anyone in Tarchna to remember me so kindly.

Taking just one guard, I walked towards the Forum. The king's palace was just across the square from the villa where I had grown up. Seeing it brought back so many memories. Mostly sad. I wondered who lived there now, and if it was haunted by the ghosts of Brid and my mother.

The guards at the door remembered me as the healer who had saved the king, and so sent a message to his son, Prince Arruns, who allowed me to meet with him. He wore a black mantle in honour of his dead brother, but his boots were red. He told me my father had been injured by a spear thrust to the belly, and that he was not expected to live.

'May I see him?' I asked.

Arruns nodded and shrugged and gestured to a slave to show me the way to the stables which had been turned into a makeshift hospital. 'You must realise we have had many wounded,' he said as a way of apology.

Dozens of men lay on straw pallets on the cold ground, one harassed-looking slave doing his best to tend their wounds. It took me a long while to find my father among the crowd. A festering bandage was wrapped about his abdomen. The smell of it made me sick. I had to force myself to go close enough to unwind the linen bindings and check the wound. My father did not recognise me or respond to my voice, but moved his head fretfully on the pillow, plucking at himself with skeletal fingers.

This, I thought contemptuously, was his payment for his loyalty to the king.

I had my father moved to a clean bed in a clean room, gave him a cool tisane of thyme and feverfew to drink, and cleaned out his suppurating wound. A poultice of marigold would hopefully help with the infection. The prince's slave agreed to watch over him, sponging his face and hands and trickling more tisane into his mouth. It troubled me to leave the wounded men, but I needed to find Alektrona and there was nothing more I could do for them just now.

Prince Arruns arranged some funds for me, perhaps because he was ashamed at the poor treatment my father had received. I was able to pay the innkeeper for her kindness and restock my basket of herbs. I also bought a little posy of late-blooming violets to lay on the stone above the bones of the white-haired boy who had been buried alive there. I knew all too well his terror and pain.

When it was dark, I went out into the courtyard to look up at the night sky and check the phase of the moon. She was dwindling fast.

225

Soon I would be able to look in the scrying bowl again. Till then I would have to use my wits, instead of magic.

I guessed that Alektrona had come to Tarchna to search for Fatima. When the slave girl had been freed, she had said that she was going to try and find her mother Nasrin, who had been sold by my father before we left for Velzna. I summoned my guard, and wearily set out for the slave dealer's quarters. I knew only a little about the slave trade, just that most were sold at public auction and that the dealer had to issue a warrant which was hung about the slave's neck. It was my hope that the dealer had kept his records.

He lived in a vast villa on the eastern slope of the hill, and received me in his opulent receiving room with an obsequious air. 'The daughter of Lord Cassius is always welcome,' he said. 'Please, have some wine, some candied figs. What can I do for you?'

'I am trying to track down a slave you sold on behalf of my father eight years ago,' I began. I expected him to prevaricate and make excuses, to protest it was impossible for him to know what had happened to Nasrin, but instead he heaved a weary sigh.

'Another one of you? Why is this slave so important? Does she know the secret hiding place of some treasure trove?'

'Others have come looking for her?'

'Yes, yes, first the former slave girl, the dancing girl given her liberty, and then another daughter of Lord Cassius, one of your sisters. Both asking after her, both insisting I dig through my records. Luckily for you, I remembered her, a tasty morsel she was, despite getting rather long in the tooth.'

'So you know where she is?'

'I know where she was. I sold her last year to her daughter, the dancing girl.'

I was startled. 'Fatima bought her? But how?'

226

'That I do not know. Former slaves do not usually come to me with bags of money demanding to buy other slaves – it is most unusual. That is why I remember them.'

'Do you know where they are now?'

'Why would I know that? I have no interest in my stock once it is sold. Is there anything else I can help you with, my lady? I have two pretty boys that would make a striking addition to your household, being almost perfectly matched. Or a good strong barbarian that would make you a fine bodyguard, better than that lanky youth.' He waved one pudgy hand at my guard, standing against the wall and staring stolidly ahead, trying to pretend he was not listening.

'No. I have no need of slaves.' I rose, trying to express my contempt and dislike by my coldness of voice and stiffness of demeanour, but he did not notice, only gesturing for me to be shown out. I walked back to the king's villa, thinking over all I had learned. I was no closer to finding Alektrona, but I was very glad to know that Fatima had found her mother and been able to buy her freedom. I wondered how she had found the money. Slaves did not come cheaply.

I looked in on my father, and then went back to the inn to sleep. I thought of Ambrose, as I did every night when the darkness closed over my bed. Where was he? What was he doing? Did he understand why I had to leave? Was he upset with me? I remembered the robin that had led me to the kind innkeeper, and was comforted.

The next two weeks were spent tending my father, who was agitated and delirious. Any spare moment I had was spent looking for Alektrona. I walked along Graveyard Street, my guard at my back, I visited every inn and every theatre, and I asked everyone I met to pass along a message to my sister. Every night I went out into the garden and looked up at the night sky, watching the moon dwindle. At last it was the night of the dark moon again. I had just enough lake water left in my leather bottle to fill the scrying bowl. Lighting my lamp, I gazed down into its glimmering surface and spoke the spell. 'Where are you, Alektrona?' I whispered. 'Show yourself to me.'

A room of men, lying at their ease on couches, were drinking wine, smoking opium pipes and choosing tidbits from trays offered by near-naked slaves. Musicians played double flutes, lyres and tambourines, and a woman danced in the centre of the room, dressed in crimson gauze. Her black hair was cut in a straight fringe across her forehead. My heartbeat accelerated. It was Fatima.

Another woman stepped out of the shadows and began a slow sensuous dance around the first. She was dressed in men's clothing, fitted carefully to show her slight feminine curves. Her hair had been cut short like a man's too. Even so, I recognised her at once. It was my sister. Together Fatima and Alektrona danced like lovers might, swaying and turning in each other's arms, eyes fixed on each other.

A singer sang a haunting song of love and longing. It told the story of Iphis, born a girl but raised a boy after her father had threatened to put any daughter of his to death. Iphis was in love with the beautiful Ianthe, and yearned to be a man so they might marry. The singer – dressed as the goddess Isis in cloth-of-silver with a crescent moon on her brow – took pity on the lovers. She transformed Iphis into a man. At once Alektrona's manner changed. She began to leap high into the air, seizing Fatima and spinning her around, bending her back over her arm. The dance ended when she lowered Fatima to the floor in a simulacrum of the love act, lying between her thighs and pressing her lips to her breast.

The men clapped and cheered. Fatima and Alektrona rose and bowed, flushed and laughing. The musicians began another tune, and two handsome boys carried around more food. They were almost identical in height and colouring, and wore little but loincloths and jewels. Their eyelids had been painted gold. I wondered if they were twins.

Where are you, Alektrona? I asked silently. *Give me a clue.*

Then I saw a fresco on the wall. It showed a banquet, with naked men and women reclining on couches, eating grapes and drinking wine. I recognised it. For a moment I could not remember where I had seen it before, then suddenly it clicked into place. It was painted on the wall of the slave dealer's receiving room. At once I recognised other details. The red silk couch piled with cushions. A tall urn with black figures of dancers. And the slave dealer himself, half-obscured behind clouds of smoke billowing from his opium pipe.

Anger blazed up in me. He had lied. He had known where Fatima and Alektrona were all that time. I got up, pacing back and forth, thinking. Perhaps Fatima had gone into debt bondage to secure her mother's release? If so, she would have to work for the slave dealer till he deemed the debt cleared. That could take a lifetime. Alektrona could be helping her clear the debt, which meant she was in bondage too.

One thing was clear. I would need a lot of money.

The next day I went again to see Prince Arruns, and offered him my services to tend his father's wounded army. For men who lay suffering and dying in his stables were not men who could fight on his behalf. 'I will need to be paid in advance,' I said.

He smiled thinly and gave me a heavy bag of coins. I could not stop the grin spreading across my face. Now I could pay the slave dealer and bring the rest of my family home.

VI

To See and Be Seen

'Alektrona,' I whispered from the shadows.

My sister half-turned towards me, then recoiled with a shriek.

I shushed her hurriedly. I wanted no-one who might be spying on me to know I had found her. Alektrona backed away. Even in the ill-lit street I could see the expression of terror on her face.

'It's me,' I said, not understanding her fear.

'Psykhe? You're . . . you're alive?'

At once I understood. She had thought me a ghost. I stepped a little closer, putting back the hood. 'Yes. I'm alive. I escaped the dragon. I've been looking everywhere for you.'

She put one hand to her heart. 'You almost killed me! What are you doing here?'

'Looking for you,' I repeated. 'Can we go inside? I don't want anyone to know I'm here.'

Fatima had been standing stock still, her hands held out in a gesture that was half surprise, half rebuff. She took a deep breath now, and put her hand in a pocket to withdraw a key. 'Come in,' she said in a voice that was not quite steady, and unlocked a door set into the wall behind her.

Within was a small room, furnished only with a few old sticks of furniture. It was warm and cosy, though, and filled with the comforting smell of soup. Nasrin was stirring a pot on the fire, dressed in an old, patched gown, with a shawl wrapped about her shoulders. She looked much older than I remembered, with deep lines on her face and swollen, crooked hands. Life must have been hard for her these past seven years. She stared at me in astonishment, then gave a broad, gap-toothed smile. 'Why, it's little Psykhe grown into a woman! And such a beautiful one!'

'We thought she was a ghost,' Alektrona said, unwinding the scarf from her hair and hanging it from a hook. Fatima locked the door behind her, and pushed home a bolt. I understood her precaution. Their tiny home was in the poorest, roughest sector of Tarchna, a place where rats rummaged in the rubbish left in piles in the corners.

'Come, sit,' Nasrin said, drawing out a low stool for me. 'Fatima, take her cloak.'

Her daughter obeyed her, still with that wary expression on her face. I sat down, and held my cold hands to the fire. Alektrona sat down too, frowning at me. 'I cannot believe you are here! How did you escape the dragon? And how did you find me?'

'I knew you'd come in search of Fatima,' I said, smiling at her. 'I'm so happy to have found you at last.'

'And I'm happy you are alive! I can't quite believe it. But how?'

'It's a long story,' I answered. 'I'll tell you another time. What's important is that I've come to take you home.'

'Home? What do you mean?' Alektrona waved at the dark little room. 'This is home now.'

'I've paid off the slave dealer,' I said eagerly. 'You aren't in debt bondage anymore. And Father never sold the house in Velzna. Khrysanthe and Cesar are there now, safe and sound.'

'Khrysanthe!' Alektrona exclaimed in astonishment. 'But she escaped Roma with Lucius, didn't she?'

I shook my head. 'Lucius was killed by one of Brutus's men, and then he had Khrysanthe and her baby thrown into the street. They were destitute.'

'The bastard! Minerva's spear, I never liked him. I knew he was not such a fool as he pretended to be, but I never guessed he could be that ruthless. What did Khrysanthe do? How did she escape the war?'

Quickly, I explained all that had happened. Alektrona pestered me with questions that I did my best to answer.

'What of Father?' she asked eventually. 'Does he know I am here too?'

I shook my head. 'No. He was sorely wounded. He's at the palace. I think it'll be a slow recovery for him.'

'You saved his life?' Her voice was hard.

'I couldn't just let him die.'

She turned away, shrugging one thin shoulder. 'Why not? He left us to rot in Roma. Rode off with the king without even a backward glance. I was lucky to escape with my life.'

'I'm so glad you did,' I said softly, 'and glad to have found you. I've been searching for months.'

At that she embraced me fiercely. 'I'm sorry. I was just surprised. I thought you . . . I thought you must be dead.'

'So you'll come home to Velzna?' I was puzzled that she was not as happy and excited as I had expected her to be.

'It's just . . . well, we've made a life for ourselves here. On our own terms. We're happy.'

'Couldn't you be happy in Velzna too?'

'What do you think?' Alektrona looked to Fatima, who was crouched on the far side of the fire, rolling flatbread.

'We will not make such good money dancing in Velzna, where there are no drunken sailors to fill our purses,' Fatima replied, not looking at me. 'How will we earn enough to pay your sister back?'

'You don't need to pay me back!' It had not occurred to me that Fatima would consider her debt had been transferred to me. I jumped up in my agitation. 'You are like a sister to me. I could not know you were in trouble and not help you. When I think what my father did to you . . . please, Fatima! You owe me nothing.'

She looked up at me. 'What of my mother?'

'Nasrin is welcome in Velzna too. There is plenty of room there. She can help Khrysanthe with the baby. The garden is there. You can grow most of your own food and sell the rest at the market, or I could teach you to make wreaths like I used to . . .'

'You would not be there to do it?' Alektrona interrupted.

I did not know how to answer. I had promised Ambrose to tell nobody about us, but it was very difficult to keep sidestepping my sisters' questions. I made some vague answer, and redoubled my efforts to persuade them to return to Velzna. At last, Alektrona and Fatima agreed, but only if I allowed them to repay the money I had given to the slave dealer.

'I am a free woman now,' Fatima said proudly. 'I don't wish to owe anybody anything.'

The next day I set to work setting up the hospital for the wounded soldiers.

I soon had the stables scrubbed out and properly organised, and simple wooden beds made so that the soldiers were not lying on the cold floor. Nasrin came to work with me, and I taught her how to grind herbs and distil their essences to make simple remedies. She showed such aptitude I had hope that she would be able to help the people of Velzna as Nocturna and I had once done. Every evening as I came home, worn out and footsore, Alektrona and Fatima went out to dance for the sailors and merchants. When I woke in the mornings, it was to find the lumps of bronze and silver they had earned in a neat pile beside my bed.

My father slowly recovered, though he was not pleased to see me. I simply told him that I had escaped the dragon, and he was too weak to do much more than frown, move his head fretfully on the pillow and tell me the gods would be displeased.

'Then sacrifice yourself instead,' I said, and turned to go. I hoped never to have to see him again.

My biggest problem now was how to leave Tarchna without drawing any attention to myself. There was only one road into the walled town, freshly repaired after the tidal wave that had almost drowned me. Seagulls flew above it every day, while pigeons and sparrows darted about everywhere in the square before the gate. They were all birds sacred to Venus, and so, I suspected, her spies. Or perhaps Venus was watching me through the round hand-mirror that she was always depicted holding in paintings. It made me feel fearful all the time, imagining I was being watched. I swathed myself in a heavy cloak, kept my hood pulled over my head, and bought gloves to hide my hands.

It was the month with no name, and growing colder every day. Once again the moon was pared away to nothing. I was tempted to look for Ambrose in my scrying bowl. I missed him so much. I had been away much longer than I had ever expected. I longed to see where he was, what he was doing, whether he missed me. One part of me feared he would have found another lover by now, another rejected that thought fiercely. He loved me, I told myself. He would wait for me.

One day I was leaning over the back fence, scratching the back of the piglet kept penned there. The inn's serving-maid came out carrying a bucket of scraps. As she threw them over the fence, she said, 'He's sweet, isn't he? Such a shame he's for the knife next week. Though we can't have the Saturnalia feast without roast pork!'

At once I knew what to do.

On the night of the Saturnalia, everything was turned topsy-turvy.

Men dressed as women and women as men. Slaves wore silks and jewels and their masters served them with bended knees. Musicians played their instruments upside down or back to front. People sang and danced and played leapfrog, dressed as gods or beasts or birds.

I had bought us all disguises too, our faces hidden behind masks. All night we feasted and danced, like everyone else. At midnight, when the masks were meant to be removed and the rightful order restored, we slipped out the portal gate and along to the city of the dead, where hired horses were tethered in the shadow of the tombs. We left our masks there and, wrapped in dark cloaks, went quietly through the frosty marshes, the icy mud crunching under our horses' hooves. By the time the sun rose, the sea was far behind us and we were safe.

We rode hard all that night and the next day, stopping only to rest our horses and eat the food I had packed for us. At last we saw Velzna rising in the distance. By the time we had led our horses through the gate and up the steep road, it was dark, and I was so sick with weariness that I could scarcely put one foot before the other.

Khrysanthe welcomed us joyously. 'You're safe!' she exclaimed. 'I've been so worried.'

She led us into the hall, where Cesar sat up sleepily, rubbing his eyes. He saw me and his face lit up. He held up his arms, and I lifted him and cuddled him close.

'Are you hungry?' Khrysanthe asked. 'I don't have much, I'm sorry.'

'We bought some fish in the market,' Nasrin said. 'I will get it ready for us.'

Khrysanthe smiled at her. 'Welcome home,' she said gently, and I felt a swelling of love in my heart for my sister. It was wonderful to be back here at Velzna, knowing my family was safe. I did not know how I was going to tell them that I was not staying. I needed to go back to the pale mountains, though, I needed to see Ambrose. I longed for him with every iota of my being.

We gathered by the fire to prepare our supper. Khrysanthe wanted to know everything that had happened to Alektrona, and was delighted by her account of earning her living as a dancer.

'How bold!' she cried. 'Father would be horrified.'

'That was an added bonus,' Alektrona replied with a grin.

Inevitably, the talk turned to me. They wanted to know how I had escaped the dragon, and I found it very difficult to explain without breaking my promise to Ambrose. I told them I had managed to wriggle free of my bonds, and then crept away down the mountains.

Alektrona frowned. 'Minerva's spear, you must not have been tied up very tightly. Did they want you to escape?'

'No. No. They fear the dragon, fear his wrath. If he is not fed once a year, he shoots out jets of flames and destroys their town.'

Alektrona was not satisfied. 'But why does the dragon only threaten them once a year? Is it not hungry all the time?'

'I don't know. Maybe dragons only eat once a year.' Then I remembered what Misurina had told me. 'He's not always a dragon,' I blurted out.

'What?'

'He's a sorcerer. He changes shape into a dragon, whenever he wants to burn things up, I suppose. The dragon is just one of his forms.' I was speaking wildly, saying the first thing that came into my head.

'So he's a sorcerer, not a dragon,' she said thoughtfully, propping her chin on her hand. 'He's a man that can change shape.'

'I suppose so. I mean, that's what I was told.'

'Does he still eat the girls he takes?' Khrysanthe wanted to know.

'I don't know. Maybe. I was told that nothing is ever found of the girls they sacrifice. No bloodstains, no bones.' My stomach churned. I averted my eyes from the fish Nasrin was gutting. Even the smell made me feel sick.

'So he unchains them and takes them away somewhere else.'

'Maybe.'

'Perhaps the dragon is just a trick, to get girls into his power.'

'Maybe.' My body felt too hot, my clothes too tight.

'They'd be slaves to him,' Fatima said. 'The poor things.'

'You were lucky to escape,' Alektrona said.

'Yes.' I was unable to meet their eyes. Nasrin had finished gutting the fish and rose to empty the bowl. It was a slimy bloody mess. My stomach lurched. Before I could stop it, vomit erupted up my throat. It was thin, acidic, bitter. I pressed my hands over my mouth.

'Well, I think that answers that question.' Alektrona came and put her arm about me, led me to a chair. Fatima found a cloth and began to mop up the mess.

'Who's the father?' Khrysanthe asked.

I stared at her blankly.

'The father of your baby.'

I could not answer her. The shock was too great.

'You didn't know?' Alektrona spoke gently.

I shook my head.

How could I not know? I was a midwife. I had spent a whole season making love every night. I had taken no precautions, had not even given it a thought. None of it had felt real. It was as if I had been bespelled.

I had not bled once while at the castle, but I had thought that had been because I had lost so much weight on the long, hard journey. How could I have been so stupid?

Ruin of all, the Sybil had called my bridegroom. I had not expected her words to be literally true for me. I pressed my hands against my belly. Looked down at myself. I could see my breasts were swollen, pressing hard against my bodice. I could feel that they were hot and sore. And I had been so tired. Every day had been like dragging a heavy weight behind me. I had thought it was because I had been working so hard.

'I'm an idiot.' I said the words out loud.

'Psykhe, who's the father?'

I shook my head.

'You don't know?' Khrysanthe was half-horrified, half-titillated.

'You can't say?' Nasrin's voice was so gentle, so understanding, tears sprang to my eyes.

'Psykhe, is it the sorcerer?' Alektrona asked.

My eyes flew to hers in horror. I shook my head. *No. No.*

Yet my thoughts buzzed about like angry bees. The Sybil had warned me that my bridegroom was one feared by all, and that none could escape his arrows of flame. He had never let me see his face, he had come and left in darkness, he would not let me know his name. I had been kept locked in, forbidden to see or speak to anyone else. He had given me the key and the means to see my family only after I had persisted in my pleading.

How did I know my lover was the boy I had known? I had not seen him. It could be someone pretending to be him. It could all

238

be a wicked trick, a cruel lie. And, even if it was the boy I had known, how did I know that he had not seduced me with his charms and spells, pretending to be my friend, pretending to rescue me? Perhaps Ambrose was no god, no immortal, but just an evil magician ensnaring me in his nets? Perhaps he was the sorcerer of the old tales, the one who had tricked the warrior princess and the curious little girl named Misurina to their deaths. Perhaps the man I had loved so desperately *was* the shapeshifting sorcerer, the winged serpent of the tales.

Perhaps it had always been a lie. Perhaps it was all a plot to ensnare me and punish me, because people thought me as fair as a goddess. Perhaps the child in my womb was really a monster, like the bull-headed minotaur born to the queen of Crete in punishment for her husband's pride, or the fearsome Echidna, half-woman, half-serpent, granddaughter of snake-haired Medusa. Perhaps the gods were nothing but evil magicians? Perhaps we worshipped those who wished us nothing but harm. I remembered all the tales I had read. The boy Narcissus, condemned by Nemesis the goddess of justice to fall in love with his own reflection and stare at it till he starved to death. Actaeon, who dared to look upon Luna the goddess of the moon as she bathed, and was transformed into a stag and hunted to death by his own hounds. And, of course, poor Myrrha, cursed to lust after her own father by an arrow shot from Ambrose's bow.

He said he hadn't known. He said he loved me.

'No, no,' I cried. 'It's not true. He's a good man!'

'Who is he, Psykhe?'

'Just a man,' I faltered.

I was peppered with questions. What was his name? Where did he live? How did I meet him? What kind of man was he? What did he do?

239

I tried to construct a man out of shards of truth. He lived in the mountains not far from where my mother had been born. He had helped me escape the dragon. He had offered me a refuge. Was he rich? I suppose so. He lived in a beautiful white castle. He had given me my ring and silk dresses – he had many servants.

'How has he made his fortune?' Khrysanthe asked. 'Living so far from civilisation. He cannot have rich grain fields and vineyards, or a fleet of ships trading in furs and amber, when he lives like a barbarian in the wilderness.'

'I don't know. I suppose he must have made it like any other man and retired to the mountains for some peace and quiet,' I replied snappishly.

'But I thought he was a young man?' Alektrona asked at once.

I felt caught in a trap, unable to think what to say. My sisters looked at me, then at each other. 'Psykhe, you must know if your lover is a young man or an old one?'

'He's young,' I said, but I was by now so beset with suspicions and misgivings that my voice quavered and I began to cry. 'I don't know, I don't know. He *felt* young.'

'How can you not know?' Then Alektrona's voice changed. 'Psykhe, do you not know who he is? Did he rape you?'

'No, no. It wasn't like that.' I cried harder.

'Did you not see who it was?' Khrysanthe asked.

I shook my head.

'You didn't? You never saw him? He came to you in darkness? More than once?'

I did not answer my sister's questions.

Alektrona knelt beside my chair, taking my restless hands in hers. 'Psykhe, sweetling, can't you see the truth? The oracle said you were to be wed to some kind of dreadful winged serpent. Your mother's people sacrifice a maiden every year to a wicked sorcerer who can shape change into a dragon. It's assumed the dragon eats them, but there are never any remains left to be buried. Isn't it more likely he abducts them, takes them back to his lair, seduces them?'

'But why?' I protested. 'It doesn't make sense.'

'To fatten you up,' Khrysanthe said mischievously. 'To eat you later when you are good and plump.'

Alektrona gave her a stern look. 'To satisfy his lust, Psykhe. To have you in his power, helpless and dependent, a prisoner to his desires. To break your spirit and make you his slave.'

I felt chilled to the core of my being. 'No,' I said faintly. I clung to the memory of the bright-breasted bird that had found shelter for me in Tarchna. *He loves me*, I told myself. *He kept me safe.*

'Does he know where you are?' Khrysanthe asked suddenly. 'Will he come and try to take you away again?' She looked down at the little boy asleep on her lap, and all mischief vanished from her face.

'He knows,' I said. 'He has always found me when he wanted to.'

I stood up and went to where my cloak and satchel hung from a peg by the door.

'What are you doing?' Alektrona said in surprise.

'I am going home,' I answered. 'I need to know the truth.'

I had tried to make myself invisible as a child. I had not wanted anyone to see me.

But I was a woman now, and soon to be a mother. I did not want to be invisible anymore.

I wanted to see and be seen.

VII

Tinderbox

Three twists of the enchanted ring and I was back at the castle, standing outside the front door which stood ajar. Light spilled out through the crack.

I hesitated, clutching my cloak about me. The night air was freezing cold. My breath came in quick visible puffs. I put my hand into my pocket where my knife was hidden, its stone blade whetted as always to sharpness. In my pouch was a tinderbox, freshly stocked with dried heather, charcloth and sulphur-tipped splints. I was determined to light the lamp and look upon my lover, but still I found it hard to cross the threshold and go inside.

Would he be there? Would he know I had returned?

I took a deep breath and pushed the door open.

As I walked through the castle, lamps lit before me and extinguished behind me, I moved in a halo of radiance, able to see only a few steps ahead. I came to the tower and went up the spiral staircase. For a moment I moved in shadow before the lantern in the bedroom above flickered into life. In that moment, I once again touched my knife. I do not know what I feared most. Discovering

242

it was all a lie or discovering that it was not, and I had betrayed my lover's trust.

A fire glowed on the hearth, the quilt was turned down, and my nightgown lay waiting. A jug of warm water was set in a big bowl. I dropped my cloak and satchel on a chair near the bed, stripped and washed myself all over, and cleaned my teeth with a pine twig laid ready for that purpose. I took time over my ablutions, conscious of the heavy beat of my heart within my breast. The sheets were warmed with a hot brick. I rested my cold feet against it and lay back against my pillows. I did not bank the fire or blow out the lamp. The flames sunk lower and lower, and then snuffed themselves out.

'Psykhe.' As always, his voice sent a thrill through me.

'I am here.'

His light step, the weight of his body sinking down the side of the bed. I put my arms around him. He kissed me, stroked back my hair with both hands. 'I was so afraid you'd not come back.'

'I had to.'

'You missed me?' A soft teasing note in his voice.

'So much.' I lifted the quilt, and he slid in beside me. He was naked. I ran my hands down his body, over his back, down to his buttocks. I kissed his neck, his shoulder, moved my mouth down his chest, sucked on his nipple, swirled my tongue in his belly button. He sighed and moaned in gratifying response as I explored his whole body. Every inch of him was a man.

I had been away almost three months. I could not get enough of him – the taste, the smell, the feel of him. We did not talk, all of our energies focused on each other's bodies. Some flame was quickened in me, some new self-assurance. He was a man and I was a woman, and our bodies were made to fit together as one. Afterwards we lay still, clasped in each other's arms, trying to catch our breaths.

'I love you,' he whispered against my hair. I murmured the words back, then lay in silence as he slipped into sleep.

You don't need to do this, I told myself. *He loves you. What does it matter if you only ever meet in darkness? Half of him is better than none of him.*

I put my hand down and stroked the subtle curve of my belly. I knew I was lying to myself. This life in the shadows was only half a life, and I wanted it all. Day-light and night-darkness. Whatever joy or suffering lay ahead, I wanted us to face it together.

I slid out of bed, and drew on my cloak against the bitterly cold air. Groping in the darkness for my cloak, I found the dagger and the tinderbox. Still, I hesitated. I thought of the story of Semele, a mortal girl burned to cinders after asking Jove to show her his true divine form. Would I too be burned to ash if my lover was truly a god? Or was he a sorcerer, capable of transforming himself in a flash to a giant winged serpent with venomous fangs? I did not want to be a sorcerer's slave, and I did not want to be a god's plaything. I needed to know the truth.

Opening the tinderbox, my questing fingers found the flint and steel. I struck them together. A shower of tiny red sparks fell into the box and were caught by the charcloth. A few began to smoulder. I fed the flame with the dried heather, then lit the sulphur head of the splint. It caught and blazed up. Quickly, I lit the wick, lifted the lamp and bent over the bed.

Ambrose lay sprawled, the sheet crumpled about his naked body. One dark curl hung over his brow. For a moment I stood still, feasting my eyes upon him. He was just as beautiful as I had remembered. Then I bent and shook his shoulder. 'Dear heart, wake up. Come on, sweetling, wake for me.' He did not stir. I shook him more vigorously. 'Ambrose, wake up. I have something to tell you.'

He woke with a start, his eyes wide with shock. One arm flew up, knocking the lamp in my hand. Burning hot oil poured down upon his chest. Ambrose screamed. I gasped and flinched, the lamp flying from my hand. It fell onto the sheet. Flames raced across the bed and licked at his side. He screamed again and jumped to his feet. I stumbled against the table where I had laid my obsidian dagger, and it tumbled to the floor. Ambrose saw the lamp, the dagger, the rapidly spreading fire. His eyes met mine in one charged moment of pain and accusation. Then he sprang for the window, wings unfurling from his back.

'Ambrose!' I scrambled after him, flung my arms about his waist. He burst the shutters open and leapt out. I clung to him, swung through space, stars above, flames below. I was not strong enough to hold on. My fingers parted and I fell.

With a swoop, Ambrose caught me in his arms. He folded his wings and alighted on the ground, setting me away from him. 'Why, Psykhe? Why could you not trust me?'

'I . . . I just wanted to . . .' I tried to embrace him, but he sucked in his breath in pain, holding me away from his burned skin.

'Love cannot live where there is no trust,' he told me, his face as cold and stern as I had ever seen it. He spread his wings and soared away. I ran after him, calling his name, trying to explain, but with just a few wingbeats he was out of sight. I stumbled and fell, then struggled up and kept on running, calling for him again and again.

I had not meant to hurt him. I had only wanted to see his face when I told him we were going to have a child. I had thought I would know then what he really felt. I had hoped he would be overjoyed, that he would defy his mother and raise our child with me, that he would want to be with me always.

Instead, I had hurt him and driven him away.

I had to find him. I ran, calling till I was hoarse. Many times I stumbled and fell, able to see little in the moonless night. I wore nothing but my nightgown and cloak, and my feet were bare. Soon they were cold and numb, and I could run no more.

I looked back at the castle. The fire was dying out, and I could see only a surly orange glow through the tower window. I began to walk back. I had to find him, I had to explain. Surely he would forgive me when he understood?

The rest of the castle was empty and silent. No doors opened for me, no lanterns lit. I had to grope my way in darkness. My room was full of smoke and heat. Red embers glowered like the eyes of watching demons. I had snatched up the lamp from the front hall on my way, and now I bent and lit it from a glowing coal. The bed was a mess of charred timbers and ashes, the stone wall was scorched. Step by cautious step I made my way through the hot cinders, and opened the stout wooden chest where my clothes were kept. I found my mother's dress and cloak and the boots I had worn on my long journey. Everything else had vanished. For some reason this made me weep again.

Scrubbing away my tears, I dressed myself and fastened the silver torc around my neck to keep it safe. I found my tinderbox, blackened and buckled by the heat, and my obsidian knife. My satchel was still lying on the chair where I had left it, untouched by the flames. I shoved the tinderbox in with the scrying bowl, looked around at the ruins of the beautiful room I had loved so much, then left, carrying the lamp.

It was pitch-black outside. The stars were so bright I could see the sharp jagged peaks of the mountains etched against them. Frost glittered on the lawn.

Down the mountain I went, as fast as I dared. At last, my breath sobbing in my chest, my limbs trembling, I reached the lake far below. I filled my leather bottle to the brim, drank deeply, then filled it again and tucked it inside my satchel. Then I scooped up more water in the scrying bowl and set my lantern beside it. The water in the bowl glinted. I bent over it, whispering the spell and then, focusing as intensely as I could, *Ambrose, Ambrose, Ambrose . . .*

I saw a squalling baby, lying in a gilded cradle, being rocked by a slim goddess with golden wings, a herald's rod in one hand.

'I'm sorry, little one,' she whispered. 'You must see it is impossible. Your father, sweet as he is, is fickle as the wind. Hot one minute, cold the next. And I am the messenger of the gods, sent hither and thither at a moment's warning. A baby is just going to weigh me down.' She bent and brushed a swift kiss on the baby's soft cheek. 'You'll be fine. Venus has so many brats, what's one more to her?' Then she spread her wings and flew away, leaving a glowing rainbow in her wake.

An old woman bent over and picked up the crying baby, wrapping him in a dark cloak. 'Come on, little one,' she said. 'Let us take you to Venus. Iris is right – she'll hardly notice one more. Let us hope you are a pretty lad.'

I could not see the old woman's face. It was hidden in shadows. But I felt I knew her. 'Nocturna?' I whispered. She looked up and met my eyes. Everything shifted and whirled. I saw her searching through a cave, a flaming torch in either hand, I saw her kneeling beside a tomb, gathering grave dirt at midnight, I saw her binding a poppet with black thread. Unconsciously I recoiled. She said, 'Do not seek to see into *my* soul, Psykhe. Who is it you wish to know?'

'Ambrose.'

As I whispered his name, Nocturna's face receded into shadows. Once again I saw my lover, this time as a merry little boy, playing with other boys. Sometimes they feasted, sometimes they were forgotten and had to forage for food under tables where empty goblets rolled and drunken men snored. Sometimes they were lavished with attention, their curls ruffled, other times they were ignored. Musicians played, dancers whirled and leapt, fire-eaters and sword-swallowers and jugglers entertained the crowd, dwarves in ludicrous costumes fought with flower stalks and did clumsy forward-rolls to the sounds of catcalls and slow derisive clapping.

A woman reclined at the centre of this strange and vivid court. Her thick blonde hair hung below her hips, her eyes were as green as the ocean, her skin as white as seafoam. She wore the most extraordinary dress I had ever seen, made of some slippery green fabric that looked like it had been poured over her. It revealed her smooth arms and shoulders, and was fastened under her breasts with an embroidered golden girdle. Its sleeves hung long, concealing her hands. Golden bells at her ankles chimed at every movement. Her court bowed low to her, laughed at every word she spoke, vied with each other for her attention. She was voluptuous, seductive, adored.

She was everything I was not.

Venus, my enemy.

VIII

God of the Wild

A series of images, so swift that one scarcely came before another flicked it away. Swirling water and blood, the splash of seafoam, a slim figure springing onto the shore, naked, blonde hair swirling about her. She played in the shallows like a child, laughing. She romped with sea naiads, drew on the strand with sticks, decorated sandcastles with shells. One of her playmates was a beautiful boy with the bluest of eyes. She tried to kiss him, and he shook his head. She promised him a pair of golden wings so that he could fly to the land of the gods with her, but again he rejected her. Eyes flashing with rage, she transformed him into a sea snail.

People bowed to her, brought her strands of milky-white pearls, chunks of amber, golden chains, carved jade pendants. She clothed herself in silk, draped herself in jewels, built a palace of white marble. Whatever she wanted was given to her. She feasted and danced, hosted games, sought out all that was strange and decadent.

And then she fell in love. A shepherd boy with a comely face and a strong, young body. She wooed him and deceived him, pretending to be just a girl. But Jove wanted her for himself. Once before he had tried to force himself upon her. She had fled, and the god's seed had spilt upon the land. Jove saw she dallied with a mortal, and angrily struck the shepherd boy down with a bolt of lightning. Once fleet-footed and lithe, now he was crippled. Venus wanted only perfection. She left the maimed boy crying in pain, bore her son Aeneas in secret, and gave him away.

Jove ordered her to marry Vulcan, his black-browed, clubfooted, hunchbacked son, the blacksmith god of fire and volcanoes. She wept and pleaded, but the king of the gods would not be moved. Weeping, she was forced to Vulcan's bed.

Goddesses, it seemed, had no more right to choose their husbands than girls.

Her laughter became hard and scornful, her movements restless, her tournaments ever crueller. One day Eris, the goddess of strife, tossed a golden apple amidst the goddesses of Olympia, inscribed 'to the fairest'. All wanted the prize, and Paris of Troy was chosen to judge. Venus was so determined to win, she promised to give Paris the beautiful Helen of Troy if he judged in her favour. He agreed, and so began the Trojan war.

Men slashed and stabbed and hacked at each other. Blood sprayed. Women screamed. Fire blazed.

I did this, Venus thought. *I made men kill for love.*

No game had ever gripped her so much. She watched every battle avidly, and manipulated human and god as if they were pieces on a gameboard. She seduced the god of war so that he would fight on her side, and she saved the life of her son Aeneas when he fell in the battle. But then a spear stabbed her in the palm. She felt pain for the very first time, saw her own blood spurt. A dark mist came across her eyes, she stumbled and fell. She had to be rescued, and the other gods laughed and told her to confine herself to matters of the bed. The wound healed, but left a scar.

A mortal did that, she thought, gazing at the disfigurement. *A mortal dared stab me, and the gods dared mock me.*

She swore to make them pay.

The goddess gathered together a flock of unwanted boys, gave them golden wings and quivers of arrows. Those made of gold kindled love, those made of lead kindled hate. She petted and lavished praise on the boys, won their fervent loyalty, and set them loose on the world. No-one was safe, not even the king of the gods.

The boys were all given nicknames that meant love in one form or another. Bridal-Song, Desire, Lust, Love-Returned, Love-Not-Returned, Sweet-Talk, Longing. The last moniker was attached to Ambrose. He yearned for love, and she laughed at him for it. He wriggled into her lap, and she pushed him away. He brought her a flower, and she let it fall to the ground. Every time he won a race or a wrestling match or an archery contest, he looked to her at once, and she yawned and snapped her fingers for more wine. So Ambrose tried ever harder to please her. He ran errands for her, acted the jester in the hope it would make her laugh, fought the other boys whenever they made a crude remark about her, watched with hurt, puzzled eyes as she pitted one paramour against another.

Vulcan forged a net of chains and hung it above her bed, fashioned so that it would fall down and entrap her in the love act. She and her lover Mars were caught, unable to move, not even to uncouple. Then Vulcan called the whole court in to see. Among the jeering crowd was Ambrose, his face burning with shame, his eyes downcast.

Venus could not bear to be mocked. She flaunted her lovers in her husband's face, so enraging him that smoke and burning sparks billowed from the peak of his mountain home, turning the countryside into a wasteland. And she sent her flock of boys to punish everyone who had ever slighted her. But her cruelty came at a cost.

People no longer lavished her with love. They feared her and her flock of winged boys. Her shrines were no longer heaped with gold and amber; her strength was no longer fed with the warm blood of sacrificial doves and goats. People looked for kinder, fairer gods. With each leaden arrow he shot, Ambrose became more troubled, more doubtful. Within him, a seed of rebellion was growing, and so he had come to Velzna to see the only one he knew who had dared defy her.

Me.

I watched us laughing together, exploring the underground cellars, running hand-in-hand through the streets, my silvery hair falling loose. We danced together under the stars, and then I went to sit with Silviano and listen to his song. Ambrose hurried alone through the dark streets, back to where my ribbon had fallen. He picked it up, kissed it, tucked it away inside his tunic.

The images were spinning faster now, one snatch of a scene dissolving into another.

Venus was angry at his absence, angry that he no longer adored her. She searched his room, found the ribbon and slashed it to pieces. 'You ungrateful brat!' she screamed. 'After I took you in when nobody wanted you! You'd think you'd be thankful, but no, you're like all men. So selfish, so unkind. Who is she? What's her name? I'll kill her.'

'She's nobody,' Ambrose said. 'Just a girl.'

'Tell me her name!'

'I never asked it,' he answered, shrugging.

Venus stared at him for a long time, her eyes narrowed, then laughed. 'My boy is turning into a man,' she said caressingly. 'Very well. Just as long as it's me you love the best.'

'Yes, Mother,' he answered woodenly, staring at the ground where my ribbon lay in shreds.

Venus did not believe him. She set spies to follow him, she watched him through her mirror just as I was watching her through mine. Then I saved Fatima's life, and people called me a goddess. Ambrose had come secretly to warn me, but she had seen.

'You cannot hide from the gaze of the gods,' she told me, looking directly into my eyes.

I jerked back in horror.

Her face filled the scrying bowl. I could see nothing but her. I tried to wrench my mind away, I tried to throw the scrying bowl from me so I could escape that spiteful green gaze. But I was paralysed.

'Yes, I see you and I know you. The snow-haired girl who dared steal the dove marked for sacrifice to me! The mortal who dared resurrect the dead! If mortals can be healed, if they no longer suffer pain and illness, they will no longer fear and worship us. I cannot allow that.'

'They would still worship you if you were not so cruel,' I told her. 'You send your cupids out into the world to cause pain and heartache and suffering. It is so unfair.'

'Who are you to judge me? You are nothing. A clot of mud. And you will drag my son down to your own level. The more time he spends in the mortal world, the more mortal he will become. He will get old, and one day he will die and rot away just like any other piece of meat. Is that what you want for him?'

I was shaking, but said staunchly, 'To love someone, to be loved by them, is worth the cost.'

'Stupid fool. Love is nothing but pain.'

'I'd rather have the pain than not.'

'I will cause you such pain when I find you! How dare you raise your eyes to a god?'

'He loves me. We could be happy. Why don't you want him to be happy?'

Her eyes flared. 'Happy with you? A mortal? I took him in, I raised him, I gave him everything, I made him powerful and feared! What could you possibly give him that I can't?'

'Love,' I answered.

Her rage was a maelstrom, sucking me in. Water spun about me. I did not know which way was up or down or out.

'Ambrose!' I cried out loud. 'Ambrose!'

His name was a magical charm.

He sprang between us, golden wings spread, an arrow set into the string of his bow, aimed directly at his mother's heart. His eyes were bright with fever, his body seared and blackened. 'Go!' he cried. 'Psykhe, go!'

Somehow I was able to shove the scrying bowl away from me. As the water cascaded out, I saw him stagger and fall. I heard her voice, faint and venomous. 'Wherever you are, I will find you and I will destroy you.'

It was dawn. The lake glimmered beneath the early morning mist, the snow-dusted pinnacles above touched with fiery rose. I trembled in every limb.

Ambrose, Ambrose.

He had spoken the truth. He had done all he could to protect me.

'I am so sorry,' I whispered. 'I did not understand. Please, please, forgive me.'

No answer.

I bent to the scrying bowl, trying to see him, to make sure that he was safe, but the water had all been spilled, the bowl was empty. I wept as if trying to fill it again with my tears. I wept till I was hollowed out, and then I did my best to compose myself. I splashed my face with icy lake water, dried it with my sleeve.

I needed to fix things.

'I'm coming, dear heart,' I promised him. 'I'm coming!'

But I did not know how to find him.

A delicate strain of music floated on the air. I looked up. It was so ethereal, so beautiful. I felt I had heard it before. Slinging my satchel over my shoulder, I followed the sound through the beech trees, a few bright leaves still clinging to the high vaulting branches. My boots crackled on the bronze carpet below, and the first light slanted through the silvery-grey trunks in long shining rays.

I came to a small clearing in the heart of the grove, where a man with the horns and hooves of a goat sat on a fallen tree, playing a set of pipes made from reeds. His grizzled hair hung in matted elflocks to his waist, his wild beard spread over his bare chest, his ears were tufted with hair. He wore nothing but some kind of skin slung about his hips.

'Silviano?' I asked in amazement.

How could I ever have thought him just a man?

He lowered the pipes and smiled wickedly at me. 'That is one of my names.'

'What name do you call yourself then?'

He laughed, his eyes dancing amidst a thousand wrinkles. 'A clever question. I call myself Silvanus.'

'Silvanus? The god of the wild?' I was amazed.

'Some call us gods, Psykhe. Others call us the fata, or the Old Ones.'

'What do you call yourself?'

He considered the question. 'A living soul, perhaps. Like you, Psykhe.'

'But . . . gods are immortal, aren't they?'

'Oh, no, sweet child. Gods can be born and gods can die.' He sighed, as if seeing some awful vision of the future. 'We can be wounded, we can be bound and flung into the pit, we can be betrayed and overcome, just like any other living soul.'

'So he could die.' My despair rose within me, lodging like a stone in my throat so that I could scarcely breathe.

'Yes, Psykhe, he could die. All living souls must die in time. Some have brief lives, lasting only a few days. Mayflies and moon moths, blue butterflies and dragonflies, they are born, they dance, they die. Other creatures live for many centuries, like these beech trees and me. It is harder for those you call gods to die. We draw strength from the land in which we dwell, we can sleep for a hundred years, we armour ourselves with protective spells or hide our hearts in secret places.'

'Can . . . can I save him?'

Silvanus gazed at me with eyes that seemed as ancient and secret as a forest pool. 'You can try. All things are possible in all the possible worlds.'

'But how?' I cried. 'I don't know how to find him.'

'Is this not the hour of your greatest need?'

I looked down at the ring I still wore. 'But can it take me to his world? The world of the gods?'

'Indeed it can, little maid. The worlds lie one inside the other, like the layers of the bulb of a lily, each separate but touching, sharing the same roots, the same heart. Where the edges of the worlds overlap there are gaps. Gateways. Those are the places where the skin between the worlds is thinnest and can be most easily pierced. Look for the edges of things, the borders of things, places where earth and sky and water meet and mingle and part once more. Find natural thresholds, caves and holes and waterfalls, and go to them at the edges of time, summer's end and winter's beginning, the dark and the bright of the moon, dawn and dusk.'

'Like now?'

'And like here.'

I glanced about me. One of the ancient beech trees had a hole in the trunk like a tiny doorway. I looked back at Silvanus. I did not have much reason to trust in the gods. 'Why are you helping me?' I asked tentatively.

He looked away from me, frowning. 'These young gods care nothing for the old ways,' he said at last. 'They do not honour the great goddess who gave life to us all. As the gods plunder and rape and pillage, so too do men in their image. The great-hearted trees are torn down and burned, the hidden riches of the earth are dug out and made waste, the air is thick with smoke and ashes, the rivers and seas are poisoned, wild beasts are hunted to extinction for sport, and the goddess's sacred serpents are slaughtered.'

I had a flash of memory. The Sibyl dancing in the king's throne room, snakes winding about her arms, striking at her throat. Her chanted prophecy. *Great Goddess, mother of us all, speak with my tongue . . .*

Silvanus's face was drawn and sorrowful. 'The Old Ones cannot stand by and do nothing. What is remembered lives. What is forgotten dies. And so a few of us old gods fight to make sure she is not forgotten. We search for those willing to work with us, healers and seers and storytellers, and we teach them all that we know so they can carry the light for us down through generations. One day, the time will come. One day, far in the future, the powers of these dark gods will be broken. The earth will be healed, and humans will once again live in harmony with the wild. Till then, we all must resist in any way we can, and that means guarding and protecting our carriers of the flame.'

I sat in silence, biting my lip. He smiled at me. 'Do not be afraid. It is never easy to walk between the worlds, but you are strong, stronger than you know. Simply fix your intention and trust in the magic.'

I took a deep breath and nodded. He lifted his flute to his mouth and began to play, haunting music filling the air. Slinging my satchel over my shoulder again, I went to the beech tree and knelt before the doorway. I bowed my head, closed my eyes and turned the ring on my finger three times, saying under my breath:

> Let me find my love
> wherever he may be
> in the hills above
> or across the endless sea.

It was the best I could do on the spur of the moment. I could only hope it would work. Then I crawled forward, into the darkness of the hollow tree.

Part IV

imago
Latin: 'an image, a likeness'

The final transformative stage of a butterfly or moth,
in which the insect casts off its mask or disguise
and becomes its true self.

. . . take this casket and . . . descend to the ghastly halls
of Orcus himself . . .
Eros and Psykhe
Metamorphoses, Lucius Apuleius

I

The Goddess's Palace

Silvanus's ethereal tune faded away. Instead, I heard dance music, the thump of dancing feet, the clink of goblets, laughter. My skin tingled all over, as if I had been whipped with nettles. I opened my eyes.

I knelt in the doorway of a room, gripping onto its gilded wooden frame. It was dark within. All I could see was a canopied bed, a carved chest, a tapestry in which gold threads glinted. I glanced about me. A hallway with high ceilings painted with rosy clouds and winged cupids with tiny bows and arrows, a mosaic floor depicting rose garlands and white birds, a pillar of pale green crystal that reflected glints of light.

I stood, giddy and disorientated, and took a few tentative steps into the room. A sickening smell in the air like burned leather. A low moan of pain. I crept forward, trying to see. The dim shape of a figure lying sprawled among tangled sheets. Another moan, a fretful movement. 'Ambrose?' I whispered. 'Dear heart?'

He did not respond. His dark hair was sweat-bedraggled. I touched his skin. It was burning hot. I needed more light. I went to the window and drew back the curtain a little. He winced and turned his face from the light. I saw his left side was red-raw and blistered, oozing a yellowish liquid that had stained his sheets.

'I'm so sorry,' I muttered, kneeling beside his bed. His lips were parched, his skin dry. I pulled out the bottle of water from my satchel and held it to his lips. He managed to swallow a few mouthfuls. His sheets stank of sweat and sickness.

I had helped Nocturna treat a burned child once. He had pulled a pot of boiling water over himself. We had worked all night to save him, but we had failed.

My hands shaking, I began to wash his wound. The pain roused him. 'Psykhe,' he whispered.

'I am here, my darling. I'm so sorry. I am here now.'

He sighed and lifted his hand towards me. I took it and kissed it. 'Let's get you cleaned up. Can you sip some more water?'

The door banged open.

An elderly maidservant stood on the threshold, guards on either side of her. 'So,' she said, 'my mistress is right. There is an intruder in the house. We know who you are, worthless girl. My mistress has been searching for you. Look what you have done to her poor boy! You shall suffer for it now.'

'No, no,' I cried. 'Please! I am looking after him. He is very ill. He could die if left untended.'

'No thanks to you,' she snorted. 'You think we do not know the truth of the matter? My lady warned him, but he would not listen. And now my lady will see you finely punished for your impertinence.'

She made a gesture with one hand, and the guards headed for me. Both were very tall and broad, and wore leather armour studded with bronze. I tried to dodge and run. They caught me easily. I could have drawn my knife and tried to stab them, but it would have been futile. They were too strong and their armour was too thick. And I would just lose my knife, my last gift from Nocturna. Smarter to keep it hidden, to wait for the right moment to use it.

Ambrose raised himself on one elbow, called my name despairingly.

It was no use. I was dragged down the stairs and through a vast banqueting hall throned with people in fantastical costumes of silk and velvet. Their faces were painted, their hair arranged in elaborate braids and coils that must have taken hours. I saw dryads and nymphs and satyrs, bedecked with garlands of roses, and young men with bare oiled torsos and gilded eyelids, lounging about on low couches and playing knucklebones. Quivers full of golden arrows rested against their chairs.

The guards flung me before a mother-of-pearl throne. Venus reclined there, dressed in green gauze that made her eyes look like emeralds. Pinned at the shoulder with a great glowing jewel, the fabric was so fine I could see the shape of her breasts within. One shapely arm was bare, the other covered with a tight sleeve that came to a point over the back of her hand.

She leant forward at the sight of me and laughed mockingly. 'So this is the little slut that has seduced my son? Why, I thought she was supposed to be a beauty. Look at her, pale and wan as a ghost. What could he have seen in her? Put some roses in her cheeks, lads.'

Casually the guard slapped me hard across the face. I was knocked sideways. I tried to scramble away, but he slapped me again across the other cheek. I was too shocked to do more than gasp, and hold my hands to my face. Blood trickled from my nose.

'Now, what shall be her punishment? Should I burn her as she so cruelly burned my darling boy? Shall I cut off those lips that dared kiss him? Shall I put her in red-hot shoes and make her dance to her death?'

The crowd laughed and applauded, calling out suggestions. One of the guards seized a torch from the wall and held it so close to me, I could feel the hairs on my arm shrivelling. I shrank away. 'Please, don't hurt me. He will die if someone doesn't care for him. He's feverish, he needs water and something to help bring down his temperature, and his wound needs to be dressed. If you hurt me, I can't save him. Please, let me go to him.'

'Presumptuous little whore,' she snarled. 'He is my son, I know what is best for him.'

'But you left him alone, sick, feverish, desperately thirsty, in dirty linen. His burns will become infected, his fever will get worse. He'll die! Let me go to him, let me care for him. Please, please, I'll do anything.'

'Anything? You'll do anything I say?'

'Yes. Of course. Just let me help him!'

'This could be amusing,' she said, tapping her cheek with one long gilded fingernail. 'Very well. I shall set you a series of tasks. If you succeed, you shall be allowed to tend my son. If you fail, then you shall dance for me in red-hot shoes. Do we have a deal?'

'Yes,' I said.

What else could I say?

Venus smiled. 'What a fool you are! Well, at least watching you labour will alleviate my boredom a little. Guards, take her to the barn! Pour before her every grain and seed we have in our store-rooms.' She turned back to me. 'If you can sort it all into the right sack by nightfall, I shall not punish you again this night. However, if you fail . . .'

'Dancing in red-hot shoes!' the court chanted.

I was taken, with lots of shoves and jeers, to a huge shadowy barn. The guards brought sack after sack, and poured out their contents at my feet. Wheat, millet, barley, poppy seeds, sunflower seeds, lentils, and beans of all colours mixed together into one massive pile, as tall as me and much wider. I was left alone, with only a small lantern to see by.

I set to work as best I could. I could not see the tiny seeds clearly and had to bring each one close to my eyes to try to identify it. It was not long before my back was aching and my fingers were cramped, yet I had hardly made a dent in the enormous pile. It seemed impossible. I sat back on my heels and pressed my fingers into my aching eyes, thinking I might as well just give up now.

Then I noticed a long line of ants marching in from under the barn door. One by one they seized a seed or grain in their tiny claws, heaved it up and scurried up the side of the sack and dropped it in. Sometimes one ant would shoulder a seed much bigger and heavier than herself, and wrestle it into the sack. Sometimes three or four would work together to carry one of the larger beans. I was humbled by their dogged determination, their persistence, their unity. I stretched out my cramped back, and set myself to help them.

By dusk, all the seeds and grains were sorted and in their right sack. I hurt all over, but felt a fierce satisfaction at the finished task. 'Thank you,' I said to the ants, now all wearily marching back the way they had come. 'Whoever sent you, thank you.'

They had scarcely vanished before the barn doors were unlocked, and Venus came to inspect my work, along with a laughing retinue. They fell silent at the sight of the clean floor and the tidy sacks all filled to the brim with the right grain.

'This is not your work, you foul creature,' the goddess said through her teeth. 'The hands that accomplished it are not yours.'

'Who could have helped me? The doors were locked and guarded by your own servants,' I replied.

'I do not know how, but whosoever's favour you have gained, it will do you little good. Tomorrow I will have another task for you.' Venus stalked away.

One of the guards threw me a stale crust of bread before he left, my first food all day. I was very hungry, but I carefully crumbled some of the bread onto the floor for the ants and other little creatures before I ate. Then I made myself a bed in the straw, wrapped myself in my heavy cloak, and slept, my head pillowed on my satchel.

In the morning, I was summoned again to the throne room. I was stiff and sore and dirty, but I lifted my head high and tried to be as proud and fearless as I could.

Venus examined me with a frowning glance. 'There is said to be a flock of sheep whose fleece are purest gold. I order you to find this flock, and bring me back an armful of golden wool. Do this, or I will shod you with shoes of red-hot iron.'

'But how am I meant to find this flock? Where is it?'

The goddess gestured towards the far end of the banqueting hall, where a huge arched door was set into a recess in the wall. It was unlit and shadowy, but I could just manage to see it was embossed with two profiles, each looking in opposite directions. 'That is the Janus gate. It will take you wherever you wish to go. Unless, of course, it takes you where you least wish to be!' She laughed.

I was shoved down the room, many in the crowd reaching out to pinch or slap me, mocking me, or tearing at my clothes. I ignored them, trying to remember all I knew about Janus, the god of thresholds. His name meant 'opening'. He was named first in all prayers and received the first offerings of wine and incense in temple rituals. In Roma, the Janus gate was left open in time of war and shut in time of peace. I wondered if it was open now or closed.

The door was made of heavy bronze, split down the middle into two, and heavily embossed with images of the phases of the moon, the sun rising and setting, the wheel of constellations, trees in flower, in leaf and bare-twigged. One of the faces, looking left, was an old man with curly hair and beard, holding a staff. The other face, looking right, was a young man. He held a key.

One of the god's faces looked to the past, I remembered, and the other to the future.

As I reached the doorway, I hesitated, afraid. There were two doorknobs, one on either leaf of the door. I did not know which one to turn.

'Open the gate!' Venus commanded. 'Else tonight you'll dance!'

Stories about golden fleeces came from the ancient past, I thought.

I raised my left hand and turned the doorknob under the profile of the bearded man. The door swung open. Beyond was a yellow field. Again I paused, but someone kicked me hard in the small of the back. I fell through onto my knees. The gate clanged shut behind me.

I was in a wide sloping meadow enclosed on three sides by high thorny hedges, with forest and mountains beyond. On the far side was a fast-running river, foaming over rocks and edged with reeds. It was autumn, and the trees and hedges were aflame with orange. The dry grass waved in the hot breeze.

At the other end of the field was a fierce-looking ram with huge, curling horns, guarding a flock of sheep with fleece that gleamed as bright as polished gold. The ram sniffed the air, pawed the ground, then began to charge towards me, horns lowered. I ran to the river and threw myself in, only seconds before the ram reached me. His horns were thicker than my arm and looked as hard as stone. His eyes were golden, inscrutable, with a strange horizontal slit of a pupil. His teeth were long and yellowish-brown, capable of administering a vicious bite. He stared at me and I stared back, clinging to the rushes to avoid being swept away down the river, the strap of my satchel digging deep into my neck.

The breeze stirred the reeds. A faint sound of music. I turned my head sharply, listening intently to the song breathed by the wind.

Psykhe, you are harrowed by great trials,
You can only win with wit and guile.
Do not rush in the heat of the day,
I beg of you, wait, be patient, stay.
When twilight comes, the sheep can be shorn,
Find their golden wool hung on the thorn.

It was Silvanus's voice, and so I obeyed, even as the fast-rushing river sought to tear my grasp from the rushes and the cold drained all strength from my body. The ram soon lost interest and wandered away to graze at the grass. The sun passed overhead and sunk behind the mountains, and the sheep began to lie down in small groups, dozing. At last the ram joined them, his nose thrust into his flank.

As dusk fell, I crawled out of the river and – cold and bedraggled – crept along the hedge plucking the tufts of golden wool caught in the brambles. When my satchel was brimming over with glowing fleece, I returned to the gate. It looked just like an ordinary farm gate, but I had to trust that it was still the magical portal that had brought me here. I stood before it and chanted a little rhyme I had composed during the long hours I had waited in the shallows:

Janus, hear my plea,
god of the threshold,
open the gate, let me return,
with the goddess's gold.

II

The Water of Death

I pushed the gate open and stepped through into Venus's banqueting hall, dripping water and river weed all over her marble floor. As I walked up the room, silence fell and people drew away, staring in amazement. The goddess sat bolt upright, eyes wide and startled.

'For you, as requested.' I opened my satchel and drew out the handfuls of golden wool, bright as the noon.

For a moment she did not speak, then her frown deepened. 'Who is helping you? Is it my traitorous son?'

'No, my lady,' her servant cried. 'He lies unconscious still, burning to the touch.'

'Oh, please! Let me go to him, let me help.' I raised imploring hands.

'What use are you to him? A stupid, ugly, bumbling mortal girl, and he a god? How dare you even raise your eyes to him?'

I was so weary I sank down to the ground and rested my head on my arms. *Ambrose*, I whispered. *I am trying. I am trying so hard.* 'Please let me go to him,' I said again. 'He is your son. You say you love him. Do you not realise he might die?'

269

'He is a god! Gods do not die!'

'And yet he is dying.' The world wavered about me, too loud and then sinking away into a buzzing silence, too close and then far, far away. 'You say you cannot be hurt, but I know that you can. Were you not once wounded by a mortal weapon? Did you not bleed, did your limbs not weaken and your sight darken? Have you not lost where once you loved, have you not felt grief? I know you have.'

The goddess sighed. Her fingers moved to rub at the scar on her hand, half-hidden by her long sleeve. 'No,' she said in a low voice. 'No. It is a lie. These mortals, how they seek to make themselves gods. We are inviolable.' Her sea-green eyes stared into nothing for a long while, then she roused herself, smiled. 'The tasks I have set you have obviously been too easy. So let me increase the difficulty. I want you to travel to the source of the Styx and fill a jug to the brim with the water of death. Bring it back to me without spilling a single drop.'

I stood as if frozen. It was an impossible task. The Styx was the river that separated the world of the living from the world of the dead. The water was poisonous and would dissolve any vessel except one made of hoof or horn. The gods feared it so much that they swore their greatest and most binding vows by its waters.

After a moment, I said carefully, 'Very well, but only if you bring me a drinking horn to fill.'

Venus gave a brittle laugh. 'The slut knows her stories. Very well. Take her to her cell now and in the morning she can go to the Styx. Get her a drinking horn, much good may it do her.'

The old maidservant brought me a drinking horn with a silver handle. My fingers were so cold and numb I almost dropped it. She escorted me from the banquet hall, my guards like a stone wall around me. I hardly cared. I was so tired, so very tired.

As the carved double doors shut behind us, I turned to the old servant, seized her skinny arm. 'Please! It is true he could die. If his fever climbs too high, if his burn gets infected. He needs water, nourishment.'

'My lady has forbidden it,' she answered sullenly. 'He should not be dallying with mortals.'

'But he is her son!'

'He's no son of hers. My lady took him in when his mother did not want him. He should be grateful!'

'He is grateful. He loves her! How can she let him die?'

She gazed at me in astonishment. 'He won't die. He's the son of a god.'

'If he can be wounded, he can die. Can't you see that?'

She shook her head and walked away. The world reeled about me. I clutched at one of the guards' arms so I did not fall. 'I need to eat. Please, bring me some food.'

No-one answered. I drew myself upright. 'I'm carrying his child! I need to eat else his child will die.'

They locked me in a cold, dank cell. I could do nothing but curl up in a corner and try to still my shivering. Everything I owned was wet through, and the cold was piercing. Then I heard the grating of iron. Someone had opened a small flap in the bottom of the door and pushed in a hunk of bread. 'Thank you,' I whispered and devoured it in a few huge bites. Somehow I managed to sleep.

The next day, I was taken again to the gate of Janus, the drinking horn safely buckled within my satchel. Emboldened by my success from the day before, I put my hand on the doorknob to the right, thinking, *The underworld is the future for all of us.*

I stepped through to a long spur of stone. A huge rock towered above me. From its jaws, far above, dark waters leapt out and cascaded down the cliff-face. Where it fell, smoke hissed and wreathed. The stones were stippled with a thousand holes.

I sat down on a stone, weary beyond belief. I could see no way to climb that cliff without being splashed by the noxious waters. There was no path, no handholds. To make matters worse, snakes slithered out from the damp hollows, winding long sinuous necks, unblinking eyes fixed on me. I could see no way to complete my task. Utterly downcast and exhausted, I crouched as far away from that deadly waterfall as I could. I had failed. That night I must dance in red-hot shoes and Ambrose would die.

I could not let that happen. I had to try. I stood back and stared up at the cliff. A few spindly misshapen trees grew out of the rocks. I could use them to drag myself up. And there were the occasional cracks and crevices that I could cling onto. I drew my knife, which I had kept safely hidden within its secret pocket, and used it to cut the hem of my dress into long rags. I bound them around my hands, hoping to protect them from the deadly spray, and used another to tie the drinking horn to my belt. I wrapped my cloak tightly around me and pulled the hood over my head. Hopefully the thick fur would protect me. Using my knife, I dug out a small groove for a foothold. I fitted in the toe of my boot and stretched upwards, grabbing at an outcropping of stone. Then I dug another foothold, and reached for a tree root. Slowly, laboriously, I climbed the cliff.

Once a snake hissed at me from a crevice in the rock. I jerked back and lost my handhold. Only a desperate grab at a tree root saved me. I clung to it, panting, till my heart stopped racing. Then on I went, every muscle screaming.

Time passed. The day faded. The moon was high in the sky, frail and blue. At last I was near the top of the cliff. The waterfall surged out of a deep cleft to one side of me. I could scarcely see it now – twilight was falling. Hooking my arm through the branch of a tree, I untied the drinking horn from my belt and reached out with it.

I was too far away. I could not reach the water. My eyes burned with hot tears. I could not creep any closer without being scalded by the steaming waters. I looked up at the thin crescent moon. 'Please, Hekate,' I whispered. 'Please, help me.'

An owl hooted, right above me. I jerked wildly and glanced up. A great white bird swooped down, wings spread wide. In a heart-beat it was right in front of me, claws extended. I screamed and flinched, but it only snatched the drinking horn from my hand. Hardly comprehending, I watched as it soared up and held the horn under the falling water. Slowly it circled back down and landed beside me, holding out the drinking horn in one feathered talon. I met its fierce marigold eyes. 'Thank you,' I whispered and very carefully took the horn which was filled to the brim with black smoking water. It dipped its head, crowned by two erect ear tufts, then spread its wings and soared away again.

Holding the horn as far away from me as possible, I said shakily:

Janus, two-faced god, open the gate,
I have a gift for the goddess of hate.

The rock split open in front of me. Beyond, the brightly lit banquet hall, music playing, people dancing. Holding the horn with both hands, I stepped through the gap and stumbled through the crowd towards the goddess's throne. People gasped and drew away from me. Silence fell.

Venus gazed at me, astonished and afraid. 'Are you a witch? Who helps you?'

I did not answer. I just stared at her.

Venus rose from her throne and began to pace back and forth. 'When I find out who has been helping you, I will make them suffer! I'll cast them into the deepest pits of the underworld!'

'Please,' I said faintly. My hands were shaking so much I was in danger of slopping the toxic water on myself. 'I have done everything you've asked. You swore that if I did as you asked, you'd let me care for Ambrose. I'm so afraid for him. Please.'

'Your care is not needed. He is my son, and must be taught to obey me. I took him in when he was unwanted, and he chose to lie and deceive me. So now he must suffer for it, and so too must you. I will make sure that no other mortal ever dares to defy me!'

Anger blazed up in me. 'I will defy you as long as I have breath left in my body! For you are fair of face but most cruel and unfair of spirit. One day, I promise you, your altars will lie in ruins and you will be forgotten.'

The crowd of revellers inhaled sharply. I expected her to order me to be beaten and thrown back in my cell, and I tightened my grip on the horn of poisonous water, ready to fling it at anyone who came near me. But to my surprise, Venus shrank back, rubbing at the scar on her hand. 'No, no,' she whispered. 'Can this be a true vision of the future? What dark powers does this witch have, that she dares to threaten me?'

She looked from my face to the horn of smoking black water, and back again. 'I will send you somewhere no-one will be able to help you,' she said slowly. 'Somewhere that will teach you what it means to be mortal.'

Dread slowly rose in me, drenching my anger. 'Where?' I asked hoarsely.

A smile grew on her face. 'I will send you to my sister. You must go to her and ask her to give you a box of beauty.'

'A box of beauty? From your sister?' It seemed too easy a task. There had to be a catch to it. I tried to remember the gods' genealogy. 'Which sister do you mean?'

'My sister Proserpina, queen of the underworld.'

My heart kicked. All my life I had heard stories about the underworld. I had seen black animals sacrificed to the gods of that dark dismal realm, hot blood gushing to feed hungry ghosts. I had banged bronze pans and chanted, 'Spirits, begone!', while my father, barefoot, his right thumb thrust into the crevice between his fingers, threw black beans into the shadowy corners where lurked the *lemures* and the *larvae*, the silent and malevolent dead.

All mortals travelled to the underworld in time.

None returned.

I tried to remember all the stories I had ever heard about heroes who had travelled to the underworld, and then returned to the world of the living. Bacchus had, but he was a god. Theseus had, but he was a god's son. Orpheus had, but he was the son of a muse. I was just an ordinary young woman. And yet it was the only way to save my beloved's life.

'If I go, will you promise to send someone to care for Ambrose?' I kept my eyes fixed on her face.

Venus shrugged. 'Very well.'

'Will you swear to it?' Inspiration struck me. 'Will you swear on the waters of the Styx?'

She frowned. 'I see no need for that.'

'I do. Swear to it, and I will go to the underworld.'

The goddess looked askance at the curved drinking horn in my hand. The black liquid within bubbled and hissed, wisps of foul-smelling smoke rising into the air. If she broke an oath sworn on the deathly waters, her punishment would be to drink it.

Desperation made me reckless. I took a few rapid steps towards her, lifting the drinking horn threateningly. 'You want me to go? Swear to it, else I'll throw the waters in your face!'

She recoiled. 'Very well. If you insist.'

'I do.'

Casting me a look of hatred, Venus went through the motions of pouring out a libation of the black poisonous water and making a sacred oath. The water burned a smoking hole in her green marble floor.

'Now go! Give my regards to my sister,' she cried. 'And may you never find your way back to the world of the living again!'

III

Nettles and Brambles

I was so afraid, so weak, so worn out, the guards had to help me limp down the hall to the gate of the two-faced god. The closer we came, the more I hung back. I had given my promise, but I dreaded having to fulfil it. Surely I was going to my death?

I'm sorry, little one, I whispered to the tiny unseen child that nestled deep within my womb. *I'm so sorry. I wish you could have known your father. He would have loved you and kept you safe, I know it. I wish I could have given you life. I wish we could all have been together. We would have been so happy.*

Tears blinded me. I stumbled and almost fell.

The old maidservant gave me a small mother-of-pearl box. I tucked it inside my satchel. The Janus gate stood before me. I had to choose which handle to turn. Once again I chose the door embossed with the face of a young man looking into the future. I turned the handle and opened the door.

Beyond, only darkness and night. I hesitated, hung back against the hands that held me, tried to back away. The guards hurled me through.

I landed on my knees in a forest. Dry leaves rustled under me. It was bitterly cold. I scurried sideways and crouched against a tree, darting looks from side to side. An owl hooted, swooping past on pale muffled wings. I shrank back, my pulse thundering. Owls were messengers of the underworld.

Had the owl seen me? Was my presence known?

I crept through the trees. Gnarled trunks, twisted roots like snakes, a great swathe of stars above.

I frowned. Were there stars in the underworld?

Before me lay a lake, drifting with mist. My frown deepened. I had never heard of a lake in the land of the dead. I looked about me more carefully, then laid my hand on the trunk of one of the trees. It was silvery-pale, smooth. Under my fingers, faint ripples. I bent and ruffled my hand through the thick layer of leaves till I found the prickly seed case of a beechnut. I stood, gazing beyond the tree branches. A faint flush of colour in the sky, and the sound of birdsong.

I was certain the sun never rose in the underworld.

I limped through trees and came out on the shore of the lake. The sun rose higher, burning away the mist, and illuminated the familiar shape of the pale mountains. I was back in the beech grove where I had met Silvanus.

What had I done wrong? Had I made a mistake, chosen the wrong door?

I did not know what to do. I had expected to find myself in the shadowy realm of the dead, not back at the same place I had departed from only three days earlier. I looked about me in bewilderment. Everything seemed subtly different, as if the beech trees had drawn up their roots and walked about while I had been gone. I could not find the fallen log where Silvanus had played his flute. Yet the mountains were the same, their snow-streaked peaks reflected in the lake as they had always been.

I was thirsty. The water was stiffening into ice, and I cracked it with my knife so I could drink, bathe my face and hands, and fill up my water bottle. I would climb back up to the castle, I decided. I needed warmth and shelter while I figured out what to do next. Somehow I had to find a way to the underworld and back, if I was to keep my promise to the goddess.

Wearily standing once more, I glanced down the lake towards the hillfort.

I felt a jolt like the shock of static. The forest no longer cradled the lake in its dark arms. The pine trees had been cut back, and bare brown fields now lay alongside the water, dusted with snow but showing the regular lines of a ploughshare. The wooden palisade had been replaced with stout walls of stone, and the town had spilled out across the hill. Instead of mud huts with thatched roofs, sturdy houses made of brick and stone now raised upper storeys of beautifully carved wood. I could see boats out on the lake, with figures bending and throwing nets, and the air rang with goat-bells.

I stared. Surely they could not have made such dramatic changes in the three days I had been away? It gave me a very strange feeling.

I began to hurry away from the lake, wanting desperately to be back at the castle, safe and warm again. The climb seemed harder than ever before. I kept telling myself that I must be mistaken, that I had somehow not noticed the hillfort growing and changing. My steps quickened, though, till I was almost running. By the time I reached the hidden valley, I had a sharp stitch in my side. My legs were aching. I bent, trying to catch my breath, then hurried towards the castle, straining my eyes, trying to see.

Step by step, my sense of wrongness grew. I began to run.

One tower was gone. The garden wall was broken under the weight of a fallen tree. Ivy hung everywhere. I clambered over the tumbled stones and fought my way through nettles and brambles, the garden returned to the wild.

By the time I found the front door, my dress was torn and filthy, my arms scratched. It hung ajar on its hinges. Within, a thick fur of dust covered everything. Filthy cobwebs hung in ragged loops, and rats had nested in what might once have been cushions.

How? How was it possible? I had left just three days ago.

One night in our world can equal a hundred years in yours, Ambrose had once told me.

I felt sick. Three hundred years? Had three hundred years passed by while I had been gone?

I searched through the rooms for some proof that I was wrong, that it was just a mistake, that I had not somehow returned three hundred years after I had left. But every room was desolate and filthy. The kitchen's thatched roof had rotted away and collapsed, and the whole long room was so overgrown with brambles I could scarcely see the walls. The dining-room where I had first been served by invisible servants was a tangle of weeds, briars looping through the windows and coiling about the table legs. A few faint figures still feasted on the walls, under the black flowers of mildew. The old library still stood, for its slate roof had not rotted away like the thatch. However, its mosaic floor was covered in leaves and twigs, the shelves were draped in cobwebs like filthy curtains, and the papyrus scrolls were disintegrating into dust.

Scarcely able to breathe, I hurried to the other tower. My sitting-room was just a pile of scorched rubble and charred timbers, my bedroom collapsed upon it. It was as if Ambrose and I had never lain in each other's arms, never kissed, never touched, never existed.

The spiral staircase wound up into nothingness. I climbed it, my boots sending stones skittering, and stood on its last step, looking down at the ruin. The staircase seemed to sway under my feet. Already the light was failing, and snow whirled past. My feet and hands were numb, my limbs trembled.

The way to the world of the dead was easy. A thrust of a sword, a sudden fall, a careless bite of toadstool, and the soul was sucked down to the dark kingdom of Orcus, god of the dead.

I should just cast myself down, I thought. *That would be the quickest way to reach the underworld.*

Yes, the way to death was easy. It was the return journey that was difficult.

Deep within me I felt a tiny flutter. I laid one hand on my belly, clutching at the central pillar in sudden fear. My baby quickening in the womb. If I cast myself into that dizzying space, I would kill my child as well as myself.

I turned and very carefully descended the steps again. I did not have much time to prepare for the bitter cold of a winter's night.

I gathered kindling and made a fire in the hearth of the old library, using the crumbling remains of some scrolls to help light it. I found an old cauldron and scoured it out, drew water from the well, and picked the last of the nettles and some wild garlic to make a thin green soup. Heather and wild thyme made a rough bed, and I swept the floor clean with birch twigs. By the time I had finished, it was dark. I was cold, hungry and very frightened.

I had seen no moon in the sky as I toiled. Had I been returned to the same phase of the moon as when I had left, though three hundred years later? I did not know. My whole sense of time had been turned topsy-turvy. All I knew was that it was winter, snow was falling, and the night was very black. I took the scrying bowl from my satchel and poured in a measure of the water from the lake. I bent over it, whispering:

Flame so bright,
open my sight,
let me see,
what's unseen by me.

With a painfully beating heart, I asked, 'My sisters? Cesar?'

I saw nothing but my own white face and hollow eyes, like a skull.

Had three hundred years really passed by? If so, my family was dead. I had not even said a proper goodbye. I'd left them with anger and resentment in my heart. I had thought them ungrateful.

Back and forth I rocked, arms crossed over my belly, panting like a wounded animal. I felt sick, as if I might vomit. The night, the darkness, seemed malevolent, as if it was alive and circling me, waiting to strike. My thoughts skittered like leaves in a cold wind. I would never see Cesar run and play, never see him grow. I would never laugh with my sisters again. What had happened to them all? How had they died? I felt it was my fault, that they would not have died if it was not for me. I know it made no sense, but my guilt was near as sharp as my grief.

My father. I would never hear my father thank me or say sorry. That hurt. I had gone to him, I had nursed him, I had saved his life, and all the time I had hoped that one day he'd be grateful.

My eyes burned, I could not snatch a breath.

If only I had embraced them before I left. I had been cold, distant, disliking them for the way they had hounded me with questions. How arrogant, how vain I had been. I had wanted them to love me because I was their saviour. I had imagined myself at the centre of the family, loved and lavished with attention, because I was the one responsible for their safety and happiness.

I realised, with a horrible sinking of my heart, that Alektrona had wanted to be the one to save Fatima. She had gone to her, she had found her, she had joined forces with her, they had danced together, making a new life for themselves. Then I had come and bought out Fatima's debt with seemingly no effort at all. I had told them we were returning to Velzna, I had made them, all of them, so indebted to me, I had not once asked them what they would like to do. I had forced Fatima to return to the place where she had been hurt and violated. No wonder Fatima had been so quiet, so with-drawn, so different from the girl I had seen dancing in my sister's arms. No wonder Alektrona had been so hesitant, so unthankful.

And what of Khrysanthe? She had not been grateful either.

I argued with her silently. *I saved your life! I saved your baby!*

But always having to be grateful can be a heavy burden. I had acted as if Cesar had been mine, and my sister a foolish maidservant who did not know how to change his nappy properly, or feed him, or care for him. She had had no chance to find her own strength, her own solutions.

Cesar, baby Cesar. I hoped he had lived long and been happy. I hoped he had found love, had babies of his own. I hoped they told him about me, that they remembered me with kindness. What had they thought had happened to me? Had they ever searched for me as I had searched for them?

I would never know.

Such a vast loneliness overwhelmed me. I was so cold, so cold. I huddled as close to the fire as I could get, but my limbs trembled, my teeth chattered. What was I to do? How could I live in a world where nobody knew me? What of Nocturna? What of Nera, whose muzzle was grey and her eyes growing dim when last I saw her? She too must be dead. And maybe Ambrose would die too, for I did not know how to save him.

Maybe he was already dead.

'Psykhe.'

My name was just a whisper, but I looked around wildly.

The water in the scrying bowl glimmered in the glow of the fire. I saw within an old, old face with fathomless black eyes. I cradled the bowl in my hands, bending so close my nose almost touched the water. 'Nocturna?'

'I am here.'

I could not speak, I was crying so hard.

'Calm yourself, Psykhe. I need you to listen to me. I know that you grieve. I know the cost has been high. But you cannot give up now. Ambrose still lives but he needs you. You must seek atonement for yourself and for him. You must travel to the underworld.'

'But how?' I cried, chest heaving. 'Should I fling myself from the tower? Cut my wrists?'

'If you do such a foolish thing, there's no chance of ever returning alive,' Nocturna snapped. 'Get yourself under control. Why surrender everything now when you are so close to the end of your tasks?'

I fought to control my sobs.

'Listen to me. There are many ways down to the land of the dead, but only one way to return alive. You must find such a gateway, but do not go into the shadows empty-handed. You will need two coins for Charon the ferryman, one to cross the Styx on your way there and one to return. You will also need two mead cakes to feed the guardian of the final gate. One for the journey there and one for the journey back. You will need to carry a cake in either hand, so put the coins in your mouth and make sure that Charon removes them with his own fingers. Do not eat of the food of the dead and do not drink of its waters. There will be traps set to ensnare you on your way. Do not stop for any reason, do not speak to anyone except the queen of the dead, and do not forget to take her a gift in return for what she will give to you.'

'Wait,' I cried. 'What gift?'

But Nocturna's face was fading away. I called her name frantically, but she was gone. Wearily I fed the fire, then sat with my arms wrapped around my knees, watching the flames and thinking.

It was too late for me to save my family. They were gone. I could only hope they had forgiven me and lived long and happy lives. I would have to mourn them and let them go.

But Ambrose, my love, my twin soul.

I still had a chance to save him, and by the goddess, I would, even if I had to go to the underworld to do so.

IV

All-heal

I had to try to remember everything I had ever heard about the land of the dead. There was a gateway in Roma, I knew, but it would take me weeks to walk there and I did not have time. There had to be another way. I thought about what Silvanus had told me about natural thresholds. I needed to look for the edges of things, the gateway times.

I went out into the starry night. Nocturna had taught me to mark the passage of time by the phases of the moon and the movements of the stars. So I searched for the Seven Sisters, one of the most recognisable clusters of stars and visible even to my dim eyes. I knew that when the Seven Sisters reached the highest point of the sky, it was the time of the midwinter solstice.

There they were, soaring like a flock of ice-blue birds away from the pursuing figure of Orion the Hunter. They were not yet at the zenith of the sky, but it would not be long. The midwinter solstice was only days away.

I had been left chained to the highest peak for the dragon on the night of the midsummer solstice. Six months ago for me, though the moon must have waxed and waned many thousands of times in those three days when I had been in the goddess's realm. I had thought that was to be my moment of death. Yet now, here I was, alive, and searching for another way to die. It would be funny if it was not so awful.

Thinking of the dragon made me think of the Raven and his daughter Misurina. They would be dead now too. I was sorry. Misurina had been kind to me. I had wished we could be friends. She had told me a story, hadn't she? About a gate to the underworld.

On the night of the midwinter solstice, the gate to the underworld opens and the blind queen and her daughter row out onto the wild lake . . .

Excitement thrummed through my veins. The wild lake. I wondered where it was. Perhaps it was not so far away. I needed to find someone who knew. My thoughts returned to the hillfort. I had been careful not to be seen each time I went to the lake, partly because of Ambrose's command and partly because I had been afraid of their anger. But I did not need to worry about that anymore. Anyone who had seen me was now dead. Again I felt that weird compulsion to laugh. I shook it off. It was because I was light-headed with hunger, I told myself. I had scarcely eaten in days. If I went to the hillfort in the morning, perhaps they would give me some food. And news. I wanted to know what had happened while I'd been gone.

I returned to my tiny fire and huddled beside it, doing my best to sleep despite the bitter cold. In and out of fitful dreams I slipped, and woke in the morning with frost on my cloak and the tip of my nose like ice.

Walking down to the lake took me most of the day, for I was so weak and faint that I needed to stop often to rest. I wondered about the hole in the trunk of the beech tree in the forest. I had passed through it once before, with the help of the magic ring. Perhaps it would open for me again?

But when I reached the beech forest, it was to find the tree had long ago fallen. I sat for a while, the red leaves the only colour in a landscape of silvery-grey. Perhaps I hoped to hear again the haunting sound of Silvanus's flute. Perhaps I looked for another hollowed beech, another magical gateway. Perhaps I was too exhausted to walk anymore. I know I sat as if in a trance, gazing at nothing.

A rustle in the fallen leaves startled me. I looked up. A girl stood staring at me, a long switch in her hands. A small herd of bristly black pigs snuffled through the roots, looking for beechmast. I stood up, and the girl stumbled back a few steps. I suddenly realised what I must look like. My white hair matted in knots, my dress filthy and torn, and, no doubt, my eyes staring like a madwoman's out of my bruised face.

'Wait,' I said hoarsely. 'Please, help me.' Without realising it, I laid my hand on the swell of my stomach.

She recognised the gesture. 'I will take you to the wise woman.'

It was a long walk, much of it uphill through a shadowy pine forest. The girl tried to hurry me along, but I was so faint now I could scarcely stay upright. At last we reached an alpine meadow surrounded on all sides by soaring grey peaks. A cottage was guarded by a hedge of elder and thorn. The girl opened the wooden gate and led me through a wild, overgrown garden. Even in the dead of winter, I recognised plants for both healing and harming – balm mint and belladonna, dandelions and deadly nightshade, feverfew and foxgloves, hedge woundwort and hemlock, meadowsweet and mugwort, parsley and pennyroyal, stinging nettle and sweet yarrow, now all died down or gone to seed.

The cottage was very small and round, with a steep thatched roof that reached almost to the ground. It had no windows, but the door stood open, showing a gleam of warm light. A young woman came out to meet us, a clay lamp in one hand. She was dressed in a woad-blue gathered skirt, a green blouse with a slit neck, and had a braided leather belt about her waist hung with pouches and a knife in a scabbard. Around her shoulders she had flung a knitted shawl. Her thick braid was red and hung almost to her knees, and at her side prowled the biggest cat I had ever seen. It had spotted tawny fur that faded to creamy-white on its chin and belly, and dramatic, black-tipped ears.

She took one look at me, then said to the girl, 'Thank you, Moira.' Then she took me by the arm and guided me within her cottage, settling me in a chair by the fire which glowed on a central hearth. The cat settled on the hearthrug, its purr a deep rumble.

'My name is Una,' the wise woman told me. 'Do not worry, I can help you. Let me brew you up a hot tisane of mugwort and pennyroyal and soon . . .'

'No,' I said abruptly. 'You mistake me. I . . . I want this child.'

'I see,' Una said after a moment of surprise. 'You know something of herbs, then.'

I nodded. 'I'm a midwife.'

Her look of astonishment deepened. 'Forgive me for misunderstanding your need. But you must know that most women who turn up on my doorstep, bruised and half-starved, their clothes torn, are in need of the herbs I mentioned.'

'Yes,' I answered with an effort.

Una considered me a moment, then said, 'Food first, I think.' In a few moments she had ladled me a bowl of thick vegetable stew from the pot that stood on an iron trivet above the coals. The bowl and spoon were crudely carved from wood, but the stew was warm and delicious and brought new life into me. 'When was the last time you ate?' Una asked, as she sliced me some bread.

I felt another bubble of mad laughter well up inside me. Three hundred years ago, I wanted to say. I restrained myself, and said, 'I haven't had much for a while.'

She nodded and brought me the bread, which I used to wipe out the bowl, then replaced the pot of stew with a copper kettle of water. 'I will make you a tisane. What would you recommend?'

I needed to sleep, and yet I was afraid of the darkness.

I looked up into the peak of her rafters, where bunches of herbs were hung to dry. 'Lemon balm, elderflowers, vervain and honey. Ground ginger root if you have it.'

'Sadly, I do not. We are a long way from the spice roads here. And a long way from your home too, I imagine.' Una raised a questioning eyebrow.

A moment ago I had wanted to laugh. Now I wanted to weep. I did not know anymore where my home was. I put down my spoon and tried to master myself. Swiftly Una strained the tisane and brought it to me, stirring in a healthy dollop of honey. I drank gratefully, and she sat down on a stool opposite me.

'I do not wish to pry, but . . . will you not tell me your story? I have heard old tales of white-haired maidens, but never seen one with my own eyes nor met anyone who has. And you come out of the winter storm, in clothes of another age, wearing a royal torc and carrying a child in your womb . . .' Her voice trailed away. 'I would like to help you if I can, but I fear your need is beyond what I can do.'

I smiled wearily. 'I'm no magical creature if that is what you fear. I'm an ordinary woman, just like you. Food, shelter, a bed for the night, that is all I need.'

'I willingly offer you food and a bed. Already it is growing dark, and tonight it will snow. Wherever you are going, know that you are welcome here for a time at least. You can repay me by teaching me some of what you know. New wisdom is always welcome.'

'Thank you.' I swallowed and looked away, grateful for a little human kindness.

'Is there some other way I can help you?'

I nodded. 'I need two coins and two mead cakes.'

And a gift for the queen of the dead, I thought but did not say.

Once again her eyebrows shot up in surprise. 'Mead cakes are easy, I can bake some for you if you wish. Coins are not so easy, for we do not use them here. However, I once accepted some as a curiosity. I wonder where I put them. If I can find them, you are welcome to them.' Una brought down a wooden box from a shelf above the fire and rummaged through its contents. 'Here you are.' She passed me some silver coins. To my amazement, they had images stamped on both sides of the coin. An owl and an olive branch on one side and a woman's face in profile on the other side.

Una watched me examine the coins with a small frown between her brows. 'Are these coins different from the ones you are used to?'

'Yes,' I answered, but did not elaborate.

She looked as if she was about to question me again, and so quickly I asked, 'How many days till the midwinter solstice?'

'The day after tomorrow.' Like all healers, Una knew the phases of the moon and the cycle of the seasons.

'Do you know of a place called the wild lake?' I asked.

Her frown deepened. 'I do. It's on the far side of the crystal mountain. A hard walk from here. It's very desolate, very remote. There is nothing there but forest and mountains.'

'A cave?' I asked hopefully.

'Perhaps. There are many caves in these parts.' She hesitated, then said without looking at me, 'The peak there is called Gateway Mountain.'

A thrill ran through me. 'Can you tell me the way?'

Una nodded. 'I could show you if you like.'

I shook my head. 'I need to go alone.' This I understood instinctively.

'I will pack you some food then. When do you wish to go?'

'I will go as soon as it is light. That is, if you do not mind me staying the night?'

'Of course. You are most welcome.'

Again, Una was regarding me questioningly, and so, to distract her, I asked, 'Can you tell me . . . what news from Roma?'

'I do not think it has fallen yet,' she answered. 'Though word is slow to come to us here.'

'Roma? Fallen?'

'Not yet,' she replied, misunderstanding my shock. 'Though their losses have been heavy. I heard that Hannibal's brother carried a great urn filled with thousands of golden rings back to Carthage and poured a flood of them out upon the floor of the council hall, saying they had all been drawn from the fingers of dead Roman soldiers.'

'Hannibal?'

'Yes, you know, the great general from Carthage.' She talked on for a while about battles and surprise attacks and some great wild trumpeting creature that had struck terror into the Roman troops, then said proudly, 'Hannibal hasn't yet managed to breach Roma's walls, unlike we of the Galli.'

It seemed a lot had happened in the years that had passed while I was in the otherworld. I stopped trying to understand and leant my head back against the chair. All the struggle and strife which had once seemed so urgent and terrifying was now nothing more than a hazy memory. It made me feel like a ghost.

Something of my feelings must have shown on my face, for Una stopped talking and said gently, 'Let's get you to bed. All will seem easier in the morning.'

I did not sleep well. My mind was worrying away at the problems that lay before me. How was I to find the gateway to the underworld?

291

What would I do if the midwinter solstice passed and I had not found it? And what gift could I possibly take to the queen of the dead?

I racked my brain for all the stories I had ever heard about Proserpina, the queen of the underworld. She was taken against her will by Orcus. While her mother Ceres searched for her, the world was turned to a wintry wasteland. Hekate guided Ceres to the underworld with two flaming torches, but by the time they found Proserpina she had eaten six pomegranate seeds and so was doomed to spend half of every year in the lower world. While she was trapped below, the world lay as if dead under the mantle of winter. When she climbed back to the upper world, the world was revived with the vital green force of spring. She loved music and was compassionate to lovers, allowing Orpheus to descend and search for his wife Eurydice.

What gift could I take her? I had no idea.

I slipped in and out of nightmares, dreaming that I was caught somewhere and could not escape. I ran, searching through endless caves, I struggled against claw-like hands, I fell into a dark river and could not drag myself free, I heard Cesar crying and could not get to him, I saw my sisters in their graves, lifting reproachful fingerbones to me, eyeholes empty in their skulls. I saw Ambrose, fevered, fretful, sobbing out my name, while the scarlet burn on his side ate away his skin like acid till nothing was left of him but smoking nothingness.

I woke, gasping and panting, tears on my face, with Una bending over me, shaking me awake. 'It's just a dream,' she whispered. 'Don't be afraid.'

She made me a chamomile tisane, but I could not sleep again. I got up and began to prepare for my journey. Una got up too. Silently we made mead cakes, then she looked through her clothes for some warm leggings and a knitted hat for me. I hardly spoke. My mind was filled with the horror of my nightmares.

'What is it that frightens you?' she asked.

'Ghosts,' I said at last, not knowing how else to explain.

'It is a shame you must go so soon,' Una said, taking the mead cakes out of the oven. 'Every midwinter eve, I go to cut all-heal. I'd like to give you a sprig to tuck in your bodice for protection. It is the best thing to protect you against ghosts.'

I stared at her. 'All-heal?'

'The druid's herb. I've heard some call it mistletoe. We hang it above our doors to protect against spirits and witches.'

I got up, went across and put my arms about her, holding her in a fierce hug.

'Why, what's this?' she asked, hugging me back.

'Thank you,' I whispered, tears falling freely.

'What for?'

'Everything.' I took a deep breath. 'And I'd love to go with you to gather mistletoe. Is it on the way?'

'To the wild lake?' She smiled slowly. 'It is indeed.'

The next day, Una and I made our way through the sombre forest to an ancient oak tree. Immense branches had sunk down to rest on the ground, making an archway that I ducked through to reach its gnarled and pitted trunk. Its branches were bare and black against the grey twilight sky, dark wheels of mistletoe suspended high in the twigs.

'Be careful cutting it,' Una told me as I began to climb, my obsidian knife in my belt. 'None of it must touch the earth.'

I nodded, and concentrated on climbing without falling. At last I reached the lowest clump, and braced myself against the trunk so that I could reach the mistletoe branch with its delicate white berries. I had to use one hand to hold the stem and the other to wield the knife, else risk it falling to the ground. I felt most precarious, so far above the ground. I looked up at the sky. The new moon was a thin silver crescent, hanging over the mountain peaks.

'Bless and protect me, Hekate,' I prayed and then sliced through the branch. It fell, and the unexpected weight made me lurch off-balance. I could not grab at a branch without dropping either the mistletoe or my obsidian dagger.

I let the knife go. It fell to the ground and shattered.

Hanging grimly to a branch far above, I nodded in understanding. There was always a price to be paid.

V

The Midwinter Gate

Wrapped in my mother's ermine cloak and hood, I was still cold to the core. My satchel was slung over my shoulder, the mistletoe tied to my girdle. The landscape was empty, frozen. My boots left deep prints in the snow.

I slept in a shelter made of fallen branches and snow as Una had taught me. I did not sleep much, it is true, but neither did I die. I rose early, as soon as the darkness began to retreat, so that I could reach the wild lake by dawn. The sky was very clear, the stars burning so bright that I could see my way forward. On either side, great towering pinnacles, clad in white robes, their faces grave and remote.

I came at last to the lake, dark between the snowy shores, ice creeping inwards from the edges. Snow blew from the high peaks, and softened the branches of the pines that crowded down the shore. Opposite, the cliffs soared straight from the water like a grey wall. I hung the mistletoe from the bare bough of a larch tree, made myself a rough shelter from old branches, and lit a fire. Una had packed me some bread and cheese. I toasted them on a long stick, and watched the sun kindle the peaks to saffron and rose. Slowly the light spread, turning the lake to deepest green. It was sunrise on the day of the midwinter solstice, an in-between time on an in-between day.

If anything was going to happen, now was the time.

Silence. Stillness. I felt an unbearable tension. If the stories were wrong, if I had followed a chimera, I would have failed to find the gateway to the underworld and failed to save Ambrose, and that I could not bear.

I heard the distant sound of splashing. I leant forward, gripping my fingers together. A low black boat slid from under the overhang of the cliff. An old woman sat in the prow, white hair billowing from under a blue crown like icicles. Her eyes were bandaged with a strip of linen. She turned her sightless face from side to side, as if listening intently. A young woman sat in the prow, rowing. Her hair and gown were black, her face deathly white, and she carried a silver bow on her back. She looked towards me, but did not seem to register my presence. It was as if I did not exist. I was transfixed, unable to move. It was such an unnerving sight.

The black boat glided about the lake, then slowly slid back under the arch of stone and was gone. In a moment I was up, and stripping off. I rolled my tinderbox, the coins and the cakes and the mother-of-pearl box inside my dress and cloak, then tied the mistletoe on top. Everything else had to be left behind. Hardest to leave was the scrying bowl Ambrose had given me, but it had to be done.

Naked, I walked into the lake.

The cold pierced like knives. Ice broke around me, floating in jagged pieces on the jade-green water. My bare feet burned as if I walked on hot coals instead of glacial mud. Doggedly I kept going. The jade-green water rose up my goose-pimpled thighs; I could

296

no longer see my feet. I stumbled forward, water up to my hips, my waist, my shoulders. The weight of the bundle on my head pushed me down. Then I was swimming. The far shore seemed an impossible distance away. I kicked hard with my legs, keeping my head as far above water as I could.

At last I reached the cliff. I had to lower the bundle from my head and pass it carefully under the overhang to make sure the mistletoe did not brush against the stone. Then, holding my arms out rigidly, I ducked my head and swam forward into a cave.

Only the faintest ripple of light shone in, enough for me to see the black boat drawn up on a rocky shelf. I laid my clothes down beside it, then hauled myself out of the water. My arms and legs felt so weak I could scarcely manage it. Trembling violently, I unfastened the mistletoe and hung it from the prow of the boat so I could unroll my cloak and wrap it about me. It took me a long time to strike a light, despite all my care in keeping my tinder dry, for my hands shook violently. At last the wick caught and a small glow shone out.

I was in a low-roofed cave, its roof hung with icicles. I drew on my clothes with clumsy fingers, and tied the mistletoe at my waist once more. I put the mother-of-pearl box in the pouch that hung from my girdle, and the two old coins in my mouth. They tasted unpleasantly metallic. Then I held the mead cakes, one in either hand.

I could carry nothing else. I had to leave my tinderbox behind. It was terrifying, leaving behind my only source of light. How was I to find my way?

All my life I had been afraid of going blind. Of not being able to see dangers coming.

My eyesight had always been dim. Sometimes, when the light was too fierce, people's faces were just shadows, and I could not read their intentions. I had to find other cues. The way they moved, the sound of their footsteps, the intonation of their voice. Perhaps that was why I had struggled so much with the darkness Ambrose had asked of me. I had not liked being made blind.

But I had no choice. I had to go on or I had to give up. And that I would never do.

I bent and blew out the little flame.

Blind, barefoot, I stepped forward, bracing my body against the hurt I knew must come.

A faint greenish glimmer fluttered into life before me. It was a pale moth, as big as my hand, with delicate feathery antennae. On each of its four wings, a glowing circle edged with darkness like a waning moon. The moth's wings cast a subtle radiance about it, enough that I could see the path. I followed it, filled with awe. It was an impossible creature. A moth that glowed like a firefly, a moth as big as a bird, a moth that knew the path to the underworld. Some spirit guided my way.

It was not easy walking, and the moth cast only a small light. But at least the scrambling helped warm me. Soon the tunnel opened up into a vast cavern, lined with great spikes and spires of rock like the teeth of some monster. On a stone bier lay the old queen, her crown upon her head, hands crossed on her breast, the bandage still concealing her eyes. Her dark-haired daughter crouched at the foot of the bier, the silver bow and an empty quiver of arrows leaning against her. She was asleep.

The light of the moth showed the faint tracery of veins at her wrist and temple. Her eyes moved a little beneath her eyelids, her chest rose and fell almost imperceptibly. Would the silver trumpets ever sound for them? I wondered. Would they ever wake to a new world?

I tiptoed past, and kept following the path down as it wound over slippery, damp rocks. On either side, lacy curtains of stone like frozen waterfalls, sharp-pointed icicles above. The moth fluttered ahead of me, casting just enough light for me to see several paces on either side.

Step after step after step. How much longer must I go on? How much deeper?

Hours passed. Perhaps days. Time had no meaning in this subterranean world. I set one heavy painful foot after another.

As I walked, I held imaginary conversations with Ambrose. I tried to explain, to excuse myself. *I did not want to be invisible anymore. I loved you with all my heart, but I did not want to be just a doll, a plaything. Please understand.*

I was not ready, he told me. *I had to find the way to break free of her. She took me in when no-one wanted me.*

For her own selfish ends! She likes having handsome boys at her beck and call.

She's my mother. She has suffered too. And I did her harm, even though I did not mean to.

I sighed. If only I had been patient. If only I had seen more clearly, listened more closely. But I had been blinded by my own urgent need to be loved.

For the first time I thought about how carefully Ambrose had planned my rescue. He had found a safe place, hidden from his mother's eyes. He had built me a place of refuge, filled with all the things I loved. Calmly, steadfastly, he had made his plans, thinking of everything I might need. He had defied his mother, someone who cruelly punished disloyalty. He had risked his home, his known place in the world, for me.

All he had asked of me was to trust him a while longer. Yet I had doubted him. I had asked more of him than he had been ready to give. I had wanted him to choose me over his mother and the life that he knew when he was still deeply enmeshed within it, trying to understand and find his own way free.

Was I any less a monster than his mother?

The moth-light blurred and swam. I sniffled, lifting my arm to wipe my eyes on my sleeve. Because of me, Ambrose was lying in pain, racked with fever. Because of me, he might die. I had to make atonement.

Wait for me, dear heart, I whispered. *I am coming to you as fast as I can.*

Space opened around me. A chill dank breath of air. The path led onto a bridge of stone flung like a girder across a void. The path glistened with damp. I began to edge my way along, hands held out for balance.

The moth fluttered forward. Its pale light showed, astonishingly, an old man limping ahead, leading a lame donkey. He was dressed in rags and leant on a gnarled staff. The donkey was heavily laden with sticks and had one leg bound in a dirty old bandage. As I stared, utterly taken aback, the donkey's hoof slipped and it stumbled to its knees. Its load of firewood slid sideways and crashed down, scattering twigs down the cliff.

'Help me, oh, help me!' the old man cried. 'Please!'

My impulse was to rush forward and help him, but my hands were full of cake. I could not even comfort him for my mouth was full of coins. *Speak to nobody but the queen of the dead*, Nocturna had told me.

'They will punish me! They will make me suffer. Please, help me!'

The moth had flitted onwards. If I hesitated even a moment, I would no longer walk within its frail circle of radiance. I set my jaw and walked on, averting my eyes, ignoring the man and his pitiful cries. As I passed him, his cries became more piercing. 'How can you be so cruel? Do you care nothing for the poor and the old?

Do you step over me as if I was nothing but a pile of rubbish? Stop! Help me! Help me!'

It was one of the most difficult things I had ever done, ignoring that old man. All my life I had tried to help people in need. But I knew that, this time, I had to choose. Ambrose's life hung in the balance. I hurried on.

Suddenly there was the scamper of quick moving feet, then a weight leapt onto my back. Strong fingers encircled my neck, squeezing. I choked and fell to my knees. My mother's silver torc pressed tight about my throat, cutting off my airways. I tried to throw the weight off my back, but it was too heavy. I smelt the reek of filthy rags, felt sharp nails raking my skin. I could not breathe. Black dots swam in my vision. The coins in my mouth were making me gag. In a moment I'd choke on them. I had to spit them out.

Resolutely I clamped my jaw shut, and threw my head backwards. I hit the old man in the face. His hold loosened. I gasped a breath and tried to lurch to my feet. He seized the torc, trying to drag me backwards. The twisted silver wires bent and flexed. I jerked my head forward, releasing my throat from its vise. The old man fell backwards, the torc still gripped in his hands. A scream of terror. He lurched over the edge of the cliff, the torc tumbling from his hands. I ran, sobbing, looking for the moth. It glimmered far ahead of me. I looked behind. The road was empty. No donkey, no fallen twigs, no old man.

But my mother's torc was gone from my neck.

The moth fluttered on ahead, remote and inexhaustible. I could not stop to rest, I could not take a sip of water to ease my sore throat, I could not eat. I could only stumble on, retching at the feel of the coins in my mouth, on and on and on.

A long time later, I heard the soft lapping of water. The mouth of the tunnel widened and opened up like a doorway. A dark slow-moving river wound its way through a vast cavern, surrounded on all sides by columns and arches and skewers of stone, fantastically formed and fretted with holes. Mist drifted above the scummy water, forming strange faces. A pier ran out into the river, with a bronze gong upon it.

The moth hovered above the gong.

No choice. I had to ring it.

My hands were clenched on the cakes, so I could not lift the mallet to strike the gong. Instead, I banged on it hard with my knuckles. The sound I made was only small, but it echoed across the water. I stared, tense and waiting. A narrow boat slid out of the dark and floated towards me. It was black, and curved up at either end into fearsome dragon heads. An old hunchbacked man stood in the stern, poling the boat along. His skin was blueish, and he peered at me from deep-set eyes. One shaking hand reached out to me, cupped like a beggar.

With my tongue, I pushed one of the coins forward between my lips, keeping the other tucked in my cheek. He plucked the coin from between my lips. His skin stank of decay. I gagged involuntarily. Turning away, I breathed deeply, try to compose myself. Then I had to step down into the boat without over-balancing, both hands still full of cake. It rocked wildly. I sat down abruptly, my cloak hanging over the edge. I could not gather it in with my hands full. The ferryman turned the boat around and began to pole across the river. To my relief, the moth flew on ahead. The black river seethed about the boat, hissing and smoking. Overhead the arch of the cave closed over us like the mouth of a monster.

Suddenly a corpse bobbed out of the water right next to me. I gasped and almost swallowed the coin. It lifted its head, gazed at me with empty eyesockets, then clutched the edge of the boat with grey rotting hands, trying to drag itself in. I shrank away, as it

302

implored me to help it. 'Pleassssse,' it hissed through blackened stumps of teeth. 'Asssssist me.'

I could do nothing but turn my face away, trying not to breathe in its sickening reek. The ferryman poled on without pause. The hissing pleas continued, then the corpse clutched at the edge of my trailing cloak and hauled on it. I was dragged towards it, unable to stop myself. I shrugged my cloak from my shoulders and pushed it away with my elbows, wriggling out from underneath. The heavy cloak slid over the edge of the boat, dragging the corpse back under the water. Both were sucked away in a swirl of scummy bubbles.

I shivered in the sudden cold.

The ferry reached the far shore, and stiffly I clambered out, both hands held high so I did not drop the cakes. I was dry-eyed, but there was a great lump in my throat. So often I had imagined the warm embrace of the cloak was my mother's arms cradling me. The cloak was gone now, and I felt naked and exposed. The skin of my arms was goosepimpled.

A faint path lay before me, winding through some kind of bog. Mud sucked and bubbled, and strange formations looked like ancient, petrified trees. The moth floated ever onwards and I trudged after it, my bare feet squelching in the mud.

In a kind of clearing among the grey fossilised trunks three old women sat on the ground, dressed in grimy rags. One was spinning with a drop spindle made from an old stick and a stone, a distaff of unspun wool tucked under one skinny arm. Another untwisted the spun thread from another spindle, measuring it from the inside of her elbow to the tip of her longest finger, then winding it into skeins. The third, the smallest and most hunched, reached out with one long-nailed finger at irregular intervals, stopping the measuring of the thread. Her sister held the thread taut as she cut it with a whetted flint.

I halted, frozen.

The spinner glanced towards me. One eyelid was twisted and scarred, half-hiding the blank white eye within. She smiled, showing toothless gums. 'Sisters dear, look! A living soul comes our way.'

The other two turned their faces in my direction. The second old woman had one empty eye socket. The third was completely eyeless.

'I can feel her warmth,' the measurer said.

'I can smell her blood,' said the cutter.

'Come join us, my dear,' said the spinner. 'It has been a long time since we have had company. Tell us what is happening in the world.'

'Who is being born?' asked the measurer.

'Who is dying?' said the cutter.

The moth fluttered past them, and darted along the path. Shadows fell about me. If I did not hurry, I'd be left behind in darkness. I took a step forward, and then another.

The three old women leant forward, peering and sniffing the air. 'Does she come?' the third one whispered.

'Will you not help us? My hands are so old, and the spindle is so heavy,' the spinner begged.

'My eye is so dim, I cannot see the thread to measure anymore.'

'My fingers tremble so much that I might cut the thread wrongly.'

I kept on walking.

'Is she here?' the third one asked eagerly.

'She comes, she comes!' The spinner reached out one claw-like hand to me. 'Sit with us, help us. This might be your thread that I am spinning. Don't you want it smooth and fine?'

'Don't you want me to measure it long?'

'Don't you want me not to cut it short?'

I began to step past them, keeping my eyes fixed on the moth fluttering so far ahead.

'She's here! I can smell her!' The third sister's hand whipped out and seized me about the wrist. She was astonishingly strong. I struggled, trying to break free. Wrenching away my wrist, I lost hold of one of the mead cakes. I lunged for it. Quick as lightning, the old woman snatched the ring from my finger. I felt it go, but could do nothing but try to catch the cake. I caught it just before it hit the ground, jerked free and ran.

As I fled down the path, I heard the old women muttering and grumbling behind me.

'I will spin her thread so lumpy.'

'I will tangle it and snarl it.'

'I will snap it so short. I will bite it!'

VI

Queen of the Dead

My ring was gone. There was nothing I could do about it. On I ran, choking back sobs, trying to catch up to the moth.

Ahead rose a strange, contorted castle, all twisted stone pinnacles and gaping hollows. Its topmost towers were hidden in shadows, the black waters of the Styx frothing about its base. Another fragile bridge arched across the torrent. The moth fluttered over it, and I had to follow. Step by careful step, I crossed. The path led through a cave mouth bristling with spikes as sharp as spears. A dog lay across the threshold, chained to a stake.

If you could call such a fearsome creature a dog. It was as big as a carthorse, and black as tar. Its claws were hooked and sharp, and its scaly tail writhed and twitched like an angry python. It had three ugly brutish heads, each with a mane of snakes, all twisting and writhing and flickering out their forked tongues. I would have to step over its serpentine tail to enter the castle.

I could creep past, hoping not to wake it. Or I could run.

The moth was no more than a tiny spark, deep within the castle's shadows.

I had to run.

As I sprinted past, the dog stirred and came to life, all three heads barking. I leapt over the writhing tail and lobbed a cake in a spray of crumbs. The monster's jaws snapped, snapped, snapped, trying to catch every last scrap. I raced past and was through the gateway and bounding up the stairs when suddenly it leapt towards me. Its hooked claws caught in my dress and tore it to shreds. My silver girdle broke. The mistletoe fell.

Somehow I managed to catch it before it hit the ground. I clutched it to me, my pulse thundering in my ears. So close, so close, and yet I had almost lost it.

The pouch tied to my girdle had also fallen. It contained the mother-of-pearl box the goddess had given me. The dog's three heads were snuffling about, looking for the mead cake crushed in my hand. I had to turn, I had to go backwards, closer and closer to those slavering jaws, in order to retrieve the box. I bent to pick it up. A wave of dizziness broke over me. I almost fell. Giddy and light-headed, I scooped up the pouch and staggered after the moth. Behind me, the three-headed dog fought against its chain, barking.

The tunnel opened out into a garden unlike any I had ever seen. Forged from gold and silver and bronze, the trees were cunningly fashioned to look like real trees. Fruit and flowers made of jewels nestled among the stiff metallic leaves. I remembered that one of Orcus's titles was Pluto, Giver of Riches, for it was in his realm that the wealth of the world was hidden.

I stood leaning against a silver tree for a while, trying to master my dizziness. The moth darted about my head as if urging me to hurry. In its uncertain light, the shining branches and berries seemed to dip and sway. I was so hungry I wanted to cram the last mead cake into my mouth – I wanted to devour it in a few huge bites. But I could not. I must not.

Half-naked, my clothes in shreds, my feet swollen and throbbing, my back smarting and bleeding from the dog's claws, my hair matted, my mouth dry as a desert, my stomach gnawing with hunger, shivering with cold, exhausted beyond my limits, I had to go on.

Step by slow step, I followed the moth. It seemed to be dwindling away, growing smaller as I grew ever more weary. I leant against the heavy silver door, too faint to stand upright. The moth floated above my head. I rang the bell.

The clank of locks and bolts. The door swung open. A woman stood smiling at me. 'Welcome!' she cried. 'Come in.'

I stood as if turned to stone. I had never expected to be welcomed here. The woman was young, not much older than me. She wore a long green gown so dark it was almost black. Soft waves of dark hair hung down her back, and her blue-grey eyes were shadowed, her skin near as pale as mine. She wore a crown of white berries on her head, and carried a wand made of a crooked mistletoe twig, carved with unreadable runes.

She must be Proserpina, queen of the underworld.

Acutely conscious of my filth and disorder, I bowed and offered her the branch of mistletoe.

'You have carried it far, and through many dangers. I thank you.' She made a graceful gesture with one hand, indicating that I enter.

Unsteadily I crossed the threshold. The door swung shut silently. She touched it with her wand, and I heard a dozen locks springing shut.

'It is not often I have the pleasure of a living soul in my banquet hall. Come in, come in. What can I offer you? Some mulled wine?'

I shook my head vehemently. I knew better than to eat the food of the dead or drink their wine.

'You are wise. If only I had been so wise. Come through.'

As she led me down a cavernous shadowy hall, I saw her feet were bare and a metal shackle encircled one ankle. It gave me a little jolt. I remembered she was a captive here, held against her will for half of every year. What was her husband like? Orcus, god of the underworld. Would I see him? I shuddered at the thought.

Proserpina showed me into a vast banqueting hall. It was lit only by greenish marsh lights that floated through the air, giving the hall a strange ghostly glow. A narrow table stretched the length of the hall. People sat, wreaths of stinking nightshade on their heads, eating and drinking. Hooded servants offered them platters of food or poured a smoking green liquid into their goblets. It reeked of wormwood and rue. Their plates were piled high with red-capped toadstools, toads on spits, writhing slugs, roasted hemlock roots, and giant jellyfish with pulsating blue tentacles that kept squirming away from the knives that sought to impale them. Vases of poisonous flowers decorated the table. Deadly nightshade, hemlock, wolfsbane.

'It amuses my husband,' Proserpina said, 'to feed the newly dead on food that would have killed them if they had still lived. He has a black sense of humour.'

Musicians played on a raised platform at the far end of the hall. It was so shadowy that I could only see that they played on harps and flutes of bone. The music was seemingly without melody, eerie and strangely beautiful. People danced to it, slowly spinning and swaying. All were dressed as they must have been at the time of their death. Many wore loose white nightgowns, their feet bare. One young woman was dripping wet, seaweed in her hair. Another man had a noose drawn tight about his throat. A soldier sat, holding in his spilling intestines with one hand and eating with his other. A girl sat, her hair loose, her lap stained with blood, cradling a tiny blue baby in her palm.

The horror of it was too much. I had one hand pressed over my mouth, the other cradling my curdling stomach. 'How can you bear it?' I whispered. It was hard to speak with the coin in my mouth – I had to clench it between my teeth. My tongue tasted of metal.

'I must,' Proserpina answered, after a moment. 'It is surprising what you can endure if you have no choice.'

'It's awful.'

'You must not speak against the rites of the underworld,' Proserpina said coldly. 'What do you know of death?'

I was so faint and dizzy I did not have the strength to answer. Besides, it was true. What did I know of anything?

She saw I was swaying on my feet, and laid a hand on my bare shoulder to support me. Her touch was icy-cold. 'They do not know it. They think they are feasting. When they have eaten of the food of the dead, they will begin to fade. Their memories of the past will loosen, and in time they will drink of the waters of the River Lethe and forget.'

I remembered the first poem I had ever read. *You will drift invisible in the underworld, a shade among the shadowy dead.*

'I do not want to forget.' I felt strange, as if my head was very light and floated above my body like thistledown, while my limbs were so very heavy.

'Many do. They want to forget the pain, the sorrow. If only they knew.'

'Knew what?'

Proserpina smiled at me. 'The pain is how they know they are alive.'

I needed to sit down, I needed to rest. She nodded at a hooded servant, who drew out a black throne for her and another little stool for me. I sank down thankfully.

'This is not the life I imagined for myself.' Proserpina looked about the cold, shadowy hall, at the musicians playing on their instruments of bone and the dancers slowly turning and bowing, their faces blank beneath the drooping wreaths of purple-veined flowers. 'I found it very hard, as I am sure you can imagine. My uncle never asked me if I wanted to be his wife, if I wanted to be queen of the dead. I was just a girl. I was playing in a meadow, making wreaths of dandelions and daisies, when he came for me. I was dragged away and trapped down here, locked away from all I knew and loved. Nobody came, though I screamed till I was hoarse. I felt I was forgotten.'

When you die, you will lie forgotten . . .

'I am so sorry,' I managed to say. 'It was very wrong.'

'I tried to flee, but there is no way to escape from the under-world. And I was so weary, so hungry, so thirsty. I hurt like you are hurting now.'

Her voice was soft and musical. It wove around me like the haunting bone music. There was such a heaviness in all my limbs. I reached out to her, touched her hand. 'I'm sorry you were so badly hurt,' I said, even knowing the words could not be much comfort.

She smiled faintly in response. 'So when the lord of this realm offered me a pomegranate, I ate a few seeds. That is all I did. I ate a few seeds. If I had only known . . .'

'It was cruel.'

Proserpina had to bend to hear my words. 'Yes,' she whispered back. 'It was cruel. If I had known the cost. If I had known my mother was coming. If I had thought there was any hope. But I did not know. I thought my life was over.'

A long silence. My thoughts drifted. *No hope . . . no longing . . .*

'The dead are outside time,' she told me. 'That is how we see that which is hidden to the eyes of living souls. We see the past and we see all the possible futures. So I knew, the first time you died, that if I saved you then you would come to me again as a living soul.'

I stared at her, startled awake again.

'Oh, yes. You have been here before. Born dead.'

I could not speak.

'Born dead,' she repeated. 'Not even a chance to take a breath. No chance to grow, to learn, to love, to sorrow. I knew that if I sent you back, you would live and you would save many others from dying before their time. And I knew that you would come again, bringing me the silver branch.'

Proserpina lifted the ball of mistletoe I had brought her.

'I have only one power here, and that is the power to revive the dead. It was the gift given to me after I lost everything. But mistletoe grows only in winter. When I am down here, in the underworld, I cannot pluck it for myself. I must wait for it to be brought to me. Yet what living soul dares travel so far, through such danger, to bring me such a gift?'

'One who loves greatly.' My voice cracked.

'Yes. One who loves greatly.'

Another long silence. Proserpina touched the white berries with one finger. 'I must choose carefully. Each berry has only one spark of life within it. If I use one of the sprigs of mistletoe on someone who has been dead too long, it is wasted. If I use one on a soul who cannot be saved, it is wasted. If I use one on a soul who does not want to live, it is wasted. Do you understand?'

I nodded.

'And each time I save a life, I anger my husband. He is the god of the underworld, and the dead are his subjects. Every soul I send back to life is one less vassal. I am afraid of my husband, I fear his anger. Yet I know now that this is my true destiny. I am given the choice. Who will return to the life they know, and who will forget and be born again in a new life? All must be born, all must die and be made anew – that is the turn of the wheel, that is the soul's journey. Yet when we die, all we have known, all we have learned is lost. And so I search not only for those who long to return, but for those who will remember and pass on what they know to others.'

'And so you chose me?' My jaw ached from clenching the coin.

'Yes. I knew you could be saved, and I knew you could save others. But I saw further, much further. I knew that if you lived, you would return here to the underworld and thence once more to the upper world. A journey few souls take. You would return and you would tell what you had seen, you would pass on what you had learned.'

'What . . . what I have learned?'

She smiled wearily. 'Who am I to tell you that? Only you can know. Now, it is time for you to go. Living souls that spend too much time in the land of the dead will die, just as immortals who spend too much time in the mortal world will grow old and feel pain and loss and suffering.'

I rose unsteadily to my feet. I still carried the mother-of-pearl box in one hand. 'Your . . . your sister sends you her regards,' I managed to say. 'I . . . I'm to ask you for a little of your beauty.'

Proserpina laughed, a cold, hard, bitter sound. 'You want beauty? Then I shall give it to you.' She took the box, and rose to leave. Then she turned and spoke over her shoulder. 'Psykhe, know that I give you this in return for the gift you gave me. You could have asked for anything. Immortality, even. But beauty is what you have asked of me and so that is what you shall get. I shall, however, give you another gift freely. Because you listened, because you cared, because you have loved greatly. You may choose a soul for me to revive. Just one soul. Choose wisely.'

She left silently, carrying the box. I stared after her, and then around the dark cavernous hall. Everywhere I looked, newly dead souls wandered, heads bowed under their wreaths of purple-veined flowers. The sickly smell hung in the air, making me nauseous. I rose to my feet. How could I choose?

I began to hurry about the room, looking into dead face after dead face. What was I looking for? I hardly knew. The possibility of life, the longing to live again. Fear gnawed at me. What if I chose wrongly?

The certainty was growing in me that Proserpina had a soul in mind for me. This was not another test, or even an empty gesture. There had been sorrow and compassion in her face. Desperately I searched the halls of the dead for one beloved face.

A small dwindling light danced in the gloom – the moth which had guided me so far. It flitted away from the banqueting table, away from the feasting dead. I followed it. Past thick pillars of stone, past vaulted arches and hanging barbs, to the door the queen had locked behind me. A naked figure crouched against it, beating feeble fists against the metal. 'Let me out,' he gasped. 'Let me go back.'

I knelt and took him in my arms, stroking his dark curls, murmuring words of comfort. He pressed his face against me, his chest heaving. 'I'm sorry,' I whispered. 'I came as fast as I could.'

The queen of the dead found us there, in each other's arms, pressed against the locked door. She looked down on us, and smiled. Then she drew a sprig of mistletoe from her crown, and touched it to Ambrose's brow.

VII

Box of Beauty

My beloved faded away, disappearing from my arms. Despite myself, I gave a sob.

Proserpina handed me the box of beauty. 'I hope you find your way back.'

I took her gift. 'Thank you,' I managed to say.

'I will see you again, Psykhe. At the rightful time for you to descend to my realm.' She gave me a faint smile, then unlocked the door with her mistletoe wand.

Back through the garden of metal trees. Back past the three-headed dog who greedily swallowed the mead cake I threw him. Back through the bog to the river, where the ferryman took the coin I gave him and rowed me over the misty waters. Up the long winding path, and through the gateways where I had lost everything that had meaning to me. Up, up, up, I toiled, barefoot and shivering in my rags. Up past the sleeping queen and her daughter, up to the cave with its black boat, up to the crack of light beyond.

I hardly knew how I made the ascent. If it had not been for the moth, growing ever smaller as it fluttered valiantly ahead of me, I do not think I could have made it. As I crept into the icicle-hung cave, the moth sparked bright, then faded away.

I could not drink. The lake was frozen solid. I had to crawl out of the cave on my hands and knees. I wore nothing but a few torn rags. The cold was sharp as a whetted blade, the light like needles in my eyes. I lifted a hand to shade my face. It was an assemblage of bones and veins within translucent skin. I tried to get up. My legs failed me.

I have travelled to the underworld and back, I have the strength to cross this lake, I told myself, and began to crawl.

It was not easy. I hurt everywhere. I welcomed the pain. A body that hurt was a body in time, a body alive.

I reached the far shore. Bloody streaks behind me. I found a stick, hauled myself to my feet. Ambrose, Ambrose, Ambrose. A syllable for each step. I found the shelter I had made, the blanket Una had given me. I crawled within, wrapped myself up. Unable to stop shuddering. Darkness folded its wings over me.

The box of beauty that I had brought back from the underworld lay beside me, mother-of-pearl glimmering like a moon. The prize I had won from the queen of the dead. I reached out one skeletal hand and drew it towards me.

The goddess of love and hate had thought she was sending me to my death. The box of beauty was just a ruse, an excuse to send me to the shadowy realm from which no mortal could come back. But I had. I had travelled deeper than any living soul, I had carried the gift of life to the queen of the dead, I had saved my beloved and found atonement, and I had struggled back to the world of the living.

I knew now the gift was meant for me.

Drawing on the last of my strength, I lifted the lid. Within, a circlet of rosehips.

My lips curved. Hips as red as blood in return for berries as white as death.

I plucked one and held it to my lips, squeezing out the soft red heart. It was the first food I had tasted in days. It gave me the strength to suck another. It gave me the strength to ward off death.

My mind wandered. It was as if I had been untethered. I saw myself, my white hair snaking down my back. I saw my thin body, curled around my unborn babe. I saw the circlet of rosehips in my hand. My white eyelashes, lying on my white cheek. I drifted higher, into the shining air. The turquoise-green lake lay below me, the sombre ring of trees, the great stony mountains with their snowy peaks. Here and there, larch trees were hung with green gossamer like fairy wedding veils. Blossoms burst open on twigs. Eggs cracked open from within. A butterfly clambered from its pupa case, drying its wings in the sun before taking flight. A snake woke from its long sleep and slid out, tasting the air with its tongue, leaving behind an empty coil of skin. Fox cubs played in the snow.

Higher and higher I flew, larger and larger I grew. I saw the curved rim of the world, turning towards shadow. Slowly it returned again into the light, only to turn once more. Darkness and brightness revolving, again and again and again. Petals blew away in the wind, fruit swelled, fell to the earth, rotted away. Seeds lay in the black earth, waiting, then put out one tiny root. A delicate sprig of leaves unfurled. Slowly, slowly, the tree grew, even knowing its time to die would come.

I flew so high the world was just a jot. Stars as far as I could see. Shivers of stars all through me. For one long moment it was as if I was that vast tingling space. I understood everything was energy, everything was connected, everything was one.

I began to spread too far. I was in danger of being stretched so thin I could never find my own shape again. Space rushed through me. Vast wheeling galaxies, sucking holes of nothingness.

I spun, falling into darkness. It was as if I had no substance.

'Ambrose,' I whispered in sudden fear.

Names had power. Ambrose's mother had mocked him and called him Longing. Yet he had called himself Ambrose. It meant not-dead. It meant life.

'Ambrose,' I called. Louder. 'Ambrose!'

'Psykhe!'

I heard my name. It meant butterfly and soul and breath. I remembered who I was. At once I was drawn back towards my own body as swiftly and irresistibly as iron filings to a lodestone. A jolt as I returned. My limbs jerked.

Ambrose's mouth was on mine, his breath was in my lungs. I opened my eyes and put up one hand to touch his dear face. He drew back, gazing down at me. I smiled at him, murmured his name. He bent his head again and kissed me.

VIII

Joy

How does one make a new life when the old one is lost? A butterfly can never return to its chrysalis.

Ambrose and I built a new home for ourselves, on a hill overlooking the lake where my mother had been born. We had never constructed a wall or thatched a roof before, but there were those who were willing to teach us. Ambrose learned to tend bees and make mead. I planted a garden with seeds from the rosehips the queen of the dead had given me, as well as many other plants that I harvested in the fields and forest. I worked with Una as I had once worked with Nocturna, easing the passing of babies into this world and the passing of their grandmothers to the underworld. She became as dear to me as a sister.

My daughter was born in midsummer in the full light of day, the scent of roses blowing through the open window. Her birth labour was hard and long, but the goddess state was upon me. I felt as if my mother was there, lending me her strength, and her mother and hers too, all the mothers back to the very beginning of time, back to the first mother of all. When that tiny scrap of life was at last laid in

319

my arms, I wept and whispered a prayer of thanks. Her hair was dark like her father's, her eyes pale like mine. We named her Joy. She had a valiant spirit and a questioning mind, and we taught her never to be afraid to be curious.

I never discovered what had happened to my sisters. I liked to imagine Khrysanthe had many lovers and many children, and died content in her bed, her family around her. And maybe Alektrona and Fatima travelled the world, dancing to adoring crowds, till they died in each other's arms. Maybe.

What I did learn is that a family carrying the name Cesar was gaining power and influence in Roma, and that it was rumoured one of their ancestors had been cut out of his mother's womb. 'Most unlikely, though,' Una said. 'Whoever heard of such a thing? Not even a midwife as skilled as you could do that, Psykhe!'

I had been afraid, at first, of building a home in the shadow of the crystal mountain where the dragon lurked. But Una told me there was an old tale of a young woman who had offered herself to the sorcerer. He had taken her back to his cave and made her his slave. She never gave up hope of getting home, however. One day, while he was absent, she had explored deep into the mountain. There she found a cave hung with bats. One of the bats fluttered down and spoke to her with a human voice. She had once been a girl named Rosa, the bat said, and she knew the secret to breaking the spell.

'Open the sorcerer's chest,' the bat told the girl, 'and take the three poorest things you find inside. Then run home as fast as you can. Whenever it seems certain the sorcerer will catch you, throw one of the things behind you.'

So the girl did as she was told. Inside the chest were gold coins and glittering jewels and silver arrows, but she only took the simplest, least valuable things: a handkerchief, a comb and an apron. Then she ran. Three times the sorcerer almost caught her, and three times she threw something over her shoulder. The comb transformed into a thorny forest, the handkerchief turned into an icy glacier, and the apron became an avalanche that swept the sorcerer away. The spell was broken, and all the bats were transformed into girls again.

'This lake was named after the brave girl who saved them all,' Una said.

'Misurina?' I asked, remembering the Raven's daughter who had told me the story of the warrior princess and her enchanted silver arrows. Without her, I would never have found the gate to the underworld. Without her, Ambrose would have died.

Una stared. 'How on earth did you guess?'

I smiled. 'I must have heard the story before.'

The years passed, full of happiness and sorrow, laughter and loss. Joy grew into a woman, fell in love, and had a child of her own that I helped deliver. In time her daughter had daughters of her own. I have taught them all how to make soup, how to stitch flesh back together, and how to squeeze out the soft red heart of a rosehip.

Ambrose's hair has turned as silver as mine. He still carries the scar of that terrible burn. Sometimes, when it is hot and he takes off his shirt to wipe his sweaty brow, our great-grandchildren ask how it happened. 'I burnt myself, a long time ago,' he says. 'Which is why we tell you not to stick your fingers into a flame!'

He is a good man. It has been a good life.

My fingers have grown so bent and gnarled it is hard for me to hold my reed pen anymore. For I have kept my promise to the queen of the dead. I have written down all that I saw and learned on my journey to the underworld.

Now it is time for me to return.

I sit by the sinking fire, my last and most beloved dog resting by my feet. It is spring, and a new moon is rising. A time for new beginnings, new adventures. Ambrose snores in his chair opposite. He is old now, wrinkled and age-spotted, his silver hair thinning, but he has never been more beautiful to me.

A dark hunched figure is waiting for me in the shadows. The candlelight makes an aureole of her white hair. 'It is time,' she says.

'Just a few more words, Nocturna,' I whisper.

I dip my reed pen in my inkpot for the last time, and think about what else I need to say.

> Do not grieve for me, my love, and do not be afraid.
> One day we are born. Another day we die.
> Bitter winter comes, but then rose briars blossom.
>> The world turns on its pivot.
> I loved you with all of my soul and I will never forget you.
> When I am gone, sing, tell stories, remember the past.
> In time, perhaps we shall meet again. All things are possible
>> in all possible worlds.
> I will be waiting for you.

I put my pen back in the inkpot, tidy my pages into a neat pile. I have always liked things to be in order. Then I turn to Nocturna and let her lift me out of the husk of my body and take me home.

Three times I have died. Once I was born dead. Once I died returning from death. This time I die at my rightful time, without fear.

I know nothing is ever lost.

Author's Note

I have loved the myth of 'Eros and Psykhe' for a very long time. It is one of the few myths in which a woman does not have her tongue cut out, or her hair turned to hissing snakes, or her life reduced to a plaintive voice echoing men. It celebrates female desire and disobedience, and its denouement leads to love and liberation, not sorrow and suffering.

When I was about twelve, I read *Till We Have Faces*, C. S. Lewis' retelling of the tale. It made a deep impression on me. Later, as a young woman, I studied myth and folklore at university and realised that 'Eros and Psykhe' was the taproot for one of my favourite fairy tales, 'Beauty and the Beast'.

The best known version of the myth was written by Lucius Apuleius in the second century CE, but archaeological evidence proves it had existed as a folktale of the ancient Greco-Roman world for much longer. The oldest known artistic representation of Eros and Psykhe appears seven centuries earlier, in an ancient tomb in the Etruscan necropolis at Tarquinia called the Tomb of the Passage of Souls. The fresco has since been lost, the passage of time obliterating the image. Luckily a British artist named James Byres drew a quick likeness of the painting in 1766. It shows Psykhe depicted with butterfly wings, her arms held out to embrace Eros. On one side of her is the tree of life. On the other, the gateway to death.

This lost painting of Eros and Psykhe was created in the fifth century BCE, when Etruscan kings ruled in Rome and the Gauls were slowly gaining strength in the Italian Alps. The tectonic plates of these three cultures were grating together, forcing change. Soon the kings of Rome would be overthrown, and the Etruscans (who called themselves the Rasenna) would be absorbed into the Roman empire and their art and stories forgotten. It is so long ago that history and myth are one, and so it seemed the perfect time and place to set my retelling of this ancient story of love, loss and atonement.

I read many different translations and examinations of the myth during my research. Some key texts for me were Dr Erich Neumann's psychoanalytic interpretation, *Amor and Psyche: The Psychic Development of the Feminine: A Commentary on the Tale by Apuleius*, Graham Anderson's *Fairytale in the Ancient World*, and Christine Downing's *Psyche's Sisters: Reimagining the Meaning of Sisterhood*. A fascinating book which helped me develop my world was *Etruscan Magic and Occult Remedies* by Charles Godfrey Leland, first published in 1892. He believed that the ancient Etruscan deities (such as Selvans, the god of the forest and the wild) still existed in Tuscan folklore as *fata*, or fairies. Selvans was akin to Silvanus, the Roman god, and to the *silvani*, magical spirits of the forest, which appeared in the folklore of the Ladin people of the Italian Alps. My primary source for their wonder tales was *The Dolomites and Their Legends* by Karl Felix Wolff, published in 1930.

Most Greek and Roman myths were told and recorded by men, and tend to focus on the heroic battles and deeds of a male protagonist, while Western wonder tales tend to be told about women by women. 'Eros and Psykhe' is therefore highly unusual, a narrative from ancient times which focuses on the heroic journey of a female protagonist. For this reason, it is often called the first fairy tale.

In folkloric studies, stories with similar motifs and patterns of action are grouped together, and 'Eros and Psykhe' is categorised as part of Tale Type 425: Search for a Lost Husband, which includes many versions of 'Beauty and the Beast', including the lesser-known variants 'The Snake Prince' from Greece and 'Zelinda and the Monster' from Italy.

Both these tales were key texts for me in helping build my story, for there are a number of crucial differences between these female-centric tales and the version recorded by Apuleius.

For example, in his story, Psykhe is condemned to marry a winged serpent but is rescued by Eros and taken to a secret palace where he visits her that night, making her 'his wife' even though she is afraid and unwilling. However, in 'The Snake Prince' the heroine must give her love willingly and wholeheartedly if the curse is to be broken; her consent is crucial and the giving of it the most powerful moment in the tale. So I have drawn as much upon the traditional wonder tales as I have upon Apuleius' literary creation.

Roses are, of course, the central motif in both 'Beauty and the Beast' tales and in myths about Aphrodite/Venus and Eros/Amor. Interestingly, they also appear in Apuleius' story. The hero Lucius has been turned into a donkey by a witch. The goddess Isis comes to him in a dream and tells him the only way he can return to his human form is to eat a rose. Lucius obeys, and the curse is broken.

Although my book is a work of imaginative fiction, it draws on ancient history as well as myth. The story of the last king of Rome, Tarquin the Proud, who was overthrown after the rape of Lucretia, was recorded by the Roman historian Livy and the Greek historian Dionysius of Halicarnassus. Similarly the burning of the Sibylline books was reported by the Roman historian Marcus Terentius Varro. And a boy with albinism and epilepsy was buried under the stones of the forum of Tarquinia, his bones only discovered thousands of years later.

All the places described in my story are real. You can visit Tarquinia and see the tomb paintings there. You can go to Orvieto, built upon the ruins of the ancient Etruscan town of Volsinii (sometimes called Velzna), and go down into the underground caves to see the dovecots and cisterns just like Psykhe did with Ambrose. You can even visit the exquisite white marble statue of the goddess Vei in the Orvieto National Archaeological Museum. In Rome, little remains of the Etruscan kings, but you can see the remains of some of the temples and monuments they built, including the Temple of Jupiter Optimus Maximus. And you can go to the small coastal village of Portovenere, named after the ancient shrine of Venus, which once stood on the promontory there.

The Dolomites were known as the Pale Mountains until the late eighteenth century. Monte Cristallo is found in the Province of Belluno, and was the location for the Sylvester Stallone movie *Cliffhanger*. You can visit Lake Misurina, as I did, and hear the story of the curious little girl who wanted a magic mirror and whose father turned himself into a mountain to please her. And the Pragser Wildsee or 'wild lake' is a beautiful turquoise-green lake in the South Tyrol, generally better known by its Italian name, Lago di Braies. This is a landscape rich in legend and magic, including the story of the warrior princess Dolasilla who died saving her people, and whose mother and sister sleep under the mountain, rowing a black boat around the lake at dawn on the winter solstice.

I have spent more than three years immersed in the haunting tale of Psykhe's journey to the underworld and back. As always, I have many people to thank.

My mother, who gave me her deep love of myths and magic. My great-aunts, Aunty Clarice and Aunty Gwen, who had a copy of *Till We Have Faces* on their bookshelves, which I read while staying with them one summer holiday. My beloved family, who endure my obsessions with such grace, and who travelled with me on my adventures to Italy. Thanks also to Elisabeth Storrs, an author, friend and expert on the Etruscans who helped me discover their world, and Ashleigh Meikle who sent me her own copy of a book of Etruscan history. A very special thanks to my lovely friend and midwife, Megan Colville, who answered endless questions about midwifery, including how to cut a living baby out of a womb in the days before anaesthesia, and to Lucy Carpenter, who gave me her own personal insights of what it is to be born with albinism. And, as always, with such love and gratitude, my agent Tara Wynne, my editor Patrick Mangan, my publisher Meredith Curnow, and the whole team at Penguin. I am the luckiest author in the world.

About the Author

D r Kate Forsyth is an award-winning author, poet and storyteller. Her most recent novels are *Psykhe*, a retelling of the Ancient Greek myth of Eros and Psykhe, and *The Crimson Thread*, a reimagining of 'The Minotaur in the Labyrinth' myth set in Crete during the Nazi invasion and occupation of World War II. Other historical novels include *Beauty in Thorns*, a reimagining of 'Sleeping Beauty' told in the voices of four women of the Pre-Raphaelite circle of artists and poets; *The Wild Girl*, the story of the forbidden romance behind the Grimm brothers' fairy tales, which was named Most Memorable Love Story of 2013; and *Bitter Greens*, a retelling of 'Rapunzel', which won the 2015 American Library Association award for Best Historical Fiction. Kate has a Doctorate of Creative Arts in fairy tale studies, and is also an accredited master storyteller with the Australian Guild of Storytellers. She has taught writing retreats in Australia, Fiji, Greece and the United Kingdom.

Powered by Penguin

Looking for more great reads, exclusive content and book giveaways?
Subscribe to our weekly newsletter.

Scan the QR code or visit penguin.com.au/signup